Book 1 of the Seeds of Civilization series

Tractrix

Second Edition

R.J. Archie (signature)

Lincoln City
Sept. 2006

R.J. Archer

NWIDI Press ~ Portland, OR

This book is a work of fiction.
All names, characters or incidents are either
the product of the author's imagination or are used fictitiously
and any resemblance to any persons, living or dead,
is entirely coincidental.

Library of Congress
Cataloging-in-Publication Data

"Tractrix" by R.J. Archer
Second Edition © 2006 by R.J. Archer. All rights reserved.

p. cm.
ISBN-10: 0-9779109-0-3 (softcover)
ISBN-13: 978-0-9779109-0-8
Science Fiction, general

823.0876   2006905118

Second edition published 2006 by NWIDI Press, P.O. Box 230154,
Portland, OR 97281, USA
©2004, 2006 by R.J. Archer.

Cover art: sphere illustration by Alvaro Fontan, Portland, Oregon.
Cover design by Diseño International, Portland, Oregon.

Manufactured in the United States of America.

"Fasten your seatbelts for an engaging joyride through a labyrinth of riddles involving the ancient Maya, a U.S. military installation in the Nevada desert, and alien visitors from centuries past. *Tractrix* is a fast-paced yarn based on intriguing historical perspectives, and it's sure to keep you guessing and wondering right up until its surprising conclusion."

Al Lohner, author of *(fear not): Venture to Inner Peace* and *October Dreams*

"If you like Clive Cussler's writing you will certainly love R.J. Archer's mesh of historical facts and culture with theories and speculations that have intrigued man for several decades."

Steven Macon, *Yellow30 SciFi.com*

Tractrix

Acknowledgements

While I accept full responsibility for any errors or omissions in this book, credit for the finished product is gratefully shared with a number of others. Jim Powell, my first non-fiction editor, taught me that writing could be both fun and profitable. Alvaro Fontan conceived and produced the cover graphics when the book was only a few chapters old.

Several friends and family members were kind enough to read early versions of the manuscript and provide much-needed feedback and support: Carol Evans, Dennis Olver, Gary Jensen, John & Judy Archer, Hal & Marilyn McGlathery, Judy Cooper, Steve Culbertson, Suzan Hall, Sebastian Fontan, Jerry Wade, and my step-sons, Sergio and Miguel Igartua.

Two people deserve a very special Thank You: my friend and co-worker Fred Ray and my wife Marty Olver-Archer. Fred not only read every chapter in its roughest form but he also inspired one of the main characters. During the course of several business "road trips", Fred helped me refine the plot and he also joined me on a scouting trip to the area around the Nevada Test Site, one of the book's primary locations. His relentless requests for each new chapter were a constant source of motivation.

My wife and best friend, Marty, read every page as soon as it slid out of the printer and her encouragement kept me going when I would have otherwise given up. Besides serving as my editor, she also helped me with every other aspect of this project from the basic concept to query letters and cover design. But most importantly, she remained my friend during my many months of all-nighters and stay-at-home weekends, making this truly a labor of love.

-- R.J. Archer

About the Series

The *Seeds of Civilization* series is loosely based on the theories of Graham Hancock and others who believe that highly developed civilizations existed on Earth thousands of years before the time currently put forth by mainstream Anthropology.

The series accepts Hancock's theories, in principal, but goes on to explore the question of how and where these ancient civilizations might have acquired their advanced knowledge of mathematics, astronomy and architecture. Why, for example, were the Maya of Mexico's Yucatan Peninsula able to predict the exact time of a solar eclipse more than 500 years before the "advanced" thinkers of Europe figured out that the earth wasn't actually flat?

If Hancock's theory that an advanced civilization existed on Earth 9,000 years ago is correct, one has to wonder whether or not there were even earlier civilizations, each lost to some global cataclysmic event. What if the Mesopotamians weren't really Earth's first civilization but merely a sprout from a carefully planted Seed?

About the Second Edition

In 2004, when *Tractrix* was first published, the course of the series was somewhat undefined. By the time Book 2, *Tsubute*, was published, Book 3 was already under development and the direction of the series was well established. This Second Edition represents the author's efforts to more closely integrate *Tractrix* into the overall theme of the *Seeds of Civilization* series. Several minor errors in the original version have also been corrected.

For more information about this and other books in the series, join us at: **http://www.SeedsOfCivilization.com**

Chapter 1

(Wednesday, March 7, 1951)

Chaak reviewed the evidence for the third time and then hung his head in sadness. Several minutes later he looked up and said, "The end has begun. Initiate the project termination protocol immediately."

***

(Wednesday, June25, 2001)

Dr. Frank Morton walked down the steps of the Oregon Lottery Commission building in Salem, Oregon, and smiled up at the mid-day sun. His hand slipped into his sports jacket and touched the check for the tenth time in five minutes. The $1 million check in his pocket was a token payment on the $86 million Powerball jackpot he had recently won. Even after giving up half the jackpot to the 'cash' option and another thirty-eight percent to taxes, his net was almost $31 million. In addition to the check in his pocket, the Lottery commission had transferred an additional $30 million to his bank in Seattle earlier that morning, making Frank a very rich man. A smile started to form on his lips but it was quickly wiped away by a wave of sadness that had been following him around for almost six months – ever since he had lost Donna, his wife of eighteen years, in an accident that had plunged him into unbearable loneliness and despair.

Just six months earlier, Donna had walked the short two blocks down the hill from their Seattle high-rise condo to a local convenience market to buy some salad dressing for a special dinner she was preparing. On her way back up the hill she slipped on a patch of ice left over from the previous day's freak snowstorm and, in the process of trying to recover her balance, she stumbled into the street. A car coming down the hill slammed her into a parked car and she was killed instantly.

For months after Donna's death Frank tried to find someone, or something, to blame for the tragic accident. The driver of the car that had hit her couldn't possibly have anticipated that she would suddenly fly out between the parked cars and witnesses had confirmed that he was driving at a reasonable speed. In fact, the driver was still in therapy to deal with the emotional trauma he had suffered as a result of the fatal accident.

For weeks after the accident, Frank had blamed himself for not being there to run that errand for her, but he had been stuck in Seattle's usual afternoon rush-hour traffic. Sometimes he blamed Donna for not being more careful or for not waiting for him to get home. For a time he even blamed God for causing the storm, but in the end there was really no one to blame and it was time to get on with his life. Maybe the check in his pocket would help.

Frank's friends had been incredibly supportive during his months of grieving and self-pity. Since they were rarely apart, anyone who knew Frank also knew and loved Donna. Frank's employer, Boeing Aerospace, had bent every rule in the employee handbook to give him the time and space he needed to heal. Frank had missed more than five weeks' work since the accident, and even when he did show up he'd been moody and difficult to work with. Only in the ten days since the lottery drawing was Frank beginning to believe that there might still be a reason to live. Not that he was over Donna's death – he would never get over that – but the prospect of being wealthy beyond belief was allowing his mind to wander to places it hadn't dared go since the accident. He found himself able to daydream about how things were going to be instead of dwelling on how things had been and he was starting to emerge from the emotional coma he had been in since the December 27th accident.

Frank shook off the momentary pang of grief as he walked to his car in the parking lot next to the state office building. It was a warm, sunny day in early June and he noticed how dirty the car was – something Donna would have never permitted. They had bought the white Volvo on a lark one Saturday last September while out for a late summer ride. To keep it looking new, weekly washings had become almost a ritual even though neither of them had really liked the car once they got it home.

Suddenly, out of nowhere, an old vaudeville routine popped into Frank's head and he blurted out loud, "My car's dirty – it must be time to buy a new one!"

His sudden outburst startled two women he happened to be passing on the sidewalk and as he opened the driver's door his face finally broke into a smile. A plan was beginning to form in a brain that hadn't done much creative thinking in months.

"I'll take that black one right there," announced Frank, as he burst through the doors of the showroom and crossed the floor towards a small desk in the corner.

"What?" asked the salesman, obviously upset by the sudden interruption of his afternoon catnap. "Can I help you?"

"I said, I'll take that black Durango right there," repeated Frank. "There's a dirty white Volvo parked out front that I want to trade in and I'll pay you the difference in cash. I'm in a bit of a hurry, so can we get this done as quickly as possible?"

An hour later, after convincing the salesman and the sales manager that he wasn't some lunatic off the street, Frank was finally headed north on Interstate 5 in his new "rig." The sales manager had ordered the black Special Edition Dodge Durango as a showpiece to attract customers into the small downtown Salem dealership and he hadn't really wanted to part with it, but a call to Frank's bank verified that he could, indeed, pay cash for the vehicle and resulted in a veritable whirlwind of activity at the dealership. The service department even recruited a team of three mechanics just to install the custom floor mats Frank wanted.

"It's a beauty, Donna!" Frank said out loud. "It's a real beauty!"

The Durango had almost every available option, including the big V-8 engine, a leather interior and a great sounding stereo system. While cleaning out the Volvo he had found one of Donna's *Chicago* CDs under the passenger seat and it was currently blasting out through the Durango's sound system. He decided he would have to stop in Portland and get some more tunes before making the 3-hour drive back to Seattle's waterfront. Besides, he had skipped lunch to buy the Durango and his 6'2", 195-pound body was starting to demand refueling.

During the brief 40-minute drive from Salem to Portland, Frank began to refine the plan that had started forming earlier and the more he thought about it the more his spirits lightened.

Frank had gone to work for Boeing Aerospace right out of college and during the past 21 years he had worked his way up both the academic and corporate ladders. With the help of Boeing's continuing education program he had received his doctorate in Aerospace Engineering from the University of Washington ten years ago. Now, at 46, he was a Project Leader in charge of a team of scientists and engineers who were designing components for the

International Space Station. Like most senior staffers at Boeing, Frank thoroughly enjoyed his work and had ignored the opportunity to retire when he reached the 20-year mark, but after Donna's accident he had lost interest in the daily routine of meetings, conferences and planning sessions. He knew he was going to miss his friends and co-workers at Boeing, but by the time Frank and his new Durango reached the southern suburbs of Portland he'd made up his mind to put in for his retirement as soon as he got back to Seattle. He was lost in thought, considering what he would do with his time when his cell phone rang and jolted him back to reality.

"This is Frank Morton," he said into the hands-free unit he wore whenever he was driving.

"Frank, this is Tony! How the hell are you?" exclaimed the familiar voice at the other end of the connection.

"Hi, Tony! I'm fine, thanks. In fact, I haven't felt this good in months. What's up?"

"Well, I'm going to be in Seattle late tomorrow afternoon and I have something I'd really like to show you," replied Tony. "Can we get together for a beer somewhere?"

"Sure," replied Frank, shaking his head to himself and smiling "What have you gotten mixed up in this time?"

"No, no, Frank, this is serious. A couple of nights ago I was in a small town north of Las Vegas and an old guy gave me something I think you'll be very interested in."

"Okay, how about tomorrow night? I'm in Oregon today, but I'll be home either late tonight or early tomorrow and I've got some pretty big news for you, too. Shall we meet at The Warf about 7:00 p.m.?" asked Frank, referring to a seafood restaurant on Seattle's waterfront that was a favorite with many of the locals.

"7:00 p.m. it is! You're sounding good, old man. I'm looking forward to it. Hey, one more thing. Didn't you have an interest in hieroglyphics a few years ago?"

"Yes, but on a very amateur level. I took a class in Mayan writing over at the University about five years ago. Why?"

"It'll keep until tomorrow night. See you then."

Frank pressed the button on his cell phone to end the call and wondered what could possibly cause Tony to be interested in hieroglyphics.

Frank Morton had grown up as an Air Force brat, the only son of Colonel and Mrs. David Morton. By the time he graduated from high school in Montana, Frank had already lived in Germany, England, Ohio, Colorado, Florida and California. Unlike most kids, Frank enjoyed the regular moves with their new places, new experiences and new friends but as a result of the vagabond lifestyle he had become a loner with a few really good friends rather than a lot of casual acquaintances and Tony Nicoletti was one of Frank's oldest and closest friends. Like Frank, Tony had moved around a lot as a child, and, as an adult, he had become a long-haul trucker and never really settled down.

Whenever Tony was in the Northwest, he and Frank made it a point to get together for a few beers and to relive their "good old days" in Southeast Asia, where they had both served during the last months of the Viet Nam Conflict. As proud members of the TLC (Thailand, Laos and Cambodia) Brotherhood, Frank had been a Pararescueman in the Air Force's Air Commandos and Tony had been a Forward Air Controller in the Army's elite Rangers. They had met in a local bar in a no-name town in the middle of the jungle during an R & R break back in 1975. While the folks back home were being told that the "war" was winding down, the Air Commandos were still rescuing as many downed U.S. pilots as they had at the height of the conflict. Not long after they met, Frank and Tony were assigned to a joint Army/Air Force Special Forces unit and they had carried out several covert operations together before the group was deactivated in the spring of 1976.

Tony always had some "hot deal" or "unbelievable opportunity" in the works, a characteristic that Frank attributed to the fact that Tony had way too much idle brain time when he was behind the wheel of his 18-wheeler, motoring back and forth across the country. This time, however, Frank was pretty sure his own lottery news would top whatever new scheme Tony wanted to discuss.

By the time Frank got to Portland, found a place to park, had lunch and browsed the music section of the downtown Border's bookstore, it was almost 4:00 p.m. He decided to spend the night in Oregon and head back to Seattle the next morning because the evening rush was already in full swing and I-5 northbound out of Portland was a real mess from an earlier fender-bender.

Frank checked into the downtown Marriott and spent the rest of the evening on a park bench in Waterfront Park, across the street from the hotel. He hardly noticed the skaters, bicyclers, joggers and pedestrians that moved back and forth on the sidewalk between his bench and the Willamette River seawall. He was lost in his own thoughts, able for the first time in months to think about what he was going to do with the rest of his life.

Frank had always been interested in the many "mysteries of history" found in the real world – the pyramids of Egypt, the Incas of South America, the Aztecs and Mayas of Mexico and even the more recent UFO phenomenon. At various times since childhood he had devoted large blocks of time and energy to the study of a particular subject. He would see a documentary on television or read an article in a magazine that would spark his interest and before he knew it he was immersed in the subject. He would read dozens of books (or, more recently, explore hundreds of Web sites), compile extensive notes and become a self-made expert on the subject. Eventually he would exhaust his resources and move on to another topic. It wasn't that he lost interest, really, but while he was growing up Frank hadn't had the means to pursue his investigations beyond the local library and as an adult he hadn't had the free time to do much more than surf the Web. The den in his condo was cluttered with boxes of papers, maps and diagrams that he had been hauling around for years. Donna had tried several times to convince him to get rid of the "Morton Archives", as he called them, but he had always refused, insisting that some day he was going to have the time and money to pursue a few of the ideas and theories he had developed.

Now, with retirement on the horizon and $31 million at his disposal, Frank would have the time and money to do some serious investigative work and the activity would provide some much-needed therapy. By the time he headed back to his hotel room, he had compiled a mental list of things he wanted to buy as soon as he got back to Seattle. He had also decided what he was going to do with his time and money for the next few years.

Thus was born, at least in Frank Morton's mind, the Northwest Institute of Discovery and Investigation – or NWIDI – an organization he planned to create to pursue the private research of unusual phenomenon.

Chapter 2

As soon as Frank arrived in Seattle the next morning, he set about acquiring some of the items on the list he had developed the night before in Portland. His first stop was the local computer store, where he purchased the most robust notebook PC they had in stock. He and Donna had bought a fancy new desktop computer as a gift to each other last Christmas, but Frank was assembling a "mobile office" and the notebook computer would allow him to connect to the vast resources of the Internet from wherever his travels took him. He also picked up a portable color printer that would pack and travel well.

His next stop was the local camera outlet where he selected a Sony digital camcorder with a built-in still camera. The unit was equipped with a high-powered digital zoom and it had the ability to take photos in very low-light situations. It could easily be connected to the notebook and printer for almost instant processing of photos and sound bites.

By the time he was done at the camera store it was almost noon. Frank had called his boss, Jerry Parks, on the way into town that morning to set up a lunch meeting. Jerry hadn't been surprised to hear about Frank's retirement plans – he actually sounded somewhat relieved – and he had suggested that they start the paperwork as soon as possible. That's fine, Frank thought. The sooner I get on the road the better!

They had agreed to meet at Lamont's, an upscale restaurant near the Boeing facility where they both worked. When Frank arrived, Jerry was already seated and he had several manila folders on the table beside him. He stood up and extended his hand as Frank approached the table.

"Good to see you, Frank. Sounds like you've made some big decisions since I saw you last."

It's amazing what winning the Powerball jackpot will do for your attitude, thought Frank. As they sat down across from each other he said out loud, "Well I think it's time for me to move on. Is that the paperwork?"

"Yes, I've actually had this retirement paperwork in my desk for three months," replied Jerry. "The big shots have been trying to get me to convince you to retire since March, but after the accident and all, well you know…" Jerry's voice trailed off and his eyes couldn't meet Frank's.

"You're a good friend, Jerry, and I appreciate everything you've done to cover for me since Donna died. Maybe my retirement will get you back into the good graces of the powers that be, huh?"

"It's probably too late for that," smiled Jerry, "and besides, to hell with them! I'd rather have the old Frank Morton back in charge of the team, if that were possible."

"I'm afraid the old Frank is gone forever, Jerry, and the new Frank wouldn't be – and hasn't been – a good team leader. I'm sorry I was so worthless the past few months. The company didn't deserve it, you didn't deserve it and the team certainly didn't deserve it. I'm really going to miss all of you."

"That brings up a good point, Frank. What are you going to do? You must have a plan or you wouldn't have called me about this retirement, right?" asked Jerry as the waitress arrived to take their order.

"Well, what *are* you going to do?" probed Jerry again when the waitress left the table.

"I haven't worked out all the details yet," replied Frank, "but I'm going to pursue some old research projects that I haven't had time to think about in years."

A worried look came over Jerry's face. "These projects, Frank – they won't violate your non-disclosure agreement, will they? You know how the company is about intellectual property."

"There won't be any problems, I promise," laughed Frank. "There are some secrets that even Boeing doesn't own! The 'projects' I have in mind are in no way related to the company or any of its interests. Actually, they're more along the lines of archeology and anthropology, rather than engineering, and they have nothing to do with outer space. Now what have you got there for me to sign?"

As the two friends ate their lunch, Frank described his partially developed plan. He told Jerry about his childhood passion for "the Great Mysteries" as he called them. He described his plan to pursue some of his old interests "just for the hell of it" and he could see the envy on Jerry's face.

"Wow!" exclaimed Jerry when Frank finished. "That's the coolest idea I've ever heard and a great way to spend your retirement money. I really envy you, my friend. What mystery do you plan to tackle first?"

"I haven't really decided yet," replied Frank, "I'm going to spend the next few days going through some of my old files and see if an idea comes to me. If not, I might just take an extended vacation and visit some of the world's classic archeological sites that I've read so much about and see what turns up. I'll have plenty of time and no pressure, deadlines or launch dates, like back at Boeing, so I'm just going to take it easy and see what develops." Frank intentionally didn't tell Jerry about the Powerball jackpot. That would become public information soon enough.

"Well, it sounds like a great plan, Frank," admitted Jerry. "Now how about letting me get back to work? I want to get this paperwork back to personnel today and I also have a four o'clock staff meeting."

They stood up to leave and as Jerry was scooping up the two-dozen documents Frank had signed he said, "Just don't forget to write once in the while, old buddy. Remember that a lot of us desk jockeys back at the plant will be living vicariously through you. And if there's anything I can do, on an unofficial basis, of course, please give me a call!"

"I will, Jerry, and thanks," smiled Frank. "Actually, you'll be doing me a huge favor if you get the retirement paperwork pushed through as soon as possible in case I decide to take off for parts unknown."

On his way home, Frank checked another item off his shopping list by stopping at the main branch of Seattle Cellular. He went in hoping to find a cell phone with a larger geographic coverage area than the Qwest phone he currently had. He came out the proud, if not poorer, owner of a Qualcomm Globalstar Tri-Mode Satellite phone – a device he hadn't even known existed until an hour earlier. The $1,500 compact unit not only functioned as a standard analog or digital PCS cell phone, but it also had the ability to send and receive calls through a private satellite network that provided nearly world-wide coverage. Only the central African continent and parts of the mid-East lacked service, and even that was planned for the near future. The satellite phone brought a whole new meaning to the phrase 'reach out and touch someone!'

Arriving home with a load of bags, Frank had just put his key into the front door lock when his neighbor, Linda McBride, came out into the hallway carrying a bag of trash.

"Hi, Frank," she smiled warmly, "I haven't seen you around for a while. Have you been out of town?"

His neighbor, an attractive, late 30-something divorcee, had been one of Donna's best friends and she had tried to look in on Frank numerous times after the accident, but he had insisted on grieving alone and he had refused everyone's help, especially Linda's. Maybe it was because Linda looked a little like Donna or maybe it was just because she and Donna had been such good friends, but, whatever the reason, Frank had been unfairly cold to Linda during the past six months, and he knew it.

"Hi, Linda. I was in Oregon the past couple of days, but other than that I've just been hanging out. How are you?"

"Oh, you know me, Frank. I'm always busy doing nothing," she replied as she crossed to the elevator. Indicating the bags Frank was struggling with, she said, "It looks like you've been doing some shopping"

Turning the key with one hand, Frank looked back over his shoulder at Linda and said "Yeah, I went a little crazy and bought some new toys." At that moment the door flung open, pulling Frank off balance and tossing him and his bags into a pile just inside his door.

Linda let out a short burst of laughter then quickly clamped her hand over her mouth to stifle the sound. Laughing out loud, Frank raised himself to his hands and knees just as the elevator door opened.

"I guess I'd better get inside before I really hurt myself," he grinned. "I'll see you later, Linda," he said as he got to his feet and closed the door.

As Linda stepped onto the elevator, she realized that this was the first time she had seen Frank laugh since Donna's death. She smiled as the elevator began its descent to the basement.

Inside, Frank gathered up the bags and piled them onto the brown leather couch that had been his bed for many nights just after the accident. He retrieved a cold beer from the refrigerator, opened the days' purchases one by one and carefully laid each one out on the dining room table along with the appropriate instruction manuals and accessories. Neat and orderly, he would call it. Donna, on the other hand, would have described it, with a smile, as compulsive, obsessive behavior. Either way, the manuals for the computer, printer, camcorder and cell phone were going to provide him with plenty of reading material for the next few nights.

Frank picked up the satellite phone and called his old cell phone to make sure the new service had been activated. He checked the caller ID number displayed on his old phone to make sure it matched the number the store had given him, and then he reversed the process, calling the sat-phone from his old cell phone. Just making sure, Frank thought to himself. He also made a mental note to check the satellite service as soon as he learned how to use it. Frank figured out how to program the new phone's telephone number memory and spent the next hour copying all the stored numbers from his old phone into the new one. By the time he had finished programming the sat-phone it was almost time to meet his old friend Tony Nicoletti for dinner.

Frank arrived at Fisherman's Restaurant about ten minutes after seven and figured his tardiness meant he would find the always-impatient Tony in the bar upstairs. As he waved off the hostess who was headed his way with a stack of menus, he heard the unmistakable laugh of his Italian-American friend, who always claimed to be Sicilian, above the normal background noises of the restaurant. As Frank reached the top of the wooden staircase he spotted Tony standing casually at the bar, his left arm around the cocktail waitress and talking to a couple of guys to his right.

"Yup, those were the good old days," he heard Tony say.

Oh no, thought Frank, I hope he's not telling war stories already! This could be a really long night if he is.

Frank tried to sneak up on his old buddy, but Tony spotted him in the mirror behind the bar. Just as Frank reached his friend, Tony jumped straight up and spun around, landing in a karate stance. He startled the waitress so bad she let out a scream and the bar went dead silent.

"Nice to see you, too, Tony," said Frank dryly, not at all impressed with the maneuver. Smiling at Tony and indicating the waitress who had shrunk back into a corner, he said, "Now apologize to the nice girl before she has a stroke."

By the time they reached out to shake hands they were both laughing and things had gotten back to normal in the room. The waitress' name turned out to be Paula and Tony coaxed her back to the bar although it was clear that she thought Tony might be a psycho.

"This is the guy I was telling you about, darlin'," Tony said as she cautiously approached the pair, "This is my old buddy Frank Morton."

The waitress nodded and smiled politely, but immediately found things to keep her busy at the other end of the bar, away from Tony and Frank.

"The usual, Frank?" asked Tony as he flagged down the bartender. "A Shirley Temple, isn't it?"

"Yeah, right, wise guy. How many nights did I drink you under the table when we were overseas?" he replied. "Bartender, I'll have a gin and tonic please. And for the rest of the night this man's money is no good. Start us a tab on this VISA card. Can we eat dinner up here?"

"Of course," said the bartender as he took Frank's card. "But no hand-to-hand combat, okay?"

"It's a deal," grinned Frank. "We're going to grab that table over by the windows. Would you pour my friend another one, too, and send the young lady over with some menus, please?"

The bartender nodded as Frank and Tony retreated to a table away from the bar, next to the windows facing the Washington State Ferry dock. From their second story vantage point they had a great view of the big green and white boats as they came and went.

"This has always been one of my favorite places on earth," reminisced Frank. "Donna and I used to come here all the time to watch the sunsets. And remember my fortieth birthday party? I thought they were going to call in the SWAT team before it was over!"

"They'd have been no match for us, my friend. Back then we were younger, stronger and, of course, really, really drunk," grinned Tony.

Frank and Tony chatted through a couple of more drinks and then dinner, reliving the good old days, and finally agreeing that they weren't so good after all. A lot of men and women had died in Southeast Asia, and the two old friends had seen more then their share of them pass. As Special Forces soldiers, their "official" task had been to rescue downed pilots when they could and return the personal effects when they couldn't. Most of these rescues involved parachuting into the jungle behind enemy lines, locating the pilot and getting him back to a safe area where he could be patched up and transported to safety. Pararescuemen, like Frank, were thoroughly trained in first aid and survival skills as well as parachuting and scuba diving. They were a pilot's best chance of survival regardless of whether he went down in the jungle or at sea.

Special Forces troops were often called on to perform "unofficial" tasks, too. Like the Navy's SEALS, the Air Force Commandos and the Army Rangers represented the best of the best and non-rescue missions often involved operating deep behind enemy lines with no hope of extraction if they got in trouble. Frank and Tony had served together on several such missions just before the U.S. pulled out of Viet Nam and working under these extreme circumstances had created a bond stronger than blood. After Donna's death, Tony was the only person Frank had shared his grief with and that had strengthened their friendship even more. It was little wonder, then, that Frank had wanted Tony to be the first one to hear the news about winning the Powerball jackpot.

After the dishes had been cleared and Paula had delivered each of them a brandy, Frank decided it was time to let Tony in on his recent good fortune.

"Tony," he started, "I assume you heard that somebody won the big Powerball jackpot a couple of weeks ago."

"Sure, some lucky bastard is walking around with an $86 million ticket and doesn't even know it!" exclaimed Tony, obviously frustrated with the nerve of this unknown person.

"Well, my friend, yesterday I waltzed into the Oregon Lottery Commission office and cashed that ticket," whispered Frank, careful not to let anyone in the room overhear.

"Get out of here!" shouted Tony, immediately drawing the attention of every person in the room.

"Hold it down, damn it!" hissed Frank as he scanned the room, "You're the only person that knows so far, and I want to keep it that way for as long as possible."

"Yeah, but…" started Tony, waving his hands excitedly.

"The Powerball folks promised to keep a lid on the news until Saturday morning, and I plan to be out of town by then," explained Frank, "so just hold it down, please!"

"Wow!" exclaimed Tony, as he leaned back in his chair. "Why the hell didn't you tell me this on the phone yesterday? What are you going to do now? Are you going to finally retire from that damn think tank and go have some fun?"

"Slow down, man. I've got some plans in the works, but you've got to promise me you'll keep this quiet until Saturday. I really don't want the press busting my chops, and you know that people are going to come crawling out of the woodwork once my name is released. Now here's what I plan to do."

Frank explained his plans to Tony in as much detail as he had worked out and every time Tony tried to interrupt Frank would hold up his hand indicating "stop!" and say "Please let me finish before you tell me I'm crazy!"

Finally, Frank finished by recounting his lunch meeting with Jerry Parks and said to Tony, "Okay, okay, you've been dying to jump in for 5 minutes, so go ahead – tell me what an idiot I am."

"No, no, Frank that's not it at all! Do you remember yesterday on the phone when I told you that I wanted to talk to you about something important? You're not going to believe what I have to tell you! This has to be fate or something..." jabbered Tony excitedly.

Tony scooted his chair up to the table and leaned forward, motioning for Frank to also lean closer. Scanning the room for potential eavesdroppers, Tony began to speak in an uncharacteristically soft voice. "Frank, about three days ago I was down around Las Vegas. I stopped for dinner in a little town called Beatty, about 100 miles north of Vegas on U.S. Highway 95. I had dinner in the restaurant and then I went into the small bar and casino to make my usual donation to the Nevada treasury. There was a pretty good crowd that night, mostly other truckers like myself, and there was a boxing match on television so I sat down at the end of the bar and ordered a Coke."

Tony paused when the waitress arrived with their refills and he didn't say anything more until she had left the table. When she was out of ear shot, he leaned back over the table and continued.

"Between the rounds of the boxing match this old guy named Al and I got to talking. I mentioned that I was a truck driver and I asked him if he was retired because he looked like he was in his seventies, at least.

"The old man shook his head and said 'No, I should be, but I work up at the mountain.'

"I had no idea what mountain he meant, so I asked him.

"'Yucca Mountain,' he replied. 'It's southeast of here, out on the range.'

"Well, at this point I was completely lost, because I'd never heard of any Yucca Mountain and I didn't think there was much range country around Las Vegas – just desert and military stuff."

"I've heard of that place," nodded Frank, "It's been in the news a lot lately. It's out near a place called the Nevada Test Site. I think they're planning to use it to store radioactive waste or something like that."

"Well, I've never heard of it. Anyway, between rounds this old guy starts telling me about a huge underground tunnel the government is building up there, all the time glancing back over his shoulder as if checking to see if he's being watched. When he started talking about how they are using it to store some *very unusual* objects, I got curious."

Tony paused and took another sip of his drink.

"Is there a point to all this, Tony?" asked Frank. "Every old timer in Nevada has a story about buried treasure or hidden gold mines. That's how they bilk drink money out of tourists – and apparently truck drivers, too."

"Well yes, my friend, there *is* a point, if you'll just be patient," whispered Tony. "Between rounds 8 and 9 of the boxing match, old Al tugged on my sleeve. 'They have alien stuff up there, you know,' he said in a matter-of-fact tone.

"I tried to humor him and explained that I'd heard stories about alleged flying saucers that had been captured by the Air Force and were being reverse engineered at a place called Area 51. 'No,' he shook his head, 'I never saw any flying saucers, but I do have a couple of these gadgets that I've been studying. Strictly hush-hush, you understand. They have more of them out there, too,' he said as he handed me what looked like a dimpled black metal sphere about the size of a major league baseball."

"I handed the object back to him with a smile and asked him how he knew it was alien. 'Well just look at these strange markings here on the side, sonny,' he said, indicating the symbols on the exterior of the sphere. 'That must be alien writing. I've never seen anything like it, have you?'

"I had completely missed the symbols because of the poor lighting in the bar. He handed the sphere back to me, and I twisted around on my stool to get some better light on it. As I examined the

Tractrix

sphere again, the markings didn't look so alien to me, Frank. They looked more like hieroglyphics or something."

"It was probably a fake, Tony," said Frank as he leaned back in his chair, smiling. "What would hieroglyphics be doing on an alien object?"

"Well I don't know," exclaimed Tony, a little frustrated with Frank's attitude. "But I thought you might want to look at it for yourself."

Tony reached into his jacket pocket, produced the very object he had been describing, and plopped it down in the middle of the table with a thud.

"Don't say I never gave you anything!" he said as he drained his drink.

As Frank picked up the sphere, Tony anticipated his "How the hell did you get this" question and explained without being asked.

"About half way through round 10 one of the fighters knocked the other one right off his feet and a roar went up from the others watching the fight. I looked up at the screen to see what was going on and when I looked back down, the old guy was gone. Everybody in the place was on their feet and had congregated around my end of the bar, so I couldn't see which way the old guy had gone. I elbowed my way out through the crowd and tried to spot him, but he was nowhere to be found. I poked my head out the back door of the place, but I didn't see him in the parking lot, so I went back to my rig and continued on north up Highway 95. I assumed you could figure this all out when I got here."

While Tony was explaining how he had come by the unusual black object, Frank had been studying the markings on the sphere. He didn't say a word for several seconds after Tony stopped talking. Then he slowly raised his head, his eyes wide, and said, "You're right Tony, I think these are hieroglyphics, all right – <u>Maya</u> hieroglyphics!"

Chapter 3

Frank awoke Friday morning with a pounding headache. He and Tony had talked until after midnight and now he was paying for the combination of too much alcohol and too much second-hand cigarette smoke in the bar. He crawled out of bed and made his way to the kitchen, where he started a pot of coffee. On his way back to the bedroom, he spotted the object of last night's discussion, the so-called "alien object" that Tony had acquired on his recent trip through Las Vegas.

Frank picked up the sphere, with its strange inscriptions, and examined the markings again. He certainly wasn't an expert in ancient writings, but he had studied the Maya calendar years earlier and he was sure he recognized several of the symbols. One of his first priorities for the day was to get some help from a real expert and friend at the University of Washington's Department of Anthropology. Even though Frank had graduated from the Department of Aeronautics and Astronautics, his keen interest in the early civilizations of Mesoamerica had made him a frequent attendee at talks and seminars on the subject. It was at one such seminar that he had first met Jim Barnes. At the time, Jim was doing his post-doctorate work and he had presented a paper on his theories about the origin of Maya writing. After the presentation, Frank struck up a conversation with Jim and they had remained casual acquaintances ever since. Jim was now a full professor at UW and Frank hoped Jim would be able to find time to see him on such short notice.

Frank put the black sphere back down on the breakfast counter that separated the kitchen from the dining area and started down the hallway toward the master bedroom. Just as he reached the door, he heard a sound from the kitchen that sounded like glass cracking. His first thought was that his coffee maker's carafe had cracked and, as he raced back to the kitchen, he had visions of coffee running down the oak kitchen counter and all over the floor.

When he reached the kitchen he was surprised to see no mess. The carafe was about a quarter full and coffee was dripping into it normally. Frank was relieved but puzzled – if the sound hadn't come from the coffee maker, where had it come from? He checked the glass items in the sink and even opened several cupboard doors to see if something on a shelf had cracked but he found nothing out of the ordinary. He desperately needed some aspirin and a shower, so he decided to postpone his search until later. As he turned to leave the kitchen, his eye caught a thin, dark line extending the entire length of the breakfast bar. When he got closer it was obvious that the Formica laminate that covered the counter had developed a hairline crack running end-to-end and passing directly beneath the sphere. The crack appeared to be perfectly straight and it was so fine that Frank could barely feel it as he rubbed his finger back and forth over it. Strange, he thought. There must have been a stress defect in the laminate that I triggered when I put the heavy sphere on it. He shook his head, partly in frustration with the countertop and partly to clear the cobwebs, and padded off down the hall for a shower. He was going to have a busy day and dealing with a defective countertop would just have to wait.

An hour later Frank was feeling much better and he was eager to get started. He had a lot of things to do if he was going to get on the road before the Lottery Commission released his name to the press the next morning. Prior to his evening with Tony, Frank hadn't had any idea where he was going – he just knew he wanted to be out of Seattle before Saturday morning. Now it was clear that he needed to go to Las Vegas to see if he could learn anything more about the sphere or the man who had given it to Tony.

Frank called Jim Barnes' office at the University. To his surprise, Jim answered the phone on the first ring.

"Hello, Frank, it's been a while, hasn't it? I was very sorry to hear about your wife's accident. How are you doing?" greeted Jim in his characteristically soft voice.

"I'm doing okay, Jim. Thanks. Listen, I'm in a bit of a time crunch here and I've got something I'd like your professional opinion on. Is there any way you could find a few minutes today to see me?" pleaded Frank.

"Well gee, Frank, today is really bad for me. I've got a lecture in about 15 minutes, another one at 10:30 a.m. and a Department meeting at lunch. And I have to leave for the airport as soon as the meeting is over because I'm on a 4 o'clock flight to Mexico City for a conference. Couldn't someone else help you?" asked Jim.

"No, I'd really rather have you *see* this. Ummm… how are you getting to the airport?"

"I usually just call Super Shuttle. They pick me up at my doorstep and drop me right at the terminal door, why?" inquired Jim.

"Listen, if I give you a lift to the airport, can I impose on you to take a look at something for me while we're driving up there? I wouldn't ask you to do this if it wasn't really important, and I think you will find what I have to show you very interesting."

"Well now that you've got my curiosity up, how could I say 'No'," laughed Jim. "Can you pick me up at the Anthropology office about 1:15 p.m.? I have my suitcase here with me so we can go straight to the airport."

"1:15 p.m. it is, my friend. And thanks, Jim, I really appreciate this."

Frank hung up the phone, took a second for a sigh of relief and then began frantically packing for his own trip. The portable color printer and the camcorder went into a small roll-on suitcase along with a pair of binoculars and the accessories for the camcorder and satellite phone. He stuffed several pads of paper, some miscellaneous pens and pencils, his address book, and his Day-timer containing his checkbook and extra credit cards into the computer bag. He packed 3 pairs of Levi's and a weeks' worth of shirts, socks and underwear into another small suitcase, which he left open on the bed to receive any last minute things he thought of.

Frank spent the next hour in the den going through his old files. He didn't know exactly what he was looking for but he ended up with a stack of papers on a variety of subjects including some Area 51 background materials, his Maya calendar research and a detailed map of Mexico's Yucatan Peninsula. He stuffed the papers into a canvas tote bag, which he tossed into the suitcase on top of his clothes. Back in the den he changed his voice mail message to say simply "You have reached 206-555-3708. Please leave a message at the tone." He expected a lot of calls when the Lottery Commission released his name the next morning and he hoped that removing his name from the message would discourage some callers. He would have to remember to check his voice mail often for the next few days to keep the mailbox from getting full.

The next thing on Frank's to-do list was to find someone to look after his condo, collect his mail and generally keep up the appearance that he was still in town. He considered several choices, but the one that made the most sense was his neighbor Linda. He finally decided that he would have to apologize for his behavior of recent months and ask her to do him a big favor practically in the same sentence. He knew she was at work, but he called her home number anyway and left a voice mail message asking if he could talk to her later that evening. If she said "No" he wouldn't have time to ask anyone else, but he was pretty sure he could convince her to help him out.

At 12:30 p.m. Frank folded a tracing of the sphere's glyphs he had made into his shirt pocket and headed over to the University of Washington to pick up Jim Barnes. He had considered taking the sphere itself, but he respected Barnes as a scholar and he didn't want to embarrass himself if the glyphs turned out to be fakes.

The traffic from the Seattle waterfront to the university campus was heavier than normal due to some construction and by the time he found a place to park the Durango it was 1:20 p.m. As he walked up the steps to the main entrance, he was met by a rather frantic Jim Barnes coming down the steps with a large suitcase in one hand and an overstuffed, worn leather briefcase in the other.

"Frank, there you are!" called Jim. "I thought you had forgotten me!"

Frank glanced at his watch, wrinkled his brow and replied, "It's only 1:20 p.m., Jim. We've got plenty of time. Here, let me help you with that."

The smaller Barnes was happy to hand over the suitcase, which was no strain at all for Frank.

"So what is it you wanted to talk to me about that's so important you would be willing to drive all the way to the airport and back?" questioned Jim.

Frank tossed the suitcase up into the back of the Durango and handed Jim the folded paper containing the tracings as they walked around to the passenger's door. Frank unlocked the door and said, "What do you make of that?"

Jim climbed in and began studying the paper as Frank walked around and got in the other side. They were back on the freeway and headed south to SEATAC airport before Jim said another word. Finally he looked up from the paper and asked, "Where did you get this, Frank?"

Frank stuttered, "Well, let's just say that it came to me through a friend who made some rather fantastic claims about its origin. I'd rather get your opinion before I say anything more. Can you decipher any of that?"

Jim took another studied look at the paper and scratched his head. "Well, I can decipher some of it, but I don't understand what it means."

"I don't follow. Are you saying that it's just random glyphs? Are they actually Maya glyphs, or something else?" asked Frank.

"Well, no, they're not exactly random and I believe they are Maya." Jim paused and then said, "At least most of them are."

"Ah hah!" said Frank. "I thought I recognized several of those symbols from some research I did on the Maya calendar years ago, but a couple of them look strange. Any idea what they might be?"

Jim Barnes was studying the paper again, turning it 90 degrees left, then 90 degrees right and finally upside down. "Very interesting," he muttered as he continued to rotate the paper this way and that. "Some of the Maya part seems to be a date ..." His voice trailed off as he reached into his inside jacket pocket and retrieved a pad, a pencil and a small calculator. He filled nearly a page with notes before he spoke again. "In fact, it appears to be the Maya date that would correspond to July 11, 1991 on our calendar."

"Wow!" exclaimed Frank, recalling his earlier study of the Maya calendar. "Didn't the Maya calendar end sometime in the 21st century?"

"That's correct," nodded Jim. "The Maya believed that the current creation cycle began on August 12th, 3114 B.C. and that it would end on December 21st, 2012. We don't really know whether or not they expected a new cycle to begin after that date, but some of their monuments record the dates of events 90 million years in the past."

"Double Wow!" exclaimed Frank, as he pulled over to the curb on SEATAC's departure level, "But what about this 1991 date? Does it ring a bell with you? And what about the other markings?"

"No, the date doesn't sound familiar. The rest of the Maya appears to be a number and some other information, but I'll need more time to decipher it. The last two symbols have a style similar to Maya but I'm pretty sure they aren't. They may be from the same origins, though, possibly Olmec," replied Jim. "By the way, you never did tell me how you ran across this inscription."

"I'm afraid that will have to wait until you get back, Jim. Thanks for the translation and if you happen to run across any reference to that date, please call me collect. Here's my new cell-phone number."

Frank handed Jim one of his Boeing business cards that he had written the satellite phone number on and then went to the back of the Durango to unload the big suitcase. As he handed it to Jim he said, "Don't forget – call me collect if you think of anything."

"Okay, Frank, I will, and thanks for the lift. I'll be back on Tuesday and then you have to tell me more about where you found this inscription. See you then!" called Jim, as he disappeared through the large revolving door and into the terminal.

By the time Frank battled his way through traffic and got back to the condo it was almost 3:30 p.m. He still had a number of things to do before he could leave, but he was fixated on the date Jim Barnes had deciphered. Why would an alleged alien object be inscribed in an ancient language with a recent date?

Frank turned on the desktop computer in the den and poured himself a tall glass of milk while it booted up. On his way out of the kitchen he stopped to examine the crack in the counter top again. It was so straight it was almost unnatural! He grabbed the sphere off the counter, wrapped it in a hand towel from the bathroom closet and carefully placed it between layers of clothes in his roll-on bag. Back in the den, he sat down at the computer, opened the Web browser and searched for 'July 11, 1991.' The search returned 1,564 results and the very first one was for 'Eclipse Chaser Home Page' – it turns out there was a total eclipse of the sun on July 11, 1991 and it was best observed from latitudes in Mexico that correspond to the Yucatan Peninsula – one of the centers of the Maya civilization!

Now curious about the eclipse, Frank browsed some of the other sites. When he came to entry number 125 in the search list, it simply said 'Mexico City.' He clicked on the link and was directed to a Web page that described a UFO sighting over Mexico City on July 11, 1991. The sighting lasted almost thirty minutes and occurred before, during, and after the eclipse. Seventeen different people in various parts of the city had videotaped the incident!

Fascinated by the apparent connection between Tony's black sphere, a total eclipse of the sun and a major UFO sighting,

Frank followed one Web link after another for another hour. He might have surfed all night had the ring of his telephone not startled him back to reality. He glanced at his watch as he reached for the phone and realized it was nearly 5:00 p.m.

"Crap!" he said out loud as he brought the handset up to his face.

"Excuse me?" laughed Linda, on the other end of the line. "It's generally considered good manners to start a telephone conversation with 'hello', not 'crap', Frank. Would you like me to call back later?"

"Oh, no, Hi, Linda. Sorry about that – I just got busy and lost track of time," stammered Frank. "I take it you got my voice mail message?"

"Yes, I did. You said something about a favor – are you okay, Frank?" asked Linda, sounding a little worried.

"Yes, yes, everything's fine, Linda. Listen, would you like to come over for dinner tonight? I know this is really short notice, but I need to talk to you and it has to be tonight. I'd offer to buy you dinner out someplace, but I need to talk to you in private," explained Frank.

"Well after a mysterious invitation like that, how could a girl refuse? What time should my carriage drop me by the palace?"

Frank looked at his watch again. "Ah, let's see. Five – six – how about around seven? Is that too late for you?"

"Not at all," she replied. "I'll bring a bottle of wine and see you at seven."

Frank hung up the phone and shut down his computer. As the monitor blinked off it occurred to him that he hadn't even turned on his new notebook computer since bringing it home and it didn't have any software on it except for whatever was installed at the factory. He rummaged through the computer desk and found his copy of Microsoft Office and a few other essential CDs. He grabbed a ream of paper for the new printer and packed it and the CDs into the carry-on in his bedroom. Glancing into the roll-on, he realized he needed a better selection of clothes, so he tossed in a pair of black slacks, several polo shirts and a pair of dress shoes.

Frank flipped on the living room television on his way to the kitchen. He went through the refrigerator and dumped out the last of the milk and a few leftovers. He loaded the dishwasher with the few dirty dishes and then collected the trash from the other rooms into the garbage bag from under the sink. He put the bag near the door where he could grab it on his way out in the morning and then settled onto the couch to catch up on the news.

At exactly 7:00 p.m. on the dot, Frank's doorbell rang. He had spent the last hour watching TV and he couldn't believe it was already seven o'clock. He ran his fingers through his hair, hoping some of it would end up where it was supposed to be, and opened the door.

"Hi, Linda. Please come in. And thanks for doing this on such short notice," he smiled. "I sort of let the time get away from me, so would it be okay if we order in Chinese?"

"Sure, Chinese sounds great," she smiled, handing Frank a cold bottle of White Zinfandel.

"You didn't really have to do this … well, actually I guess you did, since I probably don't have any wine. Let me get a couple of glasses and order the food – what would you like?" asked Frank as he headed toward the kitchen. "And please, make yourself comfortable."

"Almost anything is fine, but I really like Kung Pao Chicken. Here, I'll pour the wine while you order the food," she said, following him over to the breakfast counter that separated the living room from the kitchen. "Did you know that your counter has a crack in it?"

"Yeah, that's the weirdest thing. It happened this morning," Frank said, without going into details.

He handed Linda two wine glasses from the cupboard, ordered the food and then turned back to the counter. He picked up his glass, held it out gesturing a toast, and said, "To friends. And I'm sorry I haven't been a very good one since Donna died."

"To friends!" toasted Linda. "And it's okay, Frank. Everybody has to grieve in their own way and I assumed you knew I was next door if and when you needed to talk. I was getting a little worried about you, though. Then last night, when you tumbled into your living room, I saw the old Frank for the first time in months."

Frank took a sip of his wine and signaled toward the couch. "Let's sit – I have something to tell you."

Once they were comfortably seated on Frank's leather couch with the TV off, Frank began his story.

"Have you heard that somebody won that big Powerball jackpot down in Oregon?" asked Frank.

"No, I don't really follow that stuff. I've only bought lottery tickets a couple of times. The odds are astronomical and I'd rather spend my money on something I can eat or wear."

"Well, okay, let me back up a little further. A week ago Wednesday the Powerball jackpot was $86 million. I was in Portland that day and I bought a ticket at a 7-11 just before I crossed back into Washington on my way home."

Frank could see Linda's eyes starting to widen as she began to guess where his story was headed, so he tried to hurry.

"It turns out that I had the only winning ticket, which I claimed two days ago. I chose the cash option and ended up with $31 million. Yesterday I retired from Boeing and early tomorrow I'm leaving town for a while until the press, fake charities and relatives I've never heard of stop calling."

Frank stopped, took a deep breath and a sip of wine. Linda looked like she was in shock. Frank could see she was bursting with a million questions and unable to get any of them out.

"I know, it's been a shock for me, too. I've been living with this for over a week and I've only told one other person."

Linda drained her glass, which seemed to calm her enough to allow her to get her mouth working again.

"Wow, Frank, that's great! What are you... how... ah crap! I'm really excited for you. If you are retiring, what are you going to do?" Linda stammered.

"I have retired," corrected Frank. "I signed all the paperwork yesterday. As for the short term, I'm leaving town early in the morning because the Oregon Lottery Commission is releasing my name to the press sometime tomorrow and I don't want to be here when that happens. That's where you come in, Linda; the favor I mentioned in my voice mail. I want everybody to think I'm lying low here so they don't start looking for me elsewhere."

"Of course, Frank, I'll do whatever you need," said Linda, nodding her head. "Where are you going? How long do you think you'll be gone? "

"Oh, I'm just going to chase down a story passed on to me by my old buddy Tony Nicoletti. It's really just something to do while I hide out. I figure a week, maybe two, should do it. Actually, I thought I'd check in with you in a few days and see how it's going – I'll come back as soon as things settle down," explained Frank, intentionally avoiding any mention of Las Vegas or the sphere.

"Just tell me what you need, Frank. I'm really happy for you," she said sincerely.

The Chinese food arrived and they talked for another 2 hours. Linda agreed to empty Frank's mailbox every day and to call him if anything unusual turned up. Frank had been paying his bills on-line for months, so most of his mail was junk, but he didn't want it piling up in the box. Besides, he expected to receive the title and registration for the Durango in the next few days. Linda became only the third person to have the new sat-phone number – he had given it to Tony last night and to Jim Barnes today at the airport.

Linda also agreed to keep an eye on his condo while he was gone. He gave her a key in case there was an emergency and so she could drop off his mail. In return, Linda gave him her cell phone number. They also exchanged e-mail addresses, just in case.

After working out the details of the 'favor', they finally got around to talking about Donna's accident and Frank's behavior during the past six months. He apologized again for the way he had acted but Linda seemed to understand. More than once she said, "Everybody grieves in his or her own way."

Linda left around 10:00 p.m. and Frank was in bed soon after. He set his alarm for 4:00 a.m. and he was asleep almost before his head hit the pillow.

The alarm woke him from a sound sleep six hours later. He showered, shaved and got dressed as fast as he could. After a quick once-over to make sure he had packed everything, Frank loaded the carry-on, the computer bag and his roll-on into the Durango and slipped quietly out of the condo's underground parking garage. As the Durango came up to speed on the freeway, Frank thought he heard a faint whining sound from the back but it stopped almost immediately and was quickly forgotten – after all, he was on his way to Las Vegas!

Chapter 4

Frank had only heard the satellite phone ring once before – on the day he bought it – so when it rang at 5:55 a.m., the sound startled him. He finally reached over and picked up the phone off the passenger's seat.

"This is Frank Morton," he said, shifting the phone to his left hand so he could drive with his right.

"Frank, this is Jim Barnes calling from Mexico City. I'm sorry to call so early, but we're two hours ahead down here and I have to get into a meeting in about 5 minutes."

"That's okay, Jim, I've been up for a while," smiled Frank to himself. "What's up?"

"I just wanted to let you know that I found out something about your 1991 date. A bunch of us had breakfast this morning and I threw your date out as a question to the group. One of the local archeologists remembered that there had been a total eclipse of the sun on July 11, 1991. Apparently it was visible in many parts of the country, including Mexico City."

"Yes, I know, Jim. I ran across the same information last night on the Internet, but I appreciate your call. Did your friend happen to mention anything about a major UFO sighting in Mexico City at the same time as the eclipse?" asked Frank.

"Well, no, he didn't say anything about that, but the UFO phenomenon isn't taken very seriously in the scientific community, you know. He did mention something else that I found interesting, however."

"What's that?" asked Frank.

"Well, it seems that the 1991 eclipse was predicted and recorded by a group of Maya priests from the Yucatan Peninsula – back in the year 755 A.D.!"

When Frank ended the call from Jim Barnes, he shook his head in disbelief. The mystery surrounding Tony's black sphere was beginning to border on the bizarre. The date inscribed on the sphere coincided with a UFO sighting and a solar eclipse that had been predicted by Maya priests more than 1,200 years ago!

The call from Barnes escalated Frank's interest in the black sphere from curiosity to an obsession. Now he was hooked, just like in the old days with his 'research' projects. As he guided the Durango southeast on Interstate 82, his eyes were on the road, but his mind was focused on the mystery that seemed to be unfolding. His trip to Las Vegas was going to take three days, with overnight stops in Boise and Salt Lake City. This first day would be the longest, covering about 500 miles, and now he was anxious to get to a hotel and do some more Internet research. He limited his stops to those necessary for fuel and while the tank was filling, he dashed inside to use the restroom and grab snack food.

Frank arrived in Boise just after 6:00 p.m. local time. After the twelve-hour drive, he was exhausted, stiff and hungry. He checked into a hotel near the airport, unloaded his three bags and ordered pizza delivered to his room. While he was waiting for the pizza to arrive, he took a steaming hot shower to relax his back and shoulder muscles and changed into a pair of sweat pants and a T-shirt. He unpacked his suitcase so his clothes wouldn't get too wrinkled and when he came to the black sphere, wrapped in the towel, he unrolled it and studied it again. As he put it down on the desk he wondered where this ominous little object would lead him. He flipped on the television to CNN Headline News to catch up on the days' events and settled into the easy chair in the corner of the room.

After the pizza arrived, Frank unpacked his new notebook PC, anxious to get online and start investigating. The telephone was on the night stand and Frank was immediately frustrated by the fact that the short cable in his computer bag wouldn't quite reach from the built-in desk across to the telephone's data port. He wasn't anxious to spend all evening with the notebook balanced on his lap so he threw on his shoes and stormed off in search of a longer cable.

The hotel desk clerk gave Frank instructions to a Radio Shack store in a nearby mall. Frank bought a long telephone cord and an adapter that would allow two cords to be connected together. He also picked up a network cable, a small black mouse, a set of lightweight headphones and a package of rewriteable CDs. While the clerk was ringing up the items, Frank started flipping through a catalog that was lying on the counter. Just as the clerk was asking if there would be anything else, Frank turned to a full page spread of scanner radios.

"Do these things really work?" asked Frank, examining the table of features for the various models.

"Yes, sir!" exclaimed the clerk, as if he had invented the technology himself. "I personally have this model right here and it's really cool! It stores up to 500 frequencies and you can program it from your computer so you don't have to key everything in with the keypad. Would you like to see one?"

Before he knew it, Frank owned a new scanner. The young clerk, eager to share his experience with scanners, convinced Frank to purchase an AC adapter and a car adapter. Frank also picked up frequency books for Washington, Utah and Nevada. As Frank was gathering up the bags of merchandise, the clerk wrote something on the back of a store business card and handed it to Frank.

Glancing around to make sure nobody was watching, the clerk whispered "Don't tell anybody I gave you this, but here's a Web site address you may find interesting. It describes how to modify your scanner so it can receive some additional frequencies."

A little puzzled, Frank took the card and asked "But wouldn't that void the warranty?"

"Of course," replied the clerk, as he scurried off to help another customer, "But it's worth it."

Frank returned to his hotel room and dumped the bags out on the bed. The clerk had offered to program the Boise police and fire department frequencies into the scanner for Frank, so he turned it on as he set about the task of connecting the computer and installing the AOL software that had come with it. By the time he finally got everything working and heard that friendly voice saying, "You've got mail!" he was absolutely fascinated with the scanner. He had no idea it was so easy to listen in on the conversations of police and fire personnel as they went about their everyday business. Most of the radio chatter was pretty routine stuff like traffic stops and building security checks, but in the few short minutes Frank had been listening he had heard police cars being dispatched to a home burglary and the fire department responding to a warehouse fire. He put the scanner near the window for better reception and turned to his computer for some serious surfing.

Along with the usual array of junk mail, Frank had e-mail from both Linda and Tony. Linda's e-mail said that his name had been on the news that morning and that there had been several reporters inquiring as to his whereabouts. The condominium was a secure building, so the reporters couldn't get in and they were forced to deal with Mrs. Gravely, the manager, via the door intercom system. Linda suggested that Frank send Mrs. Gravely a fruit basket or some flowers when he had a chance, along with a note apologizing for putting her through the 'ordeal' of dealing with the press. Linda also implied that Mrs. Gravely, while outwardly upset about all the 'extra work', was secretly thrilled with all the extra attention.

Tony's e-mail was sent from a truck stop in southern Utah, where he had spent the previous night. He was on his way to Denver to pick up an eastbound load and he wanted to know if Frank had learned any more about the mysterious black sphere. Frank replied to Tony's e-mail and brought him up to date with all the facts he had learned in the short two days since their meeting at the restaurant. He described the unusual coincidence between the date on the sphere, the solar eclipse, the UFO sighting and the Maya prediction in 755 A.D. Frank had considered not saying anything about the UFO sighting because he knew that the mere mention of a UFO connection would have Tony swinging from the chandelier and shouting, "I told you so!" but he included the information anyway, because of the alleged alien origin of the sphere.

After dispensing with the rest of his e-mail, Frank went to the Harry & David Web site and ordered a fruit basket for Mrs. Gravely. He figured $42.95 was a small price to pay for not having to deal with the reporters. When he filled out the order form he indicated that the gift card should read 'Thanks for being there – I'm glad I'm not!' and he signed it simply '1202', his condo unit number.

Frank spent the next three hours browsing the Web for any additional information relating to the mysterious sphere and the events that were apparently connected to it. He discovered that there were thousands of sites pertaining to the 1991 eclipse and hundreds of sites about the UFO sightings during the eclipse, but *not a single site* that mentioned the mysterious black spheres. Although the dial-up Internet connection was painfully slow compared to the cable connection he had at home, he scanned as many of the sites as he could and made a mental note to look for hotels that offered high-speed service in the future. He looked at lots of interesting, and sometimes bizarre, sites without finding anything very useful.

By 11:30 p.m. Frank couldn't keep his eyes open any longer so he shut off the scanner and computer and climbed into bed. His mind was filled with visions of the ancient Maya cities and four-sided pyramids he had seen on many of the Web sites that evening. Maybe I should go down there and look around for myself, he thought.

"Go to *Loltún*," said an unfamiliar voice in the back of his mind as he drifted off into a fitful sleep.

Frank awoke Sunday morning to the sound of his watch alarm beeping just as it did every morning at 6:00 a.m. He turned the alarm off and rolled over to get up. He noticed that the clock radio on the nightstand said 7:00 a.m. and realized he had neglected to set his watch ahead when he crossed into Idaho. Oh, well, he thought, it's only 350 miles to Salt Lake City – I can afford to lose an hour. He adjusted his watch and sat up on the edge of the bed. He hadn't slept very well, probably because of the pepperoni pizza, and little bits of dreams from the night were coming back to him. He hardly ever had dreams but the Maya legends and pictures he had been browsing just before he went to sleep had no doubt inspired those of last night. The only really clear image he could remember seemed to be a scene from inside an underground cave or tunnel. In the dream, he was carrying a torch and crouching to keep from bumping his head on the rock ceiling overhead. He smiled as he remembered that Donna used to say that dreams were the drive-in theatre of the subconscious.

After a huge yawn and stretch, Frank headed off to the bathroom. As he showered, his mind struggled to reconstruct the rest of the previous night's dream. Suddenly, a strange word jumped the gap from his subconscious to his conscious – the word *Loltún*. The word meant nothing to him and he couldn't remember hearing it before. Knowing that the details of dreams fade fast, he hopped out of the shower and jotted it down on the small hotel notepad next to the telephone. He'd check it out on the Internet when he got to Salt Lake City that night.

After a light snack at the hotel's breakfast bar, Frank was finally on the road at 8:30 a.m. Barring any unforeseen difficulties, he would arrive in Salt Lake City by mid-afternoon. He had visited the city many times before, usually in the winter for skiing, and he was looking forward to dinner at Spencer's, one of his favorite steak houses. He remembered that it was located in the new Marriott Hotel complex, so he called the hotel to find out about their Internet service.

"Yes, sir, all our rooms have high-speed Internet access, but I recommend the Executive room. It's a corner room, with wrap-around windows, a built-in wet bar and a small refrigerator. I have one available for tonight that has a great view of the mountains. It's a very nice room, sir," replied the reservations clerk who had answered the call.

That was all Frank needed to hear – Internet access and a view of the mountains. "Book it, please. I'm in my car, so if you'll give me just a minute I'll get you a credit card number to guarantee the room," he said, digging his wallet out of his pocket with one hand while trying to juggle the phone and keep the Durango on the road with the other. He sure missed the hands-free kit he had for his old cell phone and he was beginning to understand why some states were considering a ban against the use of cell phones while driving!

Frank stopped for a quick lunch and gas in Twin Falls, Idaho, and reached the outskirts of Salt Lake City about 4:30 p.m. As he approached the city, he was once again struck by the beauty of the skyline displayed against the Wasatch Mountains. Salt Lake City always seemed to have a certain, unexplainable dignity about it. Frank drove directly to the hotel and checked in. His room was on the southeast corner of the 10th floor and the view was everything the clerk had promised. Even in June there was a trace of snow at the highest elevations and he thought the mountains looked almost as good in their summer green as they did when they were covered with snow.

Frank went through his unpacking ritual again, except this time he left the sphere wrapped in its towel in the suitcase. He locked the suitcase, put it on the floor of the closet and closed the door. He got out the Sony camcorder and took a few stills and some video from his window just to make sure he knew how to work the new camera. Satisfied that he knew which buttons to push, and when, he packed up the camera and got out the scanner. It took him almost thirty minutes to get the twenty Salt Lake City Police and Fire frequencies programmed into the memory banks. The Utah frequency book he had purchased with the scanner provided the necessary data but getting the radio to accept a frequency and move on to the next channel seemed more like luck than skill. Now he understood why the salesman had suggested a model that could be programmed with a personal computer. It would have taken Frank a lifetime to correctly enter frequencies into all 500 channels!

With the scanner finally going, Frank unpacked his computer and plugged it into the Marriott's Internet connection. He'd been given an instruction card when he checked in and fortunately he had much better luck with the computer than he had with the scanner. He was on-line in a matter of minutes and a quick check of his e-mail revealed one new message from Linda. He decided to leave the e-mail until later because he was really curious about the word from his dream the night before and he was also very hungry.

After a superb dinner and a half-bottle of Rushing River Chardonnay, the sphere and its mystery still wouldn't go away. Frank took his last glass of wine into the lounge and found a table in the corner. Someone was playing the piano on the opposite side of the room, and Frank let himself slump into the leather wingback chair, hoping to relax.

He tried to enjoy the music, but his mind kept going back to this damned word *Loltún*. Why had it showed up in a dream last night? He realized that he didn't really have a good mental picture of the geography of Mexico in general or the Yucatan Peninsula in particular. He had been on several scuba diving trips to Cancun and Cozumel, but he had never had the time to venture inland. Realizing that he wasn't going to relax until he had some answers, he drained the last of the wine and went back to his room.

Frank sat down at the computer just as it announced, "You've got mail!" Linda's message was pretty much the same as the day before – more reporters hounding Ms. Gravely and asking anybody who went in or out of the building if they knew Frank Morton or his whereabouts. The gift basket had arrived, and Mrs. Gravely seemed to be enjoying the attention from the reporters even more. Frank dashed off a quick reply to Linda and moved on to the e-mail that had just arrived.

It was from Tony, who was in Denver waiting to pick up a load bound for Atlanta. Frank could almost hear him hyper-ventilating as he read the message. Tony was more convinced than ever that his black sphere was the key to some sinister military cover-up or that it was the clue that would finally break open the whole UFO phenomena! Tony had closed by saying that his truck was due for some scheduled maintenance and that as soon as he got back to Atlanta he was going to put it in the shop and fly out to Las Vegas for a few days.

"Great!" said Frank out loud. "Just what I need is more chaos in my life!" Then again, he thought, it might be fun to kick around with Tony for a while. This sphere thing was really becoming intriguing and it might be good to have someone to share ideas with. He sent a reply back to Tony reminding him of his new sat phone number and telling him to call when he got to the Las Vegas airport. He brought Tony up to date on the previous night's dreams and smiled, knowing it would drive Tony nuts thinking about it on his long drive from Denver to Atlanta.

His administrative tasks dispensed with, he turned to the project at hand. Since his road atlas was still in the Durango, he used his computer to locate a map of Mexico on the Internet. The Yucatan Peninsula was much farther east and south, relative to the rest of Mexico, than he had remembered. He located a map on a tour company's Web site that showed just the upper portion of the peninsula, from Mérida east to Cancun. As he was studying the map, his eyes locked on to a word a little south and east of Mérida – the word *Loltún*! There it was – apparently the name of a group of natural limestone caverns in the Yucatan Peninsula. A few short hyperlinks later and he was looking at photographs of the site, officially known as the *Loltún* Caves. Along with many photographs, the Web pages provided information about the obscure site that has provided archaeologists with some of the earliest evidence of humans in the New World and is famous for its Maya cave drawings. As Frank studied picture after picture of the caverns and their ancient art, he recalled his cave dream from the night before. Impossible, he thought, this is just a huge coincidence. If I'm not careful, I'll start thinking like Tony!

Frank thought about sending another e-mail to Tony with this new information, but changed his mind, electing to keep this to himself for a while. Tony's already got enough to stew about, thought Frank. I'll hit him with this about the time he gets to Atlanta just to keep him crazy. Frank was mentally patting himself on the back for the great psych job he was doing on his old friend when he spotted something on a Web page that had just loaded. He leaned forward to study it more carefully. He refreshed the page to make sure he wasn't seeing things, but there was no mistake. Chills ran down his spine as he realized that the cave drawing shown in the photograph was identical to one of the unidentified glyphs on the mysterious black sphere!

Chapter 5

Frank dug the black sphere out of the suitcase like a dog retrieving his favorite bone. He checked and double-checked, but there was no mistake – one of the drawings on the wall of the *Loltún* Caves in the Yucatan was absolutely identical to one of the symbols on the sphere. Frank stayed at his computer until 1:30 a.m. looking for more information on the glyph, but his search turned up nothing else. Frustrated, he finally piled into bed for another restless night.

Despite working into the early morning, Frank was awake a 6:00 a.m. and on the road by 7:00 a.m. He entered Interstate 15 a few blocks from the hotel and headed south. Six hours later, after a single stop in Cedar City for gas, Frank approached Las Vegas. Just north of the city his route took him past the southern tip of the Nellis Air Force Range complex, which houses the Nevada Test Site and the infamous Area 51 facility. As he passed the exit for Highway 93, he had a mental picture of the black sphere, now securely stored in his suitcase, rocketing out through the roof and disappearing over the horizon towards 'home.'

Frank's experience with the Marriott's high-speed Internet connection the night before made it a prerequisite for any future hotels and since he was going to be in Las Vegas for a few days, he wanted a place where he could spread out and feel at home. Marriott's Residence Inn division typically has units that resemble small apartments – a kitchenette with appliances and dishes, a living room area and a separate bedroom. Just outside of town he called information and had them connect him to the Residence Inn, hoping that its Marriott ownership would translate into decent Internet access. Frank was pleased to learn that the Las Vegas Residence Inn had been upgraded only a month earlier and part of that facelift included the same Internet service provided in many of the chain's larger hotels. The only room available was called a Penthouse, but the rate was reasonable so he booked it. The hotel turned out to be just a couple of blocks off the strip, close to the Convention Center, so it would be handy and yet out of the main flow of tourist traffic.

A few minutes later, Frank checked in and surveyed his room. His Penthouse unit was similar to the standard unit except that the living room had a vaulted ceiling and there was a second bedroom and bath in a stacked, loft arrangement over the main bedroom and bathroom. The kitchen area included apartment size appliances and a small breakfast bar with two stools. Opposite the kitchen area was the living room with an overstuffed chair and couch facing a wood-burning fireplace. Frank laughed when he saw the fireplace, because it was still 98 degrees outside. This will be perfect, he thought, as he carried his bags into the downstairs bedroom. When Tony gets here he can bunk upstairs and we'll save the cost of another room.

After unpacking, Frank's first order of business was to secure his growing collection of new toys. He drove a short distance back to the strip where he had seen a discount luggage shop on his way in. He bought a medium-sized footlocker and a combination padlock for it. The lock wouldn't keep anybody from hauling off the whole trunk, but at least it would keep nosey housekeeping personnel out of his things. By the time he got the trunk out of the Durango and into the hotel, he was soaking wet with perspiration, so he jumped into the shower. After rinsing the soap off, he turned the knob over to cold and let the water run on his head until his body temperature was back to normal. He changed into clean pants and shirt and cranked the air conditioning down a couple more notches.

He wanted to get some food to stock the kitchen, but it was just too hot outside so he decided to wait until the sun went down to do his shopping. In the mean time, he located the Internet connection near the writing table in his bedroom, and set up the computer. Once it was online, he loaded the software he had brought with him from Seattle and the software that had come with the scanner radio. The clerk was right – it really was easier to set up the scanner by filling in a table on the computer screen. No buttons to push, and no mistakes. Not only that, but thanks to the Internet, the computer software could access a server somewhere and display nearly the same information found in the $30 books Frank had bought. Simply clicking on the desired frequencies loaded them into the next available channel in the scanner. Soon he had over 300 channels filled with Las Vegas police, fire, aircraft, medical and security frequencies. During his programming he discovered that the radio wouldn't accept any of the more 'interesting' military frequencies. This was probably why the clerk who sold him the radio had mentioned the modifications. He located the card with the

Web site address on it and put it in the desk drawer for later reference.

About 8:00 p.m. Frank opened his door for a temperature check. It was still really warm, but the sun had gone down behind some nearby buildings and he decided it was safe to venture out. He drove south a few blocks on Paradise Road until he found a grocery store where he bought mostly breakfast and snack foods. Frank assumed he would usually have lunch and dinner out, since he was in a town with hundreds of restaurants. He also bought lots of liquids like bottled water, soft drinks and juices. This heat would dehydrate him if he weren't careful.

Frank returned to the hotel, put away his groceries and kicked back for the evening. He was tired from the drive and he was still adjusting to the extreme heat of early summer in Las Vegas. He also wanted to map out a trip for the next morning that would take him north, along the western boundary of the Nellis Bombing Range area and on up to the small town of Beatty. He wanted to see first hand where Tony had met the old man named Al and he hoped he could find Al, or anyone else who would be willing to talk about the spheres. After about an hour of studying maps and calculating mileages, his eyes were so tired he had no choice but to call it a night.

Frank's alarm woke him Tuesday morning at 6:00 a.m. and he quickly showered, shaved and made himself a light breakfast. While he was finishing off his wheat toast and juice he made a to-do list. His top priority was to track down the old man, if he could, and try to get more information about the black sphere. When Tony had recounted the story of how he had come to have the sphere he had quoted the old man as saying that "they have more of them out there." Why did the government have these objects? Where had they come from? What was their purpose? These were all questions Frank hoped the old man could answer if he would talk to Frank.

Frank glanced at his watch as he headed out the door. His calculations of the night before told him that he should allow two hours each way for the trip to Beatty, and it was already 7:30 a.m. He wasn't very excited about another road trip so soon after his long drive from Seattle, but he was really curious to see Beatty first hand.

Frank's calculations proved to be very accurate and the digital clock on the Durango's dash changed to 9:30 a.m. just as he pulled into the parking lot of the Burro Inn on the south end of

Beatty. The sign out by the highway indicated that the establishment was a casino, a motel and an RV park. He could see from other signs that it was also a restaurant and a lounge.

Frank made a pass through the small bar and casino area, scanning for anyone that might fit Tony's description of the old guy who had given him the sphere. It was a Tuesday morning and the bar was deserted, so it didn't take long to determine that the old timer wasn't around. Frank retraced his steps and entered the restaurant, which occupied the other half of the building. He seated himself at the short counter and was greeted almost immediately by a woman wearing cowboy boots, jeans and a western-style blouse.

"Howdy, Mister. What can I git ya'?"

"Just coffee, for now," replied Frank. The waitress scurried down to the other end of the counter and returned almost immediately with a cup, a steaming pot of coffee and a small bowl containing packets of sugar.

"You get a lot of locals in here, don't you?" asked Frank, trying to act like he was just making conversation.

"That's right," she replied. "Them and truckers passing through. Folks that stop in Beatty to gamble usually wind up at the Wagonwheel, down at the other end of town."

"Well, personally, I prefer small places with some local flavor" he lied. "A friend of mine was in here about a week ago and said he really enjoyed himself. In fact, I think he mentioned that there was a big fight on TV that night."

"That would probably have been last Monday," said the waitress. "Busy night! And a strange one, too."

"How's that?" asked Frank, trying not to seem too interested.

"Well, one of the motel guests found this old guy out back about 9:00 p.m. He'd been shot and apparently left for dead. It's the first violent crime we've had in the two years I've been here."

"You say 'apparently left for dead'; I take it he wasn't killed, then?" asked Frank, barely able to conceal his real level of interest.

"Nope! He must be a tough old bird, 'cause the last I heard he was still alive. They hauled him off to a hospital in Las Vegas in a helicopter that landed right out there in our parkin' lot," said the waitress proudly, as if she actually owned the place.

"Any idea who he was?" asked Frank, knowing that he was walking a fine line between curiosity and interrogation.

"Oh, sure!" answered the woman. "It was old Al Thompson, a local who lives in a mobile home just down the road here. He's a good ol' boy and he always has some tall tale to tell. He comes in, or at least he used to, two or three nights a week, puts a $20 bill in the same slot machine and hardly ever wins. I used to tell him that if it wasn't for bad luck, he wouldn't have any luck at all," she laughed. "Excuse me just a minute," she said, as the telephone rang on the counter behind her.

While the waitress was on the phone, Frank put two dollars on the counter and slipped away. He had all the information he could process for the time being, and he was afraid his curiosity was going to tip his hand. Besides, if Al Thompson were in the hospital, he certainly wouldn't be showing up in Beatty for a while.

As Frank casually made his way back through the casino and out the back door, he had the disturbing feeling that somebody was watching him or maybe even following him. He circled around the building and went straight to the Durango. He got in, locked the door and left the casino as fast as he could without looking like he was fleeing the scene of a crime. Twice on the way back to Las Vegas he thought he was being followed, but both times the vehicles turned off onto side roads just as Frank was about to take evasive action. Since neither of the incidents happened close to the city, he wrote the whole 'being followed' thing off to an overactive imagination and returned to his hotel.

The waitress in Beatty had told him the old man had been transported to Las Vegas so Frank scanned the city's yellow pages under "Hospitals" and located the number for the University Medical Center. It was the largest hospital in the Las Vegas area and it seemed like the obvious place to start. He called the general information number and told the switchboard operator he was inquiring about Al Thompson. There was a pause while the operator looked up the name and then she came back on the line.

"One moment while I transfer you to the critical care unit, sir," she said in a monotone voice

A second later a pleasant voice answered, "Critical Care, this is Nurse Harris, how may I help you?"

"Ah, good morning," Frank said cheerfully, trying to pretend he had every right to be making the call. "I'm trying to find out how Al Thompson is doing. I just found out about the shooting."

After a pause, the nurse asked "Are you a relative, sir?"

Fortunately, Frank had anticipated this question. "Yes, ma'am, I'm his nephew. I just got in to town yesterday and I always try to look up Uncle Al whenever I can. Is he going to be okay?"

"May I have your name, sir?" asked the nurse.

Unfortunately, Frank hadn't anticipated that question, so without thinking he replied, "Of course, my name is Frank Morton."

"Well, Mr. Morton, I'm not allowed to give out any information over the telephone. I suggest you come down to the hospital and I'd be happy to discuss Mr. Thompson's condition with you."

"To the hospital? Well, yeah, I guess I can do that. Would this afternoon be okay?"

"This afternoon would be fine, Mr. Morton, but please come directly to the Critical Care Unit and ask for me by name – that's Jill Harris. I'm the CCU charge nurse and I'll be leaving at 3:00 p.m. sharp," she said curtly.

"Yes, ma'am!" responded Frank, feeling like he had just been scolded by the principal. "I'll be sure to get there before 3:00 p.m."

"Good bye, then," said the nurse.

As the line clicked dead, Frank stared into the receiver half expecting her to slither through the wire and bite him on the nose. He wasn't crazy about making a personal appearance at the hospital pretending to be a long lost nephew, but he felt that the old man was his best hope to learn more about the sphere so he decided it was worth the risk. After all, nobody in Las Vegas knew him, and the worst that could happen was that he'd end up with no more information than he currently had.

As he was putting the handset back onto the hotel room phone he heard the satellite phone ringing in the bedroom. When he answered, Tony was on the other end.

"Frank, old buddy, where are you?" asked Tony in his normal, too-loud voice.

"Hi, Tony. I'm at the Residence Inn just off the strip in Las Vegas. Are you headed this way?"

"Yes, in fact I'm calling from the plane. I left Atlanta about 11:30 a.m. this morning and I'll be in Las Vegas on Delta's flight 365 at 4:18 p.m. Can I tear you away from your busy schedule to pick me up at the airport?"

"Sure," replied Frank as he jotted down Tony' flight information. "I've got an appointment at University Medical Center this afternoon anyway, so I'll head down to the airport when I get through there. And if I know you, you'll require massive amounts of food after the long flight, so I'll ask about a decent place to eat down at that end of the strip."

"Medical Center? Are you sick?"

"No, but it's a long story so I'll bring you up to speed over dinner. I should have more details by then. For now I'll just tell you that it may have to do with the old timer who gave you the sphere. That'll give you something to think about on the way out. See you at the airport." With that, Frank pushed the End button on the sat phone and smiled, knowing that Tony would go nuts trying to figure out what was going on.

The phone rang again almost immediately. Laughing, Frank pushed the Talk button and said "Really, Tony, it's a long story and we can talk about it tonight."

"Ah, excuse me, I was calling for Frank Morton. I must have the wrong number," said Jim Barnes in his typical soft voice.

"Hold on, Jim! This is Frank! I thought you were somebody else calling me. What's up? How was your trip to Mexico City?"

"Oh, Hi, Frank. The trip was very pleasant, thank you. I tried to call you several times at home and all I got was your answering machine, so I thought I'd try this number you gave me at the airport. I have some additional information about that tracing of yours and I thought maybe we could get together for lunch today."

"Well, I'd love to Jim, but I'm out of town for a few days. This is actually my cell phone that you called," replied Frank.

"Oh, sorry, I didn't mean to interrupt you. We can get together when you get home," said the always-apologetic Barnes.

"No, no, that's quite all right. In fact, you should consider this my primary number for a while. I'm not sure exactly when I'll be coming back to Seattle. Can you just give me the information now, over the phone?" asked Frank.

"Sure, I guess so," began Barnes. "As you already know, part of the message on your tracing is a date – July, 11, 1991. And, as you discovered on your own, that was the date of a total solar eclipse visible across a wide part of Mexico, including Mexico City."

"Right," agreed Frank, "And it was also the date of a very widely reported UFO appearance, also in Mexico City."

"Yes, so you claim," continued Barnes, condescendingly. "But when I talked to you last I promised that I would show the tracing around and see if anyone in the group had any ideas. At first it drew a blank from the whole group, but Sunday afternoon, just before I left for the airport, I ran into one of the local fellows in the hotel lobby. He said he thought he might have an idea about the rest of the tracing and he jotted down some references for me. He suggested I look them up in the University library after I got home, and I did that today after my last lecture. What I found was pretty interesting, Frank. Where did you get that tracing, anyway?"

"Jim, I'm sorry, but I can't tell you that right now. I don't mean to be secretive, but I'm still checking the source myself. Once I can verify a few facts, I promise I'll fill you in. But what did you find in the library?" Frank was now up and pacing back and forth between the living room and the bedroom.

"Well, as you may know from your earlier studies of the Maya calendar, they had a special way of writing dates, known as the long count," explained Jim patiently.

"Right, right," said Frank impatiently. "They used a system of five parts, each representing a successively longer period of time, sort of like our days, months and years."

"That's correct," continued Professor Barnes. "Your date of July 11, 1991, for example, would have been written as 12.18.18.4.6 in our system of roman numbers. In Mayan, that's 12 Bak'tun, 18 K'atun…"

Frank cut Jim off. "I know, Jim, but how does that relate to the other glyphs on the sphere?" And as soon as the words were out of his mouth Frank knew he'd screwed up.

"Sphere? What sphere? Frank, do you have a Maya artifact with these glyphs on it? And if you do, how did you get it? You know it's illegal to take Maya artifacts out of Mexico. They have very strict laws about that," lectured Jim.

"Jim, I'm sorry, but like I said I can't tell you any more right now. However, to put your professional mind at ease, I give you my word that I have not taken any Maya artifacts out of Mexico. Now what about the rest of the glyphs?"

"Well, Federico Martinez, that's the researcher who gave me the library references, has been working on a theory for years that the Maya, and maybe even the Olmec before them, had a system for accurately describing positions on the ground that was at least as good as their calendar skills. I reviewed his work last night, along with some other published papers, and I think some of the other glyphs on your tracing specify a particular place that goes along with the date of July 11, 1991."

"Wow!" exclaimed Frank. "You mean they're kind of like longitude and latitude?"

"Not exactly. Their system was more like our polar coordinate system. It specifies the position of a remote location by using the distance and direction of travel from some known point of origin. It seems that your tracing not only tells you when, but also where."

"Have you had time to decipher the location on the tracing, Jim? Do you know the "where" that goes with the "when" of July 11, 1991?" Frank was becoming frustrated with Jim's apparent lack of excitement.

"No, I worked on that last night, but I wasn't able to get a handle on the origin point. So far, I haven't been able to decipher the two glyphs that I think should specify it."

"Maybe it's my tracing," apologized Frank. "Would it help if I sent you another copy?"

"Not yet. I'm going to try a different approach later today," said Jim matter-of-factly. "Since we know the date coincides with a solar eclipse in Mexico City, I'm going to assume that's the destination and see if I can work backwards to the origin. Mexico City may be the key to the puzzle here."

"And it's also where the UFO activity was observed," added Frank.

As the call concluded, Jim agreed to try to pin down the origin in exchange for Frank's promise to reveal the source of his mysterious tracing as soon as possible.

Frank left the Residence Inn about 2:30 p.m. to look for the University Medical Center. He didn't want to be late and make mean old Nurse Harris mad! As it turned out, UMC was only a few blocks west and north of his hotel, but by the time he found a place to park and located the Critical Care Unit it was almost 3:00 p.m. When he reached the nurses' station there were several staff members poring over three ring binders and stacks of paper, obviously catching up on their end-of-shift paper work. They occasionally spoke to one another, but no one looked up from their work.

Finally a short, petite woman, possibly in her late thirties, noticed Frank standing at the counter and asked in a tense, annoyed voice, "May I help you?"

"Yes, thank you. I don't mean to disturb you, but I'm here to see Jill Harris," said Frank in a low voice so as not to bother the others. "I called earlier about my uncle."

The nurse closed the binder she was working in, put a stack of papers into a filing basket and stood up. "Follow me," she said stiffly in a voice Frank thought he recognized.

Frank followed the attractive nurse down the hall several doors where she turned into a small conference room used by doctors to meet with the family members of critically ill patients in the CCU. As he entered the room the nurse closed the door harder than necessary and motioned for him to sit at the round table in the center of the room. She took the chair directly opposite Frank, leaned back, crossed her arms and said in the cold voice that Frank remembered from this morning, "Okay, Mister, just what the hell is going on here?"

Frank decided that his best strategy was to stay in character and pretend to be the nephew he had claimed to be. Maybe he could defrost this witch and get some information about the old man's condition. Maybe he could even have a few minutes to talk to him in private about the spheres.

"I don't know what you mean, ma'am. I called earlier to see how my uncle was doing and I was told to meet a Nurse Harris here this afternoon."

The nurse glared into his eyes for a moment and then said, "I'm Jill Harris, Mr. Morton, or whatever your real name is. I'm also Al Thompson's adopted daughter, and you are definitely not his nephew! Now tell me what the hell is going on with my stepfather or I'll call the police and have you arrested for kidnapping!"

Chapter 6

"Kidnapping!" exclaimed a shocked Frank, "What are you talking about lady?"

"You know damn well what I'm talking about," shouted Nurse Harris as she pushed her chair back and stood up. "You called here this morning to find out if my stepfather was in this facility and not an hour later he turns up missing from his room. Tell me what you know, and tell me now, or I swear to God I'll call the police!"

"Miss Harris, please calm down and let me explain. You're right, of course – I'm not Al Thompson's nephew but my name really is Frank Morton and I assure you I have no idea where your stepfather is. I just want to ask him a few questions and I didn't think I would be permitted into the Critical Care unit unless I was family. That's the only reason I made up that story – honest!" explained Frank as Jill Harris settled back into the chair.

Jill took a long minute to study Frank's face and decide whether she wanted to listen to his story or call the police. "All right, explain yourself, Mr. Morton, but it better be a damn good story."

In light of the fact that Al Thompson was apparently missing from a hospital ward, Frank decided he'd better take Jill into his confidence and tell her the whole story. He described Tony's meeting with her stepfather at the casino and their conversation about the alleged alien artifact. He told her about the mysterious symbols and their ties to an eclipse and a UFO sighting. He also explained that he only wanted to talk to the old man to see if he knew any more about the spheres and their origin. He described his own visit to the Burro Inn in Beatty earlier that day and he related his conversation with the waitress. He finished his story by taking his Washington driver's license out of his wallet and sliding it across the table to her.

"That's me, Frank Morton. I'm sorry I lied, but of course I had no idea I was talking to Al Thompson's daughter on the telephone this morning," apologized Frank. "Now why don't you tell me about your stepfather's disappearance and let's see if we can get to the bottom of it."

"Well, I haven't forgiven you for lying, but I'm at my wit's end and I need to trust somebody, so I guess it'll have to be you. Lousy picture, by the way," she said as she slid the license back across the table to him. "As you've already learned, my stepfather was shot a week ago yesterday. Fortunately, the bullet only grazed his head and the wound wasn't fatal. He was found soon after it happened, but he had lost quite a bit of blood and, at his age, the shock nearly killed him. He was brought here because this is the area's main trauma center and we have a heliport. I managed to pull some strings with the hospital administrators and they allowed my stepfather to remain here in Critical Care where I could look in on him often even though his condition was improving. In fact, just this morning his condition was upgraded from serious to stable, but now he's gone!"

"Gone?" questioned Frank, "Isn't it possible that he just walked out on his own? Maybe he was confused or scared and just decided to get out of here, Miss Harris."

"Jill," she said. "Please call me Jill. And I don't think he just walked out, Mr. Morton."

"As long as we're on a first name basis, Jill, please call me Frank. Why are you so sure your stepfather didn't leave on his own? What makes you think he was kidnapped?"

"My stepfather was involved in an automobile accident about eight years ago. He was a passenger in a car that was hit head on by a pickup truck one night on a highway up north and he was pinned into the wreckage. By the time the paramedics got to the accident scene, it was too late to save his right leg and he's had an artificial limb ever since," explained Jill.

"I'm sorry to hear that, but what does that have to do with the kidnapping?" asked Frank.

"His prosthesis is still in his room, which means he would have had to hop out of here on one leg. And some of the bedding is missing, as if he was transferred to a gurney and rolled out of here. *That's* why I think he was kidnapped! Can you help me, Frank?" Jill asked, a look of pleading and despair in her eyes.

"I assume you've contacted the police, right?" asked Frank as he handed Jill a tissue from the box on the bookshelf behind him.

"Well, yes, about an hour ago, but I can't file a missing persons report until he's been gone twenty-four hours. I wanted to make a thorough search of the hospital before I filed the report and after you called this morning I just assumed you were involved and that you would tell me what's going on when you got here. Besides..." her voice trailed off as if she had changed her mind about going on.

"Besides what," probed Frank. "Is there something you're not telling me?"

Jill folded her arms in front of herself and leaned forward onto the table. "Frank, I know this is going to sound less than compassionate, but my stepfather is a little on the strange side. For several years he has had an overwhelming belief that someone was following him wherever he went."

"Following him? Who?"

"He never said – but he was terrified of them, whoever they are. He's gone to the police a couple times and they think he's suffering from dementia," explained Jill. "In light of your friend's conversation with my stepfather, it's possible that he was just feeling guilty about taking the sphere."

"No, I don't think so," said Frank thoughtfully. "Tony had the impression that your father had the sphere, or spheres, with the full permission of their owner, whoever that is."

Jill laughed and said "Frank, my stepfather retired about ten years ago. He'll be seventy-five this October! If he really did steal anything, he's kept it hidden for a long time."

Jill explained that her mother had married Al Thompson during Jill's last year of nursing school at UNLV. After graduation, Jill and her new husband had moved to Houston, Texas, where he did his internship and she began her nursing career. Jill's mother died a couple of years later but her stepfather was a strong individual and seemed to be quite capable of living alone. Several years later, when Jill's marriage ended in a bitter divorce, she moved back to Las Vegas but by then her stepfather was retired and she didn't know many details about his time at the Test Site, as the locals called it. The 5,500 square-mile area north of Las Vegas was actually several adjoining federal properties: Nellis Air Force Bombing and Gunnery Range, the Nevada Test Site, the Tonopah Test Range and, allegedly, the super-secret base known as "Area 51." It was at the Nevada Test Site that the U.S Government conducted more than 900 atmospheric and underground nuclear tests between 1951 and 1992.

In her letters, Jill's mother had mentioned that Al was a security guard at the Test Site, but she had never gone into detail about his work. Jill had always assumed that this was because the work was routine security guard stuff, but now she was wondering if there was more to Al than she knew.

As Jill was relating what she knew of her stepfather's background and history, Frank was paying more attention to the way her mouth curved when she smiled than what she was saying. He also noticed how intense her dark eyes were when she spoke about her family, especially her stepfather, and it was clear that she was deeply concerned about his welfare.

"And you're sure he was retired, huh? Tony had a strong sense that your stepfather was still working – at a place called Yucca Mountain, I think. Have you ever heard of it?"

"Of course I have – everybody in Nevada has heard of Yucca Mountain. The Feds want to create a nuclear garbage dump out there. I can't believe my stepfather would have anything to do with that place, unless…"

"Unless what, Jill?" prodded Frank.

"Well, maybe he took a part time job as a security guard out there just to pass the time. Apparently he had plenty of guard experience and a prior history of working around classified installations, so maybe they made him an offer he just couldn't refuse."

"Maybe," nodded Frank, thoughtfully. "If so, we should be able to find someone at this Yucca Mountain place who can confirm his employment. Unless, of course, it's the Yucca Mountain folks who have been following him. We should probably be careful who we talk to until we learn a little more about your stepfather's recent activities, just in case."

Frank glanced down at his watch and was surprised to discover that he and Jill had been talking for almost an hour and it was now 3:50 p.m. Since she had officially gone off duty at 3:00 p.m., Frank suggested that she accompany him to the airport and that they pick up the search for Al Thompson as soon as they collected Tony.

"What about notifying the police?" asked Jill.

"Let's talk this over with Tony. If we don't turn up some clues tonight you can file the missing persons report first thing in the morning. In the mean time, why don't you notify hospital security and have them be on the lookout, just in case he's still here in the hospital?" suggested Frank.

Tony's plane was right on time and Jill and Frank greeted him at the gate. After a brief introduction, the three of them headed for the exit while Frank brought Tony up to date on Al Thompson's disappearance. When Frank turned towards the baggage claim area Tony grabbed his arm and said "No bags, Frank. This is all I brought." He indicated the large piece of carry-on baggage he had brought off the plane.

"Traveling pretty light, aren't you?" laughed Frank.

"Actually, this is just for a couple of days. The rest of my stuff is packed in a trunk that's in the back of a friend's truck – it should be here the day after tomorrow. There are some things you just can't carry in checked luggage, you know," smiled Tony, as he shielded a wink from Jill. "Let's get some chow and you can finish bringing me up to date. Then we'll see if we can figure out what has happened to the old man."

At Jill's suggestion they drove to a Chili's restaurant on West Sahara Boulevard not too far from the Medical Center where her car was parked. As Frank brought Tony up to speed, he was amazed at how much had happened in the short five days since the two had last met in Seattle. Some of the glyphs on the sphere were clearly Maya and had been interpreted as the date July 11, 1991, while other glyphs didn't appear to be Maya at all. Then there was the coincidence of the solar eclipse and the UFO sightings, the mysterious signs directing Frank to the Yucatan's *Loltún* Caves and the shooting of Al Thompson at the casino. And last, but not least, there was today's disappearance of Jill's stepfather from the University Medical Center Critical Care Unit.

As Tony stuffed the last remnants of the devoured chili burger into his mouth he looked at Frank and said, "It sounds like you've been busy, my friend, but have you noticed that the more you investigate, the more mysteries you uncover?" He grinned at Jill, who was hearing many of the details for the first time and said "I guess it's a good thing I showed up to bail him out, huh?"

Tony's comment jolted Jill out of her deep concentration and she smiled. "Yeah, I'd say he needs some help all right. This morning the poor boy actually thought he was my cousin!"

"Maybe he was hoping to be a kissing cousin," said Tony, causing Jill to blush and Frank to choke on his last gulp of beer.

"Stow it, Tony!" managed Frank after he got the beer down. "Do you have any constructive ideas about Jill's stepfather? I was thinking that we should probably get the cops involved if he doesn't turn up by tomorrow morning. What do you think?"

"Well," said Tony, leaning back in his chair and fixing a stare on Jill that made her blush again, "let's review what we know. Old man Thompson somehow came into the possession of ancient and/or alien artifacts which probably belong to the U.S. government. Somebody's been tailing him, maybe for several years, and the night he gives one of those gadgets to me he gets shot in the head. Now, I'm no genius, folks, but I think I know where I'd be looking for the old chap."

As Tony downed the last of his Rum and Coke he surveyed the questioning looks on the faces of his two companions. "What? Isn't it obvious? Come on, you two, surely you realize that the Feds must have him, right?"

Frank shook his head and said, "Tony, what makes you think the government has him? And even if there's a connection between the spheres and Al's disappearance, why would they wait several years to nab him?"

"There you go again, with another mystery! I don't know why, Frank, but I think I *do* know where. I need to make a few phone calls to be sure, but if I'm right we're going to have a tough time getting him back." Looking back to Jill, Tony asked, "Exactly how much do you know about your stepfather's past, Jill? Specifically, what do you know about his work for the government? Did he ever mention a place called Area 51?"

"Area 51?" laughed Jill. "Most folks around here don't believe there is such a place. As far as I know, my stepfather was a security guard at the Nevada Test Site, where they did all that nuclear testing up until the early 1990s. After my mother died he moved up north, closer to the Test Site, so he wouldn't have to drive back and forth to the city every day. I was away at school and then I lived in Texas, so I don't know much else. By the time I moved back to Nevada, he was living the life of a hermit in a mobile home up in Beatty. As far as I know, he was retired. At least that's what he told me, Mr. Nicoletti."

"Oh, ouch!" exclaimed Tony, grabbing his heart in mock pain. "Please call me Tony. The only person named Mr. Nicoletti was my late father, God rest his soul."

"Okay, Tony. Anyway, that's about all I know. My stepfather and I were never very close, although we did see each other at Christmas time and on a few other special occasions, like the anniversary of my mother's death. We always made a trip out to the cemetery together to put flowers on her grave."

Tony excused himself from the table and headed off in the direction of the restrooms, leaving Frank to settle the tab. Frank and Jill had been standing near the entrance for nearly 10 minutes when Tony finally reappeared.

"Damn," said Frank, "I thought we were going to have to call in the rescue squad! Are you all right?"

Tony wrinkled his brow as if he didn't understand the question. "Of course I'm all right. I was just tracking down Al Thompson. Sorry if I kept you waiting."

Halfway out the door, Jill spun on her heels and exclaimed "What did you say?" She grabbed Tony's arm and demanded, "Did you find him?"

"Well," said Tony, looking down into Jill's pleading eyes, "it took a few more phone calls than I expected, but yes, I found him. He's safe and sound out at O'Callaghan – exactly where I thought he'd be."

"Where the hell is O'Callaghan?" asked Frank. "Is that a military hospital?"

"Yes," replied Tony. "I think the official name is Mike O'Callaghan Federal Hospital. It's across the road from Nellis Air Force Base."

"Well let's go get him!" exclaimed Jill, heading for the door.

"Hold up there, Jill!" called Tony. He caught Frank's eye and shook his head from side to side just slightly. "I'm afraid they have him locked in the psychiatric ward."

Chapter 7

"In the psychiatric ward," cried Jill, "they can't do that to him!"

"Now, Jill, just settle down for a minute," said Tony as he guided her out the restaurant door and into the hot Las Vegas evening.

Frank followed close behind and when they were safely out of hearing range of other customers Tony put his hand on Jill's shoulder to stop her.

"Jill, I know you're upset, but I have it on good authority that your stepfather is fine, that he's being treated well and that he is just being held for his own safety," explained Tony. "My contact at the hospital suggested that someone within the government felt your stepfather was in danger and didn't think the University Medical Center could provide the appropriate security. Are you sure you've told us everything you know about his work?"

"Of course I have! I told you I was out of the state for most of the time he worked up there. I think those bastards have been following my stepfather for years and now they're trying to kill him. If you two won't help me, then I'm going to the police. The government has no right kidnapping him from a civilian medical facility!" shouted Jill angrily as she spun away from Tony and Frank and started for the Durango. "Please take me back to my car right now!"

Frank ran to catch up with her and managed to get her to stop. Tears were trickling down each cheek and she pulled a tissue out of her purse.

"Jill, I don't know what's going on with your stepfather, but if Tony says he's okay, then I've got to believe he's okay. Tony has obviously talked to someone he trusts, so let's hear him out. Maybe somebody else tried to kill your stepfather, in which case he's probably better off where he is."

"That's right, Jill," nodded Tony. "Until we can get a better handle on what's up, we shouldn't rock the boat. My friend promised to keep a close eye on your stepfather and to call me immediately if the situation changes out there. In the mean time, we need to figure out who tried to kill him and why. I'm betting it has something to do with those black spheres, but we don't know that for sure."

Frank put his arm around Jill's shoulder to console her as they walked to the Durango. "Jill, I think you should go home and let Tony and me work out a plan of action. What's your work schedule tomorrow?"

"I'm off tomorrow and Thursday – it's my week-end – but, Frank, I'm really worried about him. I don't think I'll be able to sleep. Isn't there something we can do tonight?" she asked.

"Not unless you're willing to storm into a military hospital and take your stepfather by force," replied Tony. "And like I said, he's probably safer where he is for the time being. The whole clandestine feel of this situation makes me believe there's more to your stepfather than you know. I think he should stay where he is until we have more information."

"Everything's going to be fine, Jill. Go home, try to get some sleep, and call me first thing in the morning," added Frank, handing Jill one of the restaurant's business cards he had written his satellite phone number on. "Meanwhile, we'll make some calls and see if we can get a lead on who's interested in your father, and why."

As the three of them settled into the Durango, Frank and Jill up front and Tony in the back seat, Tony remarked for about the fifth time how much he liked the new rig and how out of character it was for Frank.

"I never expected to see you in an SUV, Frank," commented Tony. "With all that new money, I would have expected you to buy a Ferrari or a Porsche or some other low-slung, exotic sports car."

Frank glanced into the rear view mirror to get Tony's attention and signal him to shut up about the money, but, as usual, Tony was in his own world. Fortunately, Jill was lost deep in thought and hadn't picked up on Tony's comment.

"So has your name been released to the media yet?" Tony asked, finally looking into the mirror for Frank's response.

This comment had not escaped Jill and before Frank could answer she looked over her shoulder at Tony and asked "The media? What about the media?"

Frank finally caught Tony's eye in the mirror and gave him an unmistakable 'shut up' look. The expression on Tony's face indicated that the message had finally gotten through and he stammered to create a cover story.

"Ah, well, you see, back in Seattle Frank is somewhat of a celebrity. I'm sure he'll tell you about it one of these days."

Before Jill could ask any more questions Frank turned the corner onto the street that ran in front of the Medical Center.

"Jill, you'll have to tell me where your car is parked. I don't know my way around here," said Frank to throw her off the line of thought that Tony had initiated.

Jill directed Frank into the staff parking lot and apparently forgot the issue of the media. After they dropped Jill at her car, Frank and Tony headed back to the Residence Inn.

"Damn it, Tony, did you have to bring up that lottery thing in front of her?" asked Frank. "I'd really like to keep that quiet, if you don't mind!"

"Sorry, old buddy," laughed Tony, "I didn't realize it was still a secret. But how 'bout it? Did your name get released?"

"Yes, last Saturday, right on schedule. My neighbor, Linda McBride, is covering for me until the dust settles. I'm going to call her tonight to see if she can dig up something on Al Thompson for us and I'll find out how things are going with the press. It seems that my landlady gets off on chasing the reporters away from the building."

"Linda… is that the same Linda that was Donna's friend – the one that lived down the hall?" asked Tony, completely missing the landlady comment.

"Well, she actually lives next door, but yes, that's her. She's a really nice person and I was pretty cold to her after Donna died. I guess I subconsciously distanced myself from anything or anyone that I associated with Donna to keep from remembering,"

"Yeah, that's right, it was next door. She's a hottie, if I remember correctly," mused Tony, obviously in his own world again.

When they got back to the Residence Inn, Frank got two cold bottles of beer out of the refrigerator while Tony looked around the suite like a burglar casing for a heist. When he finally picked up his beer and sat down on the other bar stool, he smiled and said, "Well, it's no Motel 6, but I guess it'll do."

Frank pointed to the upper loft with the neck of his beer bottle and said, "Your bed is up there, and if you snore I'll stuff a dirty sock in your mouth, old buddy. So what do you think about this missing stepfather thing?" he asked as the two old friends toasted with their bottles.

"I'm not sure what to make of it yet. There's not enough information to put together a motive, a plot or any suspects. Like I told Jill earlier, I think it's all tied up with those spheres, but I'm not even sure who the teams are yet, much less the players. And that includes your little friend Jill, there. I've been going over my conversation with the old man and I'm sure he indicated that he had more than one of those things, so I suggest we check out his place first thing tomorrow and see if we can find any others. Where's the one I gave you, by the way?"

Frank pointed to the footlocker, barely visible through the downstairs bedroom door, and said, "It's locked up in there, along with a new police scanner, a new digital camcorder and a new notebook computer."

"So, you've already parted with some of that money I'm not supposed to talk about, huh?" laughed Tony. "Let's see the scanner – I used to keep one of those in my rig but it was such a hassle reprogramming it every time you went into a new area that I finally sold it to a guy in a truck stop about a year ago."

Frank retrieved the scanner from the footlocker and explained to Tony how it could be programmed from stored lists of frequencies using a computer. While Tony was playing with the scanner, Frank went in to his desk and called Linda, who sounded glad to hear from her infamous neighbor.

"Hi, Frank!" she greeted in an upbeat, happy voice. "Are you back in town?"

"Hi, Linda. No, it doesn't look like I'll be back for a few more days. How are things going with the press and Mrs. Gravely?"

"Oh, the media folks have pretty much given up on you, Frank. There was a state ferry boat accident yesterday and now there's going to be a big investigation into the safety of the whole system, so the reporters have lots to write about. I think poor Mrs. Gravely misses the attention!" replied Linda. "How's your trip going?"

"Well, it looks like I'll be doing a little detective work before I come back. In fact, Linda, I could really use some professional help from you. Can you spare a few minutes to do some background investigating for me?" asked Frank, careful not to give away too many details.

"I think I can handle that, Frank. What exactly do you need? And where are you, by the way?" responded Linda.

Linda's question about his location reminded Frank that he had never told her he was going to Las Vegas – only that he was looking into something for Tony. Since he needed Linda's help digging into Al Thompson's background, he decided he'd better fill in at least some of the details. He told her how Al and Tony had met in a casino north of Las Vegas, that Al had been shot that same night, and that someone associated with the government had grabbed the old man from the Medical Center and stashed him securely away in a military hospital. Frank intentionally neglected to mention anything about the black sphere or its related mysteries. The facts about the sphere were just a little too bizarre to discuss yet.

Linda listened to the whole story without saying a word. When Frank finally finished there was a pause and for a second Frank thought they had been disconnected. Finally, Linda spoke.

"Wow, Frank, it sounds like you might be poking around in places where you don't belong," said Linda. "Why don't you just call the police and let them handle it?"

That would be the logical thing to do, thought Frank, if it weren't for the sphere. He couldn't very well go to the police and tell them he was in possession of government property and he wasn't ready to part with it yet. There were still too many unanswered questions about its origin and purpose.

"Ah, hell, Linda," he said with a sigh, "there's a few details I left out. But you've got to promise me that you won't repeat a word of what I'm about to tell you to anyone, do you understand?"

"Of course, Frank. I'm a researcher for a major newspaper, remember? I hear all kinds of strange tales in the course of my work."

Frank filled in the missing pieces regarding the mysterious black sphere and he even included the claim by Al Thompson that it was alien in origin. That part of the story caused Linda to chuckle out loud.

"Well, I don't know about the aliens, but I'm sure I can dig up something on your Mr. Thompson. But you be careful, Frank, you hear? Regardless of the origin of that sphere, it sounds like somebody doesn't want it in the hands of others. I mean, what if they knew you had it? They might be after…"

Frank cut Linda's motherly lecture off in mid-sentence. "Thanks, Linda. I'll be careful, I promise. Besides, my old buddy Tony Nicoletti arrived this afternoon, and we're working on this thing together. And thanks for doing this research for me. You've got my new cell phone number – call me if you turn up anything, okay?"

They said their good-byes and Frank walked back into the kitchen/living room portion of the suite where Tony had Frank's new police scanner radio partially disassembled on the breakfast bar.

"What the hell are you doing?" cried Frank in shock. "That's a brand new radio!"

"I can see that. And you obviously haven't made the standard modifications necessary to make it totally functional," replied Tony, as he took another tool out of the small kit he had laid out on the counter. "Don't panic – this will just take a second."

A few minutes later he tightened the last screw securing the back of the radio and programmed in a frequency, apparently from memory. "There!" he announced, obviously proud of whatever he had done. Every few seconds voices came from the radio that sounded like normal police radio traffic.

"So what have you done to my new radio?" asked Frank. "And what are we listening to?"

As Tony crossed to the refrigerator for another beer, he explained. "All I did was modify the tuner so it can receive 'half-channels' – the frequency right between two 'normal' channels. Oh, and I also removed a filter that blocks certain government and military frequency ranges. The FCC makes the manufacturers put them in, you know."

"So what are we listening to?" asked Frank again.

"Well, that happens to be the frequency used by the security team out at O'Callaghan Hospital – I thought it might be a good idea if we kept an eye, or ear, actually, on things out there for a while."

Frank settled onto the couch and put his feet up on the glass coffee table between the couch and the fireplace. Tony handed him another beer and dropped into the overstuffed chair at the end of the room.

"So what do you make of this deal with Jill's stepfather – pretty weird, huh?" asked Frank rhetorically.

"Yeah, it's something, all right," replied Tony as he rubbed his neck to work out the stiffness created by five hours in an airplane seat. "I didn't want to go into details in front of Jill, but my contact at the base really did say they were holding the old man for his own protection. I don't think the guys who grabbed him and took him out to O'Callaghan are the bad guys – I think they are genuinely concerned about his safety, and they obviously think he's worth protecting. My contact also implied, without really saying so, that the Air Force wasn't involved in the old man's abduction, so that means it had to be one of the federal agencies – Department of Energy or Defense, maybe. There's more to this Al Thompson character than we know and we need to be careful we don't get confused with the real bad guys because those dudes up north don't screw around."

"By up north I assume you mean…?" asked Frank.

"Nellis Bombing Range, Nevada Test Site, Area 51… Call it whatever you like, but I'm telling you those guys play for keeps and I don't think they're the ones who tried to take out the old man. For one thing, they wouldn't have made the mistake of leaving him alive out behind the casino. They would have removed the old man and any evidence that he ever existed. And even if they had botched the attempt, why would they have left him at the Medical Center for nearly a week before grabbing him? No, there's another interested party at work here, Frank"

"Okay, then let's assume someone else tried to kill Al. Do you think it has to do with the spheres he had in his possession or is it just a coincidence that the attempt on his life was made the same night he handed a sphere off to you?"

"Until we know a little more about him it's hard to say, but I don't believe in coincidences. I think we'd better watch our own backs for a while, and we need to be sure Jill does the same. Maybe we shouldn't have sent her home alone," grinned Tony, winking at Frank.

Frank ignored Tony's innuendo, although he found himself suddenly worried about a person who only this morning was going to have him arrested for kidnapping!

"We should have some info on the old man tomorrow. I called Linda a few minutes ago and asked her to do some digging.

She's a researcher for the Seattle newspaper and she has access to information and sources that would amaze you."

"Her assets certainly do amaze me, you're right about that! Maybe you should have her fly out here and join us. I'd be happy to let her bunk with me so she wouldn't have to listen to your snoring," laughed Tony.

"I said access, not assets, knucklehead. Maybe you should take a trip out to one of the local brothels tonight so we can concentrate on business tomorrow," grumbled Frank, half seriously. "And speaking of tomorrow, let's talk about that. You know Jill is going to want to do something about her stepfather, so we'll have to deal with that first thing. We need to convince her to stay away from the military hospital and I agree that we ought to pay a visit to the old man's house, if Jill can get us in. Any other suggestions?"

"That depends on what your friend Linda comes up with, I guess, but let's start with the trip to his house. I don't know if we'll learn anything or not, but I wouldn't mind seeing the country-side again. The trip will be good for Jill because she'll feel like she's doing something to help her stepfather. And who knows, maybe we'll run into somebody in Beatty who actually knows the old man," said Tony as he yawned and sunk further back into the comfortable chair.

"You look beat, pal. What happened to the G.I. who could carouse and drink all night and then walk 20 miles through the jungle the next day?" asked Frank, stifling a yawn of his own.

"He got old and lazy and right now I think he's going to hit the hay. It's almost eleven, Atlanta time, and I was up at the crack of dawn this morning. What time do you want to get started tomorrow?"

"That sort of depends on Jill, since I don't know how to reach her at home, but my alarm is set for 6:00 a.m., and I've been having a light breakfast here," replied Frank as he began turning off the lights.

"Okay, 6:00 a.m. it is. Let's hope Jill calls early because I think that trip up north will take the better part of a day," called Tony as he headed up the stairs to the loft bedroom.

As it turned out, hearing from Jill wouldn't be a problem. Frank's cell phone woke him from a sound sleep at 5:45 a.m. the next morning and the caller was a hysterical Jill.

"Frank, you've got to get up here right away. They've ransacked my stepfather's house and I think there's someone outside right now!" cried Jill.

Chapter 8

"Jill, where are you?" asked a semi-conscious Frank, as he sat up in bed and tried to blink away the sleep.

"I'm at my stepfather's trailer house, Frank, and I'm scared. I think I heard noises outside a couple of minutes ago!" replied a panicked Jill.

"Jill, put down the telephone and go make sure the doors are locked right now. I'll hold on – you go!" instructed Frank. He heard the phone being placed on a table or counter and while he waited for Jill to come back he opened his bedroom door and shouted to Tony.

"What's up?" asked Tony, as he entered the room. He was fully dressed and had obviously been up for a while. "I heard your cell phone ring – what's going on?"

Before Frank could answer Jill was back on the line. "Okay, Frank, the doors are locked, but I'm scared to death. The door on this mobile home wouldn't stop anybody who wanted in very badly."

"Try to stay calm, Jill. I know you're scared, but that won't help." Frank tried to sound calm and reassuring. "I want you to tell me exactly where you are and then I want you to call 911 and get the police over there. Be sure you tell the dispatcher that you think there's a burglar outside so they don't stop for doughnuts along the way."

Frank grabbed a notepad off the desk and wrote down Jill's directions. He made sure she understood his instructions about calling the police and he told her to call him back as soon as she had done that. He hung up and filled Tony in while he was getting dressed. "Let's go," he said, as he stuffed his feet into his untied shoes and headed for the door. "Grab the scanner, will you?"

The cell phone rang again just as they reached the Durango, and Tony said "You'd better let me drive. You're going to have to stay on the line with her until the cops show up." Tony shoved the scanner into a black backpack he had been carrying and put it on the seat behind them.

Jill's voice was only slightly calmer when Frank answered the call. "The police are on the way. They said they would be here in about 5 minutes, Frank."

"Okay, Jill, now listen. Tony and I are on our way, but it'll take us a couple of hours to get there." He kept Jill talking to keep her from becoming hysterical until the police pulled up out front. "Damn fool woman," muttered Frank, as he pressed the end button on the phone. "Why did she go up there by herself?"

Beatty was almost 120 miles northwest of Las Vegas, along the southwestern border of the Nevada Test site. Once they hit Highway 95, Tony kept the speedometer needle on 90 until they reached the exit for the government town of Mercury, where the road changed from a four-lane divided highway to a standard two-lane road. Tony slowed to 75 hour for the last 60 miles and it took them another 10 minutes to find Al's mobile home once they reached Beatty. They might never have found it if Frank hadn't recognized Jill's car in the driveway. There were no police cars in sight, so Tony honked the horn as he pulled the Durango up in front of the trailer to let Jill know they had arrived. As Frank and Tony approached the steps, Jill burst out the door and practically leaped into Tony's arms.

"Oh, God, am I glad to see you guys!" she cried as she threw her arms around his neck and gave him a big hug.

"And what am I, chopped liver?" asked Frank, in mock anger.

Jill let go of Tony and gave Frank a peck on the cheek. "Thanks for getting here so fast. Please come inside, but I've got to warn you, it's a mess."

As they entered, it was clear that Jill wasn't exaggerating. Cupboard doors were standing open and kitchen drawers had been emptied onto the floor. In the living room, couch cushions were on the floor and a large number of VHS tapes had been swept out of the small entertainment cart that held the TV.

While Frank and Jill were surveying the chaos in the kitchen, Tony headed down the hallway toward the back of the mobile home. He stuck his head in the small bedroom door and everything looked to be in order, but as he passed the bathroom door he noticed that the small frosted bathroom window was up just slightly. One glance into the bathtub under the window confirmed his suspicion. "Here's where entry was made," he called down the hall to no one in particular. He closed the window and swiveled the latch. He gave the small cupboard under the sink a quick once over but nothing appeared to be disturbed.

As Tony left the bathroom he met Jill and Frank in the hallway. "What did you say?" asked Frank.

Indicating the bathroom window with a nod of his head, he said "The window was open just a crack and there's signs of a shoe print in the tub. I'm guessing this is where entry was made." And then to Jill, he asked "Did the police see this?"

"I'm not sure, Tony," she said as she peered into the tub. "If they did, they didn't say anything to me about it. There were two of them – one asked me questions while the other took a few Polaroid pictures of the mess. Then they did a quick walk-through together. The guy who had asked me questions took some notes but he explained to me that since I couldn't give them a detailed list of what, if anything, had been taken, they probably wouldn't be able to do much."

"And that's true, of course," nodded Tony, "but they should have secured the window or at least let you know it was open. Small town amateurs," he mumbled, shaking his head in disgust as he led the group into the master bedroom that occupied the back portion of the mobile home.

Clothes had been pulled out of the built-in dresser and the nightstand drawers were dumped in the middle of the bed but the search didn't appear to be as thorough as the one that had taken place in the kitchen.

"This must have been where I interrupted him," said Jill as she slid a nightstand drawer back into place. The closet doesn't look like it has been disturbed at all.

Tony, having arrived at the same conclusion, was already at the closet door. He inspected the closet shelf, moving objects around to look behind them. He opened boxes and bags, but found nothing out of the ordinary. Jill and Frank watched in amusement as Tony got down on his hands and knees and went to work on the closet floor.

"Doesn't that remind you of a bull dog looking for a lost bone?" laughed Frank. "Except, of course, that a bull dog has a nicer looking ass!"

Tony backed out of the closet, looked at them over his shoulder and made a growling sound. "And a prettier face, too," Jill added. "Tony, what are you looking for?"

Still on his hands and knees, Tony shuffled back from the closet door enough to wrestle a one-foot square safe out into the room. "This, I hope. I don't suppose you have the combination to this, do you?" he asked Jill as he stood up and rubbed his shoulder. "Damn, that thing must weigh 100 pounds!"

Frank and Jill helped Tony lift the safe up onto the bed where they could examine it more closely. "No, sorry – I didn't even know this existed. But then, like I've said before, we weren't all that close" replied Jill. "I wonder what's in there?"

"Well, I'm hoping it contains the other black sphere your stepfather told me he had. And I bet that's what the intruder was looking for when you showed up, Jill," said Tony as he brushed his hair back into place and sat down on the corner of the bed. "Whoever was in here must have slipped out the bathroom window as you were coming through the front door."

Frank examined the safe, rolling it around on the bed to look at the back, sides and bottom. "Well, it's a good one," he said as he rolled it onto its back, with the door and combination lock facing up. "These Meilink safes are tough to crack. We had several of the larger models back at Boeing that we kept classified documents in. They have over a million possible combinations, so let's hope old Al wrote this one down and hid it somewhere around here."

"Yeah, and let's hope whoever was in here didn't find it before Jill scared them off. Let's put the old man's things away and look for the combo at the same time. Otherwise, we're going to have to convince a locksmith to drill this thing," said Tony as the two men went to work on the contents of the nightstand drawers piled on the bed.

Watching them in disbelief, Jill put her hands on her hips and asked "Guys, why don't we just ask him?"

Frank and Tony both looked up at her and asked, in unison, "Ask who?"

"My stepfather, of course! Have you forgotten that he's being held hostage by the government in a military hospital against his will? I say we put this safe back where we found it, drive back to town and demand his release. Then he can open the safe himself, if he wants to. You guys are acting like my stepfather is never coming back here!" Jill turned her back to the bed to wipe away the tear of frustration that was trickling down her cheek.

Frank went around the foot of the bed and put his arm around her shoulder. "Jill, we haven't forgotten about him, but for all we know it might have been the government that did all this," he said, indicating the mess in the room. "And if it wasn't, then it's probably a good thing he wasn't here during the break-in. Let's go put the kitchen back together and see what we can find. We'll leave Tony in charge of this room."

Reluctantly, Jill followed Frank the length of the mobile home, back to the kitchen, and began picking items up off the floor and putting them back into drawers.

"Keep your eyes open for anything that looks like three numbers, Jill. Anything from 0-0-0 to 99-99-99 could be the safe combination," said Frank, joining the cleanup.

"I'd still rather just ask him," muttered Jill, too softly to be heard.

An hour later Frank, Tony and Jill had the old man's house looking more or less normal, but they hadn't found anything resembling a safe combination. Sitting around the small dinette table, they shared the only beer that had been in the refrigerator.

"Well, now what?" asked Jill, sounding almost glad that the combination hadn't turned up. "Are we going to blast the safe open or are you two ready to admit we should go get my stepfather?"

"Jill, we've already discussed..." started Frank.

Tony interrupted with a wave of his hand. "You know what, Frank, maybe Jill is right. Why don't the two of you take her car, go over to O'Callaghan Hospital and see if you can at least talk with her stepfather. If they let you see him, Jill will feel better and maybe you can find a way to ask him about the combination."

"That's crazy, Tony! You know damn well they aren't..." protested Frank.

Again, Tony interrupted Frank, but this time he caught Frank's eye while Jill was looking away and Frank realized what Tony was up to.

"Frank, just trust me on this one, okay?" continued Tony, as if he were still trying to persuade Frank. "I'll stay here, because I have a strong hunch our visitor might come back to finish the search that Jill cut short. If you learn anything at the hospital, come back up here. If not, I'll take the Durango and meet you in the city. Then we can figure out what our next step is."

Jill, figuring that at least one of the two stubborn men had finally come to his senses, was already heading for the door. "That's a good idea, Frank. Come on; let's get over there before it gets any later."

As Jill headed down the steps towards her car, Frank turned and shook his finger at Tony. "Thanks a lot, buddy! What the hell am I going to do with her when we get to the hospital?"

"Oh, you'll think of something, Frank," smiled Tony. "You always do."

After Frank and Jill left, Tony moved the Durango down the street so it would appear that the mobile home was once again empty. What Tony hadn't told them earlier was that he not only expected the intruder to return, he *wanted* him to. Once back inside, Tony reopened the bathroom window a crack, found a two-year old Field and Stream magazine under the coffee table and stretched out on the couch to wait. The open black backpack from the Durango rested on the floor near his right shoulder.

Meanwhile, Frank and Jill made their way south, back towards Las Vegas. At the north end of the city they turned east and then north again, to the hospital. During the trip they had nearly come to blows over the approach to take when they arrived. Jill seemed to think she could just flash her University Medical Center credentials and they would let her waltz right through the front door. Frank, on the other hand, wanted to play dumb and not tip their hand. By the time they reached the parking lot, Frank had convinced Jill to play it his way first and if that didn't work then she could try her approach.

Inside, the hospital looked like a typical civilian facility. There was a large waiting area with a reception counter in the back right-hand corner. Several closed doors led out of the main room, but there was also a wide hallway to the left of the reception counter that appeared to provide access to the rest of the hospital. As they approached the counter, Frank looked down and said under his breath, "Just let me do the talking, okay?"

After waiting briefly behind an Airman at the counter, Frank stepped forward and explained that they were relatives of Mr. Al Thompson. He said they had heard that he had been transferred from UMC to O'Callaghan and they wondered if it might be possible to visit with him for a few minutes.

The receptionist gave Frank a puzzled look and typed something on the keyboard in front of her. A few seconds later she looked up at Frank and said "I'm sorry, sir, but there is no one named Thompson currently admitted here. Are you sure you have the right hospital?"

"Okay, Jill, I guess you're on," said Frank as he turned to let Jill flash her civilian ID. He had assumed she was standing behind him while they had waited in line, but when he looked around she was nowhere in sight. Frank guessed that she must have slipped away while he was talking to the receptionist and out of the corner of his eye he saw a door across the room closing, but it was too late to see if it had been Jill. Sheepishly he turned back to the receptionist, who was shaking her head.

"Did you happen to notice the woman that came in with me?" asked Frank persistently.

"No, sir, I didn't, and if you don't have an appointment please step aside so I can help the next person in line."

"But you must have seen her, she was standing right here just a minute ago!" he exclaimed, raising his voice a little too loud.

"Sir, would you like me to call security or are you going to leave on your own?"

"No, no, I'm going. Sorry to have bothered you, Miss," said Frank as he turned and headed slowly back toward the hospital's main entrance, his hands stuffed into his pockets.

Frank found a chair near the entrance that provided a view of the entire waiting room and sat down. Since they had come in Jill's car and she still had the keys, there was no point in going out to the parking lot in the mid-day heat. Maybe she's just gone to the restroom, he thought.

When Jill still hadn't returned in fifteen minutes, Frank began to get worried. Damn fool woman, he thought. She's going to get herself busted and ruin any chance we have of talking to the old man. And she's not going to do her stepfather any good, either. Damn her!

He carefully scanned the room one more time, but there was no sight of her. Then he caught a movement from outside, where the large front window joined the wall of the building. He pushed his sunglasses up onto his head and recognized Jill peeking around the corner and motioning for him to come outside.

Slowly, so as not to alert anyone who might be watching him, Frank got up and casually strolled to the entrance. As he stepped through the automatic sliding glass door he glanced back over his shoulder and noticed a uniformed soldier standing behind the counter talking with the receptionist. They both looked up at him and even across the length of the large room Frank could see the soldier's white AP armband that signified he was a member of the Air Police. Frank walked quickly to Jill's car and when he reached the vehicle she was already behind the wheel. As Jill pulled out of the parking lot onto Las Vegas Boulevard Frank noticed the AP standing outside the entrance of the hospital with his hands on his hips.

"Where in the hell did you disappear to?" demanded Frank as they headed south.

Jill pulled a small, folded piece of paper out of her blouse pocket and handed it to Frank without a word.

As Frank unfolded the paper he recognized it immediately as a safe combination. "23-14-87," he read out loud. "Jill, how did you get this? Did you talk to your stepfather?"

"Only for a minute," she said, as she wiped a tear from her cheek. "I didn't even ask him for the combination. Before I could say a word he nodded to a pencil and pad on his nightstand. He repeated these number several times and then told me about the safe in his mobile home. 'Give them back,' he said to me. 'It's the only way they'll ever leave me alone.' About then there was a commotion down the hall, so as soon as the coast was clear I slipped out of his room and ducked out through the loading dock around back."

"How did you find him?" asked Tony. "And how did you get in there? What if you had been seen?"

"Relax, Frank. Tony isn't the only one with contacts, you know. Most of the nursing staff is made up of civilians and I have a friend who worked out there for a while. Last night I called her and got an idea of the layout. She even told me which door led directly into the correct wing. I have my civilian credentials from UMC, so if I had been stopped I would have just said I was there on a consultation or something."

"Well why didn't you clue me in on your little secret agent operation?" asked a frustrated Frank as he handed the combination back to Jill. "I had no idea where you had gone or even if you were okay!"

"Because you would have tried to talk me out of it, Frank," replied Jill. "Nothing – and no one – was going to stop me from seeing my stepfather. You would have been too obvious inside the hospital and if they'd challenged you, you would've had no logical reason for being there."

"Yes, but…" started Frank.

"But nothing!" interrupted Jill. "You got what you wanted and I got to see my stepfather. Now all we have to do is return whatever is in that safe and things can get back to normal."

Frank was about to take issue with Jill's line of reasoning when his cell phone rang. "That must be Tony," he said to no one in particular, and he was surprised to hear Linda's voice when he answered the call.

"Hi, Frank! I've got some information for you on that gentleman you asked me to research," came Linda's pleasant voice.

"Hi, Linda. I'm in a car right now and I can't take notes, so why don't you just give me the highlights now and maybe you can e-mail me the details," replied Frank, trying to sound casual about the call. He hadn't told Jill about his inquiry into her stepfather's background and he didn't think she was in any mood to hear about it right now.

"Well," began Linda, "it turns out that your Mr. Thompson has had quite a career. He did his undergraduate work at Michigan State University and got his doctorate in Nuclear Physics in 1961 from MIT. He did post-doc work at the Stanford Linear Accelerator Center, and then he spent some time at JPL in Pasadena. In March of 1975 he went to work for a company named EG&G Special Projects in Las Vegas, but I also found some indications that he may have transitioned to a company called Bechtel, a huge international civil engineering and construction company headquartered in San Francisco. Bechtel has a facility in Las Vegas that provides support services to the Nevada Test Site and something called the Yucca Mountain Site Characterization Project."

"Are you sure about this?" asked a puzzled Frank. "No chance we're talking about a different subject, is there?"

"If by 'subject' you mean another person, I don't think so. The Al Thompson I found was married in 1985 to a Margaret Anderson, now deceased, who had a daughter named Annabelle Jill from a previous marriage. Oh, and he lost his right leg in an automobile accident in 1989. Does any of that sound familiar?" asked Linda.

"Uh, yes, that would be the case," replied Frank, still trying to disguise the true nature of the phone call.

"Frank, you're talking funny. Are you where you can't speak freely?"

"Yes, that would be correct," said Frank matter-of-factly, "but I'll look for your e-mail with all the details. Thank you for your help on this, Linda."

"Roger, Wilco and out, good buddy," laughed Linda. "And you had better reply to my e-mail and let me know what's going on down there. This cloak-and-dagger stuff is too funny. Bye, Frank." Linda hung up and Frank laid the phone on the seat, a million questions racing through his mind.

"Who was that?" Jill's voice derailed his train of thought and it took him a second to formulate a cover story.

"Oh, just someone from Boeing, where I used to work," lied Frank. There's been some foul-up with my retirement papers and she's trying to get things fixed. Listen, before we open that safe back at your stepfather's house, would you mind going over what you know about him again?"

"No, I don't mind, but why? I've already told you what little I know. What are you looking for?" answered Jill, a little annoyed at Frank's request.

"Nothing in particular, Jill. I was just thinking of something you said a few minutes ago. You said your stepfather told you to give the contents of the safe, which we believe to be at least one more sphere, back to 'them.' Are you sure he wasn't more specific?"

"Well, I assumed he meant the government – or whoever he took these mysterious spheres from, if that's what's really in the safe. And no, he wasn't more specific. It was like he assumed I knew – or would know – when I opened the safe," she added, starting to doubt her own idea of who 'they' were.

"All right, as long as we have some time before we get back to the mobile home, why don't you tell me again everything you can remember about him? Start when you first met him and don't leave out any details. I have an idea there's more to old Al Thompson than meets the eye."

Chapter 9

Meanwhile, back in Beatty, Tony had almost dozed off when he heard a faint noise from outside the mobile home. Slowly, so as not to make any noise of his own, he got up off the couch and reached into his open backpack. The object he withdrew was about eight inches long, two inches wide and a half-inch thick. It vaguely resembled a flat electric shaver except that Tony's Stun-Master taser was capable of discharging 625,000 volts into an opponent and rendering him completely helpless for several minutes.

Tony heard another noise, this time from the vicinity of the bathroom window. He made his way down the hall and positioned his back against the wall, just outside the bathroom door. Holding the taser in his left hand, he waited. A moment later a figure stepped through the door. Tony jammed his weapon against the other's right thigh and fingered the trigger button. A violent convulsion shook the intruder and a sharp gasp escaped his mouth before he fell to the floor, arms and legs jerking wildly. Tony stepped back out of kicking distance and waited until the thrashing body gradually curled into the fetal position and the muscle reactions became just a slight twitching. As he watched the body on the floor more closely, Tony observed that the man had the light brown skin, straight black hair and round facial features characteristic of many Native Americans.

Tony retrieved two pairs of handcuffs from his backpack – one for the intruder's hands and one for his feet. When the handcuffs were securely in place, he called Frank.

"Where are you?" he asked when he heard Frank's voice at the other end.

"We're on highway 95, about 40 miles away. What' up?"

"Our thief returned a few minutes ago and he's currently bound hand and foot in the hallway wearing off a rather serious taser stun. As long as you're headed this way, I'll just keep him quiet until you get here. How'd the visit to the hospital go?" reported Tony.

"Interesting, to say the least. I'll tell you all about it when we get there, but to make a long story short, Jill spoke with her stepfather and he gave her the combination to the safe. If you have something to write with I'll give you the combination now."

"No Thanks. I think we ought to all open it together. At least Jill should be here since it's her stepfather's property. My visitor is beginning to come to his senses, so I think I'll ask him a few questions while I wait for you. See you soon," said Tony as he positioned himself where he could keep both eyes on the figure on the floor.

Tony clicked his cell phone back into his belt and moved to the feet of the now relaxed and more straightened body on the floor. As the intruder opened his eyes, the first thing he focused on was Tony standing over him, smiling. "Welcome back," said Tony, his smile turning to the meanest look he could muster. "Did you have a nice nap?"

The intruder moved to stand and run and abruptly discovered his restraints. With a look of panic on his face, the man tried to shuffle back away from Tony on the floor. Tony raised his left hand, palm out to signal "Stop!" but the terrified intruder continued to squirm down the hall on his back. "Stop, damn you, or I'll get the taser again!" shouted Tony, to no avail. Then, on a hunch, he shouted *"Alto!"* and the figure froze in place.

"So, you understand Spanish!" said Tony to the man on the floor. As Tony approached, the intruder started to squirm again. *"Quieto!"* shouted Tony, which he hoped meant quiet or something similar. Again, the figure on the floor stopped moving and appeared to understand.

"Now we're getting somewhere," said Tony, motioning for the man to stay down on the floor. *"Tranquilo,"* said Tony in a calmer, less threatening tone. *"Tranquilo, amigo."*

Although far from fluent in Spanish, Tony did know enough to ask the intruder some simple questions and when he finally answered, the other man's Spanish was almost as bad as Tony's. Clearly, it wasn't his first language. Over the course of the next thirty minutes, Tony was able to get some basic information out of the man, whose eyes were constantly darting about looking for signs of the taser.

Tony learned that the man's name was *Ahmok* and that he was looking for a missing *jajal dyos* that had been stolen from him several days earlier. Beyond that, the intruder couldn't, or wouldn't, elaborate. It's like he's giving me his name, rank and serial number and not a bit more, thought Tony. And he couldn't get a description of a *jajal dyos*, either. Apparently the man only knew the one word to describe whatever the object was. Either that or it had no counterpart in Spanish.

By the time Frank and Jill arrived, the intruder had settled down considerably and Tony had propped him up against the wall and brought him some water. When the Indian heard the door to the mobile home open he panicked again and Tony had to forcibly hold him on the floor.

"I'm in here, guys," called Tony from the hallway, "But take it slow. Our friend is a bit nervous."

Frank and Jill joined Tony and he brought them up to date on his interrogation. As the intruder began to realize that the newcomers weren't going to cause him further harm, he settled down again. Jill moved to his side and tried to reassure him in Spanish. While he obviously didn't understand all of what she was saying, the fact that she was a female and that she hadn't just zapped him with 625,000 volts of electricity gave her a big advantage over Tony.

"So, you speak Spanish, too. Clever girl!" remarked Tony as he stood up and backed away to ease the intruder even more.

"I lived in Texas for a number of years and it was almost a necessity," replied Jill. "But I'm not sure how much Spanish this guy speaks. It's like he doesn't even recognize some words, and yet he clearly gets others. What are we going to do with him?"

"Well, I suppose we should hand him over to the police, but I'm not sure how much more they will get out of him," said Frank. "He seems to be here on what he feels is a very important mission and I don't think he intended to hurt anyone. He just wants his *jajal dyos* back, whatever that is."

"Well, can we at least get him up off the floor and onto a chair?" asked Jill, standing slowly, so as to not frighten the man again.

"Sure, there's no need to treat him like a common criminal. After all, he only broke in here twice," muttered Tony as he removed the cuffs from the intruder's ankles and pulled the man to his feet. With a firm grip on the man's arms, Tony guided him into the living room and settled him into a chair. He showed the man the handcuffs he had removed, shook his head "no" and put them in his hip pocket. This seemed to relax the intruder, who acknowledged Tony's act with a slight nod.

"All right, folks," said Frank, "We need a plan. This little adventure of ours has suddenly gotten very complicated and we don't seem to be getting closer to any answers. Anybody have any ideas?"

"Let's start by opening the safe in the other room," replied Tony. "I'm curious about what the old man thought was so important. One of us needs to stand guard here, though."

"I agree with that," added Jill, "although I don't like the idea of holding him prisoner here. Either we should turn him over to the police or let him go."

"All in good time, Jill," nodded Frank. "But if we let him go I have the feeling he'll be right back in here the minute we leave. He is clearly very focused on this mission of his. I'll stay here while you and Tony go open the safe."

When Jill left the room, the intruder became agitated about being left with a stranger. Frank sat down to appear less threatening, and that seemed to help a little.

A couple of minutes later, Frank heard Tony's voice from the bedroom. "Holy shit! Look at this!"

Frank wanted to dash to the room and find out for himself what the other two had found, but he didn't dare leave the prisoner alone. "What is it? What did you find?" he called back to them.

"You're not going to believe this, Frank!" he heard Tony say. And then Jill called out, "And there are two spheres in here too, Frank!"

"Damn it, you two, tell me what you found!" shouted Frank down the hall, startling the intruder. "Either that or one of you can come down here and watch this guy so I can look."

"Be right there, Frank," called Tony. A minute later Tony and Jill entered the room. Tony had a sphere cupped in his large hand and Jill was carrying a double hand full of banded packets of money.

"What the…" stuttered Frank as he saw the money.

"Frank, there must be a million dollars in there," whispered Jill, as if she were trying to keep the fact a secret. "Where on earth did a retired security guard get that much money?"

Ahmok, the Indian Tony had apprehended an hour earlier, briefly eyed the money in Jill's hands but when he spotted the black sphere Tony was carrying he went crazy again. Pointing at the sphere, he kept repeating *jajal dyos* excitedly.

"Well, I guess that clears up one question, doesn't it?" said Tony, extending the hand containing the sphere toward the Indian. "Apparently these spheres are called *jajal dyos* in his language."

"And since Jim Barnes has already confirmed that at least some of the hieroglyphics on the sphere are Maya, I'm betting our friend here is also Maya," commented Frank. "Jill, are those bundles of hundred dollar bills you have there?"

"Yes, and I just don't understand it! Where would my stepfather have gotten this much money? And why would he live here," she said, indicating the mobile home, "if he had this kind of money stashed away?"

Frank crossed to Jill, gently put his hands on her shoulders and eased her down on to the couch. "Jill, I'm afraid I haven't been totally honest with you today. That call I received from Seattle earlier was actually a friend of mine who works as a newspaper researcher in Seattle. I asked her to see what she could find out about your stepfather and what she turned up is pretty amazing."

Clutching the money close to her, Jill tentatively asked, "What about him?"

"Yeah," said Tony as he joined the group, "What about the old man?

"Well, it turns out that Al Thompson is a nuclear physicist with a doctorate from MIT. He had a number of government-related jobs before hiring on in 1975 with the contractor that manages the Nevada Test Site, among other places. Linda is e-mailing me all the details, but those are the high points. I'm sorry I didn't tell you this earlier, Jill, but you seemed so upset after seeing him that I didn't think the timing was right. I was actually going to wait until I had Linda's e-mail in case you didn't believe me."

"What?" said both Jill and Tony at once.

"It's true. Linda checked him out and that's what she came up with. She even knew about the car accident and the amputated leg, Jill, so I'm afraid there's no mistake. For whatever reason, your stepfather lied to you about his employment."

"And who knows what else! I wonder if my mother ever knew about any of this?" snapped Jill, as she dumped the packets of bills on the couch and stood up. "That bastard!" she added as she stomped into the kitchen and turned on the water.

Frank picked up a packet of bills that had slipped onto the floor and put it with the others. He glanced into the kitchen and noticed that Jill was leaning over the sink with her head hung down and the water still running.

"Are you all right, Jill?" he called to her.

Without turning around, Jill nodded her head and Frank guessed she was crying and didn't want the others to know. He started for the kitchen, but Tony waved him off. "Give her a minute, Frank," said Tony quietly. Frank nodded in agreement and turned to face the Maya, who was still in the chair where Tony had parked him. Next to him, Tony was casually rolling the sphere around from one hand to the other.

Tony's handling of the sphere was clearly upsetting the Indian, so Tony carefully placed it on the coffee table, out of reach. "*Mejor*?" he asked the man, "Is that better, *amigo*?"

The Maya nodded and settled back in the chair a little. "He's pretty attached to that thing, isn't he?" observed Frank. "I'd really like to question him about the sphere in detail, but he didn't seem to understand much of what Jill was saying to him earlier."

"What are we going to do with him?" Frank asked Tony. "Now that he knows we have the spheres, he'll keep breaking in here until he gets them back."

"Well, so far he only knows about this one, Frank," said Tony, indicating the sphere on the table. "He doesn't know about the other one in the bedroom or the one you have back in the city. Maybe if we give him this one he'll go away happy and leave the place alone."

"An interesting idea, but what if he came here with a shopping list? What if he knows about the other two? We have no way of knowing what he's up to," countered Frank.

"True, and we don't know how many there are altogether. We've located three by accident. There could be dozens more that we don't know about. It's too bad we don't know anybody who speaks Maya."

"Of course!" exclaimed Frank. "Jim Barnes – why didn't I think of him earlier?" Frank dashed into the kitchen where he had left his satellite phone, startling Jill in the process. As she turned around, Jill's red eyes confirmed Frank's suspicion – she had been crying.

"What's going on?" asked Jill.

"I'm calling a friend in Seattle who's an expert in everything Maya to see if he can communicate with our friend here. We need to know what it's going to take to get rid of him so he doesn't keep breaking in here," explained Frank.

"Oh," said Jill and she turned back around to the sink. This time she retrieved a glass from the cupboard and filled it with water from the tap. She turned back around and leaned against the counter as Frank dialed Jim Barnes' office.

"Hello, this is Professor Barnes," said the voice at the other end on the connection.

"Jim, this is Frank Morton. Listen, I'm in Nevada and I really need your help. Do you have a minute?" asked Frank, hopefully.

"Well, I have a lecture in about thirty minutes, but what's up? And what are you doing in Nevada?" replied the soft-spoken archeologist.

"That's a good question, but I don't have time to give you all the details. I'll fill you in later, but for now just trust me. Are you familiar with the Maya phrase, *jajal dyos*?" asked Frank.

There was a long pause, and then Jim replied "I think that means something like truth, but not the common truth, as in truth vs. lie. I think *jajal dyos* actually means 'the real truth', as in from a deity or a god. Why, Frank? Does this have anything to with that hieroglyphic tracing you gave me?"

"Yes, sort of. Actually, it's a lot more complicated than that. Jim, I'm going to try to put someone on the phone and I'd like you to ask him about this *jajal dyos*. Ask him why he wants ours and how many of them there are all together. Can you do that for me?" asked Frank.

"How many of what, Frank? What are you talking about?" asked a puzzled Barnes.

"Jim, just pretend that *jajal dyos* is an object, ask him what he wants with ours and how many of them there are altogether, okay? I'll explain all this to you later," replied Frank.

"Okay, Frank, I'll play along, but why don't you just ask him yourself? Why do you want me to talk to this person?" asked a very confused Jim Barnes.

"Because we think he only speaks Maya, Jim. And please don't ask about that, either – I'll tell you later," replied Frank as he moved back into the living room next to the intruder in the chair.

"*Sabes qué es?*" asked Frank, indicating the cell phone, "Do you know what this is?"

Apprehensively, the man nodded as he withdrew slightly from Frank. Tony moved closer to the chair in case the intruder decided to bolt.

"*Habla!*" commanded Frank, as he moved the phone to the man's ear. And then, loud enough for Jim Barnes to hear him, he said, "Okay, Jim, go ahead."

The native tried to move his head away, but with Tony's help they managed to get the phone and the Indian's head connected together long enough for the man to recognize Maya coming from the instrument. Once he recognized a few words, he settled down and Tony stepped back to present less of a threat.

Eventually the Maya uttered a few words into the phone, and then a few more. When it sounded like Jim had successfully drawn the man into a conversation, Frank signaled for Tony to remove the handcuffs from the man's wrists. After a silent argument of headshakes, nods and shrugs, Tony finally complied and Frank let the man hold the phone himself.

After about five minutes, the Maya held the phone out to Frank without a word. Frank took the phone and asked, "So what did you learn, Jim?"

Frank was surprised to hear an angry tone in Jim's voice. "Frank, what is going on down there? Why are you holding this man hostage?"

"Jim, this guy broke into a private home, not once, but twice. The second time we nabbed him and now we just want to know what he's after. Please tell me what you learned."

"Well, according to him – and his name is *Ahmok*, by the way – he's there to recover a sacred item that was stolen from him recently. What is it that you have of his?" asked Jim, the anger draining from his tone.

"We don't exactly know, Jim. My friend Tony came into possession of an object that carried the glyphs I showed you back in Seattle. Since then, we have recovered two more of the objects, and we're pretty sure they are what this guy calls the *jajal dyos*. We don't really want to turn him over to the cops, but we can't have him breaking in every few hours, either. Tony suggested just giving him one of these objects in the hope he would go away, but if he knows how many there are, one won't satisfy him," explained Frank patiently.

"Why not give him all you have, Frank? If they belong to his people, you have no right to them anyway. Stealing artifacts is a crime, you know," replied Jim, the anger starting to creep back into his voice.

"Jim, we didn't steal them from anybody, except possibly the US government. We're trying to find out where they came from, what they mean and how they relate to the shooting of a government scientist. Did he tell you how many there are all together?"

"I couldn't get a straight answer from him, but I don't think he knows how many there are. He knows you have the one he came to get because he can see it, and I think he knows there are others in existence, but I can't be sure. I'm not familiar with his dialect so I couldn't understand some of his comments," replied Jim. "I get the impression he is on some sort of religious mission, so he probably won't take "No" for an answer."

"I was afraid of that," said Frank. "Okay, Jim, I'm going to hand the phone back to him and I'd like you to tell him that we want to help him. Tell him we will give him back his *jajal dyos* if he will behave himself. That means he has to stop breaking in here so we can go back to Las Vegas and check some things out."

"Okay, let me talk to him again," said Jim.

Frank handed the phone back to the intruder, who immediately said something to Jim in Mayan. While the two were talking, Jill joined Frank and Tony, looking a little embarrassed.

"Sorry," she said. "It was just a shock to learn that my stepfather isn't who he claims to be. And when I think about my mother, going to her grave not knowing the truth…"

Frank put his arm around her shoulder and Jill leaned her head against him. "Sorry," she said again.

"Don't worry about it, Jill. Tony and I will help you get to the bottom of this. Just hang in there."

"Yeah, Kid, there may be a perfectly good explanation for all this," smiled Tony. "From what I know about the Nevada Test Site, this may all boil down to a national security thing. Maybe old Al wasn't allowed to talk about what he did. And maybe your mother knew the truth and couldn't talk about it either."

Tractrix

That seemed to cheer Jill. "Yes, maybe you're right! Maybe they didn't tell me because they didn't want me to worry about them," said Jill, mostly to herself.

Once again the Maya abruptly extended the phone to Frank, but this time he made eye contact and said, "Funk," which Frank took to be his own name in broken English.

"How'd you do?" asked Frank into the phone.

"He says he will leave the place alone if you give him the *jajal dyos* you have and promise to let him go free. Otherwise, there's no deal. And one other thing – I'm on the next plane to Las Vegas."

"Is that part of his deal, too?" asked Frank.

"No, that's part of <u>my</u> deal," replied Jim. "I'll be damned if you're going to have all the fun. I don't know what you've stumbled onto, but it's obvious that you need someone who can speak and read Mayan and I am intrigued with these *jajal dyos* things. I will be there later today."

"I guess I don't have a lot of choice, do I? Can you get away from the University?" asked Frank.

"It's summer term and I'm beginning a year of sabbatical leave but for this I'd resign, Frank. You could be on to something really, really big," exclaimed Jim.

"Yes, and out of this world, too," said Frank without explaining. "I'm going to give the phone back to this guy. Please tell him we have a deal. Thanks, Jim, and I guess we'll see you soon. Call me when you know what flight you're on and bring your passport with you – I have a feeling we'll be making a trip south of the border real soon."

Frank handed the cell phone back to the Indian and brought Tony and Jill up to date on Jim's negotiations. "Before he gets out of here with this one," Frank said, indicating the sphere on the coffee table, "I need to copy down the glyphs for Jim. We'll keep the one in the other room a secret, along with the one back in the city. Let's pick up this money, too. Jill, you should take all of it back to Las Vegas and get it into a bank for now. You can figure out what to do with it later."

The three each got busy with their chores. Jill scooped up the packets of bills and headed back to the bedroom where the safe was still lying open on her stepfather's bed. Tony collected his handcuffs and taser and began repacking his backpack while Frank got a pencil and paper from the kitchen and began the painstaking job of drawing the glyphs from the sphere.

Before Frank had finished the first glyph, the Maya was standing beside him with the cell phone extended again. Frank put it up to his ear, but Jim had already disconnected. The Maya noticed that Frank was trying to recreate the writings on the sphere and he laughed. He picked up the sphere, rotated it once, and then set it down and drew all nine glyphs on Frank's paper with amazing speed and accuracy. When he finished, he pointed to the third glyph in his drawing and then to the one Frank had partially completed. He held up three fingers, shook his head yes, held up one finger and shook his head no. From this, Frank deduced that he had started with the wrong symbol. Then, without another word, the mysterious man picked up the sphere and marched out the front door, leaving Frank staring at his artwork in awe. Tony made a move to stop him but Frank said, "Let him go, Tony. At least he's out of here, and a deal is a deal."

"But he's got one of the spheres!" protested Tony.

"I know, but this is all we really need." Frank held up the paper containing the Maya glyphs so Tony could see it. "As far as physical spheres go, we still have two. Losing that one is worth it if it keeps him out of here. We need to get back to town and try to figure out what these things are and where they came from. What's keeping Jill?"

Tony shrugged, as if to say, "Who knows" and slung his backpack over one shoulder.

Frank carefully folded the piece of paper and put it in his pocket. "Jill, are you ready?" he called to the back bedroom.

When there was no answer, Frank and Tony looked at each other in surprise and they both headed down the hallway at the same time, almost colliding.

Jill was sitting on the bed in front of the open safe. A small box about two inches square and half an inch deep was lying open next to her and she was clutching a gold locket.

"Jill, what is it?" asked Frank, as the two men stormed into the room.

As she looked up a tear trickled down each cheek. "I found a small box in the safe under the rest of the money and this was in it," she said holding out the locket for them to see. "It belonged to my mother. She was wearing it the day she died."

"Oh, sorry, Jill. But it's nice that Al kept it, don't you think?" said Tony. Why don't we take all this stuff back to town and you can go through it privately?" he said as he moved to start gathering up the packets of bills she had dumped on the bed.

As the locket turned on the chain, Frank noticed a glint from the back when it caught a beam of sunlight.

"Jill, does that locket have an inscription on the back?" asked Frank, stepping closer to the bed.

Jill turned it around and studied the back for a moment. "Yes, it does. I never noticed this before, but it says 'Remember *Loltún*.' What do you suppose that means?"

Chapter 10

Frank, Tony and Jill packed the contents of Al Thompson's safe into a small carry-on they found on the shelf of the old man's closet. Without really knowing why, Jill wrote out a note and locked it in the safe before they returned it to its original position on the floor of the closet:

The contents are with me. Love, J.

Tony gave the mobile home a security once-over, checking all the windows and doors. He found the lock broken on the bathroom window, so he used the small saw blade on his pocket knife to cut a piece off a broom handle and he wedged it into the frame to secure the window. After a final once-over, the three left through the front door and Jill locked up.

"Crap!" said Frank, as they approached Jill's car in the driveway. "I forgot that we have two vehicles up here! Tony, how about following us to Jill's place so we can make sure she gets home safely?"

"Okay," replied Tony, digging the keys to the Durango out of his pocket. He handed Frank the bag containing the money, the remaining sphere and the box of keepsakes and said, "You take this with you and I'll bring up the rear."

As Jill pulled away from her stepfather's mobile home, Tony hung back for a minute. Comfortable that no one was following Jill and Frank, Tony pulled away from the curb and soon caught up with them.

On the way back to Las Vegas, Jill wondered out loud at the recent discoveries relating to her stepfather. The spheres, the money and the whole identity secret were almost too much for her to handle. Frank consoled her as best he could, but he really didn't know how to tell someone that everything was okay when it obviously wasn't.

While Jill was lamenting the events of the day, Frank counted the money they had found in the safe. Each packet of bills contained one hundred $100 bills, for a total of $10,000 per packet. Frank counted them twice before interrupting Jill's monologue.

"Fifty-one," he said, as he stacked the packets back into the carry-on.

Jill continued talking for a second and suddenly realized that Frank had said something. "I'm sorry, Frank. What did you say?"

"Fifty-one," he repeated, "There's fifty-one packets of bills. That's $510,000 altogether. Not quite the million you estimated back at the mobile home, but a nice nest egg, just the same."

"Wow!" exclaimed Jill. "Where did he get a half-million dollars, Frank? And why would he keep that kind of money in his trailer – why wasn't it in a bank account somewhere – or at least in a safe deposit box?"

"Well, that's certainly the question of the day, isn't it?" replied Frank, as he took the remaining sphere out of the bag. "A lot of things don't add up yet, like the two spheres he had. Counting the one he gave Tony, your stepfather had three of these things that we know of," said Frank, as he turned the sphere in his hands and studied it carefully.

"Is this one just like the one my stepfather gave Tony?" asked Jill.

"Well, the sphere itself looks the same, but the hieroglyphics are definitely different," replied Frank. "The symbols go all the way around and, of course, I don't know which one is first. When the Maya wrote out the glyphs from the other sphere he got an obvious kick out of the fact that I had started with the third symbol instead of the first."

Frank pulled the piece of paper containing the Maya's transcription out of his pocket and began comparing the symbols on the paper to those on the sphere in his hand. After a second he said, "Well, I'll be damned! There are 2 glyphs on each sphere that match exactly and they're always in the same order. And if I'm not mistaken, they are the same ones that Jim hasn't given me an interpretation for. And I think…"

Frank was interrupted in mid-sentence by the ring of his satellite cell phone. "Hello, this is Frank Morton," he said into the phone.

"Frank, this is Jim Barnes. I'll be on Alaska Airlines' flight 638. I arrive at 7:21 p.m. tonight – can you pick me up at the airport?" asked Jim.

"Of course," replied Frank. "Hey, I was just talking about you. Some new facts have come to light that I think you will find interesting. Have you had any luck with those other glyphs from the first sphere? The glyphs your Mexican friend didn't recognize."

"Well, I've been working on that, but I don't have a definite answer for you yet. They're not Maya, but I still think they are closely related. They might be Olmec or some pre-Maya form," explained Jim. "I'm bringing some research material with me tonight."

"Okay, Jim, we'll see you tonight at the airport. Look for us right outside the baggage claim area on the sidewalk."

Frank pressed the End Call button on the phone and leaned his head back against the seat's headrest. "This thing gets more bizarre by the minute!" he said. He glanced at his watch. It was nearly 3:00 p.m. and he was starving, but at Jill's 55 MPH pace they were still a good two hours from the city. "Jill, can you pick it up a bit? We need to get this money secured before all the banks close. Do you happen to have a safe deposit box?"

Jill begrudgingly increased the car's speed to a steady 60 MPH, but she was obviously uncomfortable driving above the speed limit and she clutched the wheel as if it could be torn out of her hand at any minute. "Yes, I have a small one, but it won't hold all that money, if that's what you have in mind." Glancing at her own watch she said, "Besides, my branch is near the Medical Center and, with rush hour traffic, I doubt if we'll make it. Can't we just hang on to this for the night and deal with it tomorrow?" she said, indicating the bag on the floor at Frank's feet.

"Jill, we're talking about a half million dollars! Don't you think having that kind of money lying around your apartment is a little risky?" asked Frank.

"Well, I suppose, but I was actually thinking that maybe you and Tony could keep an eye on it," replied Jill, with her first smile of the day. "I'm not sure I really want to have anything to do with that money until I know a little more about where it came from."

"Jill, I'm living in a hotel and everybody and their brother has a key to my room. We'd have to pack it out with us every time we went down the street to 7-11. No, we need a better solution than that. Let me see what I can do," said Frank as he reached for his phone again.

After a series of phone calls, Frank finally announced, "Okay, I've found a place to keep the money until we decide what to do with it. When we get to town, go directly to the parking lot behind the Mandalay Bay hotel."

Before Jill could ask any questions, Frank was on the phone again talking to Tony who was following a few car lengths behind them. "Change of plans, Tony," said Frank into his phone. "We're going to take the cash to the Mandalay Bay hotel out on the strip for safe keeping until we decide what to do with it. A guy I knew from Boeing is in charge of security out there and he's going to arrange for storage in their vault."

"Are you sure that's a good idea, Frank?" asked Tony. "Are you sure they'll give it back to you?"

"They do this all the time, Tony. As far as anybody at the hotel knows we're just a couple of high rollers in town for a good time. We'll deposit the money with the hotel in a private account and this guy told me that $500,000 in cash wouldn't even raise an eyebrow. Apparently it's done all the time."

"Well, it beats the hell out of storing it in that footlocker of yours, I guess. Okay, I'll stay on your tail as best I can, but once we get into heavy traffic I may lose you. Where are you meeting this guy?"

"I'm supposed to call him when we pull into the back parking lot. He said he'd meet us at the door and make the appropriate introductions. A deposit of this size apparently includes a complimentary suite and considerable special attention, so try to act the part, okay?" jabbed Frank.

"Hey, I'm Italian, remember? I can act like a gangster without even trying. See you there, Godfather Morton!"

Frank was laughing as he ended the call with Tony and Jill asked him what was going on. "Oh, nothing, just a little Sicilian humor, that's all," said Frank. "Okay, here's the new plan, Jill. The three of us are going to pose as high rollers in town with our bag of mad money – we'll be what the casino industry refers to as 'whales.' When we get to the hotel a guy is going to meet us and introduce us as Frank and Jill Dayton, from Chicago. Tony will pose as my 'assistant.' The three of us will be shown to a suite and then I will be escorted to an office where the money will be counted and stored in the casino's vault. I'll be issued a line of credit against the cash and then we can figure out what we're going to do. Oh, the hotel is going to send one of its limos to pick up a Mr. Jim Barnes, a business associate who's flying in to meet with me tonight,"

Frank smiled. He reached into the bag and removed one of the packets of $100 bills. "You don't mind if we borrow this for pocket change, do you? I'll replace whatever we use."

When Frank looked up Jill was shaking her head and laughing. "Hell, Frank, do what ever you want with it! The last two days seem more like a Hollywood movie than real life, anyway. I've discovered a stepfather I didn't know, been face to face with a real live Maya Indian, acquired a half million dollars from an unknown source and now I'm married to a high roller from Chicago. This is too funny!"

It was nearly 5:00 p.m. when Jill turned off I-15 onto Tropicana Avenue. A quick right turn took them down a private street that runs behind the Excalibur, Luxor and Mandalay Bay hotels and provides access to the three hotels' huge off-street parking structures. Frank instructed Jill to park in an area where there weren't too many other cars and they waited for Tony to catch up.

When Tony pulled into the lot a couple of minutes later, Frank reached over and signaled him with the headlights on Jill's car. Tony pulled into the space next to them and rolled down his window. "Okay, boss man, what's up?"

"Try to remember to call me Mr. Dayton whenever there's anybody else around, Tony. Jill you can call me Frank but remember that we're supposed to be married, so you'll have to act the part," instructed Frank.

"You just watch your manners," smiled Jill. "Are we actually going to stay in this suite tonight? And what about the fact that we don't have any luggage?" asked Jill as she and Frank climbed out of her car.

"Our contact has prepared some kind of cover story, but I don't know what. We'll have to clear out of here tomorrow or they will start wondering why we aren't gambling more. Before I call my contact let's get the sphere and box of jewelry out of this bag – I don't want the boys in the counting room to find that stuff. Tony, open your backpack and we'll stow it in there," said Frank as he set the bag on the trunk of Jill's car and unzipped the bag.

Just as he dropped the sphere and box into the backpack, a voice startled all three of them. "Everything all right here, folks?"

Tony spun around in a defensive stance and came face to face with a hotel security guard. Startled himself, the guard took a step back and his hand started to move toward his gun. A quick-thinking Tony held up both hands and said, "Hey, easy, there. You just surprised us, that's all. We're checking in to the hotel."

The guard relaxed a bit, looked at Frank and asked, "Mr. Dayton?"

Frank, still recovering from the guard's arrival, was slow to respond to the unfamiliar last name. Jill nudged him and said, "Frank, the man is talking to you, for God's sake!"

"Oh, yeah, that's me. I'm Frank Dayton," Frank finally stuttered.

"Welcome to the Mandalay Bay, Mr. Dayton. Mr. Young asked me to escort you to the hotel, sir. This way please," said the guard as he motioned toward the Hotel's back entrance with an extended arm.

The three fell into step and headed toward the door a few steps ahead of the guard. Jill leaned close to Frank, so the guard couldn't hear, and whispered, "You almost blew it, buster. Some husband you are!"

Frank detected the sarcasm in her voice, so he put his arm around her shoulder, leaned close and whispered, "Stow it, lady, or I'll have my boys rub you out!" They were both laughing naturally as they reached the door and Frank slowed his pace to allow the guard time to pass and open the door for them.

A few feet inside the door they were greeted by an elderly man dressed in a very expensive suit. "Frank?" he asked.

"Wes? Wes Young?" asked a surprised Frank. "I can't believe it!" The last time Frank had seen Young, he was wearing a security guard's uniform at Frank's Boeing office complex.

"How do you like the new uniform?" he asked, smiling and extending his hand.

Frank took Wes Young's hand and shook it firmly. "Yeah, it's a big improvement, Wes. And, hey, thanks for helping us out here. Like I told you on the phone, we stumbled across the money this morning and we were at a loss what to do with it. I really appreciate you covering for us."

"It's my pleasure, Frank. I was lucky to get this job and I'm sure the recommendation you gave me helped a lot. I'm glad to have the opportunity to help out," beamed Young.

"Well, thank you again. Maybe we can get together for dinner sometime while I'm in Las Vegas." Stepping back to introduce his friends, he said, "Wes Young, this is Jill, the lady with the money dilemma, and this is my old friend Tony Nicoletti.

After brief pleasantries, Wes opened an unmarked door near the main entrance and said, "Right this way, folks."

He led them down a hallway and into an elegant office with gold letters on the door that read 'VIP Reception.' He indicated that they should be seated on a large sofa facing the desk and said, "Ms. Landis will be right with you. If there's anything else you need, just give me a call, Frank. My cell phone number is printed on the front of this card and I'll write my home number on the back. I spend most of my time here at the casino these days, but I'll take you up on that dinner sometime. Nice to see you again." He wrote his phone number on the back and handed the card to Frank. "I've got to get back out on the floor – nice meeting you all," he said to the others and then disappeared out the door.

Frank looked at the card. "Chief of Security! Wow, I guess he *did* get a good job," he said, as he put the card in his pocket.

A moment later a tall, well-dressed woman about 30 years old walked through the door. Instinctively, Frank and Tony stood up but she motioned them back into their seats. "Please be seated, gentlemen. We are very happy to have you staying with us, Mr. and Mrs. Dayton. Looking towards Tony and then back to Frank, she asked, "Will there be just the three of you?"

"Well no, actually. I believe your limo is picking up an associate of ours at the airport," replied Frank.

"Ah, yes. I'm sorry. I didn't notice the notation in your file. A Mr. Barnes, Alaska flight 638 at 7:21 p.m., is that correct?" she asked very business-like.

"Yes, that's right, but he's going to be looking for me, so he won't be expecting a hotel limo," said Frank.

"We'll find him, Mr. Dayton," she smiled, "and we'll take good care of him. If you will all follow me, I'll show you to your suite."

An hour later, with the money safely stored in the casino's vault, Frank, Tony and Jill were sitting in the living room of the suite sipping champagne and laughing at their good fortune.

The 3,200 square foot suite on the 41st floor had a curving staircase that led from the entryway down into the large, vaulted-ceiling living area that faced two-story windows looking out over Las Vegas Boulevard and McCarran International Airport.

The interior, two-story portion of the suite included a master bedroom upstairs and a smaller bedroom and bathroom downstairs. The sectional they were sitting on faced a 36-inch, high-definition television built into a huge entertainment center and there was a large formal dining table and a fully stocked wet bar at the far end of the room.

"Well, this certainly beats the Residence Inn!" laughed Tony as he leaned back on the leather sectional unit and folded his hands behind his head. "Good move, Frank."

"I'll second that," chimed in Jill. "I had no idea these suites were so elegant! How long before your friend gets here?"

Frank glanced at his watch. "He won't be here for a couple hours and I'm starving! How about if we order some food and figure out what our next move is going to be?"

The room service was as elegant as the suite itself, served on fine china with sterling silver. After the meal, Frank found a pad in the drawer of the telephone table and took notes while all three reviewed the events of the week that led up to their current situation.

About 7:50 p.m. there was a knock at the door and Frank got up to answer it. "I'll get it. That's probably Jim Barnes," he said as he climbed the stairway to the foyer. He opened the door to greet a very surprised and flustered Jim Barnes accompanied by a tall man in a dark suit.

"Mr. Dayton?" asked the man.

"Yes, I'm Frank Dayton. Come in, Jim, and welcome to Las Vegas." Frank pulled Jim through the door into the foyer and started to close the door.

"Your friend seems to be a little confused, sir," said the man in the hallway. "I had a hard time coaxing him into the limousine – he insisted he was supposed to meet a Frank Morton and even though we knew his name and flight information he didn't want to come with us."

"Sorry about that," explained Frank. "Morton is my mother's name and I sometimes use it in complex business deals, if you know what I mean," winked Frank. He slipped a $100 bill into the man's hand and closed the door. When he heard the man leave, he heaved a sigh of relief and ushered Jim down the stairs to where Tony and Frank were waiting.

"Damn, you almost blew our cover!" he said to Jim as they reached the bottom of the stairs.

"Cover? What's going on here, Frank?" asked a nervous and confused Jim Barnes. "I thought I was being kidnapped at the airport!"

"Jim, I'm really sorry about that, but there was no way I could give you a heads up. I tried to call your office in Seattle, but you had already left by the time I knew what was going on and they wouldn't give me your cell phone number. Let me explain all of this to you. This is Jill Harris and Tony Nicoletti. Are you hungry? Can we order you anything?"

Jim looked around the suite in awe. When he noticed the wet bar he said, "I'll take a double Scotch on the rocks, if you don't mind." Jim plopped down on the couch visibly shaken by his limo experience.

Tony headed to the bar for the drink and Frank sat opposite Jim in a large leather chair. He knew his friend was not the adventurous type and apologized again for the confusion at the airport.

Tony returned with the Scotch and Jim drank the entire contents of the glass in a series of long gulps. Setting the glass down on the coffee table between them, he looked across at Frank and said, "Okay, what the hell is going on?"

Frank picked up the note pad he had been using and said, "We were just recapping when you arrived. Here's where we are: We now know of three spheres, and we suspect there are more. Someone tried to kill Jill's stepfather, probably because of the spheres. The government has kidnapped the old man 'for his own protection.' This same stepfather turns out to be a nuclear physicist instead of a security guard and he also had more than a half million dollars stashed away in his mobile home. An angry Maya Indian, who broke into the old man's mobile home, is now in possession of one of the spheres. Oh, and all three spheres seem to have two hieroglyphic symbols in common. I think that about sums it up, right guys?" asked Frank as he looked from Jill to Tony.

Tony and Jill nodded silently as Jim put his head in his hands and tried to process all the information. Suddenly his head snapped up and he said, "What did you say? What was that about the symbols?"

"The two symbols you never decoded on the first sphere seem to appear in the same order on both of the new ones. Did you ever figure out what they meant?" asked Frank as he removed the

Maya's copied symbols from his pocket. "Tony, will you get the other sphere out of your backpack, please?"

Jim opened his brief case and removed the original piece of paper Frank had given him back in Seattle and the four of them moved to the large dining table to spread everything out. Jim was carefully comparing the two pieces of paper when Tony set the sphere down on the table with a 'thud.'

Jim's jaw dropped. "Is this … is this one of the spheres – a *jajal dyos*?" he asked as he picked it up and cupped it carefully in his hands.

"Yes, this is what all the fuss is about," replied Tony. "Odd looking thing, isn't it?"

At first Jim just stared at it, taking in the shape, size and weight. Soon he began to study the glyphs around its circumference and compare them to the two pieces of paper on the table. Finally, he set the sphere back down on the table and looked up at the others.

"Well, you're right. There are two glyphs on each sphere that are exactly the same." He commented, matter-of-factly.

"Any guesses as to what they might say?" asked Frank hopefully.

"No offense, Frank, but your copy of the first sphere was pretty bad. Now that I see the Indian's version and this actual sphere, the symbols make a little more sense," explained Jim, pointing to the last two symbols on the Maya's paper and the corresponding two on the sphere itself.

"Well," asked an impatient Frank, "What do you think they mean?"

"I'm not positive, but if I had to guess I'd say that the first one means 'flower' and the second one means 'rock' or 'stone' – something like that."

Frank picked up the sphere and held it at arm's length. "How would you say that in Mayan, Jim?"

Jim thought for a moment and then replied, "Well, flower is '*lol*' and the Maya word for stone is '*tun*', so I guess it would be pronounced '*lol-tun*', why?"

"*Loltún!*" said Frank, almost dropping the sphere, "There's that damn word again!"

"Of course!" shouted Jim. "There is a complex near the ancient Maya city of *Uxmal* called *Loltún*. It's an extensive area of interconnecting caverns that contains some of the very earliest Maya writings. And it also appears to be the common denominator between these spheres!"

"*Loltún*?" asked Jill, as she retrieved the small box from Tony's backpack. "Isn't that the same word that's inscribed on my mother's locket?"

Chapter 11

With the discovery that each of the three spheres carried a pair of identical hieroglyphs and that these glyphs represent the Maya name *Loltún*, Jim immersed himself in the books he had brought from Seattle. As he began scribbling notes on three different pads of paper, the others retired to the living area. Tony made each of them a drink from the wet bar – a gin and tonic for Frank, a screwdriver for Jill and a rum and Coke for himself – and settled on the leather sectional next to Jill. "What do you think this all means?" he questioned out loud.

"Do you mean the mystery glyphs?" asked Frank, "Or the various references to this place called *Loltún*?"

"Both," answered Tony. "And what's up with Jill's stepfather, his secret background, all that cash, and then there's the spheres themselves – what do you think they are?"

"Your impromptu stop in Beatty a couple weeks ago has certainly opened a huge can of worms," said Frank, "and we need a plan if we're going to get to the bottom of any of this. I'm intrigued by this *Loltún* connection and since Jim is the expert on all things Maya, I think he and I should make a trip down there as soon as possible. That is, if you wouldn't mind staying here and helping Jill figure out what's going on with her stepfather. How soon do you have to be back in Atlanta? You never did tell me how long you planned to stay here in Vegas."

"Oh, I've got a few days – I put my truck in the shop on Monday and it won't be ready until the middle of next week. I expect Jill and I can figure out what's going on here while you and Jim vacation in Mexico," laughed Tony.

Jill had been quietly studying her Mother's locket with the strange inscription on the back. "Don't I get a say in any of this," she asked, looking up from the locket.

"Of course, Jill, sorry. But don't you think Tony could be some help? And some of the circumstances relating to your stepfather also connect to our sphere mystery. And didn't you say you had to go back to work on Friday? Tony could continue to follow up any leads while you are at work."

"Hey, I didn't say I didn't want his help," she smiled as she put her hand on his arm. "I just think I should have a vote. Of course I'd welcome Tony's help because, frankly, I don't have any idea where to start. I have tomorrow off and then I go on nights beginning Friday. That's the 4:00 p.m. to midnight shift."

"Well, if everybody is agreed, I think I'll see if I can get Jim and me on a flight to the Yucatan tomorrow. Is that okay with you, Jim?"

Jim was so absorbed in his work that he didn't hear Frank. "Jim!" called Frank a little louder.

Jim lifted his head from his work for the first time in several minutes and looked at the three at the other end of the room. "Huh?" he asked, lost in thought.

"Are you game for a trip to the Yucatan tomorrow?" repeated Frank.

"Ah, yeah, sure," stammered Jim, still not quite into the conversation. "The Yucatan? Sure. Does anybody have a computer?"

By this time Frank, Tony and Jill were all laughing at Jim. He was clearly very focused on whatever he had been studying.

"I have a laptop back at my hotel," replied Frank, "and there's a high speed Internet connection, too. Are you on to something, there, Professor?"

"Ah, yes, maybe, but I need to check out some data using the University library back in Seattle. Can we go to the computer now, please?" asked Jim, with the sound of pleading in his voice.

The three laughed again and Frank got up off the couch. "Okay, come on, Jim. I'll take you down to my hotel." And then to Jill and Tony, he said, "Tony, that packet of bills is still in your backpack, so why don't you and Jill go spread some of it around down in the casino so nobody gets suspicious. You two might as well stay here tonight, if you want. It might look fishy if we all bail and nobody stays in the suite."

"Dibs on the Jacuzzi!" yelled Jill, as she jumped up off the couch. "And the big room upstairs!"

Tony rolled his eyes at Frank and said, "Great! You get to go study interesting anthropology stuff and I have to stay here in this suite with a pretty lady and $10,000 in cash! How come you get to have all the fun?" he laughed.

As Jim was gathering his papers and stuffing them into his worn leather briefcase, Tony picked up the sphere and handed it to Frank. "You should probably take this back and lock it up with the other one," he said.

During the mile or so drive back down the strip to the Residence Inn, Frank questioned Jim about what he thought he had found. "I assume it has to do with the matching glyphs, right?" asked Frank.

"Yes, but I can't be sure until I can verify some distances," replied Jim. If you remember, we determined from your tracing of the original sphere that the glyphs specified a date – July 11, 1991. We also decoded some other numbers but we didn't know exactly what they meant. And then there were the last two glyphs, undecipherable due to the quality of the drawing, which we now know mean *Lol* and *Tun*."

"Yeah, sorry about that, but I did the best I could," apologized Frank.

"Oh, I wasn't being critical, Frank. Anyway, I've decoded the dates on the other two spheres. They are August 8, 1496 and June 26, 884. We know that the date on your first sphere corresponds to a total solar eclipse, right?"

"Right," replied Frank, "And an unusual UFO sighting."

"Yes, whatever," dismissed Jim. "Well, I'm betting that these two new dates also mark total solar eclipses, but I need to check with the library to be sure. Assuming my hunch is correct, each sphere specifies the date of a total solar eclipse and a specific location, namely *Loltún*. Can you guess what the other numbers might represent?"

"Well, when you called me from Mexico the other day you mentioned something about a polar coordinate system that was based on distance and direction, right?" Frank thought for a minute, and then banged his fist on the steering wheel. "Of, course!" he shouted, "The location is relative to *Loltún*! Each sphere tells the date of a solar eclipse and its location relative to *Loltún*."

"That's what I'm guessing," said Jim. "Of course I can't be sure until I can look at some maps. We don't know what unit of measure they used for long distances, or exactly how they measured angles, but we do know that they were keenly aware of the value 360. Maybe we'll get lucky and find out they divided their circles up into 360 degrees, the way we do."

"Well, it all makes sense, doesn't it?" asked Frank. "I mean, weren't the Maya interested in solar eclipses?"

"Not just interested, Frank, they were obsessed with them. Some of my colleagues believe the whole reason they developed their sophisticated and incredibly accurate calendar system was so they could predict eclipses of the sun and moon. We assume that a shaman, or religious leader, was able to command the respect of the common people by predicting a natural phenomenon like a solar eclipse."

"But if a shaman had one of these spheres, he wouldn't need a calendar, right?" asked Frank. "He could just read the date from the hieroglyphs."

"So it would seem," replied Jim, scratching his chin and studying his notes.

***

Meanwhile, Tony and Jill had freshened up and headed down to the casino for a little fun. In the elevator Jill confessed that even though she had lived in Las Vegas for almost eight years, she had never actually been in a casino to gamble. Since her divorce, she had been struggling to make a life for herself and gambling always seemed like such a waste of money.

"Well, we've got $10,000 here and orders to act like big spenders, so I'd say it's time you got your feet wet at the craps table. You're supposed to be the high-roller lady and I'm supposed to be the bodyguard, so you take the money and I'll whisper in your ear at the table. Ten grand isn't a lot of dough for a real high roller, but it's sufficient for a girl friend or wife to have. Since you only have hundreds, I suggest we play at a table with a $100 minimum – it will look like we brought the large bills on purpose. Besides, the average tourist doesn't play the high-limit tables, so you'll be more conspicuous."

"Jeeze, Tony, I don't want to be in the spotlight! You take the money and pretend it's yours," said Jill, trying to give it back to him.

"No, Jill, we have to do this my way. The boss is away on business so I'm escorting his wife to make sure nobody gives her any grief. You'll do fine," reassured Tony.

As Jill started to protest, the elevator door opened onto the main casino floor and they found themselves face to face with a group waiting to get into the elevator. Jill stuffed the packet of bills into her purse and they moved past the elevator passengers and into the casino crowd.

Tony and Jill walked the casino floor, stopping here and there to observe various games for a few minutes. Besides getting Jill used to the feel and tempo of the casino, Tony was looking for just the right table.

Finally, Tony settled on a craps table that was moderately busy. Most of the players were well-dressed elderly folks who appeared to know their way around a casino and there was a pit boss observing the play.

"This table will do, Jill," said Tony quietly. "Just pick any number and lay a bill on it. I'll let you know what to do next."

"Tony, are you sure about this? I don't believe in gambling, you know," she protested.

"You heard what Frank said. We need to do this to keep up appearances. Now just pick a number," he said as he gently pushed her up against the rail.

Jill leaned over and put a hundred dollar bill on the first number her eyes fell on – which happened to be the number 12 with a circle around it. She looked over her shoulder at Tony to see if she had done what he wanted and he nodded slightly. At that moment someone at the other end of the table threw the dice and startled her.

"Twelve, the number to make is twelve" said the man next to her who was holding a stick with a curved end. Across from her, another casino employee picked up her hundred-dollar bill and replaced it with three poker chips. She looked back at Tony again and he nodded slightly, which she took to mean, "Leave it alone." A second later the dice flew again and the shooter shouted happily.

"Twelve it is!" shouted the man again, as Jill's three chips became nine. Again she looked at Tony and this time he nodded, "No" so she reached out and slid the small pile of chips back against the wall of the table in front of her.

Tony stepped forward next to her and said "Nice work, Mrs. Dayton!" loud enough for those around them to hear. Then very quietly, he said to Jill, "Just bet one chip at a time, and move your bets around. That's all there is to it." Tony stepped back and stood with his hands clasped in front of him, trying to look the part of a vigilant bodyguard.

Jill was getting into the swing of the game and actually enjoying herself. Sometimes she would skip a roll or two, then place a bet on the Field area in front of her. As Beginners Luck would have it, she won more often than she lost and after about forty-five minutes she had twenty chips in front of her. The nice man with the stick had given her a red plastic tray that held chips in neat rows of ten. With a nod of her head she signaled Tony to step closer and quietly asked, "Can we try something else?"

"Of, course Mrs. Dayton, anything you like," said Tony out loud. Softer, he said, "Make one more bet and then tip the stickman and the two dealers each one chip. Be sure you take your chips when you step away from the table so they will know you're done betting."

Jill looked around the table and noticed an area on the table right in front of the stickman labeled Horn. She leaned over and handed him a chip. "Could you put this on that Horn in front of you, please?" she asked in a pleasant voice.

"Of course, Ms. Dayton," replied the stickman. He had obviously been paying attention to Tony's conversations. The next roll of the dice was a two and the stickman announced, "Craps, new dealer." Then to Jill, he smiled and said, "Nicely done, ma'am!"

The man sitting directly across from the stickman, who seemed to be in charge of all the chips, slid three piles of chips across to Jill. She gave the stickman a questioning look and he answered by saying, "Thirty-to-one odds, Ma'am. Very nicely done."

Still a little confused, Jill loaded the chips into her tray and started to back away from the table. Tony moved in close, as if to help her, and whispered, "Don't forget the tip."

Jill gave each of the three casino employees a chip and walked away with the remaining chips. When they were a few yards from the table she stopped and asked Tony, "So, how did I do?"

Tony glanced at his watch. "Well, you managed to turn $100 into $4,600 in less than an hour, so I'd say you did okay for a beginner, Mrs. Dayton." He emphasized the fake name for effect.

"You mean that these little chip things are…"

"One hundred dollar chips, that's right, Jill. So please be careful where you leave them, okay?" smiled Tony, enjoying the excitement of Jill's first gambling experience.

"But that means that I tipped those guys a hundred dollars each!" she exclaimed.

"Anything less would have been impolite and called negative attention to you," smiled Tony. "Did you notice that the stickman picked up on your name? I'm betting the pit boss did, too. Frank would be very proud, Jill."

"Well, then, Wise One, which game shall we conquer next?" laughed Jill as she headed towards a roulette wheel that had caught her eye.

Tony caught up with her and put his hand on her shoulder. "Not roulette, Jill. The odds are stacked against you and it's just a game of chance."

"And what would you call what I was just doing, since I didn't have a clue how that game was played? I'll just bet one chip." Jill stepped up to the table between two tall guys dressed like cowboys and put a chip on number 36. "My age," she said to the cowboy on her right when he looked down at her. The dealer spun the wheel and after what seemed like an agonizingly long time, the ball dropped into the wheel.

"Thirty-six is a winner!" he called down the table. He collected various losing bets from around the playing field and then slid Jill four stacks of chips, one half the size of the other three.

Surprised, she began loading her winnings into the tray.

"Oh, don't leave, little lady. You might bring me some luck!" laughed the cowboy on her left. As he reached over to put his arm on her shoulder Tony stepped out of the mass of people moving back and forth in the aisle and said louder than necessary, "Ready to go, Mrs. Dayton?"

Seeing Tony, the cowboy lowered his arm, smiled at Jill, and said, "Evening, Ma'am." He touched the brim of his hat and turned back to the roulette table.

"So I take it I won again, huh?" said Jill with an 'I told you so' grin.

"You're the luckiest person I've ever seen," said Tony as they left the roulette table. "You just netted another $3,400! When Frank told us to have fun in the casino, I don't think he meant break the bank, Jill! Let's find a nice quiet bar and have a drink. Watching you win all this money has made me thirsty."

"Yeah, me, too," replied Jill. "And I'll even buy the fist round," she laughed.

***

A few miles away, Frank was having a much less exciting time watching Jim Barnes scratch notes on his yellow pads. "Anything definitive, yet, Jim?" he asked with a huge yawn.

"Not yet, but I think I'm on the right track. I just need to correlate some numbers and check them against known geographic coordinates. I shouldn't be more than another two or three hours," replied Jim without taking his eyes off the screen of Frank's computer.

"Well, you know what," said Frank, "I've been up since very early this morning chasing after nurses and Mayas and I'm really, really tired. I'm going upstairs to take a nap on Tony's bed. If you come up with anything concrete, call me. Otherwise, I'll be back down in a couple of hours."

Frank started out of the downstairs bedroom where his computer was set up when Jim looked up and said, "Huh? What was that?"

"Nothing, Jim, I'll be back in a few minutes," laughed Frank as he turned and headed up the stairs. As he put his head down on the cool pillow he could hear Jim's fingers clicking on the computer keyboard downstairs.

Frank awoke with a start to the sound of his watch beeping. He laid his head back down to collect his thoughts when he realized he could hear computer keys clicking downstairs. "Jim!" he said out loud. "Oh, crap, I've slept all night and left the poor guy downstairs working!"

As Frank entered the downstairs bedroom where he had left Jim Barnes seven hours earlier, Jim looked up with a smile and said, "Morning! Did you have nice nap?"

"Jim, I'm really sorry! I didn't intend to leave you working by yourself all night. You must be exhausted!" apologized Frank. "I'll start a pot of coffee. Can I get you some juice, or anything?"

"No, just coffee will be fine, thanks," replied Jim. "And after you get it started, I have something to show you."

Frank reentered the room a few minutes later with two cups of steaming coffee. "So what have you come up with, Jim?" he asked as he set one cup down next to his computer for Jim.

Jim had used every sheet of paper on two of the three pads and there were only a few sheets left on the third. He rummaged through the loose pages scattered all over the bed until he located the one he was looking for. "Ah, here it is. Frank, I think I've determined the locations referred to on all three spheres. Some of this is speculation, but it all fits an emerging pattern, so it's pretty good speculation."

Jim took a sip of the hot coffee and continued. "At first I tried to determine the three locations by just comparing the relative magnitude of the numbers, but that kept yielding too many possibilities. Early this morning the obvious finally occurred to me and, after a little Web surfing, I found this site." Jim brought up a page on Frank's computer that had a box at the top that said Eclipse Home Page.

"As we guessed last night, the dates all represent solar eclipses and the locations are all places where these eclipses were visible. With the help of this NASA Web site I was able to locate maps showing the paths of our three eclipses. Next, I superimposed known Maya sites onto the maps and computed the relative distance from *Loltún* to each of the sites. After that, it all sort of fell into place. Here, see what I mean?" Jim asked as he handed Frank a roughly drawn map of the Yucatan with three Xs on it. Beside each one was a date, a set of latitude/longitude coordinates and another number that Frank assumed was the distance taken from the sphere.

According to Jim's calculations, the original sphere indicated that the July 11, 1991 eclipse was visible from *Palenque*, and the two other spheres described eclipses of August 8, 1496 and June 26, 884, which were visible from *Tikal* and *Quingua*, respectively. All three locations were the sites of ancient Maya cities.

"Wow, Jim, this is great detective work!" said Frank. "And what happened to our earlier theory about Mexico City?"

"Just a coincidence, probably. The July 11th eclipse was visible across much of Mexico, and would have been just as dramatic in *Palenque* as it was in Mexico City. But the distance and angle data on that sphere clearly point to *Palenque*."

"But what about the UFO sightings?" asked Frank.

"That's your theory, not mine," replied Jim. "After studying this data all night, I'd stake my professional reputation on the places I just mentioned."

"So the spheres told whoever possessed them not only when an eclipse was going to occur, but also where. That kind of information had to make whoever knew it pretty powerful in the eyes of the common people."

"That's for sure! And I'd be willing to bet that the individual, or possibly it was a group of individuals, lived at or near the *Loltún* Caves," commented Jim.

"What makes you say that?" asked Frank.

"Well, as far as we know, *Loltún* was never a significant Maya center. There are no ancient ruins there, and I wasn't able to find any reference to it in Maya literature. So if *Loltún* wasn't important to the Mayas in general, it must have been important to whomever controlled the spheres," explained Jim.

"Sure, that makes sense," reasoned Frank. "But what doesn't make sense is why they didn't store these spheres at one of their major centers, like *Chichén Itzá* or *Uxmal* or even *Tulum*. Or, conversely, if the spheres were stored at *Loltún*, why didn't it become a significant Maya center?"

"Well, I think the answer to that question lies with the spheres themselves, Frank."

"What do you mean?"

"I believe the spheres predate the Maya cities you just mentioned by hundreds of years, maybe more. Especially *Uxmal*, which is fairly close to *Loltún*. Besides, I've studied a lot of Maya artifacts in my day, and I can tell you beyond any shadow of a doubt that these spheres are definitely not Maya in origin."

Chapter 12

Frank could see that the "all-nighter" had taken a toll on Jim Barnes. The anthropologist had made significant progress in unraveling the mystery of the spheres, but now he was exhausted. Frank finally talked Jim into going upstairs and crawling into the bed that Frank had slept on top of all night. After Frank stored the two spheres in his footlocker and collected Jim's papers into a neat pile, he logged on and checked his e-mail.

Along with the numerous junk e-mails he always got, Frank found the message from Linda McBride detailing Al Thompson's secret background. She had told him nearly everything on the telephone the day before, so there were no surprises, but he printed it out anyway, for Jill's benefit.

After dashing off a couple of quick replies to some other routine messages, Frank researched flights to the Yucatan. He found an afternoon flight on AeroMexico Airlines to Cancun with a connecting flight to Merida the next morning. Normally, Frank preferred to book all his own travel online, but since he didn't know anything about the hotels in either city, he decided to use a local travel agent. It was only 6:30 a.m., so Frank jotted down the flight information and made himself a light breakfast. He would call the travel agency later.

After several cups of coffee and thirty minutes of CNN Headline News, Frank showered, shaved and dressed for a new day. At 8:30 a.m. he called Mandalay Bay's in-house travel agent and booked the flights for Jim and himself. He asked the agent to select the hotels in both Cancun and Merida and he made arrangements to pick up the tickets at 11:00 a.m., since the flight to Cancun was due to leave at 2:10 p.m. Once the trip was booked, Frank called the suite where he had left Jill and Tony to see how their casino adventure had gone. After about four rings, Jill finally answered the phone.

"Hello," she said in a very sleepy voice.

"Good morning, Jill," replied a refreshed and rested Frank. "How did you do in the casino last night?"

"Hello, who is this?" came her sleepy reply. "This is Jill."

This time Frank thought he detected a hint of hangover mixed with some serious sleep deprivation. Frank decided to give up on Jill and try Tony, who was always up early in the morning. "Jill, this is Frank Morton. Is Tony there? Please put Tony on."

"This is Tony," came another sleepy reply almost immediately. "Who's this?"

"Tony, this is Frank. I gather that you two stayed up late last night. How was your casino visit?"

"Ah, good morning, Frank," said Tony, trying to clear his head. "Yeah, we stayed up pretty late. It was about 2:30 a.m. before we got back to the room. Jill won almost $8,000 in the casino last night, but my head feels like we drank up $4,000 of it!"

"What do you mean, she won? I thought you guys were going to spread some of that $10,000 around the casino for appearances," said Frank.

"Well, we tried, but the more Jill played, the more she won. I finally decided that the only way to keep the casino solvent was to get her off the gambling floor and into a bar!" laughed Tony. "The biggest damn case of beginner's luck I've ever seen."

"Well, while you two were partying, poor Jim worked through the night on the sphere translations," said Frank. "I think he's come up with a pretty plausible theory that I'd like to go over with you..."

Hold on just a minute, Frank," interrupted Tony. "Let me go down to the living room so Jill can sleep – she's really zonked."

Tony came back on the line a few seconds later. "Okay, that's better. Go ahead, Frank. You were saying?"

Realizing that Tony had answered the phone from the master bedroom, Frank said, "Tony, I hope you didn't take advantage of that poor girl!"

"Hardly!" replied Tony. "If anything, it was the other way around. She's a real tiger, that one. What were you saying about the spheres?"

Frank explained Jim's discovery of the correlation between the dates of solar eclipses and the locations of Maya cities on each sphere. He also explained Jim's belief that the spheres weren't Maya in origin.

"Well, I told you what the old man said, Frank. He told me the spheres were extraterrestrial. That dense black metal isn't like anything I've ever seen, and I showed it to a friend of mine before I gave it to you in Seattle and he hadn't seen anything like it either."

"Well, I'm not buying into your extraterrestrial theory, yet," said Frank, "But it does look like some kind of modern alloy and certainly not Maya. I've booked Jim and me on a flight to the Yucatan this afternoon – maybe we can learn something about the origin of these spheres at this place called *Loltún*."

"What about the money on deposit here at the hotel?" asked Tony.

"I'll be over around 11:00 a.m. to take care of that," said Frank. "In the mean time, you need to get Jill awake and ready to go. I'm going to use my unexpected trip to Mexico as reason for our sudden departure, but you two will have to clear out of the suite once I reclaim the money."

"Okay, I can handle that," said Tony yawning. "I'll help Jill get the cash into a safe deposit box today and then I'll work on the Al Thompson part of this puzzle while you're gone. Any idea how long you and Jim will be in Mexico?"

"No, not really," replied Frank. "Which brings up a good point – how long can you be away from work? Can you stay here in Las Vegas while I'm gone or should I look for some place to store the Durango and my stuff?"

"Don't worry about me, Frank," replied Tony. "As you know, I work for myself, and I'm way past due for a vacation. I'll make a call today and clear out the next couple weeks in case you run into a snag. Besides, I want to keep an eye on Jill until we figure out what's up with this stepfather of hers."

"That would be great, Tony, but I don't want you to jeopardize your business over this."

"Frank, I'm going to share something with you, but this is strictly between you and me," said Tony, in a hushed voice. "About a year after I got back from 'Nam I got a call from my old Special Ops C.O., Colonel Richardson. Somehow he had heard I was driving and he needed someone who had a Top Secret clearance to haul some freight for him. To make a long story short, I bought a tractor and I've been working on that same government contract for almost 25 years. I can pretty much call my own shots at this point."

"What the hell kind of freight requires a security clearance and Special Ops training?" asked a surprised Frank. "Especially if you're hauling it inside the United States!"

"Sorry, Frank, but I can't tell you any more than that. The point is that you don't need to worry about my business. And now you understand how I can pull a military contact out of my hat every now and then."

"Like your call to locate Jill's stepfather the other day!" exclaimed Frank. "That's how you found out he was out at the Base hospital!"

"Exactly," replied Tony, "And that's why I think I might be able to do some good by staying here. I'll call in a few favors and see what I can turn up while you're in Mexico."

"Okay, but we're not finished with this conversation, old buddy! I'm really curious about this mysterious freight and someday, over a beer, I'm going to get you to spill the beans," said Frank.

"That will never happen, my friend. I think I hear Jill crashing around upstairs, so I'll see you about 11:00 a.m., right?"

Frank ended his call with Tony and immediately called Linda McBride in Seattle.

"Hi, Linda, I hope you don't mind me calling you at work, but I've got another project for you," he said when he heard her voice on the line.

"Oh, Hi, Frank!" replied a surprised Linda. "No, that's okay. Did you get my e-mail about your Mr. Thompson?"

"Yes I did," he said, "And thanks. We're still not sure what it all means, but it was certainly interesting information – especially for his stepdaughter, who thought he was a retired security guard. This time, I'd like you to dig up whatever you can on a place called *Loltún* in the Mexican state of Yucatan. And the older the information is, the better. I'm looking for ancient history, if possible."

"Shall I e-mail you whatever I come up with, Frank?" asked Linda.

"No, you'd better call me on my satellite phone. I'm actually leaving for Mexico this afternoon and I don't know what kind of e-mail service I'll find down there."

"It sounds to me like you're having way too much fun now that you're retired, Frank. Maybe I should come down there and make sure you don't get into any trouble," laughed Linda.

"There are plenty of folks doing that already, Linda. Tony is here from Atlanta and Jim Barnes, a friend and anthropologist from the University of Washington, flew in last night. We're sort of taking over Las Vegas, one hotel room at a time!"

"Now I'm really jealous!" laughed Linda again, "I'll get on this *Loltún* research as soon as I can, but it probably won't be until later this afternoon. I'm working on a big project for one of the senior editors here at the paper and his piece runs in tomorrow's issue."

"Oh, that's fine, Linda. Thank you very much. And maybe when I get back from Mexico you can fly down here for the weekend and see what this Maya fuss is all about," offered Frank.

"You're on! I could use a break and, besides, I've never been to Las Vegas. I'll call you when I have some information on *Loltún*, okay?" she said, suddenly excited about the prospect of the trip.

"Great, and if you get my voice mail it just means that we're still in the air or that the phone is out of satellite range. Leave me a message and a phone number and I'll call you back as soon as I can. Thanks again, Linda."

Frank's next order of business was to pack for the Yucatan trip but, since he hadn't gotten around to going shopping yet, it wasn't much of a project. He decided to take his computer, his digital camcorder and, of course, the satellite phone. He debated about whether or not to take the spheres but he decided he'd better leave them with Tony. Thanks to Jim, they now had accurate copies of the hieroglyphics from all three spheres, including the one the Maya had taken, and Frank was concerned about getting the spheres through airport security and customs inspections. Instead, Frank set the camcorder on the breakfast counter, positioned each sphere in front of the lens, one at a time, and rotated them slowly with the tape rolling. He also shot several stills of each sphere from different angles.

After Frank reviewed the video and stills, he removed the tape from the camcorder, labeled it and packed it safely in his roll-on suitcase. He reloaded the camcorder with a fresh tape, packed it into its case and put it on the bed with his suitcase and computer bag.

At 10:00 a.m. Frank apologetically woke Jim and explained the details of the trip to Mexico. Jim was a little groggy from lack of sleep, but he was also excited to be off on an adventure to the land of the Maya. He quickly showered, shaved and dressed while Frank checked in with Tony to make sure he and Jill were ready to go.

Jim came down the stairs carrying his small, well-traveled brown suitcase. "I need to collect my papers from last night and then I think I'm ready, Frank," he said as he approached the breakfast bar. "What's this?"

"Oh, I decided it was best to leave the spheres here, so I took some video and still shots in case we need them as reference," explained Frank.

"No, I mean this crack. I don't remember seeing this last night," said Jim, rubbing his fingers back and forth over a section of the counter top.

"What! Let me see that!" shouted Frank, sprinting across the room to where Jim was standing. "Well I'll be damned! The same thing happened to my counter back in Seattle when I left the original sphere on it."

Frank picked up the sphere that appeared to be responsible for the crack and examined it. Handing it to Jim, he asked, "Which one is this?"

Jim studied the sphere and handed it back to Frank. "This one has the 1991 date. That's the one you brought from Seattle, isn't it?"

"Yep! That's the same one that cracked my counter back home! I need to mark this so Tony can check it out while we're gone." Frank wrapped the 1991 sphere in a paper napkin from the counter and locked both spheres back into his footlocker. "Let's head down to Mandalay Bay and see what kind of trouble Tony and Jill got into last night," laughed Frank as he and Jim left the room. "According to Tony, Jill won a bunch of money."

When they arrived at the hotel, Frank went to the front desk and asked to speak with someone in VIP Services. A minute later Ms. Landis, the same woman who had greeted them yesterday, came through a door at the end of the long reception desk.

"Good morning, Mr. Dayton!" she smiled as she joined Frank and Jim. "How may I help you?"

"I'm sorry to say that I've been unexpectedly called out of the country on business, Ms. Landis," Frank lied. "Mr. Barnes and I have to catch a 2:00 p.m. flight, so we need to leave almost immediately. I would like to thank you and the hotel for the generous hospitality, though. You have a beautiful facility here and

I look forward to returning sometime soon when I can enjoy the amenities."

"We look forward to seeing you again, too, Mr. Dayton. If you will follow me, I'll arrange to have your account closed and your funds returned to you. This way, please."

The woman led Frank and Jim through the same unmarked door they had used the night before and into her private office. She tapped a few keys on the keyboard and then looked up with a smile. "Your funds will be here momentarily, Mr. Dayton. After you've had an opportunity to verify the amount would you please be kind enough to sign this release?" she asked, as she removed a sheet of paper from a printer on the corner of her desk and slid it across to Frank. Jim was gawking around like a kid in a toy store, and his amazement was not lost on the woman.

"Is this your first time with us, Mr. Barnes?" she asked.

Surprised that she even remembered his name, he stammered, "Yes... yes it is. I'm a university professor and an anthropologist so I don't spend much time in Las Vegas. This is quite lovely," he said, indicating the artwork on the walls of the woman's office.

The woman smiled. "Well, this is a side of Las Vegas that most visitors don't have the privilege of experiencing, Mr. Barnes. The VIP facilities are reserved for a select few of our guests. It's too bad you weren't able to stay longer and get to know us," she said, stealing a glance at Frank, who was reading the release document and didn't notice.

At that moment there was a light tap on the door and a young security guard entered with Frank's bag that he had left with the hotel the night before. Ms. Landis stood up and took the bag from the guard who nodded and left the room without a word.

"Here we are, Mr. Dayton. I'll wait outside while you inspect the contents. Just tap on the door when you are ready," she said as she started for the door.

"Please, Ms. Landis, that's not necessary. I'm sure everything is in order." Frank scrawled his name on the document, catching himself just before he wrote "Morton." Jim noticed the $500,000 amount at the bottom of the document and shot Frank a look of disbelief, realizing for the first time that the old man's half-million dollars was in cash.

"I know, my handwriting is terrible, isn't it?" said Frank, attempting to cover for Jim's look of surprise. Frank stood and handed the document to Ms. Landis. "Well, if that's all, Ms. Landis, I guess we'll be on our way. We still have to collect some things from the suite, including my wife and associate."

"Of course, Mr. Dayton," she smiled, "And, thank you again for staying with us. I'll walk you to the elevator."

Once they were on the elevator and alone, Jim looked at Frank and demanded, "Okay, what the hell was that all about? First there's the limo at the airport, a lavish suite and an alias, now there's a half million dollars in cash in a carry-on bag. All this cloak-and dagger stuff is starting to freak me out, Frank!"

"Jim, I promised I would explain this all to you, and I will, but not here and not now. We'll have plenty of time on the trip and I'll lay it all out for you from top to bottom, I swear. There's a perfectly good – and legitimate – reason for all this. Just trust me for a few more hours."

When the elevator door opened onto the 41st floor lobby, Frank and Jim were greeted by the young security guard who had just delivered the bag a few minutes earlier.

"Hi!" said a surprised Frank. "Didn't we just meet downstairs?"

"Ah, yes, sir, that's correct. Could I speak with you for a minute?" the guard asked, motioning Frank down the hall a few steps.

"What is it, son?" asked Frank, a little annoyed by the delay.

"Well, I don't know if I should say anything or not, but…"

A few minutes later, when he was safely inside the suite, Frank burst into loud laughter. Tony stuck his head out the door of the master bedroom and asked, "What's so funny?"

"Well, apparently you and Jill were caught necking in the elevator last night by a security guard who felt I just had to know that somebody was fooling around with my wife. I'm afraid I'm going to have to shoot you on the spot, Tony!" laughed Frank again. "Are you two ready to go?"

"I think so," said Tony, stepping out of the room. There's some stuff downstairs in the living room we need to collect, but otherwise I think we're both ready."

"I'll get it – you round up Jill and let's get going. Technically, Jim and I need to check in two hours prior to departure, which gives us about fifteen minutes to get over to the airport."

Tony drove the Durango and dropped Frank and Jim off in front of the AeroMexico ticket counter. They had agreed on the way over that it wouldn't be a very good idea to leave a bag containing $500,000 in the rig alone. Jill was very quiet on the short drive to the airport but she kissed Frank on the cheek as they were saying their good-byes and Frank whispered into her ear, "Take care of Tony, will you? He's a good friend, but he's not too bright."

She laughed and realized immediately that Frank knew about last night and that he was okay with it. She hugged him and climbed into the passenger's seat of the Durango. As the Durango pulled away, she leaned out the window and blew a kiss in the direction of the two travelers.

Frank and Jim checked in and made their way toward the gate. Jim was amazed that every concourse in the airport had double rows of slot machines down the center. He was even more amazed that many of them were in use. "Don't they get enough of this on the strip?" he remarked as they turned into a restaurant to wait for their flight.

"Some of these folks don't get into town, Jim. I've often scheduled flights through Vegas just so I could play the slots between flights. Hell, I used to fly from Seattle to L.A. via Vegas on Southwest Airlines for just that reason," smiled Frank, remembering his days as a junior engineer at Boeing.

After they ordered lunch, Frank described in detail the events of the past ten days, starting with the Powerball jackpot and ending with Tony and Jill's apparent fling at the Mandalay Bay high rollers' suite. Some things, like the details of the spheres, Jim already knew. Other things, like the fact that Frank was now a multi-millionaire, came as a complete surprise.

As they left the restaurant for the gate, Frank said, "I'm sorry to have been so secretive about all this, Jim, but you can understand why I couldn't discuss some of this stuff until now. What started as a random meeting between Tony and an old man has mushroomed into quite a mystery, you must admit."

"Not to mention the apparent attraction between at least one of the spheres and Formica counter tops," laughed Jim. "What do you suppose that's all about?"

"Oh, crap!" said Frank. "I forgot to mention that to Tony!" Frank dug around in his computer bag until he located his phone and called Tony's cell phone. After several rings, Tony's voice mail message came on.

"Hi, Tony," he said. "Hey, I forgot to tell you about something. This morning I took some photos of the spheres on the breakfast counter in case Jim and I need them for reference on our trip. Anyway, just before we left Jim noticed that the original sphere, the one you got from the old man, had cracked the Formica just like it had at my place in Seattle. Anyway, I wrapped the 'counter-cracker' in a piece of paper so you'd know which one it was. Maybe you could check that out when you have a minute. Have fun – I'll call you from Mexico as soon as we know what our plans are."

Frank ended the call and clipped the phone onto his belt in case Tony called back. "Voice mail," he answered before Jim had a chance to even ask. "Anyway, back to our conversation. I think you now have all the facts surrounding the spheres. Maybe when we get to this place called *Loltún* we can figure out what they are and how three of them ended up in the possession of an old man in Nevada. I'll fund this little expedition, Jim, but I'm counting on you to be the real brains of the operation."

"Speaking of funding," said Jim, slapping his knee, "I meant to stop at a cash machine when we first got here. I don't think I've got more than $30 on me."

Frank opened the front of the corduroy sports jacket he had on and pulled out slightly on the top of the inside pocket to show Jim a packet of bills. "Don't worry about it. I had Tony give me back most of the cash I gave them to gamble with last night. There's about $9,000 in here, I think."

As the pre-boarding announcement for their flight was being made, Frank's phone rang. It was Tony.

"Sorry I missed your call, Frank, but I was on the phone. I got your message and I'll look into the sphere thing if I can, but we have a new problem."

"What's that?" asked Frank.

"Well, I just got an 'unofficial' call from my contact out at O'Callaghan Hospital. Jill's stepfather died about an hour ago."

Chapter 13

Frank and Jim settled into their seats on AeroMexico Flight 447 for the long six-hour flight to Mexico City, where they would change planes for another two-hour flight to Cancun. Even if everything went perfectly and there were no airline delays, they wouldn't arrive in Cancun until 10:45 p.m. local time. Frank had only slept about five hours the night before and Jim was running on even less rest, so both men were asleep before the plane reached cruising altitude.

The next time Frank opened his eyes he was staring into the face of a flight attendant who was asking him to put his seat back up for landing. Jim was already awake but he looked very groggy and his hair was a mess.

"I hate sleeping on airplanes," he said when he noticed that Frank was awake. "I always get a stiff neck."

"Yeah, me too," mumbled Frank, rubbing his own neck. "I can't believe I slept the entire trip. I'm sure glad we ate before we left Vegas."

When Frank and Jim went through customs in Mexico City, they both got green lights, which meant that they weren't required to open any of their bags for inspection. A few quick questions about the purpose and length of their stay and they were through customs and into Mexico. They grabbed a cup of coffee on their way to the next flight and their plane for Cancun pushed back from the gate at 8:50 p.m., exactly on schedule.

Frank checked his watch as the wheels left the runway and noticed it was two hours off. "Better set your watch ahead, Jim," he said. "We've picked up a couple of hours." Frank glanced over to see if Jim had heard him and found the professor fast asleep, his head against the window.

It was 11:30 p.m. before Frank and Jim got checked into the Cancun Oasis Playa resort. Frank had let the travel agent at Mandalay Bay book the hotel and his only stipulation had been that it be near the airport. As it turned out, there were no hotels close to the airport, but the Oasis was only about five miles away, on a beautiful beach and facing the Caribbean Sea. At $200 per night per room, Frank felt compelled to sit on his balcony and stare out across the moonlit water while he sipped on a Heineken from the room's mini-bar.

Frank watched the fluorescent white caps break on the beach below and marveled at the events of the past few days. Less than two weeks ago he was in Seattle, plugging away at a job that had lost all meaning since his wife's death. Tonight he was in Mexico chasing an ancient mystery and for the first time in months he was thinking about something other than his own misery and loss. He wondered where the trail of the black spheres would lead, of course, but he was happy just to be on the quest and he was sure Donna would approve.

The next morning, Frank and Jim met in the hotel lobby at 7:30 a.m. A cab delivered them back to the Cancun Airport for the forty-minute flight to Merida. After the plane took off, Jim asked what the plan was once they arrived in Merida.

"Well, the travel agent has booked us at a small place in Merida called the Caribe," said Frank. "After that, it's your show. You're the expert, so I'll take my lead from you." Frank noticed a smile cross Jim's face when he mentioned the hotel. "Do you know the Caribe?"

"Yes, I stayed there once a long time ago, actually," replied Jim. "It's small, colonial and very pleasant. It's a far cry from the resort we were in last night, but it'll suit our needs perfectly and it's close to the museums and the University of Merida. The *Loltún* Caves are about 80 miles away, so we'll have a bit of a commute, but you'll find the ruins there at *Uxmal* absolutely amazing."

"I was reading about *Uxmal* on the plane last night," said Frank. "I would love to explore around there for a day or so. That place has quite a history."

"It sure does. The last carbon dating they did put the earliest ruins at 569 AD and it was home to about 25,000 Maya by 900 AD. *Uxmal* actually means 'thrice built' or 'thrice occupied' in Mayan, but the famous Pyramid of the Magician is actually five separate structures, so the name *Uxmal* may be an understatement."

"Well, since this place is so interesting and closer to *Loltún*, maybe we should head straight down there and forget Merida," said Frank.

"If you don't mind, I'd like to do some research at the university library first," said Jim. "Other than the one brief trip to *Uxmal* while I was still in school, I've never been to that part of the

Yucatan and I'd like to do a little research on *Loltún* before we go. I think you'll find plenty to do in Merida while I'm busy. The Spanish founded the city, which is named after Merida, Spain, in 1542 and it's built on the site of the ancient Maya city of *Ichcaanzihó*. The Regional Museum of Anthropology is really quite magnificent."

"Oh, I'm sure I can stay busy," said Frank. "And like I said, you're the boss. What do you think we might find at *Loltún*? Is there really any chance of discovering the purpose or origin of the spheres?"

"To be honest, Frank, I'm not very optimistic. I've never run across any reference to artifacts like the spheres, which probably means there's never been any discovered before and in a very short period of time you've discovered three. I think the most plausible explanation is that the spheres are somebody's idea of a joke or a hoax."

"Well, if that's true, whoever created them certainly went to a lot of trouble to research the solar eclipse and relative location information," said Frank, "but I see your point. The odds of us finding something three times in a week that no one else had discovered in 500 years are pretty high, aren't they?"

During the remainder of the flight, Jim gave Frank a crash course in Maya culture and history. As the plane touched down in Merida, Frank was shaking his head. "They were an amazing people, that's for sure. What a tragedy that the Spaniards destroyed so much of the Maya history in the name of religious reform. Apparently it was more important to convert the Maya to Catholicism than it was to preserve a thousand years of cultural history."

After a short taxi ride from the airport, Frank and Jim arrived at the small, colonial Hotel Caribe. The architecture made generous use of the arch, especially in the lobby and the walkway that opened onto the central enclosed courtyard. Bright colors, mostly yellow and white, gave the place a crisp, bright feel. In the lobby the black and white tiles arranged in a checkerboard pattern were polished and shiny.

The rooms certainly weren't as plush as the rooms in Cancun, but they were more than adequate and at only $54 per night, they were also a real bargain. After an early lunch, Jim headed off to the university library and Frank took a walk through the area surrounding the hotel. Using his new digital camcorder Frank took pictures of some of the beautifully preserved colonial buildings.

When Frank returned to the hotel, he sat down at one of the tables at the "El Meson" outdoor café. It was hot and humid, but the umbrella over the table and a stiff breeze blowing down the street made the temperature bearable. A tall woman in her early forties approached the table with a smile. "May I bring you a refreshment, *Señor*?" the woman asked in perfect English.

Surprised by the woman's lack of an accent, Frank answered by stating the obvious. "You speak English."

"Yes, *Señor*, I was educated in the United States. May I get you something to drink?" she asked again.

Frank ordered a local beer and when the woman returned with it she asked, "Are you on vacation, *Señor*, or are you here to study the Maya culture?"

Frank was caught off guard by her boldness. "Actually, a little of both. And please, call me Frank. My associate and I checked into the hotel a little earlier," he said, indicating the entrance to the Hotel Caribe. "He's the archeologist – I'm just along for the ride."

"Yes, I saw you arrive," she said, nodding at the empty tables. "It's been very slow today."

"You said earlier you were educated in the US – how did you happen to end up here in Merida, if you don't mind me asking," said Frank.

Laughing, she said, "It's a long story, Frank, are you sure you want to hear it?"

Realizing for the first time that he was the Café's only customer, Frank said, "Of course! Please join me and keep me company until more customers arrive." He indicated the chair across from him and she sat down.

"My father was a young American engineer sent here to help renovate the city's water system. He met my mother while he was working on the project but eventually his work was completed and he returned to Houston." Looking down in embarrassment, she continued, "I was born about eight months after he left. My mother had been too ashamed to tell him she was pregnant so when he left he had no idea he had fathered a child. My mother died a few months after I was born and I was raised by her sister, my Aunt Carmela."

"Did your father ever learn the truth?" asked Frank.

"Yes, but not for a long time. Soon after he returned to the States his company sent him to work on a big project in Brazil. By the time he was able to get back here to visit my mother, she was already dead and my aunt was afraid my father would take me away to the US, so she never told him about me."

"So how did he find out?" asked Frank, now genuinely interested in the woman's story.

"When I was about 17, my aunt got very sick with tuberculosis. Just before she died she told me the truth about my mother, whom I had believed was my aunt all those years, and she gave me the name of my father and the company he had been working for when he was here in Merida. After my aunt died, I decided to go find the father I had never known. He was still working for the same engineering company, only now he was a vice president, and he had never married. We became very close and since I no longer had any immediate family here, I stayed in the US. After high school my father encouraged me to attend Rice University where I eventually graduated with a Masters of Art in Teaching. I taught in the Houston school system until my dad passed away three years ago. That's when I moved back to Merida and bought this Café." She sighed and stared down at the table top for a moment, obviously saddened by discussing her father's death.

"That's a really fascinating story, uhhh, I'm sorry but I don't know your name."

"Alejandra," she replied looking up with a smile. "My mother named me after my father, Alexander, and my friends call me Alex. I'm sorry to bore you with such a long story, Frank. I don't know what got into me."

Having suffered his own loss only a few months earlier, Frank guessed her motivation. "When did your father pass away?" he asked.

"Three years ago today," said Alex. She tried to hide a tear that trickled down her cheek, but Frank reached across the table and wiped it away with a linen napkin from the table. Alex sobbed once and excused herself from the table.

Frank finished off his beer, slid down in the chair and clasped his hands behind his head. Alex's story had awakened some old feelings and he closed his eyes to keep from crying himself.

When Frank heard the scraping of a chair he opened his eyes and found Jim Barnes sitting across from him. Frank snapped upright in his chair and looked around, but there was no sign of Alex. Instead, a young girl, no more than 17 or 18 was waiting on three elderly women at a table a few yards away.

"She said to tell you she was very sorry for taking up your valuable time," said Jim, "But she seemed embarrassed or ashamed about something. What happened?"

Frank looked at his watch, but he had lost all track of time while he was on his walk so he had no idea what time it had been when he first entered the café. "Damn," he said, sitting up straight in his chair. "I must have dozed off and now she probably thinks her story put me to sleep!"

***

Back in Las Vegas, Tony ended his call to Frank and crossed the room to sit beside Jill. "Is there anything I can do?" he asked.

Jill shook her head and said, "No, I just need some time alone, Tony. I appreciate your concern, but I'm really confused right now and I need to work this out. I don't know whether I should be grieving for my stepfather because he's dead or mad at him for lying all these years. Would you mind taking me back to Mandalay Bay to get my car? I think I just want to go home for a while."

"Of course, Jill, but are you sure you want to be alone right now?" asked Tony. "And what about the cash? You need to get that into a bank box where it'll be safe. In light of your stepfather's death, that money is yours now."

"I don't want to have anything to do with that money until I know where it came from," replied Jill. "For all I know, it could be stolen or laundered money. Would you take care of it for now? I'll deal with it later, after I've sorted out the rest of this."

"Well, I suppose, but you really should be the one to…"

Jill cut him off abruptly. "Please, Tony, will you just take care of it for me? We can talk about all the details later, but right now I just want to go home."

Tony grabbed the bag of money as he followed Jill through the door and out into the mid-day heat. After taking Jill to her car and making her promise to call him later that day, Tony located a

Bank of America branch and asked to see the manager. Since Tony banked with Bank of America back in Atlanta, he was able to talk the manager into renting him a large safe deposit box on the premise that he was going to be moving his accounts from Atlanta to Las Vegas in a week or two and until then, he just needed the box to store some items he had brought with him on this trip.

Once the money was safely stored in the safe deposit box, Tony relaxed a little. He stopped at a restaurant a couple of blocks off the strip and had a hearty, if not late, breakfast. While he was devouring his food, he hatched a plan.

After he finished eating, Tony returned to the Residence Inn and picked up Frank's scanner. He drove north through town on Las Vegas Boulevard and continued on until he passed O'Callaghan Hospital on the left side of the four-lane road. He turned left at the next intersection and pulled over to the side of the street. With a series of rapid keystrokes he programmed the standard military support services frequencies into the scanner and laid it down on the seat, out of sight. There was plenty of radio activity from Nellis Air Force Base, across the street, as well as from the hospital, but he listened for almost an hour before he finally heard something that peaked his interest.

"Unit 7, this is Base. One John Doe ready for transport. Over," said the radio operator's voice.

"Roger, Base, We're on our way," was the reply.

Tony suspected that the John Doe was Jill's stepfather and that the call was to alert a waiting ambulance that the body was ready to be moved to another location. Tony was very curious about where that location might be and he intended to find out.

With the scanner still operating, Tony moved the Durango into the hospital's guest parking lot and waited patiently for any sign of an ambulance. Ten minutes went by and there was still no sign of any emergency vehicles. Just as he was about to give up his waiting game, the radio came to life again. Base, this is Unit 7. Leaving Oscar with one John Doe, over."

"Ten-Four, Unit 7. I will show you ten twenty-six to UMC. Over and out," came the reply.

As Tony scanned the hospital grounds for the vehicle identifying itself as Unit 7, he guessed that Oscar was probably a code name for O'Callaghan Hospital and he knew from his Viet Nam duty as a Forward Air Controller that ten twenty-six meant 'in route.' UMC, of course, was University Medical Center, where Jill worked. That made sense, since UMC was the local public health facility and county morgue, but why were they referring to Al Thompson as a John Doe? Normally, the term 'John Doe' was used to refer to an unidentified person or body and they must know who the old man was, since they had kidnapped him from UMC in the first place.

Tony was so focused on the radio broadcast that he almost didn't see the black Chevy Suburban as it pulled out of the hospital parking lot and headed south on Las Vegas Boulevard. The only reason it caught his eye at all was because the side and back windows were heavily tinted. In an instant he made the decision to follow the suspicious Suburban, knowing that he might be chasing the wrong vehicle. If his hunch were wrong, he would lose any chance of tracking down the old man's body.

Careful to keep at least one car between himself and the Suburban, Tony followed the large vehicle through downtown Las Vegas. He let out a sigh of relief when it turned west on Charleston Boulevard toward the University Medical Center – he was, indeed, on the tail of the vehicle known as Unit 7. When the Suburban turned into the emergency room entrance, Tony parked the Durango on the street and followed as close as he could on foot. Staying in the shadows, he found a spot where he could see the back of the Suburban and the emergency room doors. There was no activity for several minutes, and he imagined that the occupants were checking in with whomever "Base" was. Finally the driver's side door opened and a man dressed in black with a shaved head and the physique of a pro-football linebacker walked around to the back of the rig. When the driver opened the back doors, Tony could see that the interior of the vehicle was outfitted more like the inside of an ambulance than a luxury SUV. As he was wondering why O'Callaghan would need an unmarked medical transport unit, three hospital staffers in white lab coats appeared from the far side of the Suburban and began unloading a gurney from the back of the vehicle. Two of the white-coated staff members wheeled the gurney out of sight and Tony could see that the sheet was pulled up to cover the body's face. The driver and the remaining hospital worker discussed something for a minute and when the driver turned to close the back door of the Suburban, Tony got his first good look at the third hospital worker's face. It was Jill Harris!

Chapter 14

Frank insisted that he and Jim wait at the outdoor café for a few minutes in case Alex returned, but when there was no sign of her Frank called the young waitress over to the table.

"Excuse me, *Señorita*, but is Alex still here?" asked Frank.

"No, *Señor*, she has left for the day, but she will be here tomorrow morning at 7:00 a.m. when we open. May I give her a message?" asked the girl in perfect English.

"No, that's all right," replied Frank. "I'm afraid I owe her an apology so I'll look for her tomorrow."

The teenager nodded and started away from the table. "Does everybody in Merida speak such good English?" he called after her.

"No, *Señor*," she smiled back over her shoulder, "Just my mother and me. I'll tell her you inquired about her."

The comment caught Frank off guard and his jaw dropped. Jim laughed out loud and slapped his friend on the back. "Let's get you out of this heat before you embarrass yourself any further. Besides, I have some interesting news for you," he said as he led the way into the hotel's lobby.

The temperature inside the thick-walled concrete hotel building was much cooler and the large ceiling fans kept the air moving. Frank followed Jim through the lobby and the deserted restaurant into the small cocktail lounge in the back. After the bartender brought each of them a cold beer, Frank asked Jim about his news.

"Well, I did some poking around over at the University library today," Jim began. "I wasn't really looking for anything in particular, but when I asked the librarian about reference materials on *Loltún*, she took an unexpected interest in my quest. It seems that a number of years ago a professor at the University tried to establish a connection between *Uxmal* and *Loltún* other than the obvious physical proximity."

"I don't follow you," said Frank.

"Let me give you some background on *Uxmal* before I go on. One of the most prominent structures at *Uxmal* is called the Pyramid of the Magician. It's also called the Temple of the Dwarf and it has quite a legend attached to it. The librarian showed me a copy of an account recorded by an English explorer named John Stephens who visited *Uxmal* in 1840. According to an ancient Maya legend, the Dwarf/Magician was hatched from an enchanted egg by a witch who took the hatchling as her son.

"Eventually the dwarf ascended to the throne by beating the king in a challenge with the help of his mother, but she died in the effort.

"The legend continues that in the town of *Mani*, a short distance from *Uxmal*, there is a deep well that opens into a cave that leads all the way to Merida. In this cave, on the bank of an underground stream, sits an old woman with a serpent. This old woman is the mother of the dwarf.

"According to the librarian, the professor was trying to prove that the cave in the ancient legend was actually *Loltún* and he spent years looking for the passage to Merida," concluded Jim as he finished off his beer and signaled the bartender to bring another round.

"That's interesting, Jim," said Frank with a wrinkled brow, "But how does that relate to our mysterious spheres?"

"In the early days of the professor's studies, he was permitted unrestricted access to the *Loltún* Caverns. Today, of course, public access is restricted to just a few upper chambers. In the process of browsing through the old man's notes in the library archives, I ran across two seemingly unrelated facts. First, he privately recorded finding some objects that he called "orbs", but he never published anything about the discovery," answered Jim.

"Really!" exclaimed Frank, suddenly very interested in Jim's dialog. "Do you think those could have been our little black spheres?"

"Well, the thought did cross my mind," replied Jim, "but it's a big jump from an obscure note in a professor's journal to an actual connection. If we could just get into those caverns and do a little exploring, maybe…"

"Didn't you say public access was restricted?"

"Yes, but I seem to remember you telling me that I was the archeologist on this trip and that you would take care of everything else," smiled Jim, "so doesn't that make it your job to figure out how to get us inside?"

"You said you ran across two facts – what's the other one?" asked Frank, already pondering how he could get the duo into the caves for an extended, and unaccompanied, period of time.

"Well, from what I was able to learn, it would seem that the professor is still in the caverns," said Jim, matter-of-factly.

"What was that?" asked Frank, mentally working on an angle to get into the caverns.

"One day he made a routine trip out to the caverns and that was the last time anybody ever saw him. He never came back and his body has never been found."

"That's unfortunate," said Frank, "But there are several possible explanations for his disappearance – a fall in the caverns, bandits along the road... hell, maybe he finally discovered the underground tunnel to Merida and just walked away."

"I don't think he walked away because in his notes from the previous day he indicated that he was planning to bring one of the orbs back to his lab for further study," explained Jim. "And his associates confirmed that he went out to the caves the next morning and he never came back. That was almost ten years ago, on a date that may be familiar to you."

"Which date would that be?" asked Frank.

"July 11, 1991 – the date of the last total solar eclipse visible in the Yucatan," said Jim softly, glancing around to make sure no one in the cantina was listening to the conversation.

"And the date of numerous UFO sightings in Mexico City and elsewhere," added Frank. "Wow! I'd say you've had quite a day Professor Barnes. Now for our next challenge... how are we going to get into the caverns to see if any of those orbs are still there? I'm betting that at least three of them have somehow made their way to Nevada."

"What I don't understand," Jim said, "is why nothing has ever been published about these spheres. Even if we assume that this local professor was the first to discover them in modern times, the Maya must have known they were there. I want to spend at least another day at the library in case there's some record in the literature that I'm not aware of. For me, the obscurity of these objects is almost as interesting as the objects themselves."

"Well, I guess I'll spend my time trying to figure out how to get us an unofficial visit into the caverns," said Frank reluctantly. "In fact, I should call Linda this evening and see if her research has turned up anything we can use. Shall we meet down here for dinner about 8:00 p.m.?"

"Yes, that's fine. I borrowed a couple of books on local history from the library that I'd like to take a look at and then maybe I'll take a swim," said Jim. As they stood to leave, the bartender signaled to Jim that he had a telephone call at the bar. He shrugged his shoulders at Frank's raised eyebrows. "Must be an admirer," he said, "I'll see you down here later."

Back in his room, Frank turned the air conditioner up to maximum and took a cold shower. He hadn't realized how hot it was until he had passed the open double doors in the lobby. He dressed in a pair of khaki shorts and a tee shirt and called Linda in Seattle.

"Any luck on the *Loltún* research?" he asked when Linda answered the phone.

"Hi, Frank!" replied Linda, obviously pleased to hear from him. "I tried to call you a couple times today, but all I got was a message saying your phone was out of service. Where are you, anyway?"

"Jim Barnes and I are in the city of Merida, Mexico. Sorry about that out of service thing; I had to turn the phone off for the flight over from Cancun this morning and I forgot to turn it back on. I just noticed it was off when I called you. Any luck?"

"Not too much, really," she replied. Some basic stuff, but I don't have much more. The name *Loltún* is really made up of two Maya words, *Lol* and *Tún*."

"Yes, I know. *Lol* means flower and *Tún* means stone," interrupted Frank. "It translates as Flower Stone, which doesn't make any sense to me."

"Well *Tún* can also mean year if you're talking about a calendar or dates," corrected Linda, "and at least one reference I ran across suggested that *Lol* means flower when used as a noun, but that it can also mean blooming, blossoming or even reawakening when used as an adjective."

"So *Loltún* could really mean Reawakening Year rather than Flower Stone!" exclaimed Frank. "That makes a whole lot more sense in light of some of the things we've discovered down here. We really have to get access to that place and have a good look around. Jim has turned up some information that seems to link

Loltún to the spheres, but we need to get into some restricted areas of the site to confirm his suspicions."

"Well, I have the name of the local official who administers the caverns, if that would help," replied Linda, "and from what I've learned, he has a reputation for accepting bribes in exchange for granting favors."

***

As the black Suburban, now absent its "John Doe" passenger pulled away from University Medical Center's emergency room door, Tony slipped out of his hiding place in the shadows and made his way back to the Durango. He wasn't sure what he had just witnessed, but he was certainly upset with Jill for lying to him. Just a couple of hours earlier she had pretended to be so distraught that she had to go home and yet here she was, in her crisp white coat, receiving a corpse under very suspicious circumstances. On the one hand, Tony wanted to storm into the hospital and demand to know what was going on, but on the other hand he knew he had to stay cool and keep this information to himself until he saw how things played out. Fortunately for Jill, the latter scenario prevailed.

Tony had arranged to have a friend haul some of his personal belongings out from Atlanta and when he glanced at his watch, he realized that he was supposed to meet the truck in fifteen minutes. He sped away from the Medical Center and jumped onto Interstate 15 northbound. He exited at the Las Vegas Motor Speedway and turned into the truck stop at the foot of the freeway ramp. He smiled at the fact that he had come full circle this morning because the truck stop was no more than a mile or two from the hospital parking lot where he had picked up the trail of the mysterious black Suburban.

After cruising the lot twice he finally spotted his friend Jack's rig parked at the far end of the lot. In a matter of minutes the men had Tony's wooden crate loaded into the back of the Durango. The box was about the size of a large footlocker, but with the back seat down it fit with room to spare.

Tony helped his friend swing the big trailer doors shut and then the two men shook hands. "Thanks again for bringing this out," said Tony.

"No problem," replied Jack, glancing over at the box they had just loaded into the Durango. "You planning on staying for a while?"

"I'm not sure yet, but if you run into any of the other guys, don't mention that you saw me here in Vegas, okay?" asked Tony. "I don't want anybody to think I'm getting lazy in my old age."

"You got it," said Jack, as he climbed back up into his cab. "And if you need any help, you call me, you understand?"

An hour later, Tony had muscled the box into the Residence Inn and up the stairs to his room. He opened it and removed the clothes he had packed on top. From the bottom of the, box he retrieved "Gert", his western-style 45-caliber Colt Cowboy revolver, and a box of ammunition. He strapped the leather quick-draw holster and belt on and checked himself out in the mirror. After taking a couple of practice draws, he loaded the gun with five rounds and slipped it back into the holster. He closed the crate and double-checked the two padlocks that secured the lid before sliding it over against the foot of his bed. Still wearing the gun belt, he went into the bathroom to take a shower. Lugging freight in 100-degree temperatures had left him soaking with perspiration.

Tony had just stepped out of the shower when he heard his cell phone ring.

"Tony, it's Jill. I need to talk to you; where are you?" she asked, sounding a little frantic.

"I'm at the hotel. I just got out of the shower, though, and I'm dripping all over the carpet. Can I call you right back?"

"Don't bother. I'll be there in ten minutes – don't go anywhere," she replied and hung up before Tony could reply.

Tony toweled off, dried his hair and got dressed. As he was brushing his teeth, he noticed his gun belt still hanging on the hook behind him. He checked to make sure the hammer was on the empty cylinder, returned the weapon to the box it had arrived in and re-secured the locks. Tony went downstairs to get a beer and just as he closed the refrigerator, there was a knock on the door.

He unlocked the door and Jill burst through, ducking under his arm. "Tony, I've just come from the Medical Center. You're not going to believe who showed up in the morgue this afternoon!"

"Oh, really," said Tony, pretending not to know about the mysterious Suburban and the John Doe it had delivered from the Air

Force hospital earlier in the day, "Well, my first guess would be your stepfather."

"Well, yes, his body was brought in, too," she said. "That's actually why I went over to the Medical Center in the first place. They paged me not ten minutes after you dropped me off at the Mandalay Bay and asked me to come in to formally identify his body. The police are treating his death as a homicide, so they asked me a bunch of questions. I still don't know what to make of his secret life, so I decided not to share any of Frank's discoveries with them."

"That was probably a good idea," said a confused Tony. "So, are you saying you saw another body at the morgue today? Somebody other than your stepfather?"

"Yes, that's what I came over here to tell you. While I was talking to the police, I heard a coded hospital page that means a body is arriving at the ambulance entrance, so I excused myself from the questioning and went down to check it out. This large, black, ominous-looking SUV was dropping off a John Doe – that's an unidentified body, you know – that was found by a security team out at the Nevada Test Site yesterday afternoon. I talked to the driver and tried to find out exactly where the body was found, but he didn't have any idea. Maybe one of your G.I. Joe friends out at the base can tell you."

"Maybe, but why do we care? Was it someone we know?" asked Tony, more confused than ever.

"Didn't I mention that?" asked Jill, acting more like an airhead than a critical care nurse. "Oh, sorry! Yes, the Joe Doe is none other than our Maya burglar friend from yesterday morning!"

Chapter 15

Frank met Jim Barnes for dinner in the hotel restaurant at 8:00 p.m., as arranged. The room's architecture matched that of the lobby – a high ceiling with a generous use of arches and brightly painted in yellow with white trim. The tables had round ceramic tile tops and the wrought iron chairs matched the ironwork trim used elsewhere in the room.

"How was your swim?" asked Frank, as he sat down across from the anthropologist.

"Actually, I never got to the pool," said Jim. "That call I received was from the librarian who helped me earlier today. She had discovered another box of the professor's notes and she thought I might want to see them."

"She certainly has taken an interest in your research, hasn't she," laughed Frank. "Or maybe she's taken an interest in you!"

Jim blushed slightly and said, "I suspect the former, rather than the latter, but I think she may have a personal interest in the professor."

"What makes you think that?"

"These notes she's been letting me look through. They're all being stored in brown cardboard boxes – the kind you would get at the grocery store. They're not at all what you would expect a library to keep historical records in. I've been into their archive room and they normally use standard containers similar to the Banker's Boxes we have back in the States. All clearly labeled and organized. But the only thing written on the box she showed me today was 'Sr. Garcia.' No date, no shelf location, nothing."

"Almost as if the boxes were somebody's personal property and not part of the library's holding at all," contemplated Frank.

"Exactly! I wonder if she's a distant relative, hoping to clear the old man's reputation."

"Or maybe not so distant," said Frank. "How old is this woman, anyway?"

Jim thought for a minute and then said, "I'm a terrible judge of age, especially of women, but I'd have to guess that she's about my age, give or take a couple of years."

Up until a couple of weeks ago the two men had only met at university seminars, and Frank had no idea how old Jim was. "And how old would that be, Professor?" joked Frank.

"I turned 36 about a month ago," replied Jim, as the waiter arrived to take their drink order.

Frank realized that he had always viewed Jim as just a scholarly Professor of ancient studies and he was surprised to learn that his new friend was 11 years his junior.

After the waiter left to get their drinks, Frank picked up his train of thought. "Do you know how old the professor is, or was, I should say?" asked Frank.

"Yes, he was born in 1919, so that would make him…"

"82, if he were still alive today," finished Frank. "That makes him more than forty years older than your librarian friend. Hmm, he could be her father or uncle, but more likely he's another generation back, don't you think?"

"Aren't you jumping to conclusions, Frank? We don't even know if they're related. Maybe he was a former teacher, or a neighbor, or just an old guy who spent a lot of time in the library," countered Jim.

"Well, my dear professor, this is clearly a socio-cultural question and, like you said earlier, you're the anthropologist on this trip, so while I'm busy trying to get us into *Loltún*, I suggest you turn on the Barnes charm and get some more information out of your girl friend. Cheers!" Frank raised his glass to make a toast.

"I told you, she's not interested in me," blushed Jim again, as he raised his glass and clinked the side of Frank's.

After the waiter had cleared away the remains of their tasty and filling meal, they each ordered a brandy. Frank asked Jim to write down the professor's full name on a note pad so he could put Linda to work on some background information. As he studied it, he said, "Professor Eduardo Torres. Well, that's certainly not Garcia, so I wonder whose name is on the boxes. What is the librarian's name?"

"I don't have any idea, Frank. I called her *Senorita* and she called me Professor. As I told you, our meeting was strictly formal and professional."

"Yeah, right! That's why she trotted out the family secrets in a plain brown wrapper… I mean box," teased Frank. "Well, add that to your list, Romeo – find out the lady's name."

The two finished their drinks and retired to their respective rooms about 9:30 p.m. It had been a long and interesting first day in Mexico, thought Frank, as he kicked off his shoes and settled into an overstuffed chair in the corner of his room. And maybe – just maybe – they were on to something that would shed some light on the mysterious spheres.

Frank waited until 10:00 p.m. (8:00 p.m. Seattle time) to call Linda at home. They chatted for several minutes about how the trip was going, what Merida was like and other touristy things before Frank gave her the professor's name.

There was a pause and then Linda said, "You know, that name sounds familiar. I wonder if I ran across it earlier today when I was researching *Loltún*."

"That's possible," replied Frank. "Apparently he spent a lot of time down there. Until he disappeared, that is."

"This guy is missing?" asked a surprised Linda.

"Yup, and he has been for almost ten years. In fact, Jim thinks he may have turned up missing on his way to *Loltún*. Jim was given access to a couple of boxes of the professor's personal notes and files today and it turns out this old guy was trying to substantiate some ancient Maya legend about a dwarf. Jim explained it all to me, but I don't remember the details. Anyway, find out what you can and let me know. I hate to ask you to do this on your weekend, but it would really help us out. I'll try to remember to keep my phone turned on tomorrow," laughed Frank.

"Okay, I'll do what I can. I have to go in to the office for a few minutes anyway, so I'll do it then."

"What? I just assumed you were doing this research from home. Have you been taking time from your job to do this?" asked an embarrassed Frank.

"Well, yes, because I can't access some of my professional resources from anywhere except work due to security restrictions."

"Really! Well, when I get back I'm going to build you your own private research center," promised Frank.

That made Linda laugh and pretty soon Frank was laughing, too. When he finally signed off, he glanced at his watch and realized that they had been talking for almost thirty minutes.

"Ouch!" he said out loud, "that will cost a bundle." He realized for the first time how much he enjoyed talking to Linda and he realized for the millionth time how much he missed talking to Donna.

The next morning, Frank and Jim met for coffee at the sidewalk café in front of the hotel. Jim was already seated when Frank came through the front entrance. As Frank approached the table his head was bobbing from side to side and he had a worried look on his face.

Jim laughed and said, "Sit down and relax, Frank. She's here. She just went to get a fresh pot of coffee."

"I don't know if that makes me feel more or less nervous," replied Frank as he drained the last half-cup of coffee out of the pot on the table. "Are you going to be able to get into the library on a Saturday? I had sort of forgotten what day of the week it was until Linda reminded me last night."

"The university library is normally only open until 1:00 p.m. on Saturdays, but I have a special 'all day pass'," smiled Jim, blushing again.

"I see!" laughed Frank. "Well, take her to lunch and find out a little about her family history, will you?"

"It's already arranged," smiled Jim. "She called me this morning to make sure I was still coming."

Frank opened his mouth to make a rude comment but stopped short when his nose caught the scent of lilacs. He looked over his shoulder and right into the bare midriff of Alex, who was leaning across to put the fresh coffee pot on the table.

Smiling, Alex set the pot on the table and stepped back a pace. "So, we meet again, Frank. And I must say, each time is more interesting than the last."

Frank tried to apologize, but all that came out were one-letter syllables. Jim had seen Alex approaching the table, of course, and he burst into laughter at Frank's nose-to-navel encounter.

Frank finally composed himself and shot Jim a 'Thanks a lot!' look, which only made him laugh harder. Alex stepped around to the side of the table, where Frank could see her. She put her hands on her hips and in mock seriousness said, "I understand you wish to speak with me, *Señor*?"

Frank stared down at the table for a second and then looked up directly into her large brown eyes. "Yes – I would like to apologize for yesterday. We had been up very late the night before, and I guess I just dozed off. I'm really sorry."

"I shouldn't have bored you with my life history. I'm the one to be sorry," she said as she picked up the empty pot from the table.

"No, really. Please accept my apology. Your story was very interesting and I was a cad for falling asleep like that. Is there any way I can make it up to you?"

Alex thought for a minute and then said, "It's Saturday and we close early today. You could join me for a drink at, say, 4:00 p.m."

"I would love that! 4:00 p.m. it is. Shall I meet you here at the café?"

"Yes, that would be fine. See you then." And with that, she was gone.

"Well, well, well," nodded Jim. "It looks like I'm not the only one with a girl friend, *amigo*."

This time it was Frank's turn to blush. "Let's get out of here and get some work done, Professor."

***

"The Maya! What the hell was he doing out at the Bombing Range?" asked a surprised Tony. "Did they find the sphere Frank let him take?"

Jill shook her head. "I have no idea. In fact, I'm not even sure who found the body, Tony. The military gave us absolutely no details except that he was found dead in a restricted area on government property. The morgue staff is doing an autopsy right now to determine the cause of death, but after that he'll just get a county burial and be forgotten." Jill sat down on the sofa and put her face in her hands.

"Did you tell anybody about the encounter at the mobile home? Does anybody know you saw this guy yesterday?" asked Tony, sitting down across from her.

Jill shook her head "No" without lifting it out of her hands. Tony sensed that the death of her stepfather was starting to sink in. He retrieved two cold beers from the refrigerator and sat down beside her. "Here," he said, "you look like you could use this."

Jill leaned back against the couch and accepted the bottle. "Thanks." she said, "This has been a stressful couple of weeks. First my stepfather was shot, then he was kidnapped and now he's dead.

In the middle of all that it turns out that he's not even the person I thought he was. It's been an emotional roller coaster, you know?" Jill took a long drink of beer and laid her head back on the couch.

"Yeah, Jill, I know. And it's not over yet, because now you will have his personal things and the mobile home to deal with. And the money – don't forget about the money. I wonder if he has any other relatives. Frank has an e-mail from Linda somewhere, but I didn't read it so I don't know if she was able to find out that kind of information."

"I don't think he does because I found his will in that box of stuff we pulled out of his safe," Jill said as she pulled a folded piece of paper out of her purse. "He left everything to my mother and if she died before him it was all to go to me. This document is dated just shortly after he and my mother were married, while I was still away at nursing school."

Jill handed the paper to Tony, who studied the will for a minute and handed it back. "It certainly appears to be in order, but we need to be sure he came by the money legally. I mean, if he robbed the Las Vegas National Bank last year, you'd have to give the cash up. Do you have an attorney?"

"There's a firm here in town that helped me during my divorce, but that was six years ago."

"I think you should take this will to them and let them start the probate process but don't mention the money just yet. You can always tell them you found it in your stepfather's safe, which is true. We'll just fudge on the exact time of the finding, that's all. And if it turns out that the money isn't yours to keep, then it's better not to mention it in the court documents."

Tony dug the safe deposit key out of his pocket and handed it to Jill. "Here, you should keep this. The money is in a box in my name at the Bank of America out on West Tropicana. You can leave it there until we figure out what to do with it. If it turns out to be legally yours, we'll move it to your bank and you can report it 'discovered' to your attorney."

"How are we going to find out where the money came from?" asked Jill.

"When you take that will to your attorney, they will probably start an investigation to determine the extent of Al's assets. Maybe that will turn up something. In the mean time, I'll see if my contacts out at the base know anything and maybe we can ask

Frank's friend Linda, back in Seattle, to dig a little deeper. Maybe one of us will get lucky," smiled Tony.

"You know, I've been meaning to ask you about these mysterious 'contacts' of yours. How is it that you know people on the inside at Nellis?"

"There's nothing mysterious about them, Jill. I was in the service back in the early 70s – that's where I first met Frank – and I worked with a lot of Air Force guys. Some of them made a career of the military and we've stayed in touch, that's all."

"You've stayed in touch for almost thirty years, huh? That's amazing. What exactly did you do in the military?" she pressed, wondering what exciting job he might have had.

"I was in the motor pool," he lied. "I drove an ambulance in 'Nam and that's why I know some of the folks at the hospital. That's also why I became a truck driver after I got out."

"Oh," replied Jill, a little let down that she hadn't discovered a secret side to Tony. "Well, I'll see if I can contact that attorney before they close for the weekend, and then I've got to make arrangements for my stepfather's burial before I go back to work tomorrow afternoon. I'm on second shift this week, so how about if we get together for brunch Saturday morning?"

Tony smiled, surprised that she had bought the motor pool story. "Sure, Saturday is fine. Shall I pick you up or do you want to meet somewhere?"

"Why don't I meet you here? We'll hit one of the hotel buffets out on the strip and pig out." Jill carefully folded her stepfather's will and returned it to her purse. "Okay, then, I'm off. See you about 10:00 a.m. Saturday." She handed Tony the empty bottle, gave him a kiss on the cheek and was gone.

After the door closed, Tony shook his head and laughed. It was hard to believe that the person who just left was the same one he had been locked in an embrace with the night before! She's a real piece of work, he thought to himself.

Last night's lack of sleep was starting to catch up with him, so Tony turned the deadbolt and returned to the living room to pick up the empty beer bottles on the coffee table. Next to Jill's bottle he found the safe deposit key he had just given her but by the time he got to the door, she was already out of the parking lot. "Damn!" he said as he watched her car disappear down the street. Back inside, he grabbed another beer and went upstairs to bed. Tomorrow would be another day.

Tony awoke the next morning to the sound of the maid knocking on the door. "Housekeeping!" she was shouting.

Groggy from sleeping so hard, Tony pulled on his pants and went down to the door. He mentally kicked himself for forgetting to hang the "Do not disturb" sign on the door. After dismissing the maid and hanging the sign, he wandered into the kitchen and started a pot of coffee. It was Friday and Frank would be starting his first full day in Mexico, Tony thought to himself. He was curious about what the two were learning about the spheres, so he called Frank's satellite phone. When voice mail answered, he hung up without leaving a message. Probably out of range, he thought.

Tony was showered, shaved and dressed by 9:30 a.m. After a quick breakfast, he double-checked the locks on Frank's footlocker and his own box upstairs and then he ventured out into the bright Las Vegas sunlight. Heading north on Las Vegas Boulevard, Tony used his cell phone to call Gene Carlson, his contact at the base – the same one who had tipped him off about Al Thompson's death the day before.

"Gene, good morning! This is Tony Nicoletti. Say, I wanted to thank you for that heads up yesterday, and I was wondering if you knew anything about the other body that came in from O'Callaghan yesterday."

"You mean the one from the Test Site?" said the voice on the other end of the line. "I've heard a few rumors, why? Did you know this guy?"

"No, no, nothing like that. I have a friend who works over at the Medical Center and she happened to be there when the body arrived. I was just curious, that's all. It seems strange to transport a body in an unmarked vehicle," said Tony, trying not to give out any more information than he had to.

"Actually, the transport was arranged by the Department of Defense folks up at Groom Lake, and I think every vehicle the DOD has is unmarked. It's just the way they do things."

"Groom Lake? I'm not familiar with that name – is it part of the Nevada Test Site?" asked Tony, trying to lead his contact into giving him more information.

"No, it's a separate complex just northeast of the NTS, but it's still within the boundaries of the Nellis Bombing Range."

"Is that where the body was found?"

"No, it was actually found early yesterday morning on NTS property during a routine security patrol," replied Carlson.

"So the body was first brought in to the base hospital and then later they transferred it to the Medical Center?" asked Tony, still probing for information.

"Right. That's standard procedure in cases involving civilians, especially ones who die up there."

"Really," replied Tony. "You make it sound like that happens all the time. Do you happen to know what this guy died of? My friend didn't have the details from the autopsy yet."

"I'd rather not discuss that on the phone. Let's get together for lunch today and I'll let you in on one of the most bizarre stories you've ever heard!"

Chapter 16

Frank and Jim left Alex's El Meson Café at 9:15 a.m. and set about their individual tasks. Frank had agreed to work on the problem of unrestricted, and hopefully unaccompanied, access to the underground caverns at *Loltún* while Jim's assignment was to learn as much as he could about the old professor and his connection to *Loltún*.

After a short walk through the quiet colonial streets of Merida, Jim arrived at the library at 9:30 a.m. on the dot.

"Good morning, *Señorita*," greeted Jim pleasantly, as he approached the library's main desk.

The woman behind the counter was sorting a large stack of checkout cards and hadn't noticed him come in. When she recognized Jim she beamed back a smile. "Good morning, *Señor*. May I help you find something?" she said loud enough for the two or three others in the library to hear. Then, in a much lower voice, she said, "Please follow me." She motioned Jim behind the desk and into the archive room where he had spent much of the prior day.

When they were out of sight of the other library visitors, the woman signaled for Jim to stop. She held her finger to her lips in a sign to be quiet and whispered, "No one must know you are here, *Señor*. This way, please." She led him to a small office in the back of the archive room and opened the door.

"This is my office. You may work here, but please stay out of sight. I will come back later and see you out."

"What's the problem, *Señorita*?" he asked, more than a little concerned about the sudden secrecy.

The librarian just shook her head and said, "I will explain later. Please stay in this room until I return for you." And with that, she was gone.

Jim heard the door lock behind her. With no real option but to stay, he made himself as comfortable as he could and began another pass through all of the professor's journals and notes. This time he was looking specifically for anything mentioning the orbs. He was also keeping his eye out for papers dated around July 11, 1991. There was no photocopier in the room, so he had to take notes whenever he found something that looked interesting.

Jim lost track of time and when he heard the key in the lock he glanced at his watch and was surprised to see that it was already 1:10 p.m. He had been working for three and a half hours!

The librarian closed the door behind her and smiled at Jim. She looked much more relaxed than she had earlier. "I apologize, *Señor*, but the Administrator would be very upset if he found out I had showed you the professor's personal papers. He has been away on vacation but he returned unexpectedly last night and I didn't want him to pay a surprise visit today and see you here. The library is now closed and he has gone to his ranch for the weekend, so you may relax."

"Why wouldn't he want me to look at the professor's papers?" Jim asked.

"Señor Garcia considers the professor's notes his personal property, even though Professor Torres' wife gave them to the library before she moved back to Mexico City. That's why they aren't cataloged and on the shelves like our other historical documents. He only stores them in the library because he feels this is the safest place for them."

"Why does Señor Garcia have such an interest in the papers?" asked Jim.

"I have never looked at the papers, *Señor*, so I do not know what they might contain, but I suspect Señor Garcia does. His family owns most of the land around the *Loltún* caverns and controlled the caves themselves until the government made them a tourist site a few years ago. The Garcia family has quite a history in this part of the Yucatan."

"Well, I think I've learned all I can from these notes, so could I convince you to tell me about that history over lunch, Señorita ___?" asked Jim. He intentionally left the end of his question dangling, hoping she would take the opportunity to provide her name.

"My name is Carmen Lopez, *Señor*, and it's actually *Señora*. I should have corrected you yesterday," she said, a little ashamed, "my husband was killed in an airplane accident several years ago."

"I'm so sorry, Carmen. May I call you Carmen?" fumbled Jim. "And please, my name is Jim. Now how about that lunch?"

"I don't know, *Señor*, I mean Jim. We only just met yesterday and I hardly know you. Some people might consider it improper."

"Some people might consider it improper for you to lock me in your office with these boxes of private papers, too, Carmen," smiled Jim. "Come on, please do me the honor of lunch. You may select the restaurant, if that would make you feel more comfortable."

"Well, there is a delightful new French bistro a few blocks from here that I've been wanting to try. Give me a couple of minutes to put these boxes away and I'll take you up on your invitation."

Over lunch, Carmen told Jim what she knew about the history of the Torres family and the eccentric professor. About two years before his disappearance the professor had become obsessed with his mysterious research at *Loltún* and he had started neglecting his classes. Sometimes he didn't show up for an entire week at a time. In the beginning, the other department members covered for him but after a while everybody got fed up with his irresponsible behavior. The University eventually placed him on sabbatical leave, hoping his research would lead to a discovery and attract grant money to the school, but Professor Torres refused to publish any of his findings. No one ever really knew what he was investigating, or why, and after his disappearance the University distanced itself from the professor and his work. Señor Garcia has kept the professor's notes a secret and the matter has been pretty much forgotten.

"And what is your connection to the professor, Carmen? Why did you allow me to study his papers when you knew that it would anger Señor Garcia if he found out?" asked Jim.

"I come from a family of very modest means, Jim. When I was in high school I worked for the professor and his wife as a housekeeper to help out financially at home. The professor had an extensive library and he used to let me borrow his books. He had a large collection of classic literature and history books and I became an avid reader. When I graduated from high school, the professor helped me get a scholarship here at the University. I am the only member of my family to ever attend, much less graduate from, a university and because of my education and my job at the library, I am able to care for my parents, who are both in poor health."

"But why give me, a total stranger, access to his personal research notes?" asked Jim.

"Because I had a deep respect for the professor and the University all but destroyed his name those last couple of years before his disappearance. I know he was acting strange – irresponsible, actually – but he must have believed there was something very important out there at *Loltún*. He wasn't the kind of person to ignore responsibility. There had to be something out there and I hoped your work might clear his name. I owe him that," replied Carmen.

"Well, if it's any consolation, that's exactly why my associate and I are here," said Jim with a smile. "Why do you think Señor Garcia doesn't want anyone to examine the papers? Do you think he knows something?"

"I truly don't know, Jim. Several months after the professor disappeared some Americans were here asking questions. I believe they were government men. I know they talked with Señora Torres and with Señor Garcia and they may have talked with others as well. They left after several days and have never returned but later that year, when Señora Torres gave the professor's papers to the library, Señor Garcia made sure no one ever knew about the gift. That's really all I know."

Jim and Carmen enjoyed a relaxed and extended lunch and then walked back to the library. They talked about their common interest in classical music and the subject of Professor Torres and *Loltún* was forgotten.

"Will I see you again?" asked Carmen as they arrived at the library and it became apparent that Jim wasn't coming back inside.

"Certainly! I still have several books on the Maya that you let me borrow yesterday, remember? I think my associate and I are going to visit the *Loltún* area tomorrow, but I would be honored if you would join me for dinner when we return. Maybe Tuesday or Wednesday?" replied Jim.

"It would be my pleasure, Jim. Good luck and please be careful down there. You know what happened to the professor."

As Jim walked back to the hotel, he wondered if anybody knew what really happened to the professor.

Meanwhile, Frank had struck out on his attempt to gain unrestricted access to the caverns. The official that Linda had suggested was attending a meeting in Mexico City and his substitute wouldn't even discuss granting access to the closed areas of the complex.

"I am shocked that you would even suggest such a thing, *Señor*! I could lose my job," scolded the junior clerk on the telephone. "My superior will be back on Monday, but I am sure his answer will be the same."

Frank didn't want to wait until Monday, especially if the clerk was right about his boss's attitude. Linda had been sure the senior official could be 'convinced' to bend the rules, but the new president of Mexico was trying desperately to stop the blatant corruption of local officials and maybe his message had been heard in Merida.

It was just after 1:00 p.m. on Saturday and all government offices were closed until Monday, so there was little Frank could do except wait until 4:00 p.m. to meet with Alex. As much as he wanted to get into the caverns, he was looking forward to this afternoon's meeting even more. Realizing that he still hadn't done the shopping he had planned when he left Seattle, Frank inquired at the front desk about where he could purchase some local clothing.

The desk clerk suggested a shop about four blocks away and handed Frank a hotel business card. "Ask for Alfredo, *Señor*. Tell him Juan sent you and he will take good care of you, I promise"

When Frank left Alfredo's store an hour later he had purchased several pairs of pants, six new shirts and two pairs of shoes. Frank had also bought underwear, socks and two belts, one to go with each pair of shoes. He was sure his shopping spree totaled more than the shop had sold all day, but he didn't care. He needed these things and Alfredo had seemed to be an honest sort, actually waving Frank off a couple of items, saying, "That is not correctly priced, *Señor*. May I suggest something less expensive?"

The total bill came to $485 and when Frank handed Alfredo five one hundred dollar bills, the proprietor's eye widened. "Please allow me to have your purchases delivered to your hotel, *Señor*. This is far too much to carry in the afternoon heat."

"Well, yes, you're probably right, Alfredo, but I need it there soon. I have an appointment in two hours and I would like to wear some of these items," replied Frank, a little worried that he might never see his purchases again.

"In that case, *Señor*, I will personally take both you and your purchases back to the hotel this minute," smiled the shopkeeper. He called to a young man in the back room and gave him some instructions in Spanish. "This way, *Señor*, my car is in the back."

As they pulled up in front of the hotel, Frank reached for his wallet but Alfredo waved his hand vigorously. "No, no, *Señor*. You have made an otherwise slow day into a very good one. Please put your money away! And if there is anything else I can do for you, please let me know."

Frank climbed out of the passenger's door and came around the car to where the shopkeeper was unloading the several bags and boxes.

"Well, my associate and I <u>would</u> like to get into the closed portion of *Loltún* Caves tomorrow and do some looking around on our own. Could you arrange that?" laughed Frank.

Alfredo reached into his shirt pocket and pulled out one of his shop business cards. He wrote a telephone number on the back and handed it to Frank. "Call me at this number when you are ready to leave, *Señor*. My son and I can be here in ten minutes and our fee is $100 per day each."

Stunned, Frank stared at the card and then up at Alfredo. "Are you saying you can get us through the public areas into the restricted part of the caves?"

"No, *Señor*, if you want to see the public areas you will have to pay the admission and go on one of the guided tours. But if you want to see the rest of the caverns, my son can take you in through a secret entrance once used by the Maya themselves."

***

Tony had arranged to meet Gene Carlson, an acquaintance from his Viet Nam days, at one of the restaurants at the Palace Station Casino just off Interstate 15. When Tony arrived, he discovered that the casino, which he had seen many times from the freeway, was much larger than it looked from the road. He parked the Durango and found his way to the restaurant. When he got there, Carlson and another man were in a booth near the back.

Carlson saw Tony approaching and slid out to greet him. "How in the hell are you, old man? I haven't seen you in, what, 20 years or more?" grinned Carlson, pumping Tony's hand.

"I'm fine, Gene, how about yourself?" asked Tony, eyeing the person with Carlson.

"Oh, you know, same old, same old. Tony, this is Buzz Edwards. I asked him to join us because it sounded to me like you might know more about this Maya character than you were letting on, and Buzz would like to ask you some questions."

Tony held up his hand and started to back away. "Hey, now you didn't say anything about any questions!"

"Relax, Tony. Buzz is with us. I promised to tell you a bizarre story, and I will, but Buzz is the real expert on this phenomenon, if that's what you call it, and he got to be the expert by talking to a lot of people. This is all strictly off the record and unofficial, I swear. That's why I wanted to meet you here, away from the base and the local military hangouts."

Uneasy at the presence of the stranger, Tony finally slid in next to Carlson. The waitress took their lunch order and Carlson began his story in a low voice.

"As you already know, a body was recently found on some military property north of here. As you apparently also know, the individual appears to be of Indian ancestry, possibly Maya. But what you probably don't know is that this happens on a pretty regular basis. It has happened every two or three years for the past 50 years that we know of. "

Tony's jaw dropped. "Wow!" he finally managed. "What's that all about? I mean, do you always find them dead like this one?"

"Always. And they are always in the same general area. This one was no more than three yards from where the last one was found, twenty-eight months ago," explained Carlson.

"Were they carrying anything with them?" asked Tony.

"Like what, Mr. Nicoletti? What would they have with them?" pressed the stranger, suddenly drawn into the conversation.

Backpedaling, Tony regretted his question almost before he had asked it. "I mean, well you know, like documents, or baggage, stuff like that."

Carlson looked at Buzz Edwards, who nodded slightly. "Okay, Tony, let's cut to the chase. All of the bodies have been found directly over an object buried a few inches below the surface. And we think you know what they find under each one of these bodies, don't you?"

Trying to look shocked and confused, Tony said, "What? Why would you think I know anything about this? All I know is what my friend told me. She said that the body of an Indian was delivered to the University Medical Center in an unmarked government vehicle. I thought it was unusual, so I called you to see what you knew."

Now it was Edwards' turn to talk. "Mr. Nicoletti, we have surveillance tapes from the Burro Inn showing that you met with Al Thompson a week ago last Monday in Beatty. Last Tuesday you called Mr. Carlson, here, inquiring as to the whereabouts of this same Mr. Thompson. And this morning you called Mr. Carlson again, this time inquiring about a body that was found on top of an object that we know for a fact was in Mr. Thompson's possession as recently as two weeks ago. Oh, and did I mention that this same Al Thompson, with whom you seem to be so concerned, is now dead as the result of a gun shot wound to the head which he suffered the very night you met him at the casino? I think it's time you told us what you know, Mr. Nicoletti."

Tony leaned back against the booth, his head spinning. What the hell have I gotten myself into, he thought.

"Tony, this is serious business. Please tell Buzz whatever you know," cautioned Carlson.

"Okay, but first I want to know who your friend is, and who he works for," Tony replied to Carlson.

"I work for the Department of Energy and I'm assigned to the Nellis Range facility, Mr. Nicoletti. That's all I can tell you, except to add that I'm aware of the details of your government contract and I know that your superiors hold you in the highest regard. For that reason, and that reason alone, we are treating you as a 'person of interest' rather than a suspect in the death of Mr. Thompson," replied Edwards. "But we must have your complete cooperation."

Feeling cornered by Edwards and betrayed by Carlson, Tony took a deep breath and calmed himself before making direct eye contact with the DOE agent across from him. "Okay, but let me start by assuring you that I had absolutely nothing to do with the old man's death. If you are as familiar with my past, as you claim, then you also know that it would take more than the two of you to keep me here if I decided I wanted to leave. And what I'm going to tell you is strictly off the record, is that understood?"

Edwards nodded in acknowledgement and indicated that Tony should proceed.

"The fact that I happened to be in the Burro Inn two weeks ago was a complete fluke," began Tony.

Over the course of the next thirty minutes he reconstructed the past two weeks of his life, beginning with his chance meeting at the casino and ending with his call to Gene Carlson earlier that morning.

"So that's it, gentlemen. That's the whole story. The fact that my path seems to keep crossing that of the old man is purely coincidence," he concluded.

"So it would seem," commented Edwards. "And what about your friend in Mexico, Mr. Nicoletti? What has he learned about these spheres?"

"I haven't talked to him since he left on Thursday. Maybe you should zip down there and ask him yourself," said Tony sarcastically.

"Actually, I intend to do just that, Mr. Nicoletti. But since this conversation is off the record, and because I've been assured that you can be trusted, let me fill in some blanks for you." Edwards poured another cup of coffee and began.

"You friend's background research on Mr. Thompson is essentially correct. He was transferred back and forth between various civilian contractors over the years to maintain a low profile, but he has been affiliated with the Department of Energy's operations here at the Nevada Test Site since 1975." Edwards paused while he took another sip of coffee.

"It might also interest you to know that Mr. Thompson never retired. He was on the government payroll up until the day he died. He was moved from the Medical Center out to the base hospital for security reasons and you were fed his location because we already had you under surveillance as a possible suspect in his shooting."

Tony shot Carlson a look of anger, but Carlson only shrugged.

"By the way, the money you have in your safe deposit box is all very legal and rightfully belongs to his stepdaughter, Jill Harris," continued Edwards. "In his latter years, Mr. Thompson became very distrustful of everyone, even his employers, but he was allowed to continue with his work because of the nature of his research. He has been very closely monitored these past few years, but I doubt if he was aware of it."

"Well, you're wrong there. Jill told us her stepfather believed someone was constantly watching him and when Jill saw him at the base hospital he said something about giving the spheres back so 'they' would leave him alone. He must have been on to your spies," said Tony, smugly.

"I doubt it. First of all, the spheres were in Mr. Thompson's safe with the full knowledge and approval of the Department. They were, in fact, the subject of Mr. Thompson's work for the Department. As your friend has accidentally discovered, the spheres possess some sort of energy source that is not completely understood by our scientists. Mr. Thompson was trying to determine what causes the spheres to activate periodically."

"So you let us take them out of the old man's safe to see if we knew what they were all about?" asked Tony.

"Of course. With Mr. Thompson in a coma, we really had no other option. In the past fifty years, only the dead Indians and Mr. Thompson have had any real contact with the spheres. And then you came along. The casino tapes didn't catch you receiving the first one, so we assumed you had removed both spheres when you emptied the safe. We've had your hotel room under constant surveillance ever since. We were puzzled about the one found under this latest Indian's body, but now that I've heard your story, I realize it must have been the one you allowed him to take from the mobile home. It seems that these Indians are on some 'mission' to carry these objects back to a specific place and bury them in the ground. We think they cover them with their bodies as a form of protection, but we don't know what they are protecting the spheres from or what causes the death of the Indians. Every single body has undergone an autopsy and nothing more suspicious than 'natural causes' has ever been discovered."

"What about the hieroglyphics on them?" Tony asked. "Haven't you ever attempted to translate the message?"

"Ah, well, you see, the Department of Energy is a rather focused group of people. When it appeared that the spheres might hold the key to some undiscovered form of energy, anything else, like some scribbling around the circumference of a sphere, became unimportant. Once it was determined that the symbols were some form of Mesoamerican hieroglyphics, the physicists lost their interest. The writing was Mayan, the delivery agents were Maya, so it all seemed to make sense. The question of the hour became what makes these things tick, not what do they say. In retrospect, it seems that more attention should have been paid to the alleged source of the objects."

"You mean this *Loltún* place that Frank and Jim have trotted off to?" asked Tony.

"No, Mr. Nicoletti, not *Loltún*, although that may be an intermediate storage site. Based on a closer investigation of the sphere found yesterday, there are a few of us at the Department of Energy who now believe what Mr. Thompson has contended for years – that the spheres are of alien origin."

Chapter 17

As the car pulled away from the hotel, Frank stood there shaking his head. In the process of buying a new wardrobe at Alfredo's clothing shop, he had inadvertently stumbled onto a guide who knew a secret way into the forbidden portions of the *Loltún* Caverns! Laughing to himself, Frank failed to hear Jim approach from the hotel entrance.

"What's so funny?" asked Jim in a perfectly normal voice.

Startled, Frank spun and dropped one of the bags he was holding. Seeing Jim, Frank scolded, "Geez, Jim! Never sneak up on a guy armed with a bag of new clothes!" And then, smiling, he said, "Hey, have I got news for you! Help me carry this stuff up to my room and I'll explain while I'm getting ready to meet Alex."

Jim collected several of the parcels and followed Frank into the hotel. Frank noticed that the desk clerk who had recommended Alfredo's shop to him was still on duty, so he angled over to the desk and set down his packages.

"I see your shopping trip was a success, *Señor*," smiled the young man.

"You have no idea, *amigo*, you have no idea," Frank mumbled, as he reached into his pants pocket and retrieved a hundred dollar bill he had placed there during the ride from the clothing shop back to the hotel. "This is for the great advice you gave me."

At first the desk clerk, with eyes as large as quarters, refused the bill, embarrassed to receive such a large tip for sending business to the shop of his best friend's father. Frank insisted and made it clear he wouldn't take no for an answer. As Frank and Jim walked toward the elevator, Jim asked, "What was that all about? I realize you've recently come into a large sum of money, but really, Frank, don't you think a $100 tip is a bit much for recommending a store?"

"I'll explain when we get upstairs. I think you'll agree that it was money well spent," replied Frank as the elevator door closed behind them.

Once they were in Frank's room, he explained the unlikely tour guide he had arranged for the next day. "Alfredo and his son stand to make $100 each and we get into the caverns unescorted and unrestrained. This couldn't have turned out better if we'd planned it this way," said Frank.

"It almost sounds too easy, doesn't it?" questioned Jim. "Are you sure you trust these guys? What if they take us out into the Mexican countryside, grab the $200 and leave us there. I'm not sure I'd be so thrilled about this coincidence if I were you." Jim clearly sounded worried about traveling into the remote area with strangers.

Frank pulled his suitcase down off the closet shelf and opened it. After rummaging around for a second he produced a device that looked like a dark green electric shaver with thick fangs. "Tony insisted that I bring this along. I think we'll be just fine tomorrow," replied Frank.

"What is that thing?" asked Jim.

"This is a taser. At the flip of this switch it discharges 625,000 volts into an opponent and it's pretty much 'Game Over' for anyone on the receiving end," explained Frank.

"Be careful with that thing, will you?" cautioned Jim, as Frank's finger indicated the trigger switch.

"It's just a precaution, Jim. Personally, I think this Alfredo guy is okay, especially if he knows a back way into the caverns. Our next best chance would be Monday when the government official returns from Mexico City and even then there's no guarantee. If the feds really are cracking down on bribery, that whole plan may have been a dead end, anyway. Let's just play it cool and stay on our toes. If things start to look weird, we'll abort and get the hell out of there. And now if you'll excuse me, I have to meet Alex in a few minutes and I'd like to shower first."

After showering, shaving and dressing, Frank called Tony's cell phone, but there was no answer. He tried the hotel room at the Residence Inn, but there was no answer there, either, so Frank left a message with the front desk for Tony to call him as soon as possible.

Frank was downstairs at the Café promptly at 4:00 p.m., all decked out in his new beige linen pants, aqua shirt and Italian shoes. As he was scanning the Café for Alex, she tapped him on the shoulder from behind. "Looking for me?" she asked.

Frank jumped and quickly turned to face her. "Damn, I wish people would quit sneaking up on me!"

"Sorry, Frank," apologized Alex, realizing she had startled Frank, "I thought you heard me coming up the street."

Frank, embarrassed by his rudeness, waved off her apology. "No, I'm sorry. I don't know why I'm so jumpy lately. Jim nearly scared me out of my skin earlier and we were just out here in front of the hotel. I'm sorry, Alex, I didn't mean to bark at you. Where shall we go?"

"Well, if you don't have any preference, how about if we walk a few blocks to a new French restaurant that just opened? They have a great wine selection and if you're hungry later they also have excellent food. Is that okay with you?" smiled Alex.

"Perfect," replied Frank. "I haven't eaten since breakfast and I love French cuisine."

As they walked along the tree-lined street in front of the traditional Mexican colonial buildings, Alex commented on Frank's clothes. "It looks like someone has been shopping. You look more like a well-dressed local than a Gringo tourist," she laughed. "Have you been to Alfredo's recently?"

"How did you know?" asked a surprised Frank. After all, he could have purchased the clothes anywhere.

"Just a lucky guess, but the hotel usually recommends Alfredo's because he takes good care of their guests. Besides, it's the closest place and you're on foot, so it made sense." Alex stopped and gave Frank a once-over. "I'm glad to see that Alfredo hasn't lost his touch."

"He seems like a decent guy, all right. You sound like you know him personally."

"I've known Alfredo for a long time. We went to school together, before I went to live with my father, and we've remained friends. His son, Ricardo, and my daughter, Maria, are schoolmates and friends," explained Alex as they reached the entrance to *Le Bistro*.

Once inside and seated, Frank asked again about Alex's friend. "So tell me about your friend Alfredo. He offered to give Jim and me a private tour of *Loltún* tomorrow but Jim is concerned about trusting a stranger to get us there and back safely. Do you think we will be okay?"

"I would trust Alfredo with my life," replied Alex confidently. "But I imagine Ricardo is going along, too, isn't he? He's the one who's the real expert on the Maya ruins around here.

He hopes to study archeology when he goes to the University in a couple of years."

"That's right! Alfredo did mention that his son would be going with us. How did the son get to know about *Loltún*?" asked Frank as the waiter brought their wine.

"Who knows how kids these days get interested in one thing or another. Ricardo has been interested in Maya culture for as long as I have known him and for the past two years he has found summer work as an assistant with American archeological groups working here in the area. Last summer he was hired by a group that was excavating a new portion of *Uxmal* – that's down near *Loltún*, you know – and I think he's going back to work for that same group this summer. That's probably how he became familiar with *Loltún*. Anyway, you're in goods hands with both the father and the son and you can tell your friend to stop worrying."

With that assurance, Frank dropped the subject and turned the conversation to Alex. "I think you said you returned to Merida three years ago, right? After spending so many years in the States, what made you decide to come back to the Yucatan?" asked Frank.

"This is my home, Frank. It's where I grew up and it's where some of my fondest memories are. Also, my daughter was born in the States and I wanted her to experience this culture before she gets to the age where she's ready to settle down. She may go back to the States to college and she may decide to make her life there, but at least she will have experienced this part of her heritage first hand."

"And what about Maria's father? Does he live in the U.S.?" asked Frank, trying to be tactful and failing.

"My ex-husband left us about ten years ago, when Maria was six. He's remarried now and has very little to do with us. I would have come back to Mexico after the divorce if it hadn't been for my father. He absolutely adored Maria and he was in poor health for several years before he died so it made sense to stay in Houston. Once he was gone, there was nothing keeping us in the U.S., so I returned to Merida."

Frank and Alex continued to chat through a delicious meal and more wine. Frank told Alex about his career at Boeing, about Donna's death, and about his subsequent retirement. He decided to leave out the part of the story concerning his Power Ball winnings, assuming that his retirement would adequately explain his globetrotting and financial independence. Alex was an excellent listener and Frank felt very comfortable with her. She was different from anyone he had ever known and, unlike Linda, she didn't remind him of Donna. Her dark eyes were easy to get lost in.

As they were making their way back to the hotel, Alex took Frank's hand and said, "Thank you, Frank. I had a lovely afternoon. It's been a long time since I've had someone to talk to." Frank smiled, both inside and out, and they walked the rest of the way back hand in hand.

Outside the hotel's main entrance, they stopped to say their good-byes. "Would you like to come up for a while?" Frank asked, bashfully.

Alex smiled and said, "Not tonight, Frank, but I'll take a rain check." She squeezed his hand, gave him a light kiss on the cheek and turned to leave. "Have a good trip tomorrow, and stop by to see me when you get back. I'll be right there," she called over her shoulder, indicating the now dark sidewalk Café.

Frank called Jim's room from the lobby, but there was no answer. On a hunch, he headed toward the bar where he found Jim at a table by himself.

"So, how was your date?" asked Jim as Frank approached the table.

"Amazing, actually, and what about you? Spending the evening alone?"

"No, Carmen is meeting me here in about fifteen minutes," replied Jim, checking his watch for the time. "She's taking me on a tour of the city. Would you like to join us?"

"Thanks, but I think I'll pass. I'm going to check in with Tony and then turn in early. You children have a nice time, and be home early," laughed Frank. "Oh, and guess what? Alex knows our tour guide Alfredo – seems that they're old schoolmates – and the son has worked on several archeological digs around *Uxmal* and *Loltún*. So you can relax and have a good time tonight knowing that we'll be safe tomorrow."

"Well, that does make me feel better, but I'm still a little nervous about this trip. Maybe that's just my nature. What time are we leaving in the morning?" asked Jim.

"Let's get an early start – how does 8:00 a.m. sound to you? I'll call Alfredo and arrange it when I get upstairs. And let's not mention anything about the spheres, okay. As far as they're concerned, we're just a couple of eccentric Gringos who want a special tour of the caverns. We'll see how things play out when we get there and find out what there is to see."

The next morning Frank and Jim were waiting in front of the hotel when Alfredo and his son arrived at exactly 8:00 a.m. Frank had talked the hotel into putting together lunches for the four of them and he had the food packed in his small carry-on bag, along with his satellite phone and several bottles of water. At Jim's insistence, Frank had also brought along the taser, which he had wrapped in a hand towel to disguise it. They loaded the bag into the trunk and Frank and Jim climbed into the back seat of Aifredo's Ford Escort sedan. Alfredo introduced his son to Frank and Jim and they exchanged pleasantries.

"So, *Señores*," asked Alfredo, as he put the car in gear and pulled away from the hotel, "are you also here to look for the mysterious orbs of Professor Torres?"

***

Tony looked from his Viet Nam comrade Gene Carlson across the table to the Department of Energy's agent Buzz Edwards and back to Carlson. "What do you mean *alien origin*?" Tony asked a little too loud.

"Please keep your voice down, Mr. Nicoletti," hissed Edwards. "We are only telling you this because we would like your help and cooperation. When I said that a small group of us at the Department of Energy were beginning to accept Al Thompson's theories, I meant a really small group."

Suddenly, Tony caught on. "I take it this small group is just the two of you?"

"Well, it's not *that* small, but we are certainly a minority within the Department," replied Carlson. "There are a few others who share our views, but the Department's official position is that the spheres are a foreign technology of unknown source and purpose. A policy letter has been circulated suggesting that expressing any other opinion is grounds for immediate dismissal. There's a lot of secrecy wrapped around this investigation."

"I'm sure you wondered why we asked you to meet us here, in a restaurant, rather than out at the Test Site or over at the base," added Edwards. "The fact of the matter is, we shouldn't be discussing this with you at all, so, officially, we aren't. Do you understand?"

"Yes, of course. So, Gene, does this mean that you're also working for the Department of Energy these days?" asked Tony, looking at his old Army buddy.

"Almost all civilians that have anything to do with the test site, the bombing range, or any of the other facilities at the 5,500 square mile Nellis complex are employed by the DOE, Tony, at least officially. We're all hired through a civilian government contractor to make it harder for the public to identify individuals and their duties. I'm actually part of a rather special security force these days."

"The Camo Dudes!" said Tony, again a little too loud. Both Carlson and Edwards quickly glanced around to see if anyone was paying attention to them, but the place was almost deserted and no one seemed to be interested in the trio.

"Please, Tony!" said Edwards, sternly. "We're taking a huge risk sharing this information with you, and it's very important that you keep it strictly confidential."

"Sorry," said Tony, "I appreciate being taken into your confidence, honest. It's just that this sounds so off-the-wall, you know? And, hell, Gene, I thought you worked at the Air Base. Isn't that where I called you?"

"Yes, I have a desk there, and my 'official' position is Security Liaison. As far as the Air Force is concerned, my job is to coordinate their use of the bombing range with the Department of Energy, which has overall responsibility for the Nellis complex," explained Carlson.

"You mean even the Air Force doesn't know what you actually do?"

"Well, some of them do," grinned Carlson, "but only at the highest levels. But let's get back to the subject at hand. We asked you here to share what we know about the spheres and to solicit your cooperation. It appears that you may know more about this than we do, so it's very important that we work together."

"Work together on what?" asked Tony. "You still haven't told me what your interest in the spheres is and why you're being so secretive about all this."

"I don't have time to go into a lot of detail, Tony, but we believe the spheres, directly or indirectly, may pose a threat to our national security," explained Edwards. "We would like you to give us the spheres you still have in your possession so we can store them in a secure location until we learn more about them. We would also appreciate it if you would share everything you know about the spheres or anyone associated with them. And finally, we would like you to keep this conversation and everything else you know about this subject strictly confidential."

"Now wait just a damn minute. This is beginning to sound like a pretty one-sided arrangement here. You two don't appear to have any official capacity here, so why should I hand the spheres over to you?"

"Because as long as you have them, your life, and the lives of anyone associated with you, is in grave danger," replied Edwards. "There are individuals who would kill, and probably already have killed, to gain control of the spheres. For everyone's safety, we want to store the spheres out at the complex, in a facility considered to be one of the most secure locations in the world. Out there, they won't present a threat to you or anyone else until we can figure out exactly what their purpose is. I know it sounds like we're asking a lot of you, but please understand that we wouldn't even be having this conversation unless we thought this matter was of the greatest importance. We've done our homework and we know we can trust you. We just need you to trust us until we can either confirm or dismiss our suspicions about the spheres."

"I'm not the only one that knows about these spheres, you know," said Tony, defiantly.

"We're aware of that. Like I said, we've done our homework. There's your friend Frank Morton, and Al Thompson's daughter, of course, and a Professor Jim Barnes, right?" asked Edwards.

"Yes, that's correct," answered Tony, noticing that they hadn't mentioned Linda McBride, back in Seattle. "And Jim Barnes probably knows more about the spheres than anyone else right now. He's the one who decoded the messages on the three we've had contact with."

Buzz Edwards and Gene Carlson exchanged glances and then they both looked at Tony questioningly. "What did you say?" asked Edwards.

"I said, it was Professor Barnes who decoded the messages on the three spheres we have seen. Surely you know about the messages, gentlemen," smiled Tony smugly.

"No, I mean the number. Did you say you've had contact with three spheres?"

"Yes, that's correct. The one that the old man gave me in the casino and the two we found in his safe a couple of days ago."

"Really," said a very serious Edwards. "And what about the messages?"

"Well, I don't remember the exact dates, but Jim discovered that each of the three spheres contained a unique date and some directional information. None of it made much sense until he figured out that the directional information was all relative to a single point. That allowed him to determine where the other three points were and from that he was able to deduce the significance of the dates," explained Tony.

"Please continue," said Carlson. "Where is this common point?"

"And what about the dates," added Edwards.

"Like I said, I don't remember the names of the three places, but the date on each sphere matched the date of a solar eclipse at each sphere's specified point," said Tony.

"And the common point?" asked Carlson again.

"Why, *Loltún*, of course. Why do you think Frank and Jim went down there?" replied Tony.

Suddenly, Edwards slid across the booth seat toward the aisle. To Carlson he said, "I need to get down there as soon as possible. You finish briefing Mr. Nicoletti and then get those spheres back to Yucca Mountain. I'll call you with an update as soon as I get there." And with that, he was out the door and gone.

"Where the hell is he going in such a big hurry?" asked Tony, as he moved around to the other side of the table, across from Carlson.

"*Loltún*, I imagine. Hopefully he will get there before your friends get themselves into too much trouble. Now listen very carefully, Tony. In a few minutes, you and I are going to leave here in your rig, since Buzz just took mine. I'd like you to go get the money out of your safe deposit box and then you and I will pay a visit to Jill Harris. I'll have a private chat with her, like Buzz and I did with you, and then we'll help her get to a safe location for a while. When we leave Jill's, you and I are going to go to your hotel, collect the remaining spheres and deliver them to a special place out on the Nellis complex. Once that's done, we can discuss what our next step will be."

"And what if I don't agree to accompany you on this little excursion?" asked Tony defiantly.

"Well, that's certainly your call, Tony. I know I'm asking you to trust me without giving you any real reason to do so, but at least give me the opportunity to show you Yucca Mountain. I think you'll find it very interesting, to say the least. If that doesn't convince you to join forces with us, then you can go your own way."

"And the spheres?" asked Tony, knowing the answer before he even asked the question.

"I'm afraid the spheres must stay with us whether you decide to cooperate or not, but I'm very confident that once you've seen the Yucca Mountain complex, you will be glad to be rid of them. We believe they could be very hazardous to your health."

Chapter 18

Alfredo's question about Professor Torres' spheres caught Frank and Jim off guard. "What do you mean by that, Alfredo? Have you taken someone else on a private tour of *Loltún* lately?"

"No, Señor Morton," replied Alfredo, "but Ricardo worked with an American last summer who was convinced that Professor Torres had found something out near the caverns just before he disappeared. Tell them the story, Ricardo."

Alfredo's sixteen-year old son explained. "It is true *Señores*. Last summer I worked at *Uxmal* with a group from the University of Texas. One of the American archeologists, a man named Wilson, was sure that Professor Torres had made a significant discovery at *Loltún*, and he spent all his free time searching the area near the caverns for something he called '*las esferas*' – the spheres. He went there every afternoon and when the others returned to Merida for the weekend, he would stay and continue his search alone. By the end of the summer the other members of his team thought he was loco."

"Did he ever find anything, Ricardo?" asked Jim quietly.

"No, Professor Barnes, not that I am aware of. He spent his time searching above ground because that's where he believed the Professor had been working," replied Ricardo.

"What about the caverns? Didn't you ever take him into the caverns where we're going today?" asked Frank.

"No, *Señor*. I didn't find the entrance we will use today until after the Americans had returned to the United States. It is several kilometers from the caverns, so I doubt if Señor Wilson ever found it, either.

"Wilson? That's the one who was looking for the spheres?" asked Jim.

"Yes, but I don't believe he ever searched north of the highway, in the direction of *Mani*, so he would never have found the entrance we will use today."

"*Mani*… where do I know that name from?" thought Frank out loud.

"The Legend of the Dwarf!" exclaimed Jim. "Remember, I told you about it yesterday! I ran across the 1840 account by John Stephens in the library the other day."

"That is correct, Professor," confirmed Ricardo. "The Legend of the Dwarf is a popular story among the local Maya people, especially their shamans, or priests. They believe it explains the origin of the Pyramid of the Magician, even though archeologists have determined that the original structure has actually been added on to at least four times since it was first constructed about 569 A.D."

"You're very knowledgeable, Ricardo. What made you become so interested in the Maya culture?" asked Jim.

Over the course of the next hour, Ricardo explained that his interest in archeology was a result of being one-eighth Maya. Ricardo explained that his great-grandmother, his mother's mother's mother, was full-blooded Maya and her family had lived in the Yucatan since before the Spaniards founded Merida in 1542. It wasn't long before Jim and Ricardo lapsed into a discussion of archeology in general and Frank lost interest.

As they reached the small town of *Muna* (not to be confused with *Mani*), Alfredo interrupted the archeology discussion and asked, "Professor, shall we continue south and take the road that passes *Uxmal* or would you rather go straight to the caverns?"

"What do you think, Frank? It's about 25 miles farther to go by *Uxmal*, but it's one of the best examples of Maya ruins in the Yucatan."

"I'm up for it if everyone else is. Alfredo, do you and your son have the time for a little sightseeing detour?" asked Frank.

"Of course, *Señor*. We are at your service. Perhaps Ricardo can show you where he was excavating last summer."

A few minutes later the road made a sharp turn to the left and through the trees Frank caught a glimpse of a huge stone structure with a rounded side. "Is that..." he started, as his jaw dropped in disbelief.

"Yes, that's the Pyramid of the Dwarf, Frank," said Jim as proud as if he had built it himself. "Amazing, isn't it?"

Alfredo turned off the main road and onto a well-maintained drive that led to the entrance of a resort called The Lodge at *Uxmal*. "We can stop here, *Señores*. The entrance to the site is only thirty meters from the Lodge and I suggest we have a light lunch before we head up to the caverns. The manager here is an old friend of mine and I think I'll pay him a visit while the three of you explore the ruins."

Frank, Jim and Ricardo spent the next two hours wandering around the site. Frank had never experienced anything like *Uxmal* before and he was in complete awe of everything he saw. The stone structures were much larger than he would have imagined and they were in incredibly good condition, considering they were nearly 1,500 years old. To top it off, he had two very knowledgeable experts as tour guides. Between Jim and Ricardo, there didn't seem to be a single fact they didn't know, so Frank was surprised when he asked them, "So what happened to the people that used to live here?"

Both Jim and Ricardo shrugged their shoulders and Jim explained, "Archeologists used to think that cites like *Uxmal* were eventually overrun by the inhabitants of *Chichén Itzá*, which is about 100 miles east of here, but recent discoveries of the books of the *Chilam Balam* indicate that inhabitants of the major cities of the Yucatan actually migrated from site to site in a peaceful manner. These books also make reference to a grand assembly of the lords from *Uxmal, Chichén Itzá, Itzamal* and several places as yet undiscovered, so the question of what happened to those who lived here is once again a mystery."

The three of them stopped at the entrance gate and turned to survey the site one last time before moving on. "This is truly amazing," said Frank quietly. "I wonder if our cities will hold up as well."

Frank, Jim and Ricardo entered the nearly empty restaurant and found Alfredo sitting at a table in the corner with an older man dressed in a sports jacket and tie. As the three approached, both men at the table stood to greet them.

"Señor Chaak, this is Señor Frank and Professor Jim. *Señores*, this is Señor Miguel Ortega-Chaak, the *Gerente General* of the Lodge," said Alfredo.

"That means he's the general manager," Jim whispered to Frank, translating the Spanish for him.

After exchanging greetings, they all sat down at the large round table and poured coffee from the pot. Chaak signaled a waitress over to the table and spoke to her in Spanish. She nodded and disappeared around a corner.

"Allow me the honor of sharing some typical Yucatan *botanas*, my friends. A little nourishment before your trek," smiled Chaak.

"Chaak – isn't that a Maya name, *Señor*?" asked Jim politely.

"It is, indeed, *amigo*! My family has lived in this area," said Chaak proudly, indicating the ruins just outside the restaurant's large glass windows, "for as long as time has been recorded. The happiest moment in my long life was when I was chosen to manage this facility because it allows me to be close to my home."

"If my memory serves me, there was a ruler of *Uxmal* who shared that same name, wasn't there?" asked Jim.

"Your knowledge of my ancestors is impressive, *Señor*. There are inscriptions on the Nunnery that tell of King Chan-Chaak-K'ak nal-Ahaw, also known as Lord Chaak, who was responsible for shaping most of the city of *Uxmal* that we see today."

"The nunnery was that huge structure just west of the Pyramid of the Dwarf that you found so impressive," Jim explained to Frank.

"Well, actually, I found it all impressive," replied Frank. "This is a truly amazing place, Señor Chaak, and it's easy to see why you are so proud of it and of your ancestors who built it. I could sit here and stare out at the ruins forever. There is a quiet majesty about this place that makes one feel very small and insignificant."

"In that case, *Señor*, I insist that you and the Professor stay with us as long as you like," offered the Lodge's manager. "The tourists and archeologists have all left for the season and we have plenty of room. It would be an honor to share what little I know about my ancestors with someone who could truly appreciate their role in history."

A huge grin broke out on Jim's face at the prospect of further investigating the famous Maya site, but Frank said, "Thank you very much for the generous offer, Señor Chaak, but we are headed for *Loltún* today and we did not come prepared to stay overnight. Perhaps another time."

"Ah, yes, the orbs," nodded Chaak, as several plates of appetizers were delivered to the table. "But my offer remains open. *Loltún* is only a short distance from here and our Lodge would make an excellent location from which to conduct your research. If you change your mind, just call me and I will have rooms prepared immediately."

Once they were on the road again, Frank thanked Alfredo for suggesting the side trip to *Uxmal*.

"I thought you would enjoy it, Señor Morton. Besides, I haven't seen my old friend Miguel in several months and it was good to talk with him again. He loves to talk about his ancestors and he knows many, many old legends and folk tales. He's a very colorful individual," laughed Alfredo.

"Yes, so I gather. How is it that he knew we were looking for orbs at *Loltún*, Alfredo? Did you say something to him?" asked Frank.

"I'm afraid I did, but I only wanted to see if he knew of any legends describing such objects. I meant no harm, *Señor*," replied Alfredo apologetically.

"What was his reply?" asked Jim from the back seat. "I'm curious because I've never run across any reference to spheres in my study of the Maya and I find it hard to believe that something like that wouldn't be documented."

"That depends on where such information is written," interjected Ricardo from the front seat. "Most of the early Maya writings were destroyed by the Spaniards because the writings described gods other than the one of the Spaniards. In some cases, legends are all that are left of the Maya civilization. The recent discoveries of the many surviving *Chilam Balam* are giving us our first real look at a culture that was nearly destroyed in the name of religion."

"I heard that phrase earlier. What exactly is a *Chilam Balam*?" asked Frank.

Jim nodded to Ricardo, indicating that the youngster should take the question.

"Originally, *Chilam Balam* was a great priest of the *Tixcacaydn Cavich* in the ancient town *Mani*. That's the same *Mani* that's just north of where we are going today, by the way. He died about 1430 but he left several works, of which only a few fragments remain. He also composed narratives in verse that are still sung by the Yucatec Indians. Among other things, he predicted that foreigners from the east would conquer his people and teach them the One True Religion under the symbol of the cross. Later, his teachings were taken as a prediction of the Spanish conquest.

"After his death, written transcripts of his teachings were used by Maya priests, or shamans, in religious ceremonies for hundreds of years and the texts were considered divine objects. The books themselves became known as the *Chilam Balams* and they contained the religious and moral principles of the community, the truth one should follow, the examples of the ancestors and the prescriptions of the gods. The books were passed down through the generations from one village priest to another and kept secret for fear the Spaniards would burn them as they had most of the other Maya writings."

Shaking his head, Frank said, "Everything seems to keep pointing back to this area around *Loltún*, doesn't it? I guess if the spheres really are of Maya origin, *Loltún* makes as much sense as any place."

Alfredo slowed the car and turned left at a crossroads where a sign pointing in the opposite direction read '*Loltún* Cave, 3 kms.' "Just a few more minutes until we arrive at Ricardo's entrance, *Señores*," he announced, noticing Frank's concern over the sign.

As the car turned north, Alfredo continued the earlier conversation. "And that is precisely why I mentioned the subject of the orbs to Señor Chaak. He promised me he would consult with his brother and together they would examine the *Chilam Balam* for any reference to the objects you are looking for. Miguel will notify me if they discover anything."

"You mean his brother actually has one of these books?" asked an astonished Jim.

"Of course," replied Alfredo. "You see, Miguel's brother is the shaman for what remains of the people of *Uxmal*."

***

Tony decided to play along with Gene's game until he could find out exactly who was doing what to whom. He had no intention of turning the spheres over to Gene Carlson and his strange sidekick Buzz Edwards, but he was curious about how much they really knew and Gene had certainly sparked his curiosity with the talk about this place called Yucca Mountain.

It was 2:30 p.m. when Tony and Gene arrived at the bank where Tony had stored the money. Gene waited in the Durango while Tony went in and retrieved the carry-on bag from the safe deposit box. Tony didn't see the manager in the bank, which was just as well because he didn't have to explain his unexpected return to claim the bag. When he reached the Durango, he tossed the bag in the back seat. Carlson was just finishing a call on his cell phone when Tony climbed in behind the wheel.

"I just got off the phone with Jill Harris," explained Gene without being asked. "She's at the Medical Center right now but she's going to meet us at her place in fifteen minutes. Why don't we head over that way and wait for her? I'll show you how to get there."

"You're the boss," Tony lied, as he wondered who Carlson had really been talking to. "So how did the old man come by all this cash?"

"Well, it's the damnedest thing I ever heard of. Old man Thompson has been with the Department of Energy in one capacity or another for more than 25 years, and as a research scientist, he had always made pretty good money. From the very beginning he saved aggressively, but the older he got the more he socked away. After his wife died, he began putting $3,000 a month into his 401-k, and of course, with what the government contributed it added up pretty fast."

Never good at math, Tony didn't even try to compute how much money that might be, but it didn't seem like it could be half a million dollars. "So how did it all end up in cash in a small safe in Beatty, Nevada?" asked Tony as they pulled up in front of Jill's house and parked.

"Well, we knew that old Al was starting to come unstitched at the seams, if you get my drift, but when he closed out his retirement fund he told the admin folks at Bechtel that he wanted to move it into a guaranteed savings account in case the stock market folded again like it had a few years ago. He must have been further gone than we thought to store $287,000 in cash in a home safe," laughed Carlson.

"$287,000?" asked Tony.

"Yeah, that's a lot of money to keep around in cash, huh?" laughed Carlson again. As a car pulled into the driveway of the house across the street, he said, "There's Jill. Grab the bag, will you?"

They caught up with Jill as she was unlocking her front door. She seemed surprised to see Tony, but she had clearly been expecting Carlson. She invited them into the living room and offered cold drinks. She brought a pitcher of lemonade from the refrigerator and placed it on the glass-topped coffee table along with three chilled glasses.

"So what is this all about, Mr. Carlson? On the telephone you said you wanted to talk to me about my stepfather. I assume you know that he passed away recently, right?"

"Yes, and I'd like to offer my condolences. Actually, your stepfather and I worked for the same company, so to speak."

"You mean the government?" interrupted Jill.

"Well, yes, a civilian branch of the government, that's correct. Thanks to Tony and his friends, I believe you know that your stepfather actually worked as a scientist for the Department of Energy," continued Carlson.

"So I've heard," replied Jill, throwing Tony a questioning look. Tony remained expressionless.

"And, as you also know, your stepfather had a large sum of money in his safe when he was killed."

"Yes, and at least two mysterious black spheres – maybe three, counting the one he gave to Tony, but what of it?" asked Jill, becoming impatient with the questioning.

"Well, here's the thing, Jill. The spheres were not rightfully the property of your stepfather, but the money apparently was. We would like you to forget you ever saw the spheres and in exchange we will forget we know about the money. You are Al Thompson's only living relative, so we suggest you deposit the money into several banks and enjoy it. In exchange for your silence regarding the spheres, the government is willing to overlook the matters of probate and inheritance tax. The $287,000 is yours to enjoy as you see fit."

At the mention of the amount, Jill shot Tony another questioning look, and he shrugged without being noticed by Carlson. Jill understood that Tony was suggesting she not let on how much they had really found in the old man's mobile home.

"Well, I don't have a need for any black metal baseballs, so how can I lose?" smiled Jill. And then more seriously, she added, "But I expect the investigation into his murder to proceed. Even though he wasn't really the person I thought he was, he didn't deserve to be killed and whoever did it should be punished."

"Of course, Jill. It's a police matter now, but I will do everything I can to make sure the investigation moves forward and that any guilty parties are brought to justice. You have my word on that."

Tony's eyes rolled at the last comment, but since he was now behind and to the right of Carlson only Jill could see Tony's reaction.

"Is that the money?" asked Jill, indicating the bag in Tony's hand and knowing full well what it contained.

"Yes, and it's yours as of now" said Carlson, indicating that Tony should give her the bag. As Tony started to move across the room, Carlson said, "There is one other thing, Jill." Tony had been expecting some last minute trick and stopped dead in his tracks.

"And what is that, Mr. Carlson?" she asked. Jill still didn't understand what Tony was doing with Carlson, but she now realized that Tony didn't trust the other man.

"Jill, there are those of us who think the spheres pose a significant threat to anyone who has had contact with them. One of them was apparently responsible for a death up at Nellis yesterday and Tony has agreed to return the other two to us for safekeeping. In addition, an associate of mine is on his way to Mexico to alert Tony's friends of the danger they may be facing. We're quite serious about the danger related to these things and until we find the person or persons responsible for killing your stepfather, we'd like you to take an immediate and extended vacation. Anywhere you like, as long as it's away from here. And you shouldn't tell anyone where you are going. If you must name a place, make something up. At this point, you shouldn't trust anyone. You now have substantial financial resources, so hire a security company to keep an eye on your house and get out of town as quickly as possible. Today, if you can, but by tomorrow for sure. Will you do that?"

"Okay, now you're beginning to scare me, pal. And, I can't just walk away from my job without any notice. The hospital would have to arrange for a replacement and ..."

"Jill, if you don't take my advice your employer may be looking for a permanent replacement rather than a temporary one. I'm dead serious about this," insisted Carlson.

Tony was beginning to think that Carlson might actually be on the level and might have Jill's best interests at heart. He finished his trip across the room and set the bag down beside her. "How about if I stay with Jill until she can get things worked out?" he asked the other man.

"That's a nice gesture, Tony, but you can't be with her every minute. If she's truly in danger, a killer could strike her at work, on her way to or from work or any number of other places. It is really important that she just disappear for a while. And besides, you're a potential target yourself. Putting the two of you together would invite double trouble. Two birds with one stone, and all that."

"Okay, stop it! I'm getting really scared now. I'll make the arrangements and I'll leave as soon as I can, but how can I be sure I'm not being followed. Where can I go to be safe?" said Jill, almost in tears.

"You leave that up to me, Jill. You deal with the money, make the arrangements at work and then call me at this number," said Carlson, scribbling a phone number on a napkin from the lemonade tray. "I'll arrange to get you out of Las Vegas secretly."

"Janet Airlines?" asked Tony, remembering something he had read on the Internet about an alleged "secret" airline that operated a fleet of planes out of the Las Vegas airport. Rumor had it that civilian employees were shuttled to and from secret installations on the Nellis complex and other locations each day using the fleet of six 737s and five twin-engine Beechcraft planes.

Carlson nodded and added, "Sometimes it pays to have connections in high places." Standing up, he said, "You call me as soon as you're ready to leave, Jill. I'll have a car here to pick you up within fifteen minutes of your call and the driver will take you directly to our private terminal out at McCarran. Don't tell anyone where you are headed until the plane is in the air. At that point, the pilot will need to know a general compass direction so he can take you to a commercial airport. Once you land, you can make your own connections to your final destination with the knowledge that no one has followed you. Good luck, Jill."

Carlson headed toward the door while Tony gave Jill a hug and a couple of words of encouragement. "Everything's going to be fine, Jill," he assured her. "And you call me if you need anything."

"I will, Tony. Please say 'Good bye' to Frank and Jim for me and thank them for everything." A tear rolled down Jill's cheek as Tony stepped away and moved toward the door. "And tell Frank he doesn't need to worry about paying me back," she added, forcing a smile.

As they walked across the street to the Durango, Carlson asked, "What was that all about?"

"Oh, Jill loaned Frank $10 for lunch the other day," lied Tony, knowing that Jill was actually referring to the $10,000 Frank had borrowed from the old man's stash. "I guess she doesn't need the $10 back now that she has her stepfather's money, huh?"

"Yeah, I guess not! Okay, now let's go round up those spheres and I'll show you a place that'll blow your mind. Fortunately, your current contract with the government has kept your Top Secret clearance in effect; otherwise I wouldn't have been able to get you cleared for access into the Yucca Mountain facility so quickly. As it is, I had to pull some serious strings, but my superiors really want your cooperation and I convinced them that this was the only way they would get it. You might want to pack a toothbrush, too, because we won't be coming back to town tonight."

Chapter 19

Jim's jaw dropped in disbelief. "Are you serious," he asked. "He's a real, live Maya shaman?"

"That's correct," replied Alfredo, "Of course he supports his family by giving tours of *Uxmal* and several other Maya sites in this area, but he is also the religious leader of those who still follow the old ways. If there's ever been a legend or story about your spheres, Miguel's brother will know about it."

"I'm having second thoughts about turning down Miguel's offer of hospitality at the Lodge," said Frank. "It seems like maybe we should spend some time talking to Miguel and his brother, and I wouldn't mind spending a little more time at the ruins, either."

"I'd be happy to call him, *Señor*. Why don't you decide after you have seen the caverns?" asked Alfredo.

"*Papá*, the turn is just ahead on the left! See it over there?" pointed Ricardo, as he indicated a faint trail through the underbrush on the left side of the road.

They hadn't seen another car since turning off the main highway, so Alfredo slowed to a stop in the middle of the road.

"Take a good look around, *Señores*. If you come back here on your own, you will need to know how to find this place." Looking down at the odometer of his car, he said, "We are exactly 2.3 km from the turn-off. Remember to look for the sign to *Loltún* but turn left instead of right."

Jim made notes on the small pad that always seemed to be in his shirt pocket as Alfredo put the car back in gear and eased off the road and onto the trail. He went very slowly to avoid scraping the bottom of his car as his tires made their way in and out of the many ruts and potholes. "I would not recommend this trip right after a rain," he laughed. "This road turns to deep mud very quickly."

A short distance down the brush-lined trail they came to a small stand of trees on the left side of the road. Alfredo turned off the trail and parked the car on a grassy area under the nearest tree. "Here we are, *Señores*," announced Ricardo, as he opened his door and climbed out to stretch.

Frank retrieved his carry-on from the trunk and Ricardo pulled out a full backpack. He removed four flashlights from the pack and handed one to each member of the party before his father locked up the car. Alfredo left the side windows down about an inch for ventilation because the temperature at *Uxmul* had reached nearly 100 degrees and, even with the air conditioning on, the car had become hot and uncomfortable. Here, in the shade of the trees, however, it felt oddly comfortable.

"Where does this road go, Ricardo?" asked Frank indicating the tracks that continued on to the west.

"I don't know, *Señor*. This is as far as I have ever been. One day when my father was visiting Miguel, I borrowed the car and came out this way looking for the ruins of a small Maya village I had read about. When I got to these trees, I stopped to, ah, relieve myself, and I noticed the change in temperature here. After a little exploration, I discovered the cave entrance and I lost all interest in looking for the village."

"I thought I felt cooler air!" exclaimed Jim. "Do I also detect the faint sound of water?"

"Yes, *Señor*, let me show you. Right this way," announced Ricardo, as he led the way through the trees and down a slight slope."

The hill sloped down into what appeared to be a dry creek bed, completely invisible from the road above. Ricardo turned left and led the other three men around a slight bend where he stopped and waited for everyone to catch up. The sound of running water had gotten louder and as Ricardo pulled aside a portion of a large Bugambilia plant, they could see a small cave opening in the bank of the dry creek.

"Watch your heads, *Señores*," warned Ricardo. "There is a short tunnel we must pass through and then you will be able to stand up again."

The four made their way down the dark tunnel for about 20 yards before the passage opened into a small cavern about 15 feet high. A 3-foot wide stream was rushing through the cavern and the sound of the water was amplified by the acoustics of the place. The water entered the cavern from the right, through an opening large enough to walk through. Carefully, Ricardo picked his way down to the level of the stream and, ducking under an overhang, motioned for the others to follow him downstream along the water's edge.

They passed through a series of connected caves, each a little larger than the last. They were gradually sloping down; going deeper and deeper into the earth, but the walking remained fairly easy because the underground stream had a flat gravel bank on one side.

After about fifteen minutes they entered an especially large cavern and Ricardo held up his hand for the group to stop. "Let's take a short break here. The *Loltún* caves are still about twenty minutes from here, and there won't be another good place to stop before we get there."

Frank took the sandwiches and bottles of water out of his bag and offered them around. "You would certainly never guess this underground river was here by looking at the land above," observed Frank, as they ate. "Where do you think we are, Ricardo?"

"I believe we are approximately under the highway to *Uxmal, Señor*. The trail we turned onto is almost the same distance north of the highway as *Loltún* is south of the highway and we're about halfway to the caverns. Soon we will leave this stream behind and when we get closer to *Loltún* you may be able to hear the voices of the tour groups as they are being led through the public caverns. You must be very quiet then, so you don't give away our secret," smiled Ricardo. The others nodded their agreement and, after another few minutes, they packed up their trash and continued their trek.

The next cavern was very irregular in shape, and the noise of the water was much louder here. "There's a small waterfall over there," pointed Ricardo. "We must make a short climb and exit through that large opening to your left but there is a path, so it will not be too difficult."

As they started to leave the underground stream and climb, Frank asked Jim, "Who do you suppose made this path? It seems to be worn right into the rock."

"I don't know, but it sure looks well used. So far this has been almost too easy," replied Jim.

Ricardo overheard Jim's reply and stopped the group again. "I, too, was surprised by the easy access when I first discovered this entry, *Señor*, but later I learned that the entrance used by the public today is the result of a fairly recent geologic event. A sinkhole appeared after a huge storm about a hundred years ago and the locals began exploring the caverns through it. The opening that currently serves as the pubic exit was man-made when the caverns were opened to the public in 1956. I believe that in the time of the

Maya, entrance to this complex was the one we came in through and that the caverns ahead that are now open to the public were once completely closed to the outside world. We know that many Maya hid in these caves during the great War of the Castes in the last half of the 19th century, and there are drawings on the walls of a cavern called *Huechil* that indicate a human presence here centuries before the building of *Uxmal*. Some archeologists even believe that these caves were used for shelter in prehistoric times, as much as ten thousand years ago. They have also found the bones of extinct animals, such as mammoth, bison and large cats, indicating that these caves were used during a much colder period in the Yucatan Peninsula's history."

Frank took a moment to look around and imagine the caverns filled with ancient Maya. His first day of archeology was certainly going to be one to remember – first *Uxmal* and now these caves. "I'm beginning to understand your interest in these people," he said to Jim. And then to Ricardo, he waved, "Show me more, show me more!"

After the slight climb up, they passed through a series of caverns that remained on a more or less horizontal plane with a relatively flat floor. Suddenly Jim's light caught something on a wall and he yelled out, "Look at this!"

Everybody quickly joined him, with Ricardo 'shushing' him all the way. "You must keep your voice down, *Señor*!" he admonished. "We are now close enough to be heard by others."

What Jim had found appeared to be the outline of a hand drawn on the cave wall, and Frank was a little disappointed when he saw it. "A hand? Hell, Jim, I think even I could draw something that good," he laughed softly.

"No, Frank, you don't understand. This is a classic prehistoric art form. The artist created the outline of his own hand by blowing soot around it. This was probably done before 'drawing' even existed as a human concept. This may be thousands of years old."

"There are more pictures like that ahead in the next cavern, *Señor*, but you must be quiet from now on because sound carries a great distance in these caves."

The four men moved on, and Frank could tell that Jim was also having the time of his life.

Soon Ricardo signaled for everyone to stop and remain quiet. In the distance they could hear faint voices and Ricardo mouthed the word *Loltún* and pointed up and to the left. Apparently, the public caves were a level above and close by. After the voices passed, Ricardo signaled for the others to follow him through a low opening on the opposite side of the cavern, away from the direction of the voices. Once they were all inside the next chamber, Ricardo stopped them again.

"Above us are the caverns that are open to the public. They stretch for about 2 km, from entrance to exit, and several of them are now open to the outside as the result of small sinkholes or fallen ceilings. The natural ventilation caused by these openings keeps the air fresh, even with the large number of visitors that pass through each day. The chamber we just left connects with the public portion of *Loltún*, but no one is allowed down here, not even the staff. The connecting tunnel has been blocked by a large metal gate to keep visitors from wandering down here and getting lost or injured."

"And what happens if we continue on through this cavern, Ricardo? We would obviously be headed away from *Loltún*, but where would we end up?" asked Jim.

"I don't know, *Señor*. There are many caverns in this part of the Yucatan and some may connect. There is another large cavern complex 50 km southwest of here, called *Xtacumbilxunán*, and yet another, near *Chichén Itza*, 150 km to the northeast," explained Ricardo.

"Which may explain what happened to Professor Torres," commented Frank. "He could have wandered around down here and simply gotten lost."

"That is quite possible," said Alfredo, who had been very quiet since they entered the complex back near the car. "Every time I turn a corner down here I expect to see his bones leaning against the side of the cave. It makes me very uncomfortable, *Señores*. Very uncomfortable."

"Speaking of Professor Torres," added Ricardo, "I believe this is the very cavern he was working in at the time he disappeared. Over here, I found a pencil that had rolled under the edge of this rock." Ricardo indicated a large boulder on one side of the chamber using his flashlight as a pointer. He swung the light beam around to a hole about three feet in diameter down near the floor and continued, "And in this next chamber there is something I think you will find very, very interesting."

***

Tony and Gene Carlson stopped at the Residence Inn to pick up the two spheres. Tony got Carlson a beer from the refrigerator and left him in the living room while he went upstairs to gather his shaving kit and a change of clothes into a leather travel bag he had brought from Atlanta. He started to zip the bag shut, changed his mind, and opened it again. He looked back over his shoulder to make sure Carlson wasn't watching and then quickly unlocked his crate, took his Colt revolver from the footlocker and stuffed it into the bag. After securing the crate, he went into the downstairs bedroom and unlocked Frank's footlocker. He packed the two spheres, one still wrapped in a napkin to mark it as the "counter-cracker", into the bag on top of a shirt. He zipped the bag shut, secured the footlocker and returned to the living room. "Ready?" he asked Carlson, who was gazing out the window, lost in thought.

"Ready!" he confirmed. Looking at Tony's bag, he asked, "You don't have any cameras in there do you? The folks at Yucca Mountain are pretty fussy about taking pictures of the place."

"Nope, no cameras," replied Tony, patting the bag with a smile.

During the 97-mile trip from Las Vegas to Amargosa Valley, the two chatted causally about their lives since their last meeting in Viet Nam more than 25 years ago. Realizing that Carlson and his strange friend Buzz Edwards had done some homework, Tony was truthful but guarded and he didn't bring up events in his life that hadn't already been mentioned back at the restaurant.

Carlson had apparently joined the civil service immediately after his discharge from the Army and he had been involved in security from the very beginning. This made sense, because Tony knew the other man was with an Intelligence group in Nam, but Tony wasn't taking anything Carlson said at face value. There was something about the man he just didn't trust.

"So, do you get out to Area 51 much," slipped in Tony, when there was a lull in the conversation.

"Never heard of the place," replied Carlson, without an instant's hesitation.

Tony thought he detected a slight smile on Carlson's face. I'll trip you up yet, you bastard, Tony promised himself. "You know, that hush-hush operation that's supposed to operate up near Rachel. Supposed to be flying saucers and aliens and stuff out there."

Carlson laughed out loud and said, "You've been watching too much television, my friend. In my position as Security Liaison, I'm sure I would know if such a place actually existed."

"Yes, I'm sure you would," replied Tony almost to himself.

When they reached the roadside rest area known as Amargosa Valley, where Nevada Route 373 turns south towards Death Valley Junction, Carlson directed Tony north onto a well-maintained gravel road that appeared to climb up into the foothills. Shortly after turning onto the road, they passed a sign warning that they were entering U.S. Government Property and just around the next curve they were confronted with a large guard shack and a gate across the road almost like a railroad crossing.

"Pull all the way up to the gate and then turn off the engine," instructed Carlson. "They're going to want to search the vehicle and you'll need to go inside to sign some forms."

Tony was beginning to question the wisdom of stashing his revolver in the leather bag when Carlson smiled and said, "Here, give me your bag. We don't want them going through that and finding the spheres, now do we?"

As they were walking over to the guard shack, Carlson removed an ID badge from his shirt pocket and clipped it onto his collar where it was clearly visible. Once inside, Carlson approached a small counter, handed his credentials to the guard on duty and introduced Tony. "Mr. Nicoletti will be accompanying me up to the facility. That's his vehicle, and I believe he has already been cleared for access," Carlson said authoritatively.

"That's correct, Mr. Carlson," said the man as he typed information into a computer and waited for the system to respond. After a second or two, the computer beeped and the guard said, "I'm afraid there's a small problem, though. The vehicle is registered to a Frank Morton, of Seattle, Washington, and not to Mr. Nicoletti."

Carlson looked at Tony questioningly and Tony replied, "That's correct. Frank is a friend of mine. I flew in from Atlanta to meet him several days ago and when he was unexpectedly called away on business, he asked me to take care of the Durango until he returns." Tony shrugged his shoulders as if to say, "So what's the big deal" but the man behind the counter remained firm.

"Mr. Nicoletti, you were cleared for access to the facility based on a recent background check, but Mr. Morton has not been. I'm afraid that applies to his property, as well," said the man behind the counter.

Looking back to Carlson, the man said, "I'm sorry, Mr. Carlson, but we cannot allow the vehicle beyond this point. Would you like me to call up to the site and arrange transportation for you?"

"Yes, that would be fine," replied a slightly embarrassed Carlson. "I wasn't aware that this was a borrowed vehicle. Had I known, I would have arranged for someone to pick us up in town. My apologies."

"That's quite all right, Mr. Carlson. If you'll just park the vehicle in the gravel area to the side of this building, we'll keep an eye on it until you and Mr. Nicoletti return. Just be sure to lock it and take the keys with you. While you're moving the vehicle, I have some paperwork for your guest to sign and then I'll have a temporary badge ready for him."

Tony handed Carlson the keys to the Durango and stepped up to the counter. "You guys sure are strict," commented Tony as he accepted the pen from the guard.

"Yes, sir, we are. Please sign here, here and here," he said, indicating three different forms on the counter. The man typed a few keystrokes on his keyboard and then picked up a white badge the size of a credit card from the counter behind him. In the center of the badge there was a yellow square containing the word 'TEMP' and the digits '214.' The guard handed the badge to Tony as he was finishing the last of the required signatures. "Please wear this in plain sight at all times while you on our facility, Mr. Nicoletti, and be sure you return it to us here at this gate when you leave. I'm afraid I'll also have to ask you to lock your cell phone inside the vehicle. You are not permitted to carry it onto the facility."

Tony was familiar with government security, of course, because his freight contract required that he be on and off federal facilities all the time, but he had never been asked to surrender his cell phone, and he told the man so.

"I'm afraid we do things a little differently here, Mr. Nicoletti. The use of a cell phone, even the receipt of an unexpected call, could trigger an explosion in certain parts of our facility. It's for everyone's safety."

Begrudgingly, Tony unclipped the phone from his belt, turned it off, and laid it on the counter. He heard the door open and turned to see Carlson returning from parking the Durango. "I guess this needs to go, too," said Tony, picking up his phone and handing it to Carlson.

Just then another beep came from the computer behind the counter and the guard glanced down at the screen. "Your transportation will be here in three minutes, Mr. Carlson."

Once they were seated in the back of the black Suburban, Tony turned to Carlson and asked, "You guys have some strange rules out here. Exactly what kind of place is this Yucca Mountain, anyway?"

"I'll give you more details when I take you on the grand tour, but in general terms, Yucca Mountain is a prototype for a national nuclear waste disposal facility. If Congress gives the go-ahead, and if the Nuclear Regulatory Commission approves the operating license, and if the Environmental Protection Agency approves the site, Yucca Mountain will permanently house the radioactive waste that is currently stored in temporary facilities in 35 different states."

"So that's why all the security and concern about cell phones! How much of that stuff do you have here, anyway?"

"Officially, none, because the facility is still under construction and has only been approved for very limited testing. Large-scale movement of material from around the country isn't expected to begin until at least 2010 but this facility may eventually hold 70,000 tons of high-level radioactive waste and spent reactor fuel rods," said Carlson proudly.

"And then what?" asked Tony, as the Suburban eased to a stop in front of a one-story metal building that was surrounded by a dozen or so similar buildings of varying sizes and shapes.

"Well, then the underground facility will be sealed and signs will be posted alerting the public to the danger below. Armed guards will patrol the immediate area for at least the first fifty years, and after that a new plan will have to be formulated. How's that for job security?" laughed Carlson.

As they climbed out of the Suburban, Tony grabbed the leather bag containing the spheres, his clothes and his revolver. "So how long before the buried material is safe? Are you saying everything will decompose, or whatever you call it, in fifty years?"

"Oh, no, certainly not. Some of the materials decay – not decompose – in just a few years, but most of it will remain very dangerous for tens of thousands of years. Congress only required a fifty year security plan, but obviously this area will have to remain protected for, well, forever, I guess," explained Carlson.

"Great plan," mumbled Tony. "Your tax dollars at work – forever!"

"Well, it's better than leaving the stuff scattered all over the country under the watchful eyes of minimum wage security guards, Tony. Here, let me show you why we're not too worried about anybody getting into the stuff once it's here."

Carlson led Tony around the building they had parked in front of and between two taller structures. As they came out into the sunlight again, Tony could see a trestle-like structure several hundred feet long that apparently carried a huge conveyor belt. One end fed a loading station for large dump trucks and the other end was stuck into a fifty-foot high opening in the side of the hill. A large aluminum pipe exited the tunnel entrance and turned upwards, like the exhaust pipe of a giant diesel truck.

Carlson saw Tony staring at the tunnel entrance and said, "That shaft gradually slopes down until it is 1,000 feet below the surface. There it will connect with a 100-mile long network of tunnels that are arranged as a series of concentric circles parallel to the surface. Once the facility is in operation, canisters of waste material will be carried underground by an automated rail system. At the bottom, robots resembling small automated forklifts will unload the canisters and store them in designated locations."

Tony shook his head in disbelief. "Are you supposed to be telling me all this?"

"Oh, this is all public information, Tony. Most of it can be found on the Internet. In fact, the Yucca Mountain Project has its own Web site! This is, without a doubt, the most publicly debated, openly discussed Top Secret project in the history of the world. It makes security a real challenge, as you can imagine. We'll take a ride down to the bottom and get those spheres locked up. I'm curious to see how the construction is progressing."

They returned to the building where the Suburban had been parked and Tony noticed that the vehicle was gone. Carlson opened the front door of the building and motioned Tony through ahead of him. Inside the air was cool and dry, a welcome relief from the heat outside. Carlson made his way through a maze of desks, some occupied and some empty, to an office in the back.

"Remember when I told you that I have an office over at Nellis Air Force Base for appearances? Well this is my *real* office." Indicating a chair in the corner, Carlson said, "Make yourself at home. How about a cold soft drink?"

Tony nodded and Carlson disappeared out the door. When he returned with two cans of Diet Coke, Tony was examining some of the many photos on Carlson's wall.

"Pretty neat, aren't they?" asked Carlson as he handed one of the cans to Tony. "Those were taken during various phases of the construction here. When I first arrived, almost ten years ago, this place was not much more than a 1,200-foot high, six-mile long flat-topped volcanic ridge. By the time they're done digging, this place will have cost more than 10 billion dollars."

"And why did we need to bring these spheres all the way up here to a place obviously designed for much more important matters?" asked Tony, patting his leather bag.

"Ah, yes, the spheres. Well, as I told you in the restaurant earlier today, some of us here believe the spheres represent a significant danger. We know that they have been responsible for the death of several Maya messengers and indirectly responsible for the death of Al Thompson. But a much larger threat may be the spheres themselves. Periodically they seem to 'come to life', indicating that they are self-powered, possibly by some sort of miniature reactor. Recently, our scientists were able to monitor one of these spheres during an especially 'active' period and they measured a minute amount of radioactivity being given off during the process."

"Well that's certainly intriguing, but how does that represent a danger?" asked Tony.

"Because the radiation that they measured was a little odd."

"Odd? To me, all radiation is odd. What makes this radiation so special?" asked Tony, beginning to suspect where this line of thinking was headed.

"Because it's not of this world, my friend. How's *that* for odd?"

Chapter 20

Although a large passageway on the left side of the cavern obviously connected to the next natural chamber in the chain, Ricardo led the group through a smaller opening near the floor at the back. Frank, the largest of the four men, went last and barely got his shoulders through the hole. As Frank entered the dark cave and stood up, Ricardo turned on a fluorescent lantern he had removed from his pack.

"Please be very careful where you walk, *Señores*," warned Ricardo. "This cavern does not have the smooth floor of those we just passed through."

The lantern created a circle of light about eight feet in diameter. Beyond the light's reach the cave was pitch black. While Ricardo was rummaging though his pack, Frank used his flashlight to examine the cave wall to the left of the opening they had just crawled through.

"Hey, Jim, look at this," he called quietly.

Jim and Alfredo quickly moved to his side to observe the discovery. Frank's light was panning back and forth across a number of small rounded pockets carved into the wall of the cave.

"Those are called *haltunes*, I believe," said Alfredo. "I don't know much about archeology, but I read about these in one of Ricardo's books. The Maya carved these artificial containers into the walls to collect natural dripping water. This part of the Yucatan Peninsula has very little ground water, but there is a significant amount underground and the Maya learned how to capture and conserve it. At one time, this area must have been much wetter and they probably used this cave as a source of drinking water."

Ricardo joined the others and put his arm on his father's shoulder proudly. "*Papá*, you amaze me! I didn't think you had any interest in my studies and yet you remember a small detail such as that!" he said.

As Frank continued to study the cave wall, Jim turned to Ricardo and asked, "Earlier you said you would show us something 'very interesting' in this cave, Ricardo. Were you referring to these *haltunes*?"

"Ah, no *Señor*, I didn't even notice these when I visited here before. There are some drawings on the back wall that I don't recognize. I'm not very good at Maya writing yet, but these don't look like anything I've ever seen before. They're right over here. Watch your step."

Ricardo picked up the fluorescent light and carried it to the back of the cave, leaving Frank at the front wall with only his flashlight. The mention of glyphs captured Jim's full attention and Alfredo followed close behind.

Ricardo set the light down and searched the wall of the cave with his own flashlight for a minute. When he finally spotted what he was looking for, he indicated a section of the wall to his father and Jim.

"There," he pointed. "Can you see those symbols? I tried to draw them when I was here before, but it was too hard to hold the light, a notepad and a pencil all at the same time. This time I came prepared," he said, holding up a digital camera he had retrieved from his pack."

"Good thinking, Ricardo!" said Jim, as he stepped closer to the wall to study the pictures. "You are going to make an excellent researcher. Let me take a look at these for a minute and then you can shoot some photos."

After a couple of minutes, Jim stepped back to allow Ricardo in with the camera. "I believe you're correct, my friend. These are definitely not Maya glyphs, but they are vaguely similar. I have a hunch, and it's just a hunch at this point, that these glyphs might be Olmec but we are hundreds of miles east of the recognized Olmec centers. They're more commonly associated with the area around La Venta and Veracruz."

"But if you're right, Professor, that would mean that this site was in use long before the Maya, wouldn't it?" asked Ricardo, as he continued snapping pictures of the glyphs.

"Yes, that's correct. These drawings could go back to 1,500 B.C. – maybe even earlier. That may also explain why the floor in this cavern is so different from what we experienced in the others. It's possible that the Maya never used this particular chamber. Maybe the hole we crawled through was blocked and they just never discovered it."

"Then why the *haltunes*," asked Alfredo. "Did the Olmec also use them?"

"It's possible," explained Jim. "The Olmec people are considered the Mother Culture of all of Mesoamerica and we know they passed a lot of their knowledge on to the Maya. They were excellent mathematicians and astronomers, they had an advanced system of writing and they created very accurate calendars. All of this was inherited by the Maya, so it's reasonable to assume the Olmec might have taught the Maya how to collect water, too."

"Before you get too carried away with that water theory, I think you'd better take a look at this," said Frank from across the cave.

Ricardo put the camera in a small case and clipped it to his belt. Carrying the lantern, the three rejoined Frank at the wall near the entrance to the cave.

"What is it, Frank?" asked Jim as they gathered around and looked where his flashlight was pointing on the wall.

"Ricardo, please turn that lantern off for a minute and all of you turn off your flashlights. Then watch this spot where my light is pointing when I turn it off."

Frank turned off his light, plunging the cave into total darkness. From the spot he had indicated on the wall came a very faint flickering. Compared to the relative brightness of the lantern, and even the flashlights, it was barely discernable, but as their eyes grew accustomed to the dark, it was obvious to all four that something in one of the *haltunes* was creating visible light.

"Any guesses?" asked Frank, as he turned his flashlight back on and stepped toward the wall.

"Wow," exhaled Jim. "If that's what I think it is, this is huge!"

Ricardo turned the lantern back on and held it high so Frank could see the floor better. As he reached the wall, his body blocked the *haltunes* from the view of the other three, who held their collective breath as Frank reached into the hollowed out spot.

"Well, I'll be damned!" exclaimed Frank, as he turned to face the others. He held out his arm, hand open, to display a sphere, just like the ones they had recovered from Al Thompson's safe.

"Frank, I'd be careful with that," said Jim. "You don't know what's making it glow. What if it's getting ready to explode, or something."

"It does feel slightly warm to the touch," said Frank, placing the sphere on the cave floor, "but if this thing has been here for thousands of years, what are the chances we'd happen upon it just at the moment it was going to explode? Astronomical, I'd think, no pun intended."

Ricardo bent to examine the object closer with the lantern as his father stepped back in fear.

"Maybe you should put it back, *Señor*," he whispered. "We shouldn't disturb objects of the Ancients."

"Professor, there's writing on it!" said Ricardo from his crouched position. "What does it say?"

"I'll have to study it for a while, Ricardo, but I was able to translate three others just like it, so with a little time I should be able to tell you. I have an idea it will be a place and a time, just like the others were."

Alfredo's curiosity got the better of his fear and he advanced back to join the group. "So this is what the mysterious orbs look like? What is it made from?" he asked.

"That's a good question, Alfredo," answered Frank. "I'm guessing you wouldn't find any of this material down here in the bowels of *Loltún,* or anywhere in the Yucatan, for that matter. Bring your lights over here and help me search the rest of these holes. Be careful, though, in case some critter has decided to make one a home."

Reluctantly, the other three joined in and they searched the other *haltunes*, first with their flashlights and then by hand, but they didn't find anything in any of the other cavities, not even a critter.

"So, it looks like this is the last one," commented Frank as he pointed his light at the sphere on the ground. "Maybe all the others have already found there way to Nevada."

Alfredo and Ricardo looked at each other and then back to Frank. "Who is Nevada?" asked Alfredo.

"It's not a who, it's a where," replied Frank, keeping his light on the sphere as he spoke. He gave them a brief summary of how he and Tony had come to possess, at one time or another, three of the spheres and how Jim had determined that they carried dates and places of significant solar eclipses in the Maya world.

"I wonder if Professor Torres ever got any out of here?" asked Jim, almost to himself.

"What makes you think he might have even tried?" asked Ricardo.

"His research notes for the day before he disappeared indicated that he was coming out here the next day to retrieve something he called an orb so people would take his research seriously," said Jim. And then, looking directly at Frank, he added, "I suppose you intend to take this thing with us, right.?"

"Absolutely!" replied Frank. "I have a feeling that if we don't take it somebody else will, and until we know exactly what this thing does, I'd rather it be in our hands than in somebody else's. Let's look around for anything else that might be of interest and then get out of here."

Using flashlights, the four explorers covered every inch of the cave in less than fifteen minutes, but they didn't turn up anything else. Frank counted the *haltunes* and there turned out to be an even twenty. Jim considered this significant since both the Olmec and the Maya used a vigesimal, or base-20 counting system. Frank, on the other hand, thought it just meant that there were twenty rather than nineteen or twenty-one. Encouraged by Jim's earlier comments, Ricardo took a digital photo of the section of the cave wall that contained the *haltunes*. Frank, in the mean time, stowed the sphere in the bottom of his bag for the journey back to Merida.

Finally, when there was no place else to look, the group packed up and retraced their steps to the car. On the way out, Ricardo led the way and Frank brought up the rear. Several times Frank thought he heard a sound, like a high-pitched vibration, but each time he stopped to listen, the sound disappeared. After three or four incidents like this Frank decided the sound was just his ears adjusting to the changes in elevation and humidity inside the cavern complex.

When they reached the car, Frank eased his pack into the trunk and said to Alfredo, "If you don't mind, I'd like to borrow Ricardo for another day or two. He has been very helpful and I would be happy to cover his expenses and pay his daily rate."

Ricardo's eyes lit up at the prospect of spending a few days at *Uxmal* rather than working in his father's clothing store, but then his brow wrinkled and he looked at his father questioningly. "My daily rate, *Papá*?" he asked.

"We'll discuss it later, Ricardo," Alfredo said quietly, under his breath.

As they headed back to Merida, the conversation centered on speculation about the purpose of the spheres and who had placed them in the cave. Jim wondered what the date on this sphere would be, Ricardo wondered what the glyphs he had found on the cave wall would reveal, Alfredo wondered where Professor Torres had gone and Frank wondered why he could still hear a high-pitch sound and why it always seemed to be coming from the trunk of the car.

***

Tony wasn't sure if he believed Carlson's story about the spheres emitting an "alien" radiation or not, but he did know that they had some strange powers and he was getting a little nervous about having two of them resting in his lap. He carefully picked up the bag and set it on the floor next to his chair as Carlson answered a telephone call. When Carlson hung up he had a worried look on his face.

"Something wrong?" asked Tony.

"That was Buzz Edwards. He has tracked your friend Frank Morton to a hotel in Merida, but the desk clerk says Morton and another man left early this morning in a car that picked them up out front. Nobody seems to know where they have gone."

"Well, my guess is that Frank and Jim Barnes, that's the guy with him, are headed for *Loltún*. I told you earlier that's where they were planning to go," said Tony.

"I was afraid of that. Edwards was hoping to talk to them before they left for the caverns, but it looks like he's too late," said Carlson, shaking his head.

"Well, I wouldn't worry too much about Frank – he can take care of himself. Just call Edwards back and tell him to sit tight and wait for Frank to get back to Vegas."

"Oh, Edwards is already half way to Mexico, Tony. He left this morning on a 'company' jet we keep out at the Las Vegas airport. He'll be in Merida by this evening. I hope you're right about your friend. Now let's get those spheres of yours into storage before they decide to wake up or something." Carlson pulled the plastic bag out of his wastebasket, emptied the trash back into the basket and handed Tony the bag. "Put the spheres in here and follow me," he said.

Tony was surprised by Carlson's apparent concern for Frank and Jim and he was beginning to believe that maybe Carlson, and the rest of the Department of Energy, might be on the level about the spheres and their potential danger. He decided that if they were concerned about Frank and Jim's safety, maybe he should be, too. When he told Carlson that Frank could take care of himself, what he really meant was 'Frank can take care of himself as long as I have his back.' In the time it took to bend over and grab the handle of his bag, Tony made up his mind to cooperate with Carlson, if only for the sake of his friends in Mexico.

"Gene, there's something I need to tell you," said Tony as he stood up with the bag. "Back in the city I wasn't sure what you guys were up to, so I packed a little extra security when we stopped at the hotel. I'm beginning to think you guys are on the level, so you should know that there's a hand gun in this bag."

"You mean that cowboy six-shooter of yours? No, I'm afraid I took that out back at the guard shack. It's locked in the glove compartment of the Durango, along with your cell phone. Tony, I understand your earlier distrust and I'm glad you've finally decided to come over to our side, but if you ever get back up this way, I suggest that you leave your hardware at home. *Capiche?*"

"Yeah, I get it, but you could have told me earlier! Especially if you want my trust," grumbled Tony as he took the two spheres out and placed them in the plastic bag.

"Sure, and you could have left your gun at home in the first place. Let's just forget it, okay? We're on the same side."

When the transfer of the spheres was complete, Carlson made his way to a door in the back of the building and Tony followed, carrying the bag.

As they headed toward the opening to the underground facility, Carlson explained what was going to happen next. "When we enter the tunnel up ahead, the guards are going to want to have a look through the bag. They're expecting us, and the spheres, so just hand it to them. No chatter, no jokes, nothing. Just do what they ask and we'll move right through. These folks are on the highest state of alert and if anything makes them suspicious it will cause us a significant delay."

As they reached the tunnel entrance, Tony looked back down the structure he had seen earlier. From this vantage point, the size of the conveyor belt was impressive. Just inside the tunnel, a small guard shack had been constructed against the wall. A man in civilian clothes stepped out to meet them.

"Good afternoon, gentlemen. May I see your badges, please? And I'll also need to examine that," he said, pointing to the wastebasket liner Tony was carrying.

The guard took their badges and the bag and disappeared inside the shack. Tony could feel a cool draft coming from inside the mountain and it was a welcome relief from the 100-degree heat of the outside air. When the guard returned, he handed each man a new black and yellow striped badge with a magnetic strip on the back. After they had clipped the badges to their collars, the guard handed Tony the plastic bag containing the spheres and said politely, "You may pass, gentlemen. Have a good day."

Tony fingered his new badge. "Funny color for a security badge," he commented as they walked straight into the mouth of the tunnel and away from the outside world.

"They wanted something easy to spot from a distance and this was what they came up with. From this point on, security becomes fanatical. If anyone, and I mean anyone, sees you without that badge displayed they are supposed to sound an alarm and 'immobilize' you in any way possible. Security is serious business down here, so stick close to me."

A short ways into the tunnel, they climbed into a small narrow-gauge rail car that looked similar to an old fashioned ore car except that it had a protective mesh cage over it. Carlson slammed the side door shut behind them and pressed some buttons on a small control panel attached to the front of the car.

"Hang on to something. These things lurch around a bit when they start and stop," said Carlson as the car started forward. It was apparently powered by a self-contained electric motor, because Tony could hear the telltale whine as the car came up to speed. As far as Tony could tell, the tunnel was perfectly straight and maintained a constant downward slope. Over the noise of the car's engine, Carlson said, "Even though we're only going down a thousand vertical feet, it's about a three mile ride, due to the slope. It will take us about twenty minutes to get to the bottom, so you might as well relax." Carlson indicated the bench built into the back of the metal car and both men settled back for the ride to the bottom.

The tunnel was well lit, but it was nothing compared to the area where the transporter finally stopped. The light was so bright

Tony had to shield his eyes for a minute while they adjusted. In contrast to the rounded ceiling of the tunnel, this room had a traditional flat ceiling and it was covered with light fixtures resembling the huge lights you would find at freeway interchanges.

"Why all the light?" asked Tony, as he stepped out of the car and onto a solid stone floor.

"The better to see you with, Grandma," smiled Carlson. "The security folks designed this area so it would have absolutely no shadows to confuse the cameras." Carlson indicated a surveillance camera mounted opposite their position and pointing directly at them. As Tony scanned the room, he spotted at least a dozen more cameras aimed in various directions.

As they walked toward a large stainless steel door that reminded Tony of a giant bank vault entrance, Carlson explained the cameras.

"Eventually, this part of the complex will be off limits to humans. Once they start storing large quantities of high-level waste down here, the radiation and heat will make this place deadly so all security from here on will be done remotely with hundreds of cameras. Since this is the 'lobby', so to speak, it's the best place to detect an intruder trying to enter through the tunnel. When the construction is complete, waste material will arrive here in cars similar to the one we rode in, except they won't have cages over them. Robotic devices will transfer the material to another car that will deliver it to its final storage location somewhere in the rings. The cars traveling back and forth to the surface spend as little time as possible down here so they don't become radioactive themselves. If, or when, they eventually do become contaminated, they will be diverted to a siding and permanently parked in that small tunnel they're working on over there," said Carlson, pointing to an area of construction on one side of the large room. "A new car will be installed up at the surface to replace the 'hot' one, and the process will continue."

"What happens if one of the robots breaks down?" asked Tony as they reached the massive, shinny door.

"Same thing," said Carlson. "The 'dead' robotic device will be moved to a permanent storage area down here and a replacement will be sent down from topside. The cameras, too. They have been designed to be replaceable by the machines that will inhabit this place. Once this place is operational, it will be like a scene out of a science fiction movie."

"It already is," said Tony, looking around at the endless cables and pipes and lights. "This place gives me the creeps."

Carlson punched a code into a small box on the wall next to the large door and said, "Watch the door, Tony, it swings out."

When the door had stopped moving, Carlson led the way into a large steel vault. As Tony entered the room and cleared the doorway, the big door started to swing shut. He spun on his heels at the sound but before he could react Carlson stopped him. "It's okay. We'll be out of here in just a minute. Let me show you something over here."

Reluctantly, Tony watched the door close and latch with a clang. He turned in time to see Carlson press a button on the far wall on the vault. A pair of stainless steel panels slid apart, revealing what appeared to be a small, shallow bookcase except that the four narrow shelves were made of a heavy chrome mesh. To Tony's surprise, the shelves already held a number of spheres.

"Bring yours over and let's add them to the collection, Tony," said Carlson.

Tony approached the collection of spheres slowly. "Where did you get all these?" he asked.

"One at a time, they've all turned up at about the same spot out on the Test Site. The first one was found back in 1951, not too long after the first nuclear test out here. Over the years they were stashed away in desk drawers, safes and closets all over this complex. Until about a year ago, that is, when one started to emit a strange sound. Then everybody got nervous and, since this place was available and not being used, most of them were brought here. The one we found yesterday is right here, and your two will make numbers 18 and 19."

Tony handed the spheres to Carlson, one at a time, and Carlson placed them on the top shelf next to two others. "Why is this one wrapped in paper," he asked, as he removed the napkin Frank had wrapped it in.

"Frank calls that one the counter-cracker," laughed Tony. "He has found cracks in two different counter tops that he thinks were caused by that one."

"Shit," swore Carlson, "that means it's energized! And that makes three of them that are exhibiting some form of activity."

Carlson hit a button to close the panels in the wall. "These things scare the crap out of me, Tony. Let's get out of here and I'll buy you dinner."

A large red button on the wall next to the vault door caused it to slowly open and the two men left the shiny, steel-walled room. As the door was closing the last few inches, a very loud, high-pitched sound came from inside the vault. The two men looked at each other and, without a word, started running for the rail car that had brought them down from the surface.

"Let's get the hell out of here!" yelled Carlson, as the vault door banged shut.

Chapter 21

They were about half way between *Loltún* and Merida and Frank, Jim and Ricardo were so involved in a discussion about the possible origin of the spheres that they hadn't noticed the car slowing down.

"What's the problem?" asked Frank as the car came to a complete stop.

Ricardo turned around in his seat to look out the windshield and casually said, "It's just a road block run by the *Federales* – the Mexican federal police. They're probably looking for illegal drugs and guns – we'll be on our way in no time."

Frank and Jim shot each other nervous glances but didn't say a word. The line of traffic moved fairly quickly and soon Alfredo was rolling down his window at the check point. He exchanged some pleasantries with the young man who came to the window but when the policeman noticed Frank and Jim in the back seat, he asked, "*Gringos*?" Alfredo nodded and the two exchanged a few more words.

As the policeman stood up and stepped back from the car, Alfredo said quietly, "They just want to inspect the trunk, Señor Frank. Where is the sphere?"

The look on Frank's face answered Alfredo's question without the need for words. Alfredo moved the car to the side of the road, turned off the engine and got out of the car to open the trunk for the federal agents. From inside, Frank and Jim could overhear bits of the conversation taking place behind the car, but not enough to understand what was going on until one of them exclaimed loudly, "*Qué es esto?*" – what is this?

Almost immediately there was a uniformed agent at each side of the car, motioning Frank and Jim out of their respective doors. They joined a visibly agitated Alfredo at the rear of the car and an officer wearing captain's insignia pointed into the open trunk and once again asked, "*Qué es esto?*"

Frank peered into the trunk, expecting to see the *Loltún* sphere. He breathed a sigh of relief when he discovered that there, laid out on the white hand towel it had been wrapped in, was Tony's taser.

Frank smiled and addressed the officer in English. "That's called a taser. It's a…"

"I know what a taser is, *Señor*," interrupted the man in perfect English, "and in Mexico it's illegal to own such a weapon without a permit. Do you have a permit, *Señor*?"

After nearly an hour of sometimes heated discussions, Frank was finally able to convince the *Federal* captain that they were inexperienced travelers who were only carrying the taser for self defense. Frank also made it clear that both Alfredo and Ricardo were unaware that the weapon had been in the car. When Alfredo suggested that the captain should keep the taser and "dispose of it in a proper manner," the man began to soften and soon they were on their way again, but not without a stern lecture on the importance of learning and obeying the local laws.

As the check point disappeared behind them, an unhappy Alfredo made eye contact with Frank in his rear-view mirror. "Self defense, *Señor*? Did you think that my son and I were common *bandidos*, only after your money and your jewelry?"

Fortunately, Ricardo was more used to Americans and their fear of the Mexican countryside and he was able to convince his father that Frank and Jim had acted out of caution, not distrust. By the time they reached the hotel, just after 5:00 p.m., Alfredo had forgiven the Americans and they were once again discussing the possible origins of the spheres. Ricardo had gladly agreed to join the two Americans the next day for a return trip to *Uxmal* and his father approved, subject, of course, to the daily fee of $100. As the car pulled away, Frank and Jim waved to their two new friends and entered the hotel lobby in high spirits. The trip to *Loltún* had been quite an adventure and there was much to discuss before the next day's meeting with the Maya shaman.

As they passed through the lobby to the elevator, a man sitting off to the side of the room stood and approached them. He appeared to be an American in his mid- to late-thirties and he was wearing the gold-rimmed sunglasses common among military personnel, especially pilots. His business casual dress and smooth gait made him appear relaxed, but his face told a different story.

"Mr. Morton?" he asked, as he approached Frank and Jim.

"That would be me," replied Frank, wondering who in Merida would know his name.

The stranger extended his hand and introduced himself. "Good afternoon, Mr. Morton. My name is Buzz Edwards and I'm with the U.S. Department of Energy."

Frank shook Edwards' hand and introduced Jim Barnes. "What's the occasion, Mr. Edwards?" asked Frank.

Edwards produced an official-looking government ID card from his shirt pocket and showed it to both Frank and Jim. "I just flew in from Las Vegas and I need to speak with you about something very important," said Edwards as he scanned the lobby as if to see if anyone were eavesdropping. "Is there someplace where we can talk in private?"

"Well, I guess we could go up to my room, but what is this about? Has something happened to Tony?" he asked, concerned that a government representative had tracked him down this far away.

"Tony is fine, but we need to talk. Lead the way, please," said Edwards, motioning the other two men on ahead of him."

When they reached Frank's room, he opened a bottle of cold mineral water for each of them from the small refrigerator and the three men sat at the only table in the room.

"You called this meeting, Mr. Edwards," said Frank as he eased into his chair.

"First of all, let's put this on a first name basis. Please call me Buzz. That's not my real name, but I picked up the nickname as a kid and it's stuck with me ever since. As I said, I'm with the Department of Energy, currently attached to the Nevada Test Site facility northwest of Las Vegas. A colleague and I met with your friend Tony this morning and that's how I learned that you were in Merida. Finding you in this small hotel took a bit of work, but I finally tracked you down this afternoon. I assume you've already been to *Loltún*?"

"Ah, yes," stammered a surprised Frank. "Did Tony tell you about that, too?"

"Yes, in a way. Look, I'll cut right to the chase, because I'm not trying to conceal anything and we very much need your cooperation – and yours too, Professor Barnes," said Edwards, making direct eye contact with Jim.

"As long as we're using first names," said Frank, "he's Jim and I'm Frank, but who is this 'we' you just referred to?"

"The Department of Energy. I represent a small group of people within the Agency who believe that these spheres you keep running into are potentially very dangerous objects. Dr. Thompson – you knew him as Jill's stepfather, Al Thompson – tried for years to convince his superiors and co-workers that they were alien in origin, but nobody would listen to him. Now he's dead and whatever he knew is gone with him. But our more immediate and serious concern is the fact that several of the spheres have recently activated themselves, and we don't know why. We understand that you have acquired some interesting information about several of the spheres and we hope you can help us get to the bottom of this before it's too late."

"Slow down, Buzz," said Frank, holding up his hand. "Jim and I are just here vacationing. Jim's an anthropology professor and he's just showing me some of the local ruins. We don't know anything about any spheres or Al Thompson. Are you sure you don't have us confused with some other guys?"

Edwards leaned back in his chair and took a drink of the bottled water. He smiled and said, "Okay, fair enough. I'm just some guy off the street and you don't know me from Adam. Let me spell it out in detail for you."

Edwards leaned forward and rested his elbows on the table. Over the course of the next fifteen minutes he recounted every movement Frank had made since coming in contact with the first sphere. He reminded Frank of where he stayed in Boise and Salt Lake City on his way to Las Vegas and he showed him security camera photos taken when he visited the Air Force hospital with Jill. Edwards also filled in the details that Carlson had passed on to Tony such as Al Thompson's real identity, the mysterious Maya who gave their life for the spheres and the DOE's current crusade to locate all the spheres and isolate them in the Yucca Mountain facility. When he told them that Carlson had paid Jill off with the old man's $287,000 stash and helped her flee Las Vegas for her own safety, Frank and Jim looked at each other in surprise, but neither one mentioned the actual amount that had been found in the safe. Edwards ended his exposé by stating that Tony was at the Yucca Mountain facility with Carlson at this very moment and had probably already turned over the other two spheres that had been locked in Frank's footlocker. He leaned back in his chair again, smiled, and said, "So what do you think, Frank? Do you still think I have the wrong two guys, or are you ready to work with me and help us solve this puzzle?"

Frank looked at Jim, but Jim just shrugged. Frank thought for a moment about all the information Edwards had just dumped on them and then he got up and crossed to the bed. He opened his carry-on bag and unpacked the trash left over from the underground picnic. As Edwards watched, he methodically removed four empty water bottles and balled up sandwich wrappers. Last, but not least, Frank removed the sphere they had found in the cavern earlier that day and held it out in Edwards' direction.

"So I suppose you'd also like me to share this, right?" he asked with a smile.

"My God!" Edwards was on his feet. "You found another one! Please be careful with that thing, man!"

"Relax, Buzz. It quit making noise about thirty minutes ago. I think it's taking a nap right now," Frank laughed. "How many of these things do you have back at Magic Mountain?"

"That's Yucca Mountain, Frank, and we now have nineteen, counting the two we just acquired from Tony. This one makes twenty, but, of course, we don't know how many there are altogether."

"Well, I think we can help there," said Jim. "Frank found what appears to be the original storage site in a cave deep inside the *Loltún* caverns. At first we thought the twenty cavities Frank found in the wall of the cave were for collecting drinking water, but then we found this sphere in one of them."

"Twenty, huh? That means we may have them all. Are you sure there weren't any more in the cave with this one?" asked Edwards.

"Quite sure," nodded Frank. "Jim stumbled onto the journal of a local guy who apparently disappeared the same day he was going out to *Loltún* to retrieve what he called a 'message orb' but we think he got disoriented and wandered further into the long chain of caverns instead of finding his way to the cave where we located this sphere. Eventually he would have died of hunger or thirst, or both."

"Have you had a chance to decipher the hieroglyphics on this one?" Edwards asked Jim. "I understand you have made some pretty incredible discoveries about the other three you've seen."

"No, I haven't examined this one at all. I plan to do that this evening, though, and I should have the date and place worked out for you by morning. And I'd love to get a look at the other 16 that

I haven't already seen. With that many, we might be able to piece together a pattern or a purpose."

"I think we can arrange that, Jim, but first I suggest we get this new sphere back to the Mountain. Then we can analyze the dates and places on it and the others." Edwards stood as if to leave. "I have a private plane on stand-by at the Merida airport and the sooner we get out of here, the sooner we can lock this thing up."

"Hold on there, Buzz," said Frank. "We aren't going anywhere for at least a day. Jim and I have an appointment tomorrow to meet with an authentic Maya shaman who may be able to shed some light on both the messages and the activity. You're welcome to join us, if you'd like, but I'm taking this along to show to the shaman. After that, it's all yours. As for cooperating with your team, I have no objection if Jim doesn't. We're only interested in the intellectual aspects of this mystery and if working with you and your people will help us find some answers, then I'm all for it."

Jim nodded in agreement. "I agree with Frank. The spheres seem to be at the center of a mystery that transcends several thousand years. I'm a researcher at heart, but I'm not a relic hunter. In fact, I have a professional ethics issue about these spheres being taken out of this region, but since the Maya seem intent on getting them to Nevada anyway, the least we can do is find out why."

"Well, I'm glad you're willing to cooperate, but I'd be much more comfortable if you locked that sphere up someplace where it couldn't hurt anybody," said Edwards as Frank placed it on the table and sat down.

Frank slid the sphere across the table to Jim and said, "Here you go, professor. Let's make a list of questions for our meeting tomorrow and then you can get to work on this."

Jim picked up the sphere and rotated it slowly in his hands and then put it back on the table. "There's really no question about these not being Maya, is there? They did very little with metals and this certainly feels like a metal of some sort. Buzz, have your people learned anything about the composition of the spheres?"

Edwards was struggling with being so close to an actual sphere and he wouldn't return to the table. Standing behind his chair, as if it would shield him from harm, Edwards shook his head. "We haven't learned anything yet. Other than old Dr. Thompson, nobody took these things seriously until a few months ago. That's why he was allowed to have two of them – and apparently a third he acquired on his own – at his mobile home in Beatty. When we decided to round them up, we were amazed where they had been stashed away. People had treated them like any local oddity such as an arrowhead or a four-leaf clover. They were tossed in desk drawers, filing cabinets and closets all over the Test Site."

Frank had been making some notes on a lined tablet. He slid it over to Jim and said, "Take a look at this and see if there's anything you want to add. I don't want to get back here tomorrow night and think of something we should have asked the shaman. We may not get a second chance."

Jim scanned the list and replied, "That's a pretty comprehensive list, but I'd also like to know if his book has anything to say about the cave where we found this sphere."

"Book? What book?" asked Edwards, as he slid back into his chair in spite of the sphere on the table.

Jim explained the concept of the ritual *Chilam Balam* and how they had been hidden away and survived the Spanish book burning.

"Wow!" said Edwards. "I'm definitely going with you tomorrow, even if I have to ride with this damn thing," he said, indicating the sphere.

"Okay, Buzz, but there are some ground rules," cautioned Frank. "First of all, Jim does most of the talking tomorrow. He's the expert on these people, and we don't want to open our ignorant Yankee mouths and offend the shaman. Secondly, we remember that we are guests in their country and interested in their ancestors, so we treat the shaman and his brother with respect. No demands, no threats, not even a raised voice, okay?"

Edwards nodded eagerly. "I understand that I'm way out of my league in this area, guys, and I'll try not to act like the arrogant, demanding para-military type that I really am." He smiled and added, "I'll be good, Frank, I promise. Now if you'll excuse me, I think I'll go see if I can still get a room for tonight and then call my flight crew and let them know we're staying the night. What time should I meet you in the morning?"

"Let's meet in the restaurant at 7:30 a.m.," said Frank. "We can have some coffee and recheck our list before Ricardo arrives at 8:00 a.m. That reminds me, I need to see about renting a car for tomorrow."

"Let me take care of that," offered Edwards. "I have some contacts down here and it'll give me something to do this evening. By the way, I hope it goes without saying that the two of you are welcome to fly back to Las Vegas with me on the DOE jet I came down in."

"Assuming we all go back together, we'd be happy to take you up on the plane ride, and if you want to deal with the local transportation, maybe I'll call a friend and see if she'd be willing to have dinner with me," agreed Frank. "It sounds like we may be out of here tomorrow night, and I don't want to leave without saying good-bye."

"I should call Carmen, too," smiled Jim. "Maybe she'd like to help me decode this sphere."

Edwards stood to leave, but not without another glance at the sphere. "Please be careful with that thing, gentlemen. I'll see you in the morning."

After the door closed behind Edwards, Jim said, "Well, that was certainly an interesting turn of events, huh? Who'd have thought we'd be followed all the way down here by the U.S. Government?"

"Yeah, weird, huh? I'm not too excited about the government meddling in our little investigation, but if it gets us access to another sixteen spheres, I guess it's worth putting up with this Edwards guy. Listen, let's play this close to the vest, okay? We'll share what we have to, but don't offer any unnecessary information."

"You mean like the amount of money that was really in the old man's safe," grinned Jim. "I noticed that you didn't correct him on that."

"Exactly. Edwards and his buddies think there was $287,000 in the safe, and we know the amount was really $510,000. It may be nothing, but somehow Thompson added $223,000 to the pot without the government's knowledge. I'm going to call Alex and see if she's available this evening. Do you and Carmen want to join us?"

"Let me check with her and I'll call you later. I'd really like to work on this decoding, too, so maybe we could just meet for drinks later," said Jim as he picked up the sphere and started for the door.

Frank tore a sheet of paper out of his pad and handed it to Jim. "Why don't you wrap that up so it doesn't arouse any curiosity in the hallway?"

When Jim had left, Frank called the phone number Alex had given him. A female voice answered, but it didn't sound like Alex's voice. "Is Alex home?" he asked in English.

"No, she had to leave for a few minutes," came the reply, also in English. "Is this Frank?"

"Yes it is. You must be Alex's daughter. I think we met the other day at the café," replied Frank.

"That's correct, *Señor*, I'm Maria. My mother went down to the café to drop off some supplies and if you're calling from the hotel, you may be able to catch her before she leaves," answered the daughter.

"Thanks, Maria, but if I miss her would you ask her to give me a call at the hotel?" asked Frank

"Of course," answered the daughter politely.

Frank dashed to the elevator and through the lobby like a sprinter getting ready for a track meet. The café was obviously closed but he thought he heard some movement inside the little building that served as the office for the sidewalk café.

"Alex, is that you?" called Frank, not wanting to scare her.

"Who's there?" questioned Alex, as she stepped out onto the pavement. She was wearing rubber gloves and an apron and had a scrub brush in her hand. When she saw that it was Frank, she blushed and tried to duck back inside. "Frank! I didn't expect you to be back so soon. Please go away – I'm a mess."

Laughing, Frank opened the door and joined Alex in the small room that served as kitchen, storeroom and office. Seeing that Alex had been scrubbing some pans in the sink, he asked, "Can I help?"

Accepting that Frank had already seen her at her worst, Alex relaxed and threw him a towel. "Sure, help me dry these things so I can get out of here. How did you know where to find me?"

"I called your house and your daughter suggested I might find you here," laughed Frank as he caught the towel in mid air.

"She did, did she? She's going to pay for that!" smiled Alex. "How was your trip with Alfredo and his son?"

"It was very interesting, actually. And you were right about Alfredo. He and Ricardo were very helpful. In fact, Jim and I talked

Ricardo into returning to *Uxmal* tomorrow to meet with the brother of the manager of the Lodge. It seems that the brother is a real, live Maya shaman."

"I'm glad to hear that you and Alfredo got along. Did you find whatever it was you were looking for?" asked Alex as she handed Frank the last pan and peeled off the gloves.

"We didn't really go looking for anything in particular, but we did make quite a discovery. Why don't you join me for dinner and I'll tell you all about it?"

"Frank, I'd love to, but I'm a mess. Are you sure you want to be seen in public with me?"

"What are you talking about, Alex? You look very nice – well, okay, you could lose the apron, but otherwise, you're fine. If you like, we can eat right here at the hotel."

"Okay, if you're sure I won't embarrass you," agreed Alex hesitantly. "At least give me a minute to comb my hair and fix my makeup."

Over dinner, Frank told Alex about their trek deep into the caverns and their discovery of the sphere. He also mentioned the arrival of Buzz Edwards and the fact that he and Jim might be flying back with Edwards as soon as tomorrow night.

"I was hoping you might stay a while longer," said Alex, sadly. "You only just arrived."

"I know, but we really need to get to the bottom of this sphere thing. I could always come back, though, after we wrap this up."

"That would be nice, Frank. If I knew a little in advance, maybe I could arrange for some time off and show you around the Yucatan. I'm not an archeologist, but I know some beautiful places on the peninsula. Do you by any chance scuba dive?"

"As a matter of fact, I do. I learned to dive in the military and I dive as often as I can," replied Frank.

"I have some friends that own a small dive resort on the southern tip of Cozumel. The diving is fantastic and it's close to the famous Maya ruins at *Tulum*. If you come back to Mexico, I'll meet you there and we'll return to Merida by car. That way you will also have a chance to see the ruins at *Chichén Itza*," said Alex.

"That sounds like a fantastic trip, Alex, and I'll bet you are a great tour guide. As soon as I get back to the U.S. and get this business taken care of I'll give you a call and we'll arrange it, okay?" asked Frank.

"Promise?" countered Alex.

"I promise! If Jim and I fly home in this government plane I will still have half a ticket and I couldn't let it go to waste, now, could I?" smiled Frank.

"I suppose not, Frank," Alex smiled back as she reached across the table and took his hand.

They talked about nothing in particular for another few minutes and then Frank remembered Jim's suggestion about meeting for a drink. He glanced at his watch and discovered that it was already 9:30 p.m.

"Would you like to meet Jim and his friend Carmen for a drink?" he asked.

Squeezing his hand, Alex said, "I'd rather redeem that rain check you gave me."

Frank wrinkled his brow, trying to remember. "Rain check?"

"Yes, Frank. Last night you asked me up to your room and I said I would take a rain check. I'd like to redeem it."

At 3:30 a.m. the telephone rang and a half-awake Frank rolled over carefully, trying not to wake Alex. "Hello?" he whispered, sleepily.

"Frank, it's Jim. Sorry to wake you, but I just got the last of the sphere's message decoded and I thought you'd want to see this before tomorrow morning.

Frank slid out of bed and carried the phone as far away as the cord would allow. Still whispering, he said, "Can't you just tell me what it says? I, ah, have company, Jim."

"Oh, sorry! Well, okay, here's what I found. The date is unusual because it's the first one we've seen that's in the future. Care to guess what date it is?"

"Jim, this is hardly the time for guessing games," hissed Frank, as Alex stirred and rolled over.

"Oh, right, I forgot. Well, the date is December 21, 2012. Does that ring a bell?" asked Jim

"The end of the Maya calendar! Are you sure?" asked Frank, too loudly.

"What?" mumbled Alex from the bed.

To Alex, he replied, "Nothing, Alex. Sorry to wake you."

To Jim, he whispered, "And the place? Did you figure out the location that goes with that date?"

"Well, you see, that's the thing. If my calculations are correct, and I've checked them several times, the location is somewhere inside the Nevada Test Site."

Chapter 22

Tony and Carlson piled into the small rail car and Carlson hit a large red button on the control panel. "Hold on!" he yelled as the car lurched forward and began a rapid ascent to the surface. The car was moving up about three times as fast as it had moved coming down and Tony decided that Carlson must have initiated some emergency mode. Carlson picked up a handset that hung below the control panel and began speaking in it. Finally he nodded and replaced the handset. He sat down on a small, built-in bench, his back to the spheres, and relaxed a little.

"We'll be topside in about six minutes. As you can probably tell, I pushed the panic button – literally. The security team reports that the noise in the vault has stopped, but I'd still rather not be anywhere near those damn spheres, just in case."

Tony nodded, deciding to save his questions until they were out of the noisy car. He continued to stand, holding one of the vertical posts that connected the top of the cage to the car, as he watched Carlson with some interest. The other man had his elbows on his knees and his head in his hands as if he were going to be sick. Tony was afraid Carlson was going to hyperventilate and pass out before they got to the top.

As the car lurched roughly to a stop, they were met by two civilians who came running out of the guard shack. "Are you two okay?" one of them asked.

"We're fine," said Tony, calmly. "I think he could use some water, though. Help me get him out into the fresh air."

Tony and one of the guards helped Carlson out of the car and into the fading sunshine at the entrance of the tunnel while the second guard returned to the shack for some water. When he joined the other three men, he had a plastic bottle of water.

"This is all we have," he apologized. "I drank some of it earlier."

"I'm sure Carlson won't mind," smiled Tony. He lifted Carlson's head and put the bottle up to his lips.

"What the hell happened down there?" asked the first guard. "All of a sudden our security console lit up like a Christmas tree and then the 'Evacuate' alarm went off. Fortunately, you two were the only ones down there, it being Sunday and all. Otherwise we would have a riot on our hands. There's never been an actual evacuation before."

"When Carlson put those two spheres into the cabinet down there, a couple of them started making some noise and he freaked out," replied Tony as he helped Carlson sit up.

"Sorry about that," managed Carlson as he took another sip of water from the bottle. "I don't know what happened to me down there. I've been so focused on those spheres lately that I guess I just panicked when they started making that awful noise. Help me up, will you?"

The guard who had brought the water returned to the shack and brought back Tony's and Carlson's security badges. He handed each man their original badge and collected the striped ones. To Tony, he said, "Why don't you take him into Mercury and get him some food and a good stiff drink? He's probably just been working too hard."

Carlson was on his feet now and he added, "Yeah, that's probably a good idea. We need to find you a place to stay, anyway, Tony. I'd like you to meet with the rest of our team tomorrow morning, and that drive back and forth to the city is a bitch. The Agency has some guest quarters in Mercury and there's even a modest steak house attached to the cafeteria. Give me a minute to get my head squared away and we'll take a little drive."

A few minutes later Tony and Carlson were in a white Jeep Cherokee headed southeast across the Test Site on a well-maintained gravel road. The summer sun was just starting to set behind some hills off to their right and Carlson had settled down and was actually laughing about his earlier behavior.

"What a light-weight!" Carlson said, referring to himself. "With all I saw and did in 'Nam, it's hard to believe that some little black spheres would take me down."

"Well, I have noticed that you folks up here seem to take them a lot more seriously than anyone else. Hell, I carried one around in the cab of my truck for several days, and Frank had the two I gave you today stored in a footlocker at the end of his bed. What, exactly, are you guys so afraid of?" asked Tony as he took in the countryside.

"As I mentioned earlier today, one of our research teams detected some highly irregular radiation coming from one of them.

They seem to have a self-contained source of power that nobody here – and we *are* the Department of Energy, you know – understands. We have some of the best minds in the world working for us, and they're at a loss. And then there's the issue of these Indian dudes that keep bringing the spheres up here to the Test Site. Hey, speaking of the Indians, the area where we've been finding these things is not too far from here. Do you want to take a look?"

"Sure, if we have enough daylight left," replied Tony, a little apprehensive. He had a feeling that when the sun went down it was going to get very, very dark out here on the Nevada desert.

Carlson looked at his watch and nodded. "We'll make it. The spot is just a couple of miles up this road to the left. The road isn't quite as good because it's not used much.

The jeep turned left at a crossroads and headed almost due north. Carlson was right – they had turned off a very well maintained, wide gravel road onto a simple dirt road.

"Where does this actually go?" asked Tony between potholes.

"There are roads and trails all over this part of the facility. Some were originally used to access observation posts back when they were still doing nuclear testing out here and others led to remote storage facilities or monitoring installations. This particular road is a little of both. There's some experimental equipment housed out here on the edge of an area called Jackass Flats. That's where we're headed.

About five minutes later, Carlson slowed the Cherokee to a crawl. Tony could see that the road circled back on itself and in the encircled area there were several large, metal shipping containers that had been converted into equipment sheds. Wires ran between them and one had a small satellite dish mounted on top.

As they passed the first structure, Carlson said, "I'm not exactly sure what this stuff is, but it looks like one of our environmental sensing stations. It may monitor air and soil conditions and send the information back to us through that dish, which seems to be pointed toward the Yucca Mountain facilities we just left. Our spot is just ahead, but it's really hard to see. Look for a foot path going through the sagebrush on the left."

Tony never did see the beginning of the trail, but Carlson made a sudden stop and once they were out of the Jeep Tony could see the path that traveled down a steep slope and out onto the flats.

Ahead of them was a view of some foothills in the distance and a mountain beyond the hills.

"That's Shoshone Mountain, off in the distance," commented Carlson as they walked over to the edge of the twenty-foot high slope.

"And where is the place where the spheres have been found?" asked Tony, looking down the slope to flats that spread out toward the foothills.

Carlson, rubbed his chin, looked down at Tony's feet and said, "Well, I think it's right about where you're standing, my friend."

Instinctively, Tony jumped back, an action that caused Carlson to laugh out loud.

"No need to be afraid," smiled Carlson. "They're just spheres, remember? Only we DOE types are afraid of them."

Tony shot Carlson a look that said "that wasn't funny" and got down on one knee to examine the ground. He let some of the sand run through his fingers and looked around, studying the immediate area.

"I assume you've done a soil analysis to make sure there's nothing out of the ordinary about this place," said Tony as he stood up.

"Of course. We've also checked for unusual levels of radiation but everything seems normal, or at least as normal as anything gets out here."

"What do you mean?" asked Tony.

"Well, there were over nine hundred nuclear tests done just east of here, so this whole area has a slightly higher than normal level of radiation, but this spot is well within the range of what we call 'nominal' out here," explained Carlson.

"Any unusual magnetic activity?" asked Tony as he walked the perimeter of the area again.

"Uh, I don't know. I'm not sure we ever checked for that. What are you getting at?"

"Well, look around here. This would be a damn hard place to find without a GPS, or at least a detailed map, and yet nineteen of these Indian characters have found this spot, and each one was carrying a sphere. Maybe the sphere has some way of indicating where it wants to go. The Indians could use your mountain over there, along with the setting sun, as a general landmark and directional indicator and then fine tune their positions with the sphere."

Carlson looked around the area and wrinkled his brow. "But there's nothing here except our equipment, and that's only been here a couple of years. What could the spheres be homing in on?"

This time it was Tony's turn to rub his chin. He looked down at Carlson's feet and said with a smile, "Maybe you're standing on it, my friend."

Carlson looked down at the ground and shook his head. "I suppose anything's possible, but that sounds like a real stretch. Why would anything be buried way out here?"

Tony laughed and said, "I gave up asking 'Why?' when an old man in a bar handed me a round black object and told me it was from outer space! There has to be something about this spot that draws the Indians here, though, and it has to be connected to the spheres. Since you haven't been able to determine what material the spheres are made of and you already know the radiation they emit is not normal, there may not be any easy way to test my theory short of digging a hole in the ground."

"I'll leave that up to the engineers, but you've really got me curious, now. Let's get down to Mercury so I can make a couple of phone calls. Have you seen everything you need to?" asked Carlson.

"Yeah, unless you're going to take me up to Area 51," replied Tony as they climbed back into the Cherokee.

"Never heard of it," smiled Carlson.

Tony didn't know what to expect of Mercury but he was certainly surprised to find a small town inside the boundaries of the Nevada Test Site. According to Carlson, at one time Mercury had over 1,100 buildings that included offices, warehouses, laboratories, a motor pool and housing for more than 1,200 people. It still had its own hospital, post office, fire station and law enforcement, in the form of a Nye County Sheriff's substation, but many of the older Quonset huts had been torn down in recent years because they contained asbestos insulation.

Carlson drove directly to the community food service facility and the two men went inside. The entrance to the steak house was located just inside the front door of the multipurpose building and after they had found a table Carlson excused himself and went to a white wall phone located near the door. When he returned, Tony gave him a questioning look.

"Yes, Mercury has its own telephone system, too. This is quite a place, isn't it?" he said, as the waitress brought their menus.

"It's pretty self-contained, all right. It's hard to believe that so many people worked out here, after seeing so much empty space on the way down from your office," commented Tony.

"Mercury actually supports the entire Nellis Range complex, not just the Nevada Test Site, and that's a big area – almost 5,500 square miles. You've only seen a small part of it. See anything on the menu you like?"

"Absolutely! I haven't eaten since early this morning and I'm starving, so everything looks good. Did you call for a back-hoe to dig up that spot?"

"Not exactly, but I did suggest that someone get up there first thing tomorrow and do a seismic survey of the area. That will tell us if there's anything of any mass below the surface, even if it isn't made out of materials we're familiar with," grinned Carlson. "I still think it's a long shot, but we don't have any better theories at the moment and we did ask for your input, didn't we?"

After dinner and a glass of wine, Carlson took Tony across the street to Guest Housing, which consisted of a dormitory and several small bungalows. He tossed Tony a key attached to an orange piece of plastic. "Even up here, rank has its privileges – you're in Number 2," he said, indicating the unit directly in front of the Jeep, "I've got some things to do, so I'm going to say good night. You should find everything you need inside but if you don't, just call Housekeeping. We don't have a convenience store up here any more, so there isn't any alcohol available in Mercury except here at the Steak House."

"That's okay," said Tony, patting his carry-on bag. "I carry a little in case of just such an emergency. What time should I be ready in the morning?"

"I've scheduled the team meeting for 9:00 a.m. back at my office. Why don't I pick you up at 7:30 a.m.? We'll have breakfast across the street at the cafeteria and then head back up to the Yucca complex. The meeting shouldn't last much more than an hour and then you can get back to civilization

As Tony climbed out of the Jeep, he replied, "Okay, I'll be ready. See you in the morning."

The bungalow was a small, comfortable unit similar to a studio apartment. There was a small kitchen area with a two-burner gas range, a sink and an apartment-size refrigerator. The refrigerator was stocked with several cans of soda, mixers and bottled water and the ice cube tray was full. A counter separated the mini-kitchen from a living room area that contained a couch and television. On the far, left side of the room there was a bed, a nightstand and a large armoire for clothes. The bathroom was in the far right corner and included a shower, a sink and a toilet.

Tony turned on the television and scanned the thirty or so channels on the cable service. He finally turned the set to CNN Headline News and settled onto the couch with a tall gin and tonic made from his personal supply of airline-sized bottles of gin and a can of tonic water he had found in the refrigerator. The combination of the long day, the large meal and the gin quickly took their toll, and Tony was asleep within minutes. The ringing of a telephone startled him awake and the strange surroundings disoriented him for a moment. He finally located a simple white desk phone on the lower shelf of the end table next to the couch.

"Hello," he said, still in a haze.

"Tony, this is Gene Carlson. I'm sorry to wake you so early, but we've just found something very interesting!"

Tony looked at his watch and was shocked into consciousness when he discovered that it was nearly 6:30 a.m. He had slept upright on the couch all night!

"Where?"

"Up where the spheres have been found – the same place where we stopped last night! One of our geologists stopped by on his way in this morning to see what kind of equipment they were going to need for the seismic tests and he happened to have a magnetometer with him. Based on your comments last night, I had him check the spot out and he got some very unusual readings."

"How soon can you pick me up?" asked Tony, now fully alert.

"I'm at my office and it'll take me twenty minutes to get there. See you soon." The line went dead and Tony bolted for the bathroom. Fifteen minutes later he was showered, shaved, dressed and standing in front of the bungalow waiting for Carlson. All around him he could hear the sounds of a new day starting in the strange little town. As he looked down the street he saw a white Cherokee turn the corner and head his way. Carlson screeched to a stop and waved to Tony to hurry. As he pulled away from the curb, Carlson was a bundle of excitement.

"I don't know why we didn't think of this sooner," he was babbling. "Obviously, something was drawing the Indians to the site. We should have looked in the ground years ago. But I still don't understand how they manage to get onto the Test Site grounds undetected."

"I'd be more curious about how they manage the 4,000 miles from the Yucatan to Nevada than how they walk in a few miles from the highway," said Tony. He couldn't believe how self-centered these government guys were.

"I guess you're right. They never seem to be carrying anything that would indicate they had been on a long journey. I wonder how they get here. It's too bad we can't ask one of them."

"I actually had the chance a few days ago, but how he got here didn't seem important at the time," commented Tony.

"That's right! You said you dropped one with a taser at old man Thompson's place, didn't you? Did he ever say anything?" asked Carlson.

"Oh, yes, he talked, but I didn't understand much of it. Jim Barnes – that's the guy who's in Mexico with Frank – spoke to him in Maya over the telephone and Jill found a few Spanish words he knew. It just never occurred to any of us to ask him how he got to Nevada. And two days later he ended up dead out here," lamented Tony.

The two remained silent, reflecting on the mysterious messengers and their spheres, until they approached the site. There were already a dozen vehicles along the side of the road where it looped around the equipment sheds, but Carlson drove right up to the spot and blocked the road.

"Let's go," he said, with a tone of authority Tony hadn't heard before. "They've been instructed not to move or touch anything until we get there."

Surprised by the take-charge attitude, Tony followed Carlson to the spot where a small crowd of men was standing looking down at the ground. Those who saw Carlson and Tony approach acknowledged Carlson with respect and called him Mr. Carlson.

"Okay, let us in," said Carlson, as they approached. The group separated and Tony could see several pieces of electronics equipment arranged on the ground.

"What have you found?" asked Carlson to the group in general.

"It's too soon to tell, Mr. Carlson, but something in this immediate vicinity is creating magnetic anomalies," one of the men offered. "Big ones."

"Would you say your readings indicate that something is buried here?" asked Carlson, indicating the area everybody was staring at.

"Yes sir, I would."

That was apparently evidence enough for Carlson. "Okay, I want this place gone over with a fine-tooth comb. I also want a security sweep of this area and then I want that seismic survey done. Let's get busy, gentlemen."

As the crowd quickly went about their tasks or left the area, Carlson noticed Tony staring at him.

"What?" he demanded, still operating in command mode.

Tony shook his head. "I didn't realize you wielded so much power up here," he said.

"Well, I told you yesterday that I was part of a special security force. Did I forget to mention that I'm also in charge of it?" he smiled. "Let's get out of here so the boys can get to work."

On the way back up to his Yucca Mountain office, Carlson confessed that he was, in fact, the ranking civilian in charge of security for the Nevada Test Site "and a few other places." It was his job to know everything about everybody working at the site and this sphere phenomenon was giving him an ulcer because it was a situation he just couldn't get control of.

"But surely your superiors realize that there's no way to control what's happening here. Nor would you want to until someone gets to the bottom of the sphere business," said Tony.

"My superiors only want to hear about two kinds of problems, Tony, those that have been solved and those that never happened. My ass is on the line here, and I need some answers. That's why we leaned on you and your friends so hard. If our suspicions about the spheres were to get out, Washington would lock this place down in a heartbeat. And I'd be sweeping floors at McDonalds!"

Back at Carlson's office, a small group of staffers had gathered in the conference room for the special meeting. Carlson reviewed the events of the morning and then introduced Tony, who recounted his involvement with the spheres from his first contact with Al Thompson at the casino in Beatty. After Tony finished his narrative, Carlson's team was allowed to ask specific questions. Given the morning's excitement, there were a lot of questions and the meeting ran well over the allotted one hour. Just as things were wrapping up, about 10:45 a.m., a man knocked on the door and beckoned Carlson out into the hallway. When he returned a minute later, he abruptly ended the meeting. "Okay, folks that's it. Everybody back to work."

"I know I told you that you could get back to civilization when this was over, but you may want to consider staying on a while longer," said Carlson when the room had cleared.

"Why? What's happened now?" asked Tony.

"I just received a preliminary report from the seismic team out where we've been finding the bodies. It seems that you may be correct about something in the ground," said Carlson quietly.

"Any idea what it is yet?"

"No, they're going to run another series of tests, but whatever it is, it appears to be very dense and about twenty feet below the surface. The initial estimates are that it has a square base about ten feet on a side and that it's about ten feet high."

"You mean like a big cube?" pressed Tony.

"No, it's actually shaped more like a miniature Egyptian pyramid."

Chapter 23

Frank hung up the telephone, sat down on the floor and leaned against the wall. While he was contemplating the date and location news Jim had found on the twentieth sphere, Alex rolled over to the edge of the bed and asked him what was wrong.

"Oh, nothing's wrong, it's just puzzling. That was Jim. He just finished decoding the sphere we found today and it doesn't seem to fit the pattern, that's all. Sorry to wake you."

"Are you coming back to bed?" asked Alex invitingly, as she patted the pillow next to her.

Frank looked at the clock on the nightstand. It was going on 4:00 a.m. and he had to get up at 6:00 a.m. to meet Jim and Buzz Edwards, but when he looked back at Alex he made up his mind instantly.

"Of course I am," he said with a smile.

Frank and Jim met Edwards, the Department of Energy agent, in the restaurant at 7:30 a.m. for a quick cup of coffee. The conversation centered on the sphere that had been retrieved from *Loltún* Caverns the day before.

"So I don't get it," said Frank. "Three spheres in a row are inscribed with the dates of solar eclipses and the locations of Maya cities where they were visible. Why would this one indicate a location in Nevada and specify the date of December 21, 2012?"

"Well, the significance of the date is obvious but, as far as I can tell, there's not going to be a solar eclipse in Nevada on that date – or anytime close to that date," nodded Jim Barnes. "The closest eclipse is November 13, 2012 and it's only visible in Australia and parts of the South Pacific."

"Back up a minute," said Buzz Edwards. "What's the deal with 2012?"

Jim offered a brief explanation of the Maya calendar and the fact that it ends on December 21, 2012, a date that coincides with that year's winter solstice.

Edwards whistled in amazement and said, "Maybe that explains why the spheres keep showing up in Nevada. There may not be an eclipse in Nevada in 2012, but I'll bet something's going to happen then!"

Edwards' speculation was interrupted by the arrival of Ricardo. Frank introduced Edwards and brought Ricardo up to date on the translation of the sphere that he had helped them locate the day before. Ricardo already knew about the three spheres Frank and Jim had recovered, but Frank didn't see any need to mention the others already in the custody of the DOE.

True to his word, Edwards had arranged transportation for the day. The four men climbed into a late model black Chevy Suburban with heavily tinted windows. Edwards drove and Frank joined him in the front seat. Jim and Ricardo sat in the back seat and discussed Maya history most of the way down to *Uxmal*.

As they left Merida and headed southeast through the village of *Umán*, Frank indicated the Suburban and said, "Nice ride, Buzz. Does the U.S. Government own every black Suburban that comes out of the Chevrolet plant?"

Edwards laughed and said, "Most of them, probably. The Secret Service has hundreds, maybe thousands of them, and they turn over their entire fleet every two years. When they are through with them, the rigs go to other government security agencies until they are scrapped. This one actually belongs to the Drug Enforcement Agency's field office in Merida. We let them use our plane a few weeks ago, so they owed me a favor. It's a little conspicuous, but since we're not on a covert mission I didn't figure it would matter."

"Oh, I'm not complaining. It's certainly roomier than Ricardo's father's Ford Escort. Have you seen these ruins at *Uxmal* before?" asked Frank, making conversation.

"No, I don't get out much in my line of work. And when I do travel, it's usually with a very specific purpose and on a very tight schedule. It sucks, actually," lamented Edwards.

"I know the feeling. The last few years at Boeing, when I was in charge of the team working on the Space Station, there wasn't much time to stop and smell the roses. Now that things have changed for me, I'm going to spend as much time as possible traveling. I'm really having a great time digging into this sphere mystery and there are a lot of other unexplained things around the world that I'd like to investigate. Maybe I will, when this is over," said Frank as he tilted the seat back and laid his head against the headrest.

"Yeah, you're a lucky guy, Frank. No worries about money, nobody to answer to and no schedule or agenda to keep. Pretty neat set-up, I'd say." Edwards looked over at Frank and discovered he had already fallen asleep.

As Edwards pulled off the highway into the *Uxmal* Lodge parking lot, he hit a pothole and jolted Frank awake.

"Good morning," laughed Edwards. "Did you have a rough night?"

Remembering his night with Alex, Frank smiled and replied, "Quite the contrary, my friend, quite the contrary."

As the four men entered the Lodge's lobby, they were greeted by Señor Miguel Ortega-Chaak, the manager of the Lodge. "Welcome, *Señores*! We have been expecting you! I have prepared a small, private meeting room for our visit. There's fresh *café* and *pan dulce* waiting. Please follow me."

Chaak led the group to a comfortable room that looked out onto the ruins of *Uxmal*. A table near the door was draped with a white cloth and held a large chrome coffee urn, a stack of cups and several baskets of sweet rolls. The room also contained an oval conference table that seated three on each side and one at each end. At the far end of the table sat an old man with a wrinkled, leathery-looking face dressed in the typical white cotton clothes of the locals. In front of him was a large, ancient-looking book with pages about the size of a newspaper.

When Jim spotted the book, he gasped, "Is that…"

"Yes, *Señor*, this is my brother, Ramón, and that is his *Chilam Balam*. May I introduce you, please?"

After the introductions, Jim explained to Edwards that Ramón was the local shaman, appointed by the Ancestors (the elders). His traditional duties included the curing of illness through folk medicine and looking out for the general welfare of the community. It was also the shaman's responsibility to observe certain rituals based on the ancient 260-day Maya calendar in accordance with the teachings of the *Chilam Balam*.

After serving themselves coffee, the group sat down at the table with the old man. Chaak sat on one side, next to his brother and indicated that Ricardo should sit next to him. Jim, Frank and Edwards sat on the other side, with Jim closest to the old Maya priest. Jim couldn't take his eyes off the ancient book on the table.

Chaak explained that his elder brother didn't speak very much English and that it would be best if questions were asked and answered in Spanish. Jim suggested that Ricardo should act as translator due to his knowledge of Maya history. The flattered youngster gladly accepted the responsibility and Frank pulled his list of questions out of the soft-sided brief case at his feet.

Before getting around to the specific question of the sphere, or spheres, found in the cave at *Loltún*, Frank wanted to know a little more about the large book in front of the old man. Ramón Chaak explained, through Ricardo's translations, that one version of Maya creation could be found in an ancient book called the *Popul Vuh*, or 'council book', written around 1550 in the *Quiché* area of southern Guatemala. Here in the Yucatan, at the geographically opposite end of the Maya region, the *Books of Chilam Balam* are considered the 'official' texts of the Maya. Various communities throughout the Yucatan wrote their own books, and there are now sixteen known *Chilam Balames* in existence. The one on the table in front of Ramón was the *Chilam Balam de Mani*, given special significance because *Mani* was also the birthplace of the prophet who wrote it.

Jim asked about the Maya cycles, especially the 5,125-year cycle due to end in 2012. Ramón nodded and turned to a place in his book where the Great Cycles were listed by name. According to his *Chilam Balam*, the world was currently in the 5th Great Cycle, which began in 3114 B.C. and would end in 2012. The book described the circumstances that had led up to the end of each of the four prior Cycles, but apparently the Maya gods had decided not to share some information with the prophet, because no details were given regarding the end of the current Cycle.

Edwards listened intently to Ricardo's translation of the Great Cycle explanation. Frank could see the man's interest and asked, "Buzz, do you have something to add?"

"I'm obviously out of my league here," he said, indicating the two brothers plus Jim and Ricardo, "but I recently ran across an article on the Internet that sounds very similar. The difference is that what I read is part of a Hopi Indian myth told by a 'doomsday' group trying to focus attention on the Four Corners area of the U.S. Basically, that's the Mesa Verde cliff dwellings down where Colorado, Utah, Arizona and New Mexico meet. Anyway, they had this same scheme of cycles except I think they called them Worlds.

The myth claims that we are currently in the fourth, and last, world. However, the Hopi are a little more specific about how the current World ends."

Frank waited for Ricardo to finish translating into Spanish and then asked, "And what do the Hopi think will happen?"

"Apparently each of their previous Worlds has ended with some kind of cataclysmic event, and only a few survivors made it across into the next period. They believe the fourth world will end in war and mass destruction and that the final days of this final period will be marked by the return of a group called the 'Thunder Beings'," explained Edwards. "But get this – their other name for this group is the 'Star People'!"

Frank looked at Jim, who just shrugged and said, "So, let's ask him."

Jim asked Ramón if there was any mention of people from the sky in the *Chilam Balam* or other Maya legends. Ramón listened to the question and then thought for a minute. He made eye contact with his brother and then slowly shook his head 'no.' Frank detected a reservation in Ramón's answer, so he pressed the man.

"Are you sure, *Señor*?" he asked, giving the old man a chance to change his mind. Ramón tensed and again shook his head. His brother leaned across the table and said in a soft voice that was almost a whisper, "My brother is reluctant to answer your question, Señor Frank, because the information you seek is considered 'unspeakable' by the shamans of our culture. There are some secrets that are passed from one shaman to the next and they are forbidden to discuss these with anyone except their successor. As we modern Maya stray further and further from the traditional ways, these rules seem less important, but my brother takes his responsibilities very seriously. Perhaps we should take this matter up privately at a later time," said Miguel with a wink.

Not wanting to make the old shaman feel uncomfortable, Frank nodded. "Please ask your brother to forgive me for making an inappropriate inquiry, Mr. Chaak."

After a brief exchange between the two brothers, the old man smiled at Frank and seemed to relax again.

Referring back to his list of questions, Frank asked the old man about the local population of Maya and their history. This was a subject the shaman was very happy, and very proud, to discuss and he soon overcame his shyness. It seems that in and around

Mani, where Ramón had lived all his life, there were several hundred 'practicing' Maya and Ramón was their spiritual leader and healer. As the man described his duties, Frank gained an increased respect for the shaman. The old man described several legends and myths relating to the ruins at *Uxmal* and the nearby sites of *Tical* and *Kabah*. Gradually, Frank brought the conversation around to the geography of the area and finally to *Loltún*.

Ramón described the caverns in words that translated into 'the giver of life' because it was the only large source of water in the area. Ramón confirmed that an underground stream flowed from *Loltún* north to *Mani*, as described in the ancient Legend of the Dwarf, but he could not confirm whether or not the stream continued all the way to Merida and beyond, to the Gulf of Mexico.

Ramón described a period in recent history when Maya rebels had barricaded themselves into the caverns during the War of Castes in the 1800s but Frank was interested in a much earlier period.

"Does the book mention any use of the caverns prior to the arrival of the Maya?" Frank asked, knowing he might be treading on thin ice with the old man.

"The Maya have inhabited the Yucatan for thousands of years," replied Miguel before the shaman had a chance to hear Ricardo's translation. "Who else could have used the caverns?"

"I don't know, Miguel, that's why I'm asking," replied Frank. "What about the Olmec or even some earlier culture? Are there any of them still left around here?"

Edwards and Jim could see that Frank was trying to make a connection to the Indians found at the Nevada Test Site, but Miguel just laughed at the mention of the ancient civilization, considered by many as the 'Mother Culture' of all of Mesoamerica.

"The Olmec people disappeared almost two thousand years ago, Señor Frank, and they never inhabited this part of the Yucatan. I'm sure the Maya were the only humans to visit the caves of *Loltún* until well after the arrival of the Spaniards in the sixteenth century."

Tired of avoiding the real question he had come to ask, Frank reached into his bag, snatched out the sphere and placed it in the center of the table with a thump.

"Then can you tell me who might have left this hidden in *Loltún*?" demanded Frank.

The old shaman sat back in his chair and stared at the sphere in shock. A moment later he slammed the *Chilam Balam* closed, exchanged a few harsh words with his brother and left the room with the large book under his arm.

When the door had closed, Miguel leaned back in his chair and said solemnly, "I'm afraid that's the end of the interview, *Señores*. My brother will not speak with you again."

"Well, I had to ask and we had pretty much exhausted our list of questions," apologized Frank. "At least the ones your brother would answer."

Miguel's attention was focused so intently on the sphere that he missed Frank's comment. Frank noticed this and slid the sphere across the table to Miguel. "It's okay to touch it, Miguel, it won't bite. Do you know what that is?"

"Si, *Señor*, I think I do," said Miguel as he gingerly picked up the sphere and examined it. "I've never seen one, of course, but I believe this an ancient Message Orb. I suspected this was what you were looking for when I heard you were interested in something called a sphere, but I never imagined that you'd actually find one."

"How do you know this is a Message Orb?" asked Jim Barnes, as all three men stared intently at Miguel.

"When my brother was first chosen to succeed the last shaman, he was very concerned that something might happen to him and that the sacred knowledge he had been given would be lost forever, so he shared many things with me. Not everything, of course, but many things. As Ramón grew older, he selected his own successor and now his secrets are safe with a much younger man. Since I am not tied to the old traditions the way Ramón is, I'm not bound by the shaman oaths. I can discuss these things even though he cannot."

Miguel placed the Orb back on the table and looked at the other three. "Earlier, when I told you we should discuss the Sky People later, it was because that is one of the legends Ramón had shared with me. Some of the earliest legends of our people describe a group of beings whose name can best be translated as 'the Galactic Maya.' Their leader is often referred to as the Cosmic Shaman and it is said that he has visited the earth several times since it was first created."

"The five Cycles of the Maya and the four Worlds of the Hopi!" exclaimed Jim.

Miguel nodded. "And since each visit has been accompanied by much destruction and death, the shamans are sworn to secrecy. If the common people knew the ramifications of the end of a Cycle they would destroy themselves and everything around them in a panic. Instead, the dark secret is carried by the succession of shamans, who keep the calendar and mark the days until the beginning of the next cycle."

"Okay, that might explain this Orb, since it carries the 2012 date, but what about the others?" asked Frank. "And why are the orbs being carried to Nevada and who is doing the carrying?"

"And where did the orbs come from in the first place," added Jim.

Ricardo had remained silent for quite a while, deferring to the older, more experienced men, but he couldn't restrain himself any longer.

"What if the Cosmic Shaman only comes at the end of each Cycle but others come more often?" burst out Ricardo. "Could the other spheres have been messages to the Shamans, reminding them of when these visits were to take place?"

"Well, we already know that the other spheres specify the dates of solar eclipses and the locations of Maya cities. I suppose it's possible that these returns were planned to coincide with an eclipse," offered Jim.

"Maybe it was to hide their approach," said Frank. "The Maya were very aware of the sky and all the objects in it. Something like the approach of a spacecraft, even in the light of day, would have been noticed. Maybe they used the eclipse as a diversion."

"May I make a suggestion?" asked Miguel, sitting quietly at the table, staring at the Orb.

The other three had been so involved in their own speculations they had momentarily forgotten the fact that Miguel was a Maya himself, and the brother of a shaman.

"Of course, Señor Chaak, please," apologized Frank, as he indicated that the Maya had the floor.

"As you mentioned, my ancestors were very aware of both the day and night skies. They learned to predict the exact positions of the sun, moon, Mercury, Mars, Venus, Jupiter and Saturn but they never had the benefit of a telescope. They understood motion across the sky very well, but they never fully grasped the concept of astronomical distances. Even though they could predict when an eclipse was going to occur, they never really understood why it happened and it remains a significant event in nature, even today. Timing visits to coincide with a solar eclipse would certainly make an impression on those who knew they were coming, assuming these Galactic Maya actually existed."

"Yeah, we sort of jumped right over the obvious and started assuming the existence of these folks, didn't we?" laughed Frank. "What is your opinion, Señor Chaak? Do you think there are any such beings in the universe?"

"I have no evidence one way or the other," said Miguel, his eyes focused on the black sphere on the table, "but I know that my brother believes, as did a thousand shamans before him, that the visitors exist. And I know one other thing, *Señores.*"

"What's that," asked Frank.

"I know that this object sitting here in front of me was not made by my ancestors."

Later that night, after a strangely quiet drive back to Merida, Frank, Jim and Buzz Edwards settled into the leather seats of the Department of Energy's LearJet for the trip back to Las Vegas. Jim had offered to help Ricardo secure a scholarship at the University of Washington and he had said his goodbyes to his new friend Carmen. Frank had called Alex and asked her to meet him at the airfield. They promised to keep in touch with each other and Frank swore he would be back to take Alex up on her Cancun vacation offer as soon as the issue of the spheres was resolved. As they kissed one last time at the bottom of the plane's stairs, they both knew they would probably never see each other again, and two tears raced each other down touching cheeks.

Once the small jet was at cruising altitude, Edwards unfastened his seatbelt and went to the front of the cabin. From a built-in oak cabinet, he withdrew three glasses and a small ice bucket.

"Name your poison, gentlemen," he announced. "It's either time to celebrate or time to run for cover, depending on how much you believe of what you heard today."

The men had arranged themselves in the set of opposing seats on the plane, with Frank and Jim facing forward and Edwards across from them, his back to the cockpit. As they drank, Frank commented on the luxuriousness of the aircraft.

"Yup, it's a beauty, all right," nodded Edwards. "It was confiscated from a Columbian drug lord about a year ago and assigned to the Nevada Test Site for shuttling Congressional dignitaries back and forth between Washington and Nevada. There's a lot of public relations work going on and the DOE thought this would help get Senators and Representatives to make the trip out to Nevada and have a look around."

"It would certainly get my attention," laughed Frank. "Is that a bathroom back there?"

"Yes it is. There's a full bath aft and a galley and entertainment center up front. This model can cruise at over 600 miles per hour at 41,000 ft. and it has a 2,500-mile range. It's not a bad way to go, if you have to travel.

Rubbing the gray leather armrest at his side, Frank asked, "What's something like this go for?"

"New, a plane like this sells for about $15 million, but if you're interested in this one, I can probably get you a deal."

"You guys seem to know everything else about me, so you probably also know I just came into a good bit of money but if I started spending it $15 million at a time, it wouldn't last very long. I guess I'll just have to suffer with commercial airlines," laughed Frank.

"Maybe we can work out some sort of trade," smiled Edwards as he finished off his drink and started forward to make another.

"A trade?" asked Frank. "What do I have that the DOE could possibly want?"

"Why, you, and your merry band of thieves," replied Edwards from the front of the plane. "Sometimes the government needs the services of an independent, self-sufficient team to do some 'special investigation' work. We can talk about it when we get back to Las Vegas."

Before Frank could pursue the subject further, a telephone in the galley rang and Edwards answered it. Frank couldn't make out the conversation, but it was clear that Edwards was talking to someone else in the agency, possibly an associate. After about five minutes he hung up the phone and swore loudly. When he returned to his seat he was carrying his glass, the bucket of ice and a bottle of Jack Daniels. He set the ice and bottle down on the table in front of his seat and slid in with a sigh.

Eyeing the bottle, Frank asked the obvious question. "Something wrong?"

Edwards laid his head back against the leather, high-back seat and closed his eyes. A few seconds latter he reached for the bottle and poured his glass full.

"Saturday morning we discovered what appears to be a small pyramid buried just below the surface where these damn Indians keep turning up with the spheres. I just learned that there was an accident at the excavation site about an hour ago and a civilian visitor was killed. Now I'll be up all night doing paperwork!"

Chapter 24

Carlson produced several odd looking pictures and laid them out on the conference room table. "These are the results of the seismic tests. If you look here," he said pointing to areas on two of the sheets, "and here, you can clearly make out the pyramid's shape. Each of the four sides appears to be an equilateral triangle."

Tony studied the pictures and then said, "Well, I hate to be one to say 'I told you so', but it looks like you've found your homing beacon. Something like this could explain how the Indians find their way to that specific spot on the Nevada desert. Unless..."

"Unless what?" asked Carlson as he gathered up the papers and put them back into the manila envelope they had been delivered in. "What else could explain this object?"

"Well, it could be a crashed space ship that your buddies over at Area 51 buried here to hide it from us civilians," smiled Tony.

Carlson looked up at Tony and saw the smile, but he didn't return it. Instead, he closed the door to the conference room and sat down at the table. He motioned for Tony to sit down across from him.

"Okay, look, you keep jabbing at me about Area 51 so I'm going to share something with you. I'm only doing this because you've been up front with us and, as a result of your help, we may be on the verge of the discovery of the millennium here. But what I'm going to tell you doesn't leave this room, is that understood?"

"Of course," agreed Tony, sitting down.

"There is no such place as Area 51. Not officially and not unofficially. Frankly, the government has no idea where that name originated, but it has served our misinformation efforts, so we let it become a popular fable. For one thing, when we hear somebody make a claim about Area 51, we know they have no idea what they're talking about because there simply isn't any such place. There is an Area 1, an Area 2 and even an Area 30. In fact, you're in Area 25 right now, but there's just no such place as Area 51."

"But..." stammered Tony, trying to object.

"However," interrupted Carlson, "there is an area northeast of here, just outside the Nevada Test Site but still inside the Nellis

Range area, that we call the Groom Lake Facility. Technically, it's called Air Force Flight Test Center - Detachment 3, but a number of other agencies besides the Air Force have facilities out there. Groom Lake's primary use is as an air strip for classified military aircraft that are still under development. There are two runways, each about two and a half miles long, which can take almost anything ever built except the Space Shuttle – that has to land over at Edwards on their 5-mile-long strip."

"What about the unmarked 737s that supposedly haul people in and out of there every day?" asked Tony.

"You mean the infamous Janet Airlines, of course. Well, most of those planes overnight at the Las Vegas airport and they park in plain sight right across the street from the Luxor Hotel. Their schedules are published on a number of underground Web sites and they use conventional air traffic control frequencies, so how secret can that be?" asked Carlson. "It's a private airline, used to shuffle workers between several fairly remote work sites, that's all. A private corporation would do the same thing if they had a similar type of logistics problem."

"So you're telling me that this Groom Lake is just another example of my tax dollars at work and that, contrary to popular belief, there's no crashed flying saucers or alien technology hidden out there," said a rather disappointed Tony.

"Well, no, I didn't say that. In fact…"

Carlson's explanation was interrupted by a knock on the door. A young civilian with closely cropped hair stuck his head inside the room and said, "Sorry to disturb you, Mr. Carlson, but we need to go over the excavation plans with you as soon as possible, since we'll need to borrow some heavy equipment from the Yucca Mountain project."

"I'll be right there, Jack," replied Carlson. After the man closed the door Carlson said to Tony, "We'll finish this later. I've got to look at what the engineers have come up with. By the way, my offer still stands if you want to hang out up here and see how this turns out. You can keep your room down in Mercury for a couple of more nights and hang out up here during the day. I'm afraid you can't go running around by yourself, but digging this thing out of the ground should be a pretty interesting process. What do you say?"

"Absolutely!" responded Tony, standing up. "I wouldn't miss this for the world but I should try to call Frank and let him know what's up. With my cell phone locked in the Durango, he has no way to contact me."

"Don't worry about that. I'll pass your plans on to Buzz Edwards, who can fill Frank in when they hook up. Now let's go see what the engineering geniuses have cooked up."

Tony spent the rest of Saturday tagging around with Carlson as he oversaw the preparations for the removal of the strange buried object. Normally, Carlson wouldn't get involved in an engineering project, but this one had potential security ramifications that warranted his personal attention.

About 6:00 p.m. Carlson sent his crew home, with instructions to report to work at 8:00 a.m. sharp the next morning. A large moan came from the group when they learned they were going to have to work on Sunday, but Tony expected they were as curious to see what was buried out in the sand as he was.

Tony had only packed clothes for one night so Carlson suggested they take a run into Beatty, the closest civilian town, so Tony could pick up whatever he needed. Tony was surprised when Carlson parked the Cherokee at the gate they had originally entered the day before.

"What are we stopping here for?" asked Tony.

"We don't like to take these rigs into town. Too many people have heard stories about the infamous Camo Dudes in their white Cherokees, and I don't particularly want some Area 51 fanatic snapping my picture. We'll take the Durango from here up to Beatty and from there over to the gate at Mercury. I'll get somebody to drive the Cherokee down the back way to meet us."

"So we have to leave the Durango at the Mercury gate?" asked Tony. "Can't I just park it outside my unit?"

"No, I'm afraid not. And you can't take the gun or your cell phone in, either. Sorry, but those are the rules. Of course, you could drive back to Las Vegas tonight and then back up here tomorrow morning, if you'd be more comfortable with that," offered Carlson as they headed away from the guard shack in the Durango.

"No, that's okay. The room in Mercury is fine and I want to be at the excavation site early tomorrow. I'll just pick up a few things in town and hang out here."

"Let's grab dinner in Beatty, too," said Carlson. "I get pretty tired of the cafeteria in Mercury and besides, I could use a drink. We'll stop at the Casino on the north end of town – it has good food, cheap booze and pretty waitresses."

"Perfect!" replied Tony. "My three favorite things!"

"Yeah, I thought so," smiled Carlson.

They stopped at the Beatty General Store and Tony picked up a three-pack of shorts, a package of socks and two shirts. He also grabbed a variety of snack foods, a jar of instant coffee and a paperback book. As he climbed back into the Durango, Carlson was just finishing a phone call.

"Find everything?" asked Carlson.

"I think so. I should be good for another couple of days. I also picked up some munchies and a book you might enjoy," said Tony as he tossed the paperback to Carlson and started the Durango.

"*Area 51: The Sphinx*, by Robert Doherty," laughed Carlson. "Very funny. This is a good series, though. I've read all five of the books."

After a hearty meal and plenty of red wine, Tony and Carlson headed back down U.S. 95 to Mercury. Carlson discovered he was out of chewing gum, so he asked Tony to pull into a truck stop at Amargosa Valley. While Carlson was inside, Tony unlocked the glove box and grabbed his cell phone. He checked his voice mail, expecting a message from Frank and was surprised to hear Jill's voice instead.

"Tony, this is Jill. I'm not supposed to be doing this, but I wanted you to know that I'm okay. I can't tell you where I am, but the water is blue and the breezes are warm. I've gotta go. Stay well, big guy."

Tony deleted the message and turned the phone off. He smiled, glad to know Jill was doing okay and that she was safe on St. John, in the U.S. Virgin Islands. During the course of the night they had spent in the Mandalay Bay casino and suite, Jill had told Tony about a vacation she had taken to St. John. She went on and on about how much she loved it there and she had used the same adjectives to describe it – blue water and warm breezes. Tony didn't know why, but it made him feel good that she had left him a coded message indicating where she was.

Carlson opened the passenger's door of the Durango just as Tony was locking his cell phone back into the glove box.

"Just checking my voice mail," he said. "I thought there might be a message from Frank, but there wasn't."

"When I talked with Buzz earlier he was at Frank's hotel but apparently Frank and that other guy left early this morning with two locals and haven't returned yet. I sure hope they know what they're doing. Anyway, when Buzz catches up with Frank he's going to let him know about your cell phone situation."

"Okay, then I'll quit worrying about it." said Tony, as he pulled out onto Highway 95.

About fifteen minutes later, Tony came to the clearly marked exit for Mercury, but the sign also indicated that there were "No Public Services." They crossed under Highway 95 and almost immediately came to a "No Trespassing" sign that indicated they were entering U.S. Government property. A mile down the road they came to a guard shack and gate. This gate was more formal than the one they had used to get up to Yucca Mountain but it was manned by the same civilian security agency. Tony pulled into a small parking lot to the right of the gate and found an empty spot. The two men got out and walked to the gate, where Carlson showed his credentials and went inside the base's security headquarters, leaving Tony outside under a bright street light. As promised, Carlson's Cherokee, or one just like it, was waiting just in a lot on the far side of the large security building. A few seconds later Carlson came out and handed Tony another visitor's badge like the one he had been issued the day before.

"You know the drill. Wear it at all times and always in plain sight. No wandering around, and don't talk to anyone about our little discovery, okay?" said Carlson as they walked to the waiting Cherokee.

Carlson dropped Tony at his room and arranged to pick him up at 7:30 a.m. the next morning. This time, Tony slept in the bed, rather than on the couch, and the clock radio woke him promptly at 6:30 a.m.

Sunday was pretty uneventful. Most of the morning was spent arranging for various pieces of equipment and carefully planning the method and location of the excavation. After lunch, Carlson, Tony and an entourage of staffers went out to the site and mapped out specific places on the ground. Small red flags were placed here and there and maps were marked with numbers corresponding to tags on the flags.

By late afternoon the engineers were divided half and half about how best to remove the object. Because there was a fairly steep hill on the north side of the buried pyramid, one group wanted to dig in from the side while the second group wanted to slowly remove earth from the top until the object was exposed. Carlson listened to all the pros and cons and finally decided to defer any decision until the following morning so he could mull the two plans over for a while.

Tony favored the side approach, because it exposed more of the object sooner and he was anxious to see what it was all about, but apparently the top-down approach was safer and simpler.

Back in his room that night, Tony couldn't shake the vision of a 3-D rendering one of the staffers had created from the seismic charts. Something about it bothered him, but he couldn't quite put his finger on it. Even after a couple of stiff drinks, Tony caught himself pacing, lost in thought about the buried pyramid.

By the time Carlson picked Tony up at 7:30 a.m. the next morning, he had decided to go with the side excavation plan that Tony favored. He also had big news from Buzz Edwards. It seemed that Frank and Jim Barnes had discovered another sphere inside the *Loltún* caves the day before and Jim's preliminary deciphering indicated that the location it carried matched the point where the pyramid was buried. After a morning meeting with a Maya shaman, Buzz was going to try to convince Frank and Jim to fly back with him that afternoon on the DOE's LearJet.

"Wow, so that makes a total of twenty, right?" asked Tony, "the nineteen you now have locked up at the bottom of Yucca Mountain and the one they're bringing back. I can't wait for Jim to decode the others to see if his solar eclipse theory holds."

"It does seem like all roads lead to Jackass Flats, don't they?" replied Carlson. "Speaking of the Flats, we need to go directly there. They're ready to start digging and I'm more anxious than ever to see what's buried out there. I asked a staffer from the U.S. Geological Survey (USGS) to supervise the actual excavation and he should arrive at the site about the same time we do."

"That's fine," replied Tony. "I'm pretty anxious to see what this thing is myself. Are you taking any special precautions, or are you just assuming it's dormant?"

"We're not assuming anything, but there's been no indication that anything will happen, either," explained Carlson as they headed out of Mercury for the drive up to the excavation site. "This object, whatever it is, doesn't seem to be emitting anything that we can detect. We've checked for radiation, of course, and also magnetic and electromagnetic activity. The only unusual characteristic seems to be the shape of this damn thing."

Tony and Carlson continued to speculate about the nature and origin of the buried pyramid for the rest of the trip. When they arrived at the site, it was teeming with activity and several pieces of construction equipment were being moved into place. A small group of men in suits was standing just off the road, overlooking the work.

"It's amazing what a Monday morning will bring out of the woodwork," said Carlson, shaking his head. "They probably spent all day yesterday on the golf course."

"Who are they?" asked Tony as they got out of the Cherokee and started for the group.

"Administrators, mostly. I see my boss is here, too, and a couple of desk jockeys from Bechtel. They're the equivalent of the general contractor out here. Let me do the talking and don't volunteer any information, okay? When they see your visitor's badge they're going to go ballistic."

Carlson was wearing a small two-way radio headset that looked like the type the secret service use. Carlson said something into the microphone and then Tony overheard him saying, "Roger that. Thanks for the heads up."

They approached the group of administrators and the men acknowledged Carlson with reserved respect. Carlson introduced Tony and the question and answer session began immediately, just as Carlson had predicted. After ten minutes of debate, some in private asides, the consensus of the group was that Tony could stay, but only because of the contributions he and his team had made and the fact that he had been properly cleared in advance. Tony nodded his thanks and then stepped back to watch the bureaucratic circus that was taking place around him. Privately, he wondered how this group of government employees could ever get the pyramid out of the ground without two weeks' worth of committee meetings but things somehow got organized and the first sand was finally moved just before 10:00 a.m. Tony moved back along the ridge about twenty-five feet so he could see what was going on down the slope.

Moving very slowly, a back hoe and two men with shovels began to eat into the hillside. After every scoop by the back hoe, the

USGS engineer would run up to the hill and carefully inspect the newly exposed area for any evidence of the pyramid. Eventually, he waved his hands over his head indicating that the back hoe operator should stop digging. He signaled the two men with shovels forward and pointed to a specific spot on the bank. Tony was too far away to hear what the man was saying, but he was buzzing around the spot like a mad hornet while the other two men worked at the ground very carefully with their shovels. Soon he motioned for the workers to stop and the engineer started digging in the sand with his hands.

Every eye at the site was now focused on that one spot. As the young engineer brushed away a small amount of sand, he touched a small patch of the buried object. In an instant, the exposed area emitted a brilliant, blinding white light and the engineer, who was still touching the bare surface of the pyramid, fell over backwards into the sand.

The flash was accompanied by a loud click from several of the nearby vehicles and a slight movement of the earth. It momentarily stunned the onlookers and then one of the administrators shouted "What the hell was that!"

Tony glanced over in the direction of the voice and noticed that Carlson had yanked the radio earpiece out and was holding his ear in obvious pain.

From down below, someone shouted "We need help over here! Somebody get a doctor!"

Tony scrambled down the bank and raced over to the fallen engineer. "Let me through! I had some medical training in the Army!"

Placing his finger to the engineer's neck, Tony felt for a pulse, but the man's heart had already stopped beating. Looking up at the crowd that had gathered around the victim, Tony shook his head and said, "There's no pulse at all. How fast can you get a defibrillator out here?" Without waiting for an answer, he began to administer CPR.

As Tony continued his attempt to revive the man, he heard someone at the back of the group shout "There's a chopper on the way from Mercury. ETA is five minutes."

When the medical team arrived, Tony stepped back and let them take over, but after several attempts to restart the man's heart with the defibrillator one of the medical techs stood up and said, to the group in general, "I'm sorry, but he's dead."

One of the administrators, the one Carlson had identified earlier as his boss, pushed through the small group standing around the body and addressed the medical team. "All right, get this man back to O'Callaghan immediately. On your way, call ahead and tell them to alert Dr. Anderson that another body is coming in from Area 18. And don't tell anybody any more than that, do you understand?"

The techs nodded and quickly began the task of removing the engineer's body. When the helicopter had lifted off, the administrator, now clearly in charge of the scene, called up to Carlson, "I want this place locked down right now. Nothing gets touched, nothing gets moved and not a word of this gets out until I say so. And use any means necessary to make sure that this thing in the ground stays right where it is." Looking back to the group surrounding the accident scene, he barked, "Okay, you men, clear out. And remember, not a word of this leaves this site. What happened here today, whatever the hell it was, is hereby classified Top Secret."

As the group started to disburse, the administrator motioned for Tony to stay put. When the others were a sufficient distance away, the administrator said, "My name is Patton. I'm in charge of the Nevada Test Site and I appreciate your efforts, even though you couldn't save him. Did I hear you say you were in the Army?"

"Yes, sir, Company A, 75th Infantry Regiment, and I was just doing my duty," replied Tony. "I think his heart must have stopped beating at the same instant we saw that flash. There was absolutely no pulse by the time I got to him."

Patton eyed Tony's Visitor's badge. "The 75th, huh? So you were a Ranger. Well done. I was in the Army myself. I trust you understand the seriousness of what has happened here."

"Of course, sir. I'm the one who brought the spheres in on Friday, along with Gene Carlson," responded Tony as Carlson joined the other two men.

"I see you two have met," said Carlson. "Tony and some friends of his have turned up some interesting information about the spheres, Colonel. In fact, Tony's friends are on their way back here with Buzz Edwards and yet another sphere."

"Great!" shouted Patton. "I've about had it with those damn spheres and this pyramid. We have a Congressional delegation due in here next week, and all this hocus pocus is diverting attention away from the real job of getting ready for that visit. Carlson, I want you to get this mess under control. Do what ever it takes, use whomever you need to, but make this situation go away before next week."

The gruff administrator brushed some sand off the leg of his suit pants and turned to leave. "I'm out of here. Keep me posted, Carlson."

After the man was gone, Tony said, "Did I hear you call him Colonel?"

"Yeah, he's retired Army. He claims he's a direct descendant of General George Patton, and he's certainly got the ego to match. Good administrator, though, and his contacts in Washington have helped keep a lot of projects out here funded."

Carlson stepped aside to take a call on his two-way radio. Tony couldn't hear the other end of the conversation because of the earpiece, but Tony heard him reply, "Roger, I copy that. Desert Rock Airstrip at 17:30 hours. Please pass the word that we will meet them there and also let Edwards know what's happened out here. Over."

When Carlson turned back, he said, "Buzz Edwards will be arriving at the airstrip down in Mercury about 5:30 p.m. and he has your friends, Frank and Jim, with him. They're coming directly to the Test Site rather than landing at McCarran because the sphere they found has apparently become active."

Chapter 25

As Tony watched Carlson's boss speed away, he realized that he and Carlson were the only two left at the accident scene. Carlson saw Tony's look of concern and said, "Don't worry. Right now, this is one of the most secure spots on earth. I've already ordered a lock-down of the entire Nellis Range and special surveillance and monitoring gear is headed this way as we speak. Let's take a look at the dig site before the hoard arrives."

Cautiously, the two men approached the place where the USGS engineer had been digging before he had fallen over dead. They examined the area carefully, but there was no evidence of any exposed pyramid. In fact, so much sand had shifted that it was hard to tell there had even been an excavation project there.

"That little rumble we felt with the flash must have shifted the sand enough to cover it back up and I don't think we should go digging around looking for it." observed Tony, stepping back. "I'm betting that the autopsy on the engineer will turn out identical to those you've done on the Indians."

"But the autopsies on the Indians have never turned up anything," complained Carlson as they climbed back up the slope to the road.

"Exactly."

They sat in the Cherokee until the first of the regular security forces arrived. Carlson got out and talked to one of the men in the other rig, apparently giving the man instructions. When he was back behind the wheel, Carlson suggested they drive into Mercury for lunch.

"Shall I pick up my gear from the housing unit?" asked Tony. "I assume Frank, Jim and I will be going back into Vegas after they arrive."

"Actually, I suggest the three of you stay out here tonight. I think your hieroglyphics specialist should see the rest of the spheres and there's a little experiment I'd like your help with tonight. After lunch we'll go over and arrange rooms for your friends and then I need to get back up on the hill and make some personnel arrangements."

Tony spent the afternoon 'on the hill' in the building where Carlson's office was located. He was offered the desk of a vacationing employee and, fortunately, he had brought along the book he had purchased the night before. About 3:00 p.m. Carlson stopped by to see how Tony was doing and a wide yawn answered his question.

"Bored, huh? How about taking a look at these files and seeing if you spot something we've missed," asked Carlson as he dropped a thick manila folder onto the desk in front of Tony.

Tony opened the folder and was confronted by an eight-by-ten glossy photo of the dead USGS engineer. "What the hell is this?" asked a startled Tony.

"It's the autopsy file on all the bodies we've recovered out at the pyramid site. Maybe you can find some common thread that we've overlooked. Besides, it'll keep you busy until Edwards and your buddies get here," said Carlson, as he headed back to his office.

Tony spent the next two hours studying the files. At first he just scanned the photos and he was struck by the fact that, except for the engineer, all the victims could have been brothers. Closer examination revealed that their faces weren't identical, but their features were amazingly similar. If they weren't directly related then they had to be from the same tribe or clan.

Tony found a pad of paper in the desk and began to make a more detailed comparison of the cases. Somebody had already sorted the individual files in chronological order, so Tony recorded the date each body was found in the left margin. The dates ranged from April 10, 1951, to the previous day's death of the engineer. Across the page, he listed the height and weight of each body, along with the coroner's estimated date and time of death. Tony computed the average height to be 5 feet, 10 inches and the average weight to be 155 pounds. The values were fairy normal, but what wasn't normal was the fact that none of the Indians' heights deviated from the average by more than 2 inches and none of their weights were more than 5 pounds off the average. The probability that all nineteen heights and weights fell within three percent of the median reinforced Tony's theory that the Indians must be somehow related.

There didn't seem to be any pattern to the dates, except that the deaths always occurred at least two years, and never more than three years, apart. Curious about the significance of the first death,

Tony remembered the collection of historical photographs on the wall outside the conference room. After examining the photos for several minutes he came across a grainy, black and white picture of a classic mushroom cloud. It was the caption, however, that caught Tony's eye. It read 'Able, the first atmospheric test at the newly commissioned Nevada Proving Grounds, was detonated on January 27, 1951.'

Tony jotted down the date and returned to his desk. Was it a coincidence that the first sphere arrived less than four months after the first nuclear test was conducted near the site of the buried pyramid? Tony knew there had been a lot more than nineteen nuclear tests at Nevada Test Site, so there wasn't a one-to-one relationship between tests and sphere arrivals. Maybe the first sphere and the first test weren't connected either, thought Tony, but, then again, maybe they were.

Tony read each medical examiner's report in detail, but the terminology was unfamiliar and the fact that they had been produced over a long period of time by a number of different individuals made them difficult to compare. The only thing that stuck out to Tony was the way in which all the victims, including the engineer, had died. The causes of death ranged from 'unknown' to 'apparent heart failure', but there were never any signs of injury or trauma, either internally or externally, on any of the bodies. Tony had personally witnessed the engineer's death, and if the blinding flash had been an electrical discharge there should have been burn marks on the man's hands but the report made no mention of this or anything that would indicate death by electrocution.

Carlson came out of his office about 5:05 p.m. and crossed to Tony's desk. "Did you find anything interesting?" he asked.

Tony closed the folder and handed it back to Carlson. "A couple of odd coincidences, but nothing earth shattering," replied Tony. "Let me mull it over for a while."

While Carlson returned the autopsy file to a cabinet at the far end of the room, Tony tore the sheet containing his notes off the pad, folded it up and stuffed it into his hip pocket.

"It's about time to head down to the airstrip," said Carlson as he returned. "Shall we see what the fuss over this new sphere is all about?"

Tony and Carlson waited in the Cherokee until the small jet came to a stop in front of the metal building that served as the airstrip's terminal. When they saw the door open, they walked the short distance to the tarmac and waited at the bottom of the stairs that had unfolded from inside the plane. Jim Barnes appeared in the doorway first and he looked confused by the surroundings outside. Apparently, Edwards had neglected to mention the change in itinerary.

As Jim stepped onto the tarmac, Tony shook his hand and laughed "Welcome to Nowhere! I take it you weren't expecting an airstrip in the middle of the desert?"

"Well, no, not exactly," stammered Jim as he surveyed the surroundings. "I thought we were headed for Las Vegas. Where are we, Tony, and what the heck are you doing here?"

Before Tony could answer, a very animated Frank and Buzz Edwards started down the stairs. They were obviously in the middle of a discussion that had been going on for some time.

"Now there's a marriage made in hell," said Jim sarcastically. "Those two have been yapping non-stop ever since we left El Paso. It's impossible to do any studying when those two are together."

Finally on the ground, Frank noticed Tony for the first time and greeted him warmly. "Tony, you old son of a gun! How are things back here in the good old USA? I hear you've had your share of excitement the last couple of days, but wait until you hear about Mexico! And Buzz and I have some ideas I want to run by you …"

Tony held up his hand to cut Frank off and said, "Whoa, Frank, let's get out of this sun and get your stuff stowed and then we can talk. Have you been drinking?"

"Well, maybe a little. This beauty," said Frank, indicating the LearJet, "has a pretty well stocked bar."

Tony smiled and said, mostly to himself, "Welcome to Mercury. I hope you enjoy your stay."

Carlson handed Frank and Jim each visitor badges like the one Tony was wearing and said, "You two have no idea the favors I had to call in to get you cleared to be here on such short notice! I'm afraid I'm going to have to ask you to surrender your cell phones and any weapons you might be carrying."

Due to the time difference between eastern Mexico and Las Vegas, it had been more than eight hours since the travelers had eaten so Carlson herded the group into the Cherokee and headed for the food service facility in Mercury. On the way in, Carlson had reminded everybody not to discuss the spheres or the pyramid in public, so the dinner conversation bounced back and forth between Frank's new friend, Alex, and Jim's new friend, Carmen. By the time they had finished eating, Frank was acting less hyperactive and seemed more focused on the business at hand. When they left the cafeteria, Carlson dropped Frank, Tony and Jim at guest housing before taking Edwards to his office elsewhere in Mercury.

Jim was anxious to study the spheres he hadn't already seen and Frank wanted a look at the Pyramid site, so they agreed to meet Carlson at 7:30 p.m. That would give them about an hour of sun light, plenty of time to stop at Jackass Flats on their way up to the mountain tunnel entrance. The twentieth sphere, which had been transferred to the aft baggage compartment during the Learjet's fuel stop in El Paso, was now in the back of Carlson's Cherokee and would eventually join the others in the underground vault.

After they got settled, Frank and Jim rendezvoused in Tony's room and brought him up to date about their activities in Mexico. In return, Tony explained how he had come to be a 'guest' on the Nevada Test Site. He apologized for not staying in touch, but when he explained that the Durango and his cell phone had essentially been impounded, Frank and Jim understood.

Tony removed the folded paper from his pants pocket and spread it out on the small table. He pointed out the correlation between the first nuclear test and the appearance of the first sphere and the narrow range of heights and weights of the corpses.

As an anthropologist, Jim took a special interest in the height and weight anomaly. "This doesn't make any sense," he said, rubbing his chin in thought. "The Maya aren't normally this tall, and even nomadic tribes, where there is typically a lot of inbreeding, would exhibit a wider variation than what I see here. It's almost as if these guys share a common parent – or parents."

"But that's impossible, isn't it," asked Frank. "There's almost a fifty year spread between the first and last deaths."

"It's not medically impossible, but it would certainly be unusual," admitted Jim. "Let's review what we know about them and see if a theory jumps out at us."

"Okay, well, the shaman we met at *Uxmal* didn't seem to know who they might be. He could have been hiding something, but I watched him carefully when I mentioned previous inhabitants of *Loltún* and he showed no reaction at all," offered Frank.

"And yet he clearly reacted when you presented him with the sphere," added Jim. "I came away from that meeting with the impression that the old Maya had first-hand knowledge about the spheres but I agree – I didn't get the feeling he was hiding anything about these Indians."

"So what else do we know?" asked Frank

"If the nineteen spheres stored in the bottom of Yucca Mountain came from the same cave where you two found the twentieth one, then these Indians must have had access to that cave," said Tony.

"That's right, and over a pretty long period of time. I'm guessing they brought them out one at a time according to some schedule because if they had made a one-time raid on the cave the last one wouldn't have still been there when we showed up," said Frank, scanning the column of dates on Tony's paper.

"Since we know the Maya were heavily involved in astronomy and complex calendar interpretation, we should plot these dates on an astronomical calendar and look for a correlation," said Jim. "Maybe each death, and therefore the arrival of another sphere, corresponds to positions of the planets or something obscure like that."

"Okay, but that sounds like a project for Frank, since he's the science guru here," agreed Tony. "Let's get back to the Indians themselves for a minute. This isn't some mysterious tribe that vanished a thousand years ago without a trace. Frank and I were in the same room with one of these guys less than a week ago and he died out by that buried pyramid just a few days ago. They are coming from somewhere and I bet if we figure out where that place is, we will get a lot closer to the secret of the spheres and their messages."

Before the debate could continue, there was a knock on the door. Tony refolded the paper and tucked it back into his pocket before he answered the door.

"I thought I'd find you all here," smiled Carlson, as he acknowledged the presence of Frank and Jim in the room. "Let's head up to the site before it gets any darker and then we can take a look at the spheres."

On the way to the site, Tony and Gene Carlson recounted the events of the prior day's accident in detail for the benefit of Frank and Jim, who listened intently.

"So after the flash, you could no longer see the exposed portion of pyramid?" reiterated Jim.

"That's correct," answered Carlson, "but like I said, whatever caused the flash probably caused the object to shift slightly, which in turn caused sand from the hillside to slide down and cover up the spot. That flash had to be the byproduct of the release of a tremendous amount of energy."

"Hence the dead engineer," added Tony. "In fact, the flash was actually accompanied by a slight ground tremor, like a mini-earthquake."

"Interesting," contemplated Jim. "Have you…"

"Here we are gentlemen," interrupted Carlson, as he brought the Cherokee to a stop. "Let's keep the speculation to a minimum in front of my security guys, okay? We're doing everything around here on a need-to-know basis. Frank, will you reach around behind you and hand me the sphere? It's in that paper sack."

Tony took Frank and Jim down the slope to see the site where the excavation had taken place while Carlson checked in with the two men dressed in unmarked camouflage pants and shirts. Jim tilted his head this way and that, but there really wasn't anything left to see and soon the three rejoined Carlson beside the Cherokee.

"Where's your crew?" asked Frank, noticing that the two Camo Dudes were no longer in sight.

"I sent them over to check out the equipment sheds," responded Carlson, pointing to several low metal buildings nearby. "I want to try an experiment and they don't need to see it."

Carlson retrieved the bag containing the sphere from the seat of the Cherokee and walked over to a spot on the top of the ridge that was more or less above the buried pyramid. He dug a shallow hole in the sand and buried the sphere, much the way the Indians had done for the last fifty years. When he had finished covering the sphere, he stepped back and joined the others.

"Aren't you going to lie down on top of it?" laughed Tony.

"After what happened out here yesterday, I don't think I'll take any chances," replied Carlson, seriously. "When I heard about this sphere's increased activity, I wanted to see what would happen if the sphere and pyramid were close together."

"To be an accurate experiment, you really should leave it there all night," said Jim. "And Tony's comment may be closer to the mark than he intended. It is entirely possible that the body of the Indian has something to do with whatever happens out here. And we're also kicking around the theory that the sphere has to be delivered at some astronomically correct time, so…"

"Okay, I realize this was a shot in the dark, but what the hell – we were in the area, the sphere was handy and I was curious to see if the two would react to each other. It doesn't look like anything is going to happen, so I'll get the sphere and we can get out of here."

When Carlson returned to the Cherokee, he handed the sphere to Tony and climbed in without a word. He had been sure the proximity of the pyramid would stimulate the sphere.

"What was it doing on the trip back?," asked Tony, as Carlson turned the Cherokee around and headed back down to the main road.

"It was pulsing, similar to what it was doing in the cave where we found it," explained Frank, "only the light was brighter. It was also making a high-pitched whine that seemed to be right at the threshold of human hearing. The sound was driving us nuts, and that's why we put it in the plane's baggage compartment."

"Well, it sure looks and feels dead right now," said Tony, as he examined it closely. "Maybe it'll come to life again when it rejoins its brothers at the bottom of Yucca Mountain."

When the four men arrived at Carlson's office, there was a professional looking thirty-something man waiting for them inside.

"Gentlemen, this is Dr. Ben Kingston. Ben was working with Al Thompson before his death and now he's our resident expert on the spheres. He would like to observe, if you don't mind, Jim."

Jim shook hands with the man and smiled warmly. "Not at all. I would very much like to compare notes, Dr. Kingston."

"Please, call me Ben. I would be happy to share what little I know in exchange for hearing your interpretations, Jim."

"I hope you're prepared for a long night, then, because it takes me several hours to work out the message on each of the spheres, and there are sixteen that I haven't seen. Unfortunately, all I have are some hand-written notes and a few cheat sheets to work with," said Jim, patting the leather brief case he had brought with him. "There hasn't been time to develop a computer-based tool yet."

"I'm afraid I can't allow you to stay down inside the Mountain that long, Jim, due to possible radiation exposure. I suggest that you and Ben go down and digitally photograph each of the spheres, including the ones you've already seen, and then return to the surface to do your decoding. It's time we created a permanent catalog of these things anyway. Does that sound okay?"

"I guess that would be okay, as long as we can have enough time to do a thorough job. And as an anthropologist, I certainly support making the historical record."

"I can give you three hours, which includes the ride down and back up. That's the time limit we place on all non-essential personnel, but that will give you a little over two hours to photograph. Ben brought along one of our best digital camcorders so you can also capture voice memos if you need to. Frank and Tony, can you two behave yourselves up here for a while?"

"Any chance we can get on the Internet?" asked Frank. "We have some research to do that would easily kill a couple of hours."

Carlson went to the nearest desk and logged on to the computer. "There you go, Internet access only. I'm going down to the bottom with Jim and Ben so I can unlock the vault. This way, gentlemen."

Frank and Tony were left standing in the middle of the deserted office, alone.

"He's sure a trusting guy," remarked Frank. "For all he knows, we could be poking around in all his precious secrets."

"Somehow, I think you're never alone around here," said Tony, pointing out several small, inverted black bubbles attached to the ceiling. "Those surveillance cameras are no doubt watching our every move."

"Can't say that I blame them," said Frank, as he intentionally smiled at one of the bubbles. "They have some pretty sensitive stuff out here. I've read about this Yucca Mountain project, and there's a lot of public opposition to it. Not to mention other activities that might be going on out here. Has Carlson taken you out to Area 51 yet?"

"No, he started to tell me something about a place called Groom Lake the other day, but we were interrupted. He's more or less in charge of security for the whole Nellis Range, you know. That includes Yucca Mountain, the Nevada Test Site, the Air force bombing range and anything else that may, or may not, be out here."

"Yeah, Edwards mentioned that on the way back from Mexico," said Frank. "He and Carlson, along with a few others, are also the Department of Energy's version of the X-Files unit. They have 'regular' jobs, of course, but anything out of the ordinary that comes along is given to them. Like the spheres."

"And the pyramid," added Tony. "These two seem to have their run of the place, don't they?"

"Yes, they sure do. Remind me to tell you about an interesting proposal Edwards made on the way back." Frank sat down at the computer and said, "In the mean time, let's see if we can find a good on-line ephemeris."

"A what," asked Tony, as he pulled up a chair from another desk.

"An ephemeris – a detailed catalog of astronomical events. I think the U.S. Naval Observatory has one. Where are those notes of yours?"

About an hour and fifteen minutes later, Carlson reentered the building through the back door that led to the tunnel.

Frank looked up from the monitor and asked, "Everything going okay down there?"

"Yes, I guess so," replied Carlson. "I just don't get it, though. The other day, when Tony and I were down there, several of the spheres were acting up. So bad, in fact, that I got spooked. Tonight, every single one of them is absolutely dead. I tried touching spheres to each other and grouping them together in various configurations but I got absolutely no response. Just like out at the accident site earlier."

"Well, they were sure making a hell of a racket when we were down there," agreed Tony. "I wonder what's changed since Friday."

"Well, your friend Jim has a theory, but I think he's crazy. Unfortunately, I can't prove him wrong until tomorrow," said a depressed Carlson as he sat down on a nearby desk.

"I doubt if Jim is crazy, and if I've learned anything in the last few days, I've learned to trust Jim's instincts," said Frank, turning in his chair to face Carlson. "He has a knack for getting right to the heart of the matter. So, what's his theory?"

"He thinks the discharge that killed the engineer may have also initiated some sort of automatic shutdown process," sighed Carlson.

Chapter 26

Carlson checked his watch for the hundredth time in two hours and mumbled under his breath, "Damn it, they've been down there more than three hours. I'm going over to the guard shack to see what's going on. You two wait for me here, okay?"

Frank and Tony looked at each other and laughed. "Relax, Gene," said Tony, "we're not going to run off and let you have all the fun. We're just as interested in what Jim learns about those spheres as you are."

When the back door of the office building had closed behind Carlson, Frank shook his head. "He's really a strange duck, isn't he?"

"Yes, but I suppose it comes with the territory. All this black hat stuff going on around here would tend to make a guy a little spy-shy," replied Tony, partly in Carlson's defense. "I've only been here three days and it's starting to creep me out, too. The sooner we get back to the city, the happier I'll be."

"I agree with that, and I've only been here a few hours. Hey, look at this!" said Frank, pointing to a screen full of numbers on the computer monitor Carlson had let them use.

Tony glanced at the screen and shrugged. "You know, I haven't understood a thing you've been doing since you started. What is all that crap, anyway?"

"Do you want the long version or the short version?" asked Frank.

Tony yawned. "What do you think?"

"Okay, I'll skip right to the good stuff. This is the U.S. Naval Observatory's Web site. The Observatory serves as the government's official astronomy experts. I entered the dates of the deaths from your notes and I've been trying to find a correlation to anything that might have served as an astronomical signal to our Indian friends. This data is for a near-Earth asteroid named 1998PX12, which travels on an odd shaped orbit between Earth and Mars. Because its orbit is so elliptical, it makes 'close encounters' with the earth at irregular periods that range between two and three years. A close encounter coincides almost exactly with each of the estimated dates of death from the first eighteen Indian autopsy reports. And look at this column! I calculated the number of days between the close encounter and the date of death. The differences range from eighteen to twenty-two days, and the average is 20.23."

"Twenty? That's the same as the number of spheres we think there are!" said Tony, suddenly interested in Frank's work.

"Yes, but more significantly, it's the same as the number of days in a Maya month – in *both* of their calendar systems. Their 260-day Tzolkin calendar consists of thirteen 20-day months and their 365-day Haab calendar consists of eighteen 20-day months and one 5-day month," explained Frank

"So are you saying that this asteroid may have signaled when it was time for another sphere to begin its journey to Nevada?" asked Tony. "And that it took the Indian carrying the sphere twenty days to make the trip? Aren't you grasping a little, old buddy? It must be four thousand miles from *Loltún* to the site where the bodies were found."

"Actually, its about three thousand six hundred land miles. To make the trip on foot in twenty days, you would have to maintain a brisk 7.5 miles per hour, twenty-four hours a day, for the entire twenty days," said Frank, staring at the screen.

"Well, that's just not possible," said Tony sarcastically.

"It's not *humanly* possible, that's for sure," agreed Frank. "And since this asteroid isn't visible to the naked eye, the Indians would have needed some other means of detecting its presence, but the agreement of the dates seems too close to be a coincidence. I've checked dozens of other correlations and nothing comes anywhere near this close, so I think we have to consider this a working theory until we come up with something better. It bothers me, though, that the nineteenth sphere doesn't fit the pattern. That date is about two weeks later than I would have expected."

"That's an easy one, Einstein. That sphere and its Indian somehow got separated, because we found that sphere in old man Thompson's safe, remember? According to the autopsy report, the last Indian died Thursday night, the day after you gave him back the sphere at the old man's mobile home, which means that as soon as he regained possession of the sphere he completed his quest."

"That's right!" exclaimed Frank. "Of course his date of death wouldn't fit the pattern! So, the next question is how did his sphere end up in Al Thompson's safe for two weeks?"

"And who shot the old man? By the way, that shooting was two weeks ago tonight, about the same time the Indian would have originally delivered it to the buried pyramid, according to your theory," added Tony.

"The old man obviously came into possession of that sphere prior to the night of the shooting, because we found it in his safe and we know he never went home again after he was shot. He was taken from Beatty to Jill's critical care unit and from there out to the base hospital, where he died," summarized Frank.

"Right, and when Carlson and Edwards told me about Thompson and his work for the DOE, they mentioned that they knew he had two of the recovered spheres at home for research purposes," said Tony. "But we know he actually had three spheres and that one of them, Number 19, had never been in the hands of the DOE. When you add that to the discrepancy between the amount of money we found in his safe and what the DOE thought he had, it begins to sound like old Al Thompson was doing a little freelancing, doesn't it?"

"It certainly does," agreed Frank. "Maybe he threatened to go to the authorities if his partners didn't give him more money and they shot him to keep him quiet. We may never know the real story behind the old man's death, but he obviously knew more about the spheres than the DOE gave him credit for."

"Carlson and Edwards admitted that much to me in our first meeting," nodded Tony. "They said Thompson had maintained for years that the spheres were of alien origin but that nobody at the DOE would listen to him. They thought he was a crazy old fool but they tolerated him because they were interested in his sphere research."

"Speaking of Carlson," said Frank with a nod towards the back of the office, "here he comes now – and he doesn't look happy."

"So how are our geniuses doing?" ventured Frank.

"They're finally on their way up, but I just about had to shut off the fresh air supply to get them to agree," grumbled Carlson. "I'm going to get my butt kicked tomorrow because they overstayed the three-hour limit. That's one of the things the safety people around here aren't very flexible about."

"Have they learned anything yet, or have they spent all this time taking pictures?" asked Tony, trying to put a positive spin on things.

"As far as I can tell, they've just been taking pictures and there's been absolutely no evidence of any sphere activity in the three hours they've been down there – I just don't get it," shrugged Carlson. "How are you two doing?"

"We have some ideas, but nothing concrete yet," replied Frank. "We'll lay out everything we have as soon as it makes some sense to us. What's the plan for tonight? Are Jim and your guy going to start working on the translations right away or wait until tomorrow morning?"

"I'm not sure. My guess is that they will want to start right away, but it's almost midnight and I'd just as soon get some sleep and start fresh in the morning. What about you guys?"

"I'm with you," said Frank. "With the time zone changes, my body thinks it's 2:00 a.m. already."

"I vote for tomorrow, too," added Tony, "but I'd also like to get back to civilization pretty soon. I've been up here since Friday and, frankly, it's getting a little boring."

"I understand, believe me. I live up here most of the time, and this place gets really old," said Carlson. "Maybe I can arrange for a secure conference room at the Bechtel offices in North Las Vegas. You would be able to come and go as you pleased and you could have your cell phones back. That would make life a little simpler for me, too, since I wouldn't have to run an escort service."

A few minutes later the phone rang and Carlson answered it. When he hung up, he started for the back door, saying "They're finally topside. I'll go out and get them and then we can figure out what we're doing."

After some serious protests from Jim and his new friend Ben Kingston, the group finally agreed to call it a night and move the translation operation into Las Vegas the next morning, facilities permitting. During the dark and bumpy 20-minute ride back to Mercury, Jim detailed a list of things he would need for the translation project and Ben took notes for Carlson. Ben lived north of the city and normally commuted back and forth, but due to the late hour, he had decided to stay in guest housing for the night and go into Las Vegas with the others in the morning. He added several items to Jim's list that related to the digital camera they had used to record the spheres.

"I'll need some time in the morning to make the necessary arrangements, so how about if I pick you up at 8:30 a.m.?" asked Carlson, as the four other men got out of the rig. "Ben can take you over to the cafeteria for breakfast and I'll meet you there."

Everybody agreed and headed for their respective rooms and some sleep. Twice during the night they were awakened by the roar of low-flying jets.

"Three million acres of land and they have to test their damn airplanes right over my bedroom," mumbled Frank, as he stumbled off to the bathroom after the second incident. On his way back to bed, he detoured past his window and looked out through the curtains. In the distance, he could see what appeared to be searchlights. After watching for a minute, Frank realized that someone was looking for something off in the distance but he was so sleepy he flopped down on the bed and was asleep in an instant without giving it another thought.

At 7:30 a.m. there was a knock on Frank's door and when he opened it Tony, Jim and Ben Kingston were waiting on his doorstep. They looked like zombies with their eyes half closed and Frank laughed out loud. "Apparently you heard the fly boys, too," he said.

"Yeah, and the helicopters and the trucks! What the hell was going on last night, anyway?" grumbled Tony as they started across the street to the food service facility.

"I heard the planes, but I must have slept right through the rest of it," replied Frank. "Although I think I remember seeing lights off in the distance. I just assumed it was one of the war games they have out here. Ben, do you know what was going on?"

"Not a clue, but I'm pretty sure there aren't any exercises scheduled for this month. That kind of stuff usually happens in the fall. When I talked to Gene Carlson earlier this morning he sounded pretty harried, but that's normal for him. All he told me was that he'd made the arrangements at Bechtel and that he would meet us at 8:30 a.m., as planned."

As soon as the four men entered the food service building, Tony noticed a change in the atmosphere. The place seemed busier than usual and there was a nervous buzz of conversation everywhere.

"Something's definitely going on," he commented, as they took their trays and started down the cafeteria-style line.

About 8:15 a.m. Carlson arrived and joined them at the table. He was wearing the same clothes he had been wearing the day before and he obviously hadn't slept.

"Man, you look like hell," said the always subtle Tony. "Apparently the noise kept you awake, too. What was going on last night, anyway?"

"I'll tell you later, but right now I need to get you guys on your way. There's been a slight change of plans and I need to get back up on the hill," said Carlson, as he stood and signaled for the others to follow.

Once they were in the Cherokee, Carlson twisted in his seat and looked at the three civilians in the back. A look of genuine concern managed to show through the fatigue on his face.

"What I am about to tell you is classified but since it may have some bearing on the work you're doing for us, I think it's appropriate for you to know what went on last night. But you're not to speak a word of this to anyone, understand? That goes for you, too, Ben."

The three in the back seat, along with Ben Kingston, who was in the front passenger's seat, all nodded silently.

"As I'm sure you heard, we had a little excitement around here about 1:30 a.m. There are a lot of myths and rumors about things that go on out here, and most of them are complete fantasy, but last night we had an actual, confirmed UFO sighting – at least that's what we're calling it for now. I can't give you a lot of details, but suffice it to say that the sudden appearance of an unidentified aircraft over this facility has rattled the complex to its core. The planes you heard were scrambled from Nellis and Edwards but by the time they got here our 'visitor' was gone, and so, apparently, is the pyramid."

"What!" interrupted Frank. "Are you saying that the pyramid was somehow removed from this facility last night?"

"It seems so. We're not sure exactly what happened, but during all the commotion our security team out there missed a radio check. Once things had settled down, a supervisor went out to check on them and found both men unconscious in their vehicle. In addition, the entire hillside where the pyramid had been buried was collapsed, as if the pyramid had been lifted out with a crane. That's the part that affects you, because there is suddenly a great deal of interest in what information your translation of the spheres may provide."

"Damn!" exclaimed Tony. "What about the guards? Have they been questioned?"

"They were in some sort of coma, almost like a hypnotic trance, but they seem to be coming around. Just before I came over here I was told that they would be well enough for questioning within the hour. I'll let you know what we find out, if anything.

"Gentlemen, your work, and any knowledge you have about the spheres, is now classified Top Secret in the interest of national security," continued Carlson. "I have some documents here that you must sign before you leave government property and I want you to read them very carefully because this is serious business." Carlson produced three sets of papers from a folder and handed one set each to Frank, Tony and Jim.

"Ben, you have already signed this agreement, so just let me remind you that from now on everything you know or learn about this matter is to be handled on a Need to Know basis only. You are not to discuss it with anyone except myself and these three men, do you understand?"

"Of course," replied Ben.

"I'll be providing you additional information about last night's incident as it becomes available, but for now I need to get you all to work. Unfortunately, I won't be able to go back to Vegas with you to make the introductions, but the folks at Bechtel are waiting for you and they have been instructed to cooperate in any way necessary and to provide anything you need," said Carlson, as he collected the signed documents from Frank, Tony and Jim.

Carlson handed Ben a sealed brown government routing envelope and continued with his instructions. "Since Ben is the only one actually on the government's payroll, I'm putting him officially in charge of this group, because it will make communications and resource allocation easier, but I assume you will all work as a team of equals. This envelope contains everything we know so far and some special instruction you can read later. It also includes some documents you will need to present when you arrive at Bechtel, since technically you will become contract employees of theirs until we finish this investigation."

Carlson saw the look of protest on Tony's face and continued before Tony had a chance to utter a word. "I know, and I'm sorry to 'draft' you guys like this, but this is the quickest and easiest way to get you the resources you need. Internally, we will create a special investigative unit, assign you four to it and deal with the rest of the necessary bureaucracy later. All you guys have to do is the detective work. Any questions?"

Frank cleared his throat and said, "We're all a little surprised by this, of course, but I think we're all on board. I would like to make an addition to Jim's list of resources, though. If possible, I would like to recruit a researcher from Seattle named Linda McBride to be part of our team. She has access to information and resources that may be very helpful with some of the stuff Tony and I were working on last night."

"McBride," said Carlson, thinking out loud, "I think her name came up when we ran your background check a few days ago. I can't make any promises, but I'll see what I can do. Please don't say anything to her about this until we clear her. If she checks out, we'll send a plane for her. Now, off you go. I'll drop you at the guard shack, return your cells phones, firearms and vehicle and let you get started. Good luck, gentlemen. We're counting on you to fill in a lot of missing pieces for us."

As Carlson backed out of the parking space in front of the food service building, Frank looked at Tony and asked, "Firearms?"

"It's a long story," sighed Tony, as he caught a glimpse of Carlson smiling in the rear view mirror.

On their way back to Las Vegas, the conversation in the Durango covered a broad range of subjects from the mysterious Indians who delivered the spheres to the previous night's disappearance of the pyramid.

"Jim, didn't you tell Carlson last night that you thought the pyramid was deactivated? What made you think that?" asked Frank.

"It was just a feeling, Frank. When we were out at the burial site, I felt a sense of emptiness or death or something like that. It was similar to the feeling I've had the few times I've been inside an ancient burial tomb. Down in the vault, the feeling was even stronger. Carlson had built us up with all this anticipation about sphere activity and when we got there, they were just cold, metal balls."

"So what do you think is really going on, now that you know the pyramid was somehow removed from the site early this morning?" asked Tony.

"I don't know. Maybe whatever energy source it contained or controlled had been turned off last night. That would explain the lack of sphere activity, at least. Possibly the accident involving the engineer triggered some automatic shut-down mechanism."

"Yeah, it probably just blew a fuse and last night a maintenance crew showed up to tow it in for repairs," laughed Tony, mostly to himself. "But seriously, does anybody have a take on last night? As much as it sounds like a plot for a low-budget sci-fi movie, what are the possibilities that the 'mother ship' returned last night to collect its broken pyramid?"

The Durango was quiet for several seconds before the group's newest member, Ben Kingston finally broke the silence.

"I'm pretty sure that won't be the 'official' position, gentlemen, but from the little time I was able to spend with Dr. Thompson, I can assure you that he would support that theory, or one like it. He was very much convinced that the spheres were alien in origin and I'm sure he would have made the same claim about the pyramid, if he'd known about it."

"As long as you've brought up the subject of Al Thompson, Ben, what can you tell us about him? His step-daughter didn't really know him that well, and we've turned up some unusual facts relating to the good doctor that don't seem to add up," said Frank.

"I'm afraid I don't know too much about the man, either," replied Ben, apologetically. "I was assigned to work with him about two months ago when Buzz Edwards and some of his associates convinced their superiors that Dr. Thompson was beginning to degenerate mentally. Apparently he had always been a little eccentric, but for some reason they felt he was beginning to slip over the edge."

"And what were you doing before you were assigned to Thompson?" asked Tony. "Are you also a nuclear physicist?"

"Me? Heavens, no!" replied a surprised Ben. "I assumed Carlson had told you that I'm an exobiologist on loan from NASA's Ames Research Center in California."

"A what?" questioned Tony.

"An exobiologist – someone who studies the origin and evolution of life in the universe," replied Ben, matter-of-factly.

"In other words, Tony, he studies alien life forms," added Frank. "Why in the hell would the DOE assign an exobioloist to work with a nuclear physicist who is allegedly investigating the energy source of a metal sphere?"

"I think Dr. Thompson's insistence that the spheres were of alien origin finally wore Carlson and Edwards down. I was brought in primarily to investigate whether or not the spheres might be a life form rather than an inanimate object with a mysterious power source," explained Ben.

"And what is your opinion?" asked a fascinated Jim.

"Well, in exobiology we define 'life form' in rather broad terms and I haven't yet come to a final conclusion, but I tend to think that the spheres are simply objects of an unknown origin with an unknown purpose that are sustained by an unknown power source," replied Ben.

"In other words, you don't have a clue!" exclaimed Tony.

"That's correct," smiled Ben. "The fact of the matter is that we have learned very little about the spheres since the first one was discovered fifty years ago and I've only been involved with them for the past two months. Hopefully, Jim's translations will shed some light on the purpose of these spheres, which may, in turn, tell us something about their true origin. Now that all of the spheres are locked up at the bottom of the mountain, my research is going to become a lot more difficult."

"That's true," agreed Tony. "These guys were already afraid of the spheres and, after last night, they'll be really spooked."

All the talk about aliens must have had an effect on the group, because when Jim's cell phone rang it startled everyone.

"Hi, Carmen!" said a pleasantly surprised Jim. "It's really good to hear from you. How are things in Merida?"

There was a long pause while Jim listened. In a whisper, Frank tried to explain to Ben who the caller was, but he didn't understand.

"I'm very sorry to hear that, Carmen, but I appreciate the information. Thank you for calling. Could you send me the details by e-mail when you have a chance? Yes, that's the address. Listen, how about if I call you later this afternoon? Okay, great, I'll talk to you then. And, again, my sincere condolences."

Jim folded up his cell phone and clipped it back to his belt while everyone waited for an explanation.

Tony's patience ran out first, and he finally shouted, "Well?"

"That was Carmen but I guess you know that, huh? Anyway, she called to tell me that the authorities in Merida think they may have located the remains of the long lost Professor Torres. A highway collapsed into a sink hole north of town a few days ago and while they were excavating they discovered human skeletal remains. The sink hole apparently exposed an underground river that flows north into the Gulf of Mexico and may connect to the stream we saw in the *Loltún* caverns. At any rate, the medical examiner has positively identified the bones as those of Torres."

"Did you say Torres?" asked Ben with a puzzled expression on his face.

"Yes, why? Do you know that name, Ben?" asked Jim.

"It's probably not the same person, but Dr. Thompson used to talk about someone named Torres. I think he said they met while Dr. Thompson and his second wife were on their honeymoon," replied Ben. "But it couldn't be the same person, could it?"

Frank, Tony and Jim were stunned. "Did Thompson ever mention Merida, or the Yucatan Peninsula?" pressed Frank.

Ben relaxed a little and said, "No, he never mentioned either of those. The name Torres must just be a coincidence because the only place I ever heard Dr. Thompson mention was a place he and his wife visited on their trip – a place called *Loltún*, I think."

Chapter 27

Ben Kingston's revelation about the connection between Al Thompson and Professor Torres had left Frank, Tony and Jim stunned. They looked at each other in disbelief, but as each one mulled over the events of the past two weeks, pieces of the puzzle started to fit together.

Frank was the first to speak. "The locket Jill found in her stepfather's safe, remember? I noticed an inscription on the back and when Jill turned it over it read 'Remember *Loltún*.' Al must have given it to her mother when they were on their honeymoon."

Next it was Jim's turn. "And it's no wonder Professor Torres was so intent on finding spheres, even though he had never actually seen one. If Thompson had ever mentioned that the spheres being found up here had Maya glyphs on them, Professor Torres would have taken up the challenge to find them purely out of scientific curiosity."

"But why at *Loltún*?" asked Frank. "What would have made him focus his investigation there?"

Finally, it was Tony's turn. "Maybe he asked around until someone told him about the shamans' orbs story, just like the manager of the Lodge at *Uxmal* told us. In fact, if he found out about the orbs from someone in the *Uxmal* area, *Loltún* would be an obvious place to look, wouldn't it?"

"Sure it would, and that reminds me of something Alfredo said the day he and his son took us down into *Loltún*," added Jim. "As we were pulling away from the hotel, he asked Frank if he was there to find the 'mysterious spheres of Professor Torres', or something to that effect."

"Well, I suggest we put Linda on the Thompson/Torres mysteries if the Feds let her join us. We need to learn as much about them as we can, especially what Thompson was up to during the past few months," said Frank.

The rest of the ride to Las Vegas was filled with speculation about the purpose of the spheres and the origin of the Indians responsible for carrying them to Nevada, but nobody had any convincing theories.

When they reached the city, Frank drove directly to the Residence Inn.

"Just a quick stop to pick up my computer," he said as they pulled into the parking lot.

"I'd better leave my hand gun here, too," said Tony. "I don't imagine they'd be too happy to see that at this place where Carlson is sending us."

A few minutes later they pulled up to the guard shack at Bechtel's parking lot in North Las Vegas. There was a sign out front that read 'Bechtel Nevada Special Projects.'

"Well, this must be the place," said Frank, as he rolled down the window.

Frank gave the guard his name and handed him the brown envelope Carlson had given to Ben. After reviewing the documentation, he asked Frank to pull into the closest parking space while the Durango was searched. A few minutes later they were cleared and directed to a building nearby.

"Here's a temporary pass for your vehicle, sir," said the guard. "Please display this each time you come through the gate and leave it on your dashboard when you are on the property."

Frank moved the Durango closer to the building indicated by the guard and the four entered through the nearest door. From the moment they entered the building it was obvious that they were expected, but it still took another hour before they were finally alone in a conference room and ready to begin the task of unraveling the mystery of the spheres. There had been more paperwork, photos for their new ID badges, still more paperwork, and finally a security briefing. In typical psuedo-military style, the group was assigned the code name *Special Unit Alpha* and they were given an unlisted telephone number that would ring directly into the conference room, bypassing the Bechtel switchboard.

As for the conference room, it was located one floor below the main entrance. It was a large room, maybe twenty-four feet square, with no outside windows. In the center of the room there was a large conference table with seating for ten. Three workstations, each equipped with a high-end PC and direct Internet access were arranged on small tables along one wall. Another small table on the opposite wall held a large urn of fresh coffee, a dozen plain white mugs, a tray of condiments and coffee-making supplies.

Next to the table there was an apartment-sized refrigerator stocked with soft drinks and bottled water.

During the briefing, Ben had been given the combination to the keypad that opened the conference room door, along with instructions to keep the door closed and locked at all times. He had handed the combination off to Frank before they ever left the briefing room.

The Bechtel staffers had done an excellent job of rounding up the requested items on such short notice. There was a wide-carriage photo-quality printer for processing the camera images and a number of hard-to-find books that Jim had requested. An overhead projector and screen were stored neatly in one corner and a large photocopier occupied another corner. A dozen writing pads and a box of blue BIC pens had been placed in the center of the conference table, and someone had even thought to include a calculator with a built-in printer.

When Frank had completed his survey of the room, he turned to the others and said, "Well, gang, let's get this show on the road. Ben, you and Jim should probably work down there, near the PC with the printer. Tony, how about if you help me put together a timeline and a list of unanswered questions? I think we need to convert the past two weeks into an objective outline of what we know and what we don't know."

At 12:30 p.m. a large black man dressed in cook's whites delivered a tray of sandwiches, chips, and deserts. Rather than breaking for lunch, each man snacked when he felt like it or when it was convenient. By 1:30 p.m. Jim and Ben had printed all the pictures they needed and Jim sat down at the conference table to begin work on the translations. At first, everybody gathered around to watch, but it didn't take them long to realize that watching Jim work was about as exciting as watching paint dry.

Ben offered to help Frank and Tony with their compilation and he turned out to be an excellent secretary. He had a unique combination of skills and he suggested that he key Frank and Tony's notes into a word processor for easier manipulation. As they were waiting for the first draft to print out, the telephone on the big table rang. Tentatively, Frank answered it and was surprised to hear Linda's voice.

"Frank, a very official looking person just showed up in my office and told me you had requested my presence as soon as possible. Do you know anything about this?" Linda's voice sounded like she was on the verge of tears.

"Yes, I'm afraid I do," apologized Frank, "but I didn't think you would be contacted so soon! We're in the middle of something pretty big down here, Linda, and I could really use your help if you can get away. The guy who's there with you can probably clear it with your boss and he has a private jet waiting to bring you here. How about it?"

"Sure, I'd love to! Are you still in..."

"Not over the telephone, Linda. I'll explain why when you get here," interrupted Frank.

"Okay. Man, this sounds like a real adventure. What should I pack?" asked Linda.

"Just throw together some casual clothes and personal stuff for a week or so – we'll take care of the rest. You can ask the guy who's there with you what the weather is like where we are."

"Okay, then, I guess I'm on my way. See you soon," said a relieved Linda.

Frank hung up and announced to the group, "Linda is on her way. Tony, Ben and I are just about done with our list of open issues – how are you doing on the spheres, Jim?"

Jim was so engrossed in his work that he hadn't even heard Frank talking, so Ben walked down to where Jim was hunched over a photo and picked up a sheet of paper he had helped Jim complete earlier. He scanned down the page and announced, "Jim has finished three more spheres. They're dated 1817, 630 and... Jim, what's this number?"

Jim looked up, oblivious to everything around him. He glanced at the sheet Ben held in front of him, studied it for a second, and replied, "That's 446 BC. It's the earliest one I've found so far."

Jim suddenly noticed that everybody in the room was staring at him and he asked "What? Did I miss something?"

"No, Jim, good work. Let us know if you find anything interesting, okay?"

"Sure," mumbled Jim as he quickly immersed himself back into his work.

As Ben moved back to the other end of the table, he said, "I did notice that all the spheres he's done today have a Maya city written next to them. What's that all about?"

Frank explained the theory that the dates corresponded to solar eclipses that occurred at specific Maya locations. "All except #20," he added. "That one indicates the exact location of where the pyramid was buried and the date on it is December 21, 2012. That doesn't correspond to an eclipse in Nevada."

"Wow!" said Ben. "That's really interesting stuff. No wonder Edwards wanted you guys on this case. That's more information about the spheres than the DOE has uncovered in the fifty years since they started collecting them. So, it sounds like the spheres served as a kind of post-it-note for whoever possessed them. Each one was the reminder of an important event, like the solar eclipse."

"Post-it-notes, hmmmm," said Frank. "You know, you might be on to something there, Ben. But there have been a lot more than twenty total eclipses since 446 BC. I wonder what was so special about those twenty eclipses."

"Actually it's only nineteen, since the last one doesn't mark an eclipse," corrected Tony. "And maybe the eclipses were just a cover. You already know that on one of those dates there were a large number of UFO sightings in Mexico City. What if the spheres were reminders, just as Ben suggested, not of eclipses but of the return of some aliens?"

Frank laughed and then realized that neither Tony nor Ben was smiling. "Oh, come on you guys! You don't really believe that, do you?"

"Frank, I'm an exobiologist – it's my job to believe in alien life," replied Ben. "That's why I was brought in to work with Dr. Thompson in the first place, remember?"

"And besides, Frank, how else do you explain the mysterious disappearance of the pyramid?" challenged Tony.

"Well, personally, I'm not willing to accept that idea quite yet," shrugged Frank. "I realize the spheres have some interesting characteristics, and I'd even be willing to accept that they are made from an unusual, and so far undetermined, substance, but let's not jump too far ahead, guys. What if the Maya, or whoever, found a large meteorite and forged these things themselves? Or what if this is all a carefully planned hoax? Let's not lose sight of all the possibilities in our rush to find some little green men."

After an awkward silence, Ben agreed. "Frank's right. There may be other possible explanations, and it's our scientific responsibility to eliminate them before we start creating theories of our own, because…"

"This is the oldest one yet!" exclaimed Jim from the other end of the room. "I believe this date is May 9, 922 B.C., which would be during the very earliest days of Maya history – the Early Preclassic period, we call it."

"How are we doing with locations, Jim? Do these new ones you've translated indicate Maya cities like the first three did?" asked Frank.

Jim shook his head. "Not exactly, but they all reference locations in the Maya realm of influence. The locations on the two earliest ones don't coincide with any cities or ruins that we know of, but, again, those dates are in the earliest days of the Maya. It could be that these sites have been completely eradicated by time. Or they may be so deteriorated that they just haven't been rediscovered yet. Every year another two or three 'previously unknown' sites are discovered in the forests of the Yucatan or the jungles of Guatemala."

"Okay, Tony and I can work on that a little later. And Ben, how about getting on one of those computers and seeing if you can correlate Jim's new dates to solar eclipses. We need to make sure that part of the hypothesis is still holding, too."

"Sure, I'd be happy to. Here's the printout of your questions," said Ben as he handed Frank several sheets from the printer and headed for a workstation.

Frank sat down at the table and scanned the paper. "Okay, let's go over this one more time and make sure we haven't left something out," he said to Tony.

"*Item 1: Who shot Al Thompson and why?* We need to dig a little deeper into his associations during the months before his death and explore the possibility that he might have been planning to sell information or spheres, or both, to some third party.

"*Item 2: Why the discrepancy between the amount of money we found in the old man's safe and the amount the DOE thinks he had?* The answer here is probably related directly to Item 1.

"*Item 3: Where did the spheres come from?* We're assuming they were brought to Nevada from *Loltún*, so what we really want to know is how did they get to *Loltún*?

"*Item 4: What is the purpose of the spheres?* At least some of them indicate dates and locations of total solar eclipses and we're checking each new translation as Jim finishes it. You and Ben think they may indicate extraterrestrial visits.

"*Item 5: Who is, or was, bringing the spheres to Nevada, and why?* An answer here might also answer Items 3 and 4.

"*Item 6: What caused the deaths of the couriers?* Item 5 may also answer this one.

"We think we know what happened to the Mexican professor – an unfortunate accident when he became lost in the underground stream – and the reason the spheres were being delivered to the Nevada Test Site was probably because of the buried pyramid, which brings us to the last item.

"*Item 7: The Pyramid – where did it come from, why was it here and where has it gone?*"

Frank pushed the sheet of paper across to Tony and asked, "Anything else we need to add?"

Tony studied the list for a moment and then replied, "No, I think that's plenty! If we knew what the pyramid was all about we'd probably be able to answer most of these other questions, too. There's something that's bothered me ever since my first meeting with Edwards and Carlson and now that the pyramid is apparently gone, it's even more puzzling. Apparently these Indians, or whoever they are, delivered spheres, one at a time, out to the site of the pyramid and buried them in the sand directly over the pyramid. Once their mission was accomplished, they lay down on top of the sphere, as if to protect it, and died. Am I right so far?"

Listening intently, Frank nodded agreement.

"Okay, so if these spheres are so important that they had to be hand-carried from the Yucatan to Nevada and claim the life of the carrier, then why were they still there, buried in the sand for the DOE boys to find several days later? Why didn't the pyramid assimilate them, or whatever pyramids do to spheres? Why were they left there in the ground for someone to find?"

"Good point," said Frank. "And the location was plainly marked with a dead body. Not exactly the way to hide something, is it?"

"And another thing," added Tony, "just a few hours after Carlson tried his little experiment of burying the twentieth sphere in the sand, the whole damn pyramid disappears! Do you think that was just a coincidence?"

"Okay, what if the pyramid didn't really want the spheres themselves, but instead it was programmed to depart as soon as they had all 'checked in?' How about that idea?" asked Frank.

Ben, who had been listening in on the debate from his place at the nearest computer, returned to the table with the list of Jim's new translations. "These all check out, so far," he said, as he handed the paper back to Frank. "Every one of these dates matches the date of a total solar eclipse that occurred somewhere in the Maya regions of Mexico, Belize, Guatemala or Honduras."

"Okay, thanks. Let's continue to check each new translation as soon as Jim finishes it, but I suspect the pattern will hold, since this makes seven in a row."

"You know, I was listening to your discussion just now, and if the pyramid actually was designed to leave soon after the last sphere arrived, you guys may have disrupted some grand cosmic timetable," smiled Ben. "That twentieth sphere is the only one, so far, to have a date in the future, and it certainly wasn't delivered to the pyramid by its appointed carrier or at its designated time."

"Oh, crap, you're right," said Tony. "It was still safe and sound in its little cave down in Mexico until Frank started poking around. What if it wasn't supposed to be brought to Nevada until 2012?"

"Relax, guys. I doubt very much if the presence of the last sphere made any difference. And besides, if these things really are alien, don't you think creatures capable of making them could probably afford a calendar? Now let's get back to work, here. There are several other things we need to check out while Jim finishes up on the translations."

About 5:15 p.m. there was a knock on the door. "I'll get it," said Frank, getting up from a complicated chart he had been working on. "Maybe that's Linda."

Frank opened the door to find one of the Bechtel staffers outside, with Linda timidly standing behind him. "Ms. McBride is here, Mr. Morton. It's too late to process her security credentials today, so I've issued her a temporary visitor's badge. One of you will have to escort her at all times while she is in the building the rest of the day and we'll get her paperwork done first thing tomorrow. Sorry for the inconvenience."

And with that, the Bechtel employee was gone and Linda was face to face with Frank. For a moment, she looked as if she were going to cry, but then a huge smile broke out and she threw her arms around Frank's neck.

"God, this place is spooky!" she exclaimed, as she stepped back and tried to look professional. "I mean, these people just about kidnapped me right out of my office, and the creep that took me by my condo followed me around like a puppy. He even stood at attention outside the door while I went to the bathroom."

"Sorry, Kid, but that's the way they're trained," apologized Frank, as he stepped aside and waved Linda into the conference room. "I don't like it, either, but let me catch you up and then maybe you'll have a better appreciation for why we're working with these folks."

After some introductions, Frank and Tony took turns filling in the past two weeks for Linda, who hung on every word. She had been exposed to little bits and pieces of the story as a result of the research Frank had asked her to do, but none of it had made any sense until now.

"Jim's down there translating the remaining spheres, and that about covers it," said Frank, summing up. "So now you understand why our hosts act the way they do."

"Yeah, wow, I mean ..." stuttered Linda. "Guys, this is huge! In the newspaper business, this would be called the scoop of the millennium – maybe of all time." Noticing the panic starting to set into Frank's face, she quickly added, "Of course, I realize none of this can ever become public information, but just imagine!"

"Well, we hope you can help us dig up some answers to a few very tough questions," said Frank, as he handed her the list he and Tony had been working on. "Here's where we are right now and we'd like you to start with some plain old detective work. Find out everything there is to know about Professor Torres, Al Thompson and how they might have been associated. We also need anything you can dig up on Al's recent past, although we may have to go back up to Beatty to learn very much."

Frank glanced at his watch and said, "Let's work for a couple more hours and then knock off for the night. We're all going to need food by then, and we can discuss tomorrow's game plan over dinner."

Frank called the Residence Inn and booked additional rooms for Jim and Linda. He offered to get one for Ben, but Ben declined.

"I only live about fifteen minutes northwest of here," explained Ben. "If I can get a neighbor to look after my cat, maybe I'll stay closer to town tomorrow, but I really need to get home tonight. And since my car is still up in Mercury, I guess I'll have to ask you for a ride home."

"I'll take you home, that's no problem," said Frank. "And maybe Carlson can have someone meet you tomorrow morning and run you back up to Mercury for your car. Why don't you plan on staying in town with us after tonight, though. We may be working long and unusual hours and it would be more convenient if we were closer together. If you can't find a cat sitter, bring it with you – we can always use the extra help," smiled Frank.

By 7:00 p.m., most of the team were ready to call it a day. Jim was blurry-eyed from staring at photographs of the spheres, Frank and Tony were both suffering from lack of sleep due to the UFO incident the night before in Mercury, and Ben was bored. Only Linda seemed alert and reluctant to stop.

"I'm just getting started," she protested. "After the years of meaningless stuff I've had to research for the newspaper, this is one of the few times I'm really interested in my work."

"I'm glad you're enjoying your research, but we can't leave you here alone and the rest of us are beat. You can pick this up in the morning. Come on, let's get some dinner and then you can tell me all about it on the way back from Ben's place."

Frank chose the Texas Station Hotel, a few blocks from the conference room, for dinner because the place would be bustling with activity and so noisy that it would be hard for anyone to overhear them talking. It was the first time since arriving at the Bechtel facility that Frank had been able to get Jim's attention because he had been so involved in his translations. Frank had spent the past two hours trying to correlate the translated dates with something, but there just didn't seem to be any pattern, and he asked Jim about this.

"I agree," said Jim, "it doesn't make sense that these dates would simply be random, especially if they really do correspond to some sort of visit. On the other hand, the fact that they seem to be tied to eclipses limits the possible choices. Maybe tomorrow we can spend some more time on this correlation theory. I should be finished with the last translation by noon and then we'll have the whole picture."

Tony agreed. "If the visitation theory is true, Frank, maybe the dates just fit somebody's cosmic travel plans. You know, back when I was driving cross country, if I had plotted the dates I was in any particular city it would have looked pretty random, because each trip was different and I didn't always take the same route. Maybe you're looking for a pattern that doesn't exist."

Ben added his professional two cents worth. "It's a common mistake in science, Frank. Theories are developed to fit the data and then the theoretician uses the data to substantiate his or her theory. Later, the truth turns out to be something completely different."

"Okay, maybe there isn't a pattern to the dates, but they were sure important to somebody. Important enough to warrant the creation and distribution of the spheres and important enough to justify the sacrifice of nineteen lives. I'm not done looking for a correlation but that can all wait until tomorrow. Let's get out of here and get some rest. Maybe a theory will come to me in my sleep," he said with a tired smile.

After the meal, Frank dropped Jim and Tony off at the Residence Inn and headed north with Ben and Linda in the Durango. About thirty miles north of Las Vegas they came to a new housing development along U.S. 95 and Ben directed Frank to his house.

"Man, you sure live out in the sticks," commented Frank, as they pulled up in front of a newer two-story house.

"It's the closest thing I could find to Mercury that was decent" said Ben, as he climbed down from the Durango. "A lot of my neighbors commute from here into the city, which can actually take longer than the drive to Mercury, depending on the traffic. I'll see you in the morning, but it won't be too early, because I have to go get my car. Good night!"

As Ben walked up the sidewalk to his house, Linda commented, "Nice man. He doesn't seem like the kind of guy you'd expect to find searching for little green men, though, does he?"

"No, but he does seem to know his stuff. Apparently the DOE assigned him to work with Dr. Thompson because the old man kept insisting that the spheres were alien and they wanted to cover all their bases."

"Just the same," said Linda, as she jotted down the number on the house Ben had just entered, "I'd like to check him out tomorrow. Let's make sure he's really who he says he is."

Chapter 28

The next morning Frank, Tony, Jim and Linda met at the Durango at 7:30 a.m. and stopped at a small coffee shop on Lake Mead Boulevard for breakfast. After a good night's sleep, Jim was ready to get back to work on the translations and Linda wanted to do her own background investigation on Ben Kingston before he arrived.

"You seem to be pretty suspicious of Ben," said Frank, as he finished off his three-egg omelet.

"Maybe it's just woman's intuition," replied Linda, "but something doesn't seem right there. I'll run a quick check and if nothing turns up I'll forget it, okay?"

"Take as much time as you need. You're a part of the team, now, and you need to be comfortable with the other members. Does anybody else have any reservations about Ben?" asked Frank as he scanned the faces of Tony and Jim.

Both of them shook their heads, but after he swallowed another gulp of coffee Tony reconsidered and said, "Of course, he was thrust onto us by Carlson without any real discussion and I had my own reservations about Carlson, Edwards and that whole crew up there when I first met them. There's no question in my mind that they put their own interests first."

Frank nodded. "I had similar feelings about Edwards when he first approached Jim and me in Mexico, but he has a way of making you feel like he's contributing to your cause and it's easier to trust someone who's helping you."

"Frankly," added Jim, looking up from the last of his breakfast, "I've wondered why Edwards made that trip to Mexico in the first place. He was there less than twenty-four hours, and his real interest seemed to be in what we were doing, rather than in the spheres. I'm certainly not complaining about the ride back in a private jet, mind you, but it seemed a little too convenient to me."

"Well, technically, Ben *is* the project leader, so we'll have to find a way to tolerate him, even if he turns out to be something other than what he claims. Either that or we'll have to give up our DOE support and the facilities."

On the way from the restaurant to the Bechtel facility, the four agreed to keep any new discoveries to themselves as much as they could until they had a chance to discuss them privately. Jim would continue with his translations, of course, but he wouldn't provide any personal interpretations until he had a chance to discuss them with Frank, Tony and Linda. The others all agreed to do the same – work publicly but think privately.

Once inside their temporary headquarters, the four quickly set about their agreed-upon tasks. Jim retreated into his own world as he got back into the translations, Linda took up a position at one of the computer workstations and Tony joined Frank at the conference table to continue working on the correlation of the spheres' dates. Frank still felt that there had to be some special significance to the dates but Tony was sticking to his idea that the dates just happened to coincide with some cosmic visitor's travel itinerary.

An hour later, Frank was beginning to agree. Nothing they tried seemed to agree with more than a couple of the dates. Jim had finished another translation, the ninth, and its date was November 12, 12 AD. Frank added it to the large timeline he had been constructing, but it didn't help clear up anything.

As he and Tony were standing at the table staring down at the chart, Linda got up from her workstation and wiggled in between them. Frank and Tony both thought she was just being cute until she laid a piece of paper containing a handwritten note down on top of the chart. Frank and Tony read the note, glanced at each other and at Linda with raised eyebrows. She nodded slightly and returned to her workstation, leaving Frank and Tony standing at the table.

Before either Tony or Frank could say anything, there was a knock. Linda, the closest to the door, opened it a crack to see who was there and then opened for Ben.

"Good morning," Ben said brightly. "Sorry I'm so late, but my ride to Mercury was running late and then Carlson wanted to talk to me. He said he hopes that the facilities here are adequate and that you are satisfied with the support you're getting from the Bechtel folks."

Frank nodded acknowledgement and replied, "The next time you see him you can tell him that the setup here is great."

"Oh, you can tell him yourself, Frank, because he also asked if the four of you would join him for dinner tonight at the Officers' Club out at Nellis. He'd like you to meet him at the main gate at 8:00 p.m., but if that doesn't work for any of you, you can call him and reschedule. Here's his direct line up at the Test Site." Ben handed Frank a small piece of paper with a telephone number written on it.

Frank scanned the room for objections and asked with a smile, "Anybody have other plans? No? Well, then I guess we'll dine on the government's nickel tonight." To Ben, he said, "I'll call him and confirm. Will you be joining us?"

"No, I'm afraid not. I have a prior commitment that I can't get out of. Besides, I think he just wants to get a progress report and give you all the "Welcome Aboard" talk. I've already heard that speech," smiled Ben.

"Yes, I'm sure you have," replied Frank. "Apparently you've heard it several times."

Surprised by Frank's cold tone, Ben said, "What do you mean, Frank?"

Frank picked Linda's note up off the table and handed it to Ben. "Well, it seems that before being transferred to the Department of Energy two months ago, you were assigned to the Department of Defense. You neglected to mention that yesterday. And since you purchased your house a little over three years ago, it would follow that your DOD duties were conducted on or near the Nellis complex, wouldn't it? Why don't we all sit down and listen to the real story of Ben Kingston – otherwise the four of us are out of here right now," bluffed Frank, "and *you* can explain our departure to Carlson and Edwards."

Slowly, Ben sat down and stared at the conference table, but he didn't respond to Frank's charges.

"Okay, folks, let's pack up our things and clear out. We've been on the level with these people from the beginning and if they aren't going to treat us with the same respect, then they can go to hell," announced Frank sternly.

Fortunately, Ben couldn't see the look of shock and surprise on the faces of the others in the room. "No, wait!" he said, with a tone of fear in his voice. "Please, I'll tell you what I can, but the rest you're going to have to get from Carlson or Edwards. I have very strict guidelines about what I can and can't share with you."

The others sat down and even Jim interrupted his work to join the group. Ben looked around the table at the four and then began his story.

"You're right, of course. Although I actually do work for the Ames Research Center, I was assigned to the DOD almost four years ago to assist them on a special project out at the complex. A couple of months ago I was asked to help Edwards' unit investigate this sphere thing because it had some possible connections to my work with the DOD."

Frank started to interrupt, but Ben cut him off. "Before you ask, I can't tell you anything about that work, not even a single word, so please don't ask. If you have a problem with that, you'll have to take it up with Carlson tonight. I'm sorry, but that's the way it is."

Frank nodded and motioned for Ben to continue.

"Okay, I've been holding back some information to make sure you folks were on the up-and-up. But like you said, Frank, you've been on the level with us, so I'll tell you what I can.

"When the first sphere showed up in 1951, it was considered an oddity, but the Atomic Energy Commission was in the middle of a series of nuclear tests and nobody had time to think about anything else. The incident was logged but there was never any follow-up done. By the time the third or fourth one turned up, though, folks realized that somebody was going to have to answer a lot of questions if word of the spheres ever got out, so all information relating to them was quietly swept under the carpet.

"This practice continued more or less unchanged until about two years ago – a dirty tradition passed on from one facility director to the next. There was an incident about ten years ago involving Professor Torres, but other than that the spheres became just another one of the many secrets buried out there in the Nellis sand.

"Then, about two years ago, Dr. Thompson threatened to go public if the DOE didn't take his claims seriously so a special unit was formed and an extensive cover story was concocted. All the spheres were rounded up and put under lock and key. A story was created that made the fifty-year cover-up appear to be an intentional act of super secrecy in the name of national security and Thompson was allowed to continue with his investigation to keep him quiet. As information about the spheres began to surface under the protection of the cover story, some people, like Edwards and Carlson, began to take the old man's stories seriously and eventually I was brought in to help with the investigation."

Ben ended his monologue and went to the refrigerator for a bottle of water. When he returned to the table, he looked at Frank, Tony and Linda, one at a time, and asked, "Any questions?"

All four started to talk at once, and Ben held up his hand with a smile.

Frank was the first to get his question in. "What about the incident involving Professor Torres?"

"Unfortunately, Thompson and Torres hit it off when they met in Mexico and the DOE was afraid Thompson had shared sensitive information with Torres. They sent an agent down to find out exactly how much Torres knew but the Professor got spooked and fled into the caverns to hide. It now appears that he headed down the underground river to escape and died in the process. An unfortunate accident, really, because the agent just wanted to ask the old Professor some questions."

"Yeah, I'll bet he did! I wonder if they sent an agent out to question Thompson a couple of weeks ago," said Tony sarcastically.

"No, I didn't hear anything about... oh, you mean the night he was shot," replied Ben. "You don't actually think that the DOE would shoot one of their own employees in cold blood, do you?" asked Ben in disbelief.

"Well, maybe not the DOE, but how about the DOD?" snapped Tony. "Where were you that night, Ben?"

"I was at a home owners' meeting at a neighbor's house when they called to tell me about the shooting," replied Ben in a matter-of-fact tone, "but I understand you were with him just a few minutes before he was shot."

Tony jumped up from the table in anger, but Frank intervened. "Okay, you two, calm down. We're all on the same side, I think, and we don't need any accusations. Does the government have any leads, Ben?"

"No, not really. It could have been something as simple as a drifter who just happened by as Thompson was walking home from the casino that night but I don't think robbery is considered one of the motives, is it?"

"No, we saw evidence of a robbery when we were at his mobile home a few days later, but we think we know who was responsible for that," replied Frank.

"You mean the Indian, of course," replied Ben. "I read the Sheriff's report, but I'm not sure I agree with it. The intruder you caught, Tony, seems to have been interested in one, and only one, of the spheres, right? There were actually two in the old man's safe, along with a lot of money, and yet the Indian was satisfied with the one sphere you gave him – the one he was found dead with the next day. He was clearly on a mission and not interested in the other sphere or the cash."

"That's true," agreed Frank. "We've discussed that ourselves. The second sphere, the one the Indian didn't see, had been previously recovered out at the pyramid site. The one we handed over to him was apparently taken from him while he was attempting to deliver it a couple of weeks earlier. That's why he was so anxious to get it back and as soon as he had it he completed his mission and died at the site."

"That's correct," agreed Ben. "The DOE thought Thompson had two spheres, but apparently he had three – the two he had on loan from the Yucca Mountain vault and a third one that he came by on his own. We knew the old man had passed a sphere to Tony a couple of weeks ago and we assumed that was the same one you gave to the Indian, so we were a little surprised when Tony handed over two spheres last Friday. Carlson tried to hide his surprise, but he was babbling like a child when he called me later that evening."

"So it's safe to assume that the third sphere was taken from the Indian at some point, right? We've discovered a two-week discrepancy between the time your guys found it and when we think it should have arrived, so we think it was in Thompson's hands, or at least out of the Indian's hands, for about that length of time," explained Frank, trying not to give away too much of their theory.

"That would be around the time Thompson was shot!" exclaimed Ben. "And he was home sick, or so he claimed, for part of the week before he met Tony at the casino! I wonder where he really was?"

"I'm working on that," chimed in Linda, as she closed the lid on her cell phone. "Beatty is a pretty small place but it's the largest town between Las Vegas and Tonopah so UPS uses it as a drop point. They contract a local guy to deliver packages to a number of small communities between Highway 95 and the California border and he specifically remembers that Al Thompson wasn't home the Thursday or Friday prior to the shooting, because he tried to deliver a package to Al's house. He even tried on Saturday, but there was no answer at the door and Al's car wasn't in the driveway. Monday morning he heard about the previous night's shooting, so he returned the package to the sender."

"How the hell did you find that out?" asked Ben

"Because she's a wizard," answered Frank before Linda could reply. "And a wizard's sources are confidential. Any idea who the sender was, Linda?"

"Of course," she replied proudly. "Once I got the Beatty driver to give me the tracking number, the rest was easy. The package was one of those typical nine by twelve document envelopes and it was sent from right here."

"You mean here in Las Vegas?" asked Tony.

"No, right here," replied Linda, pointing to the ground. "It was sent from Bechtel and it was picked up by UPS from this very building."

Frank gave Ben a hard stare and Ben reacted to the accusing look.

"What?" he demanded. "I don't know anything about this, I swear."

"Then how about if you see what you can find out, since you're the 'insider' on this team," said Tony coldly.

"Specifically," added Frank, "we'd like to know who sent the package and exactly what was in it."

"Okay, okay, I'll see what I can find out. Geez, you guys act as if I sent the damn thing," grumbled Ben, as he crossed the room to the door.

After the door had closed behind Ben, Frank said, "Well, that let's Bechtel off the hook. They probably wouldn't have sent the old man a package on Wednesday if they intended to shoot him on Sunday. Anybody have any ideas before Ben comes scurrying back here?"

"Clearly, we need to find out where the old man was the three days prior to the shooting," replied Linda. "Ill see what else I can learn from here, but I really ought to go up to Beatty and just start talking to folks."

"Let's save that as a last resort," said Frank. "Meanwhile, we still have a lot of leads to check out here, right?"

With that, everybody returned to their assigned tasks. A few minutes later, Ben returned and announced that the envelope in question had been sent from the Bechtel payroll office. It had contained some documents that old man Thompson had requested several weeks before he was shot – apparently he was finally planning to retire.

That night, Frank, Tony, Jim and Linda were met at the Nellis Air Force Base main gate by Gene Carlson promptly at 8:00 p.m. He handed Frank a vehicle pass for the Durango and suggested they follow him to the Officer's club parking lot.

When he joined them in front of the club, they followed his lead and were soon seated in a small, private alcove off the main dining room. After the waiter left with their drink orders, Frank glanced around the facility and remarked, "This is a very nice place, Gene. Thanks for the invitation."

"You're welcome, Frank. Between Nellis, the Nevada Test Site and Tonopah Test Range, we host a lot of visiting dignitaries, so this facility is a little more up-scale than most Officers' Clubs. But, as you've probably already guessed, my reason for getting together tonight is partly pleasure and partly business. How are things going at Bechtel? Is the space they provided satisfactory?"

"It's quite satisfactory," said Frank, answering for the group, "and it's certainly better than trying to work in a hotel room. We're only just getting started, of course, but everything we've needed so far has been anticipated in advance."

"Good," smiled Carlson, "and how about Ben Kingston? Is he proving useful?"

"Yes," nodded Frank thoughtfully, "he has provided some interesting input. In fact, we'd like to ask you a few questions about Ben before the night is over."

There was a brief interruption in the conversation as the waiter returned with the drinks and took the dinner orders. When the waiter left, Frank picked up where he had left off.

"For example, we were surprised to learn that the DOE needed the services of an exobiologist, but we were even more surprised when we learned that he was on loan to you from the Department of Defense. We're interested in why the DOD would have an exobiologist on staff in the first place."

"Well, technically ..." began Carlson, with a frown.

"Technically, he works for NASA," finished Tony. "We already know that, but Ben's been working with the DOD for the last three or four years and he told us he was assigned to work with old man Thompson because of a possible connection between the spheres and his work for the DOD. What kind of connection?"

Carlson glanced down and didn't say anything for a few seconds. When he looked back up, he made direct eye contact with Tony.

"Do you remember the other day, when you were grilling me about an alleged facility north of here?"

Tony nodded, and the others guessed that Carlson was referring to the infamous 'Area 51' complex.

"I told you then that Groom Lake was used by the Air Force, along with a number of civilian agencies and contractors, primarily for the testing of classified experimental aircraft. Well, the Department of Defense is one of those agencies. They have a modest research facility dug into the hillside up behind the main complex and that's where Ben was working before he came down to help us out."

"But what's the connection to the spheres?" asked Jim. "And why an exobiologist?"

Carlson looked over his shoulder to make sure no one else was in the small alcove and then said quietly, "Because Ben's work for the DOD involved another object, also of unknown origin. It's a classified project and Ben will probably have to go back to his DOD work soon, regardless of whether or not you four are able to help us resolve the mystery of the spheres."

"You still haven't told us why they need an exobiologist," said Linda.

"The DOD's object is somewhat larger than our spheres, Linda, and the spheres may provide some clues to the shape and size of the object's original owners. That's Ben's area of expertise and that's why he's working up there."

Before anyone could ask another question, Carlson held up his hand and said, "The subject is closed. I've already told you more than I should have, but I need you to be comfortable working with Ben for whatever time we still have him. Please, no more on this, okay?"

"Okay, fair enough," said Frank. "I think we all understand that we're outsiders and that there is some information we don't have access to, so how about if we change the subject? Yesterday morning you said you'd provide additional information about the pyramid as it became available. How about bringing us up to date on that?"

"I think our food is here," said Carlson, as he saw the waiter headed their way with a large round tray balanced on one hand. "Let's continue this after dinner."

Dinner conversation was awkward because the only topic the five had in common was off limits while the waiter and a bus boy darted in and out of the alcove filling water glasses and removing empty dishes. Finally, the last of the plates were gone and a fresh pot of coffee was on the table. Carlson advised the waiter that they would be fine for a while and asked him to check back in about fifteen minutes. The waiter got the message, thanked them all for their patronage, and disappeared.

Carlson poured a fresh cup of coffee and reopened the discussion that was interrupted by dinner.

"There isn't much news regarding the pyramid, except to confirm that it really is gone. The guards have recovered from whatever was done to them, but they don't remember a thing. They had just completed a quarter-hour radio check when they heard a sound they described as a high-pitched whine. The next thing they remember is waking up in the Mercury medical facility. Needless to say, they've been the center of attention for the last few hours, since they were the only ones physically present. What little we know, we have learned from reviewing radar recordings."

"And what is that?" asked Tony. "What did the radar see?"

"Well, as you can imagine, we have radar all over the place. It's here primarily to support the Air Force aerial dog fight exercises that are held two or three times a year, but it's also used to track the experimental flights up at Groom Lake. The UFO appeared out of nowhere about a hundred feet over the pyramid. It descended quickly to within a few feet of the ground, hovered for about five seconds, rose back up to a hundred feet and then just vanished off the screens."

"So I'm guessing the government's usual swamp gas story has been ruled out this time," said Tony, sarcastically. His comment got a chuckle out of everyone except Carlson.

"So far there have been no reports of any civilian sightings, so, officially, this event never happened, understand?" asked Carlson rhetorically, as he scanned the faces at the table for acknowledgement.

"Okay, now for some more positive news. We may have a lead regarding the activities of Al Thompson. We think he was in contact with someone off and on for about a month prior to the time he was shot. His telephone records show a number of calls from someone in Merida, Mexico – isn't that where you guys were?" asked Carlson of Frank and Jim.

"Yes!" exclaimed Frank. "Who would be calling Al from down there?"

"We don't know exactly who yet, because we just received this information a couple of hours ago. We do know, however, that the telephone number is assigned to a school in Merida called the University of the Yucatan, or something like that. Do you know the place?"

Frank and Jim looked at each other in disbelief and they both uttered the same word at the same time: "Carmen!"

Chapter 29

After learning that Al Thompson had received a number of telephone calls from the University of the Yucatan, in Merida, Frank asked Carlson to let him know as soon as the DOE identified the location of the caller. Ben Kingston had already confirmed a connection between Thompson and the University's Professor Torres, but the Professor had been dead for nearly ten years, so this recent contact was obviously with someone else – possibly someone who had information about the spheres.

As they were driving back to the Residence Inn after dinner, Frank, Tony, Jim and Linda rekindled the debate about who the mysterious Merida connection could be. Frank and Jim had both blurted out Carmen's name at dinner, but neither really expected that she was involved, especially Jim.

"She was just too helpful to be involved in anything," said Jim, shaking his head. "In fact, she risked serious trouble with her boss, a guy named Garcia, I think, when she let me go through the Professor's papers."

"Why did her boss care if you saw the papers?" asked Linda.

"I don't know. I don't think she knew what his objection was, either, but he definitely had some special interest in the *Loltún* research. When the Professor's wife donated his research papers and notes to the University library, this guy boxed them all up and hid them away in a storeroom."

"That sounds a little suspicious, don't you think?" asked Linda. "I wouldn't be surprised if this guy turned out to be our mystery caller. You think his name was Garcia, huh? I'll check him out tomorrow."

"Yes, I think so. And you know, I just remembered something else she told me the day we had lunch at that delightful French restaurant. She was telling me about the Professor and she mentioned that he had become obsessed with his research and even started skipping classes about two years before he disappeared. Wouldn't that be about the same time that Al Thompson was down there on his honeymoon?"

"That's right!" exclaimed Frank, as he turned into the Residence Inn parking lot. "Okay, tomorrow this Garcia character becomes our top priority."

The next morning Frank, Tony, Jim and Linda arrived at the Bechtel conference room to find Ben already at work at one of the computers.

"Good morning, Ben," greeted Jim, as the four entered the room to the smell of freshly brewed coffee. "You're certainly here early."

"Good morning," replied Ben. "I'm used to getting up at 5:00 a.m. because of where I live, but I stayed here in town last night, so I was here by 6:30. Besides, I want to get as much done as I can before I have to go back."

"Back? Back where?" asked Tony as he poured himself a cup of coffee.

"Back to my work at the DOD," said Ben, with a note of sadness in his voice. "I have to report back there Monday morning. I'd rather work on this sphere puzzle with you guys, but in light of the excitement out at NTS the other night, my bosses at DOD want me back on my original project."

"Any chance you're going to let us in on exactly what that project is, Ben?" asked Tony, smiling.

"No, not a chance," said Ben, quietly. "Carlson briefed me on what he told you last night, and he really shouldn't have said anything. If my bosses found out about it they would really raise hell."

"So you talked to Carlson last night?" asked Frank.

"Yes, he called me after the four of you left the Club. He asked me to document everything I could remember about Al Thompson. Every story he told me, every complaint, even phone calls I might have overheard. He said he thought you guys might be on to something and he wanted you to have the benefit of whatever I knew about Thompson. I'm trying to put it all into a memo," he said, indicating the text on the computer screen.

"I'm sure that will be very helpful, Ben," said Frank, "and we're sorry you have to leave us, but your DOD work sounds pretty important. We'll leave you alone until you finish the memo, and then I'd like to have a chat with you about the exobiology aspect of our spheres. No DOD-related questions, I promise."

Frank and Tony went back to work on their correlation chart again, hoping some answers would jump up off the paper on which they had plotted their data.

About 9:30 a.m. Jim stood up at the end of the table where he had worked for most of the last two days and announced, "Well, that's the last one."

Lost in thought, and without even looking up, Frank asked, "The last what, Jim?"

Before the words were even out of his mouth, Frank realized what Jim meant and got to his feet. "Great! Let's see what new information you have for us."

Jim handed Frank several sheets of paper. "Well, the earliest is still the year 992 B.C. and the latest is still 2012, but I think our solar eclipse theory has stood up. Every single sphere, except for the last one, of course, represents the time and location of a solar eclipse that occurred somewhere in the Maya region. Not all of the locations coincide with known ruins, but I suspect that they were all significant Maya sites at the time of the eclipse."

"And the pattern is the same on every single sphere?" asked Frank.

"Yes, it's exactly the same. There's a date, a relative direction and distance, and the two glyphs that represent *Loltún*. Even the twentieth sphere follows that pattern."

"Hold on, there. Something has been bothering me since Jim translated the first three spheres," said Tony from the coffee pot. "If every sphere includes a direction and distance from the exact same place, why would they need to record that place on each sphere? Why wouldn't the starting point, *Loltún*, just be a known constant?"

"What do you mean?" asked Frank, already guessing where Tony's line of reasoning was headed.

"Well, let's suppose I have one of these spheres and I know what type of information is inscribed on it. The only reason I would need to have the reference point on each and every sphere would be if there were other spheres somewhere that use different reference points, right?"

Jim scratched his head for a moment and then asked, "Are you suggesting that there may be other sets of these spheres, with different reference points? We certainly haven't seen any evidence of that here, and I've never heard of any such spheres in other parts of the world."

"Yes, my scholarly friend, but you hadn't ever heard of this set until about two weeks ago, and you're an expert on this part of the world," smiled Tony.

"He has a point there," added Frank. "If this set of spheres could be kept so secret for so long, why couldn't there be others. And I agree that there's really no need to keep repeating the reference point on every sphere unless there's some chance it could change. But that said, we need to get to the bottom of these twenty spheres before we start looking for others. Let's add your last dates to our chart and see if they fill in any blanks. Linda, how are you coming with Señor Garcia?"

From her workstation next to Ben's, Linda looked up and shook her head. "Not too good, so far. The university doesn't have much information about its non-teaching staff on line, and Garcia is such a common Hispanic name that it's hard to do much with the local records. It would help if we knew more about him – even his full name would be a real bonus at this point."

Frank looked at Jim and said, "How about calling Carmen and seeing what she can tell us?"

"Ah, sure, I guess I could do that. It's Thursday, so she should be at the library and I think I have that telephone number written down somewhere."

"Just don't give away too much information," cautioned Frank. "We don't know if Garcia has anything to do with this or not, but we don't want to spook him, just in case."

Jim returned to the other end of the table and rummaged through his brief case. "Got it!" he said, finally.

Jim picked up the handset on the conference room telephone but Frank waved his arms and shook his head. "Why don't you use your cell phone until we know if this is really a lead. If you use the 'house' phone, the DOE might descend on this guy like mosquitoes in a swamp, and we don't even know if he's involved yet. Besides, we don't want to involve Carmen if we don't have to."

Jim nodded and replaced the handset. "Good point."

Jim's call was longer than Frank had expected. Part way through the call Jim covered the mouthpiece and asked for the telephone number of the FAX machine.

When Jim finally ended his call, he was smiling broadly. "Carmen is going to try to send us Garcia's personnel file. She has a cousin that works in the Human Resources department who has access to that information."

"Good work, but why does that seem to make you so happy?" grinned Frank.

"Ah, well, not all of that call was business," blushed Jim. "She's coming to the states on vacation next month and I suggested we get together. We were discussing the arrangements."

"Really! That's an interesting development, isn't it?" smiled Frank.

Before he could do any serious teasing, Frank was interrupted by the sound of the computer printer. Ben collected the pages and handed them to Frank.

"This is all I can remember. I tried to organize things chronologically, as best I could, but I'm afraid it's still a mess," he apologized.

Frank was already scanning Ben's notes and as he finished a page he handed it to Tony to read. When he had completed all five pages, Frank nodded to Ben and said, "Well, done, Ben. There are some interesting details here that I'm sure will be useful."

Tony pointed to a paragraph on the page he was reading and said, "Yeah, like this statement here. You say that on several occasions the old man was 'unavailable' on Thursday and Friday. Do you mean he just didn't show up?"

"No, he always let me know the Wednesday before that he was going to take a couple of days off. I can get you the exact dates from my planner, but I think it happened at least three times in the nine weeks I worked with him. I mentioned it to Carlson, but his attitude was that if Dr. Thompson was occupied with personal business he wouldn't be around NTS threatening to go public about the spheres."

"Yes, we would definitely like to have those dates. So he knew at least a day in advance that he was going to be unavailable for two, and maybe as many as four days, if you count the weekend? Did he ever talk about what he did or where he went on those days off?" asked Frank.

"No, but he always seemed to be exhausted the following Monday. Of course he was in his seventies, so it didn't take much to tire him out, but the Mondays after one of his absences were always worse than normal."

"Nobody's ever mentioned what you guys actually did with the spheres, Ben. What kind of *research* were the two of you doing, anyway?" asked Tony.

"And, where?" added Linda.

"Well, just before Dr. Thompson's accident, we were working in a building up near Carlson's office at the Yucca complex. We were simply trying to catalog the spheres' physical properties. You know, chemical composition, hardness, density, the normal stuff," replied Ben.

"And how did that work out?" asked Frank.

"Well, not so well, I'm afraid. I can give you a copy of the preliminary report if you want," said Ben, pointing to the computer where he had prepared the earlier memo.

"Why don't you just give me the short-hand version? Did you learn anything useful?"

"Well, the spheres appear to be made from an unknown material that is harder and denser than anything we know of."

Ben saw the exasperated look on Frank's face and said, "Hey, you asked for the short version, and that's it. You know about the hieroglyphics, of course, and the unusual activity some of the spheres seem to exhibit from time to time. Some other physical characteristics you may not know are that every sphere is exactly the same size, 8 centimeters in diameter, and exactly the same weight, 1,000 grams – a little over two pounds. The weight is interesting, actually, because different spheres contain different glyphs, which you would expect to result in slightly different weights."

"Let's go back to the activity for a minute," said Frank. "Any idea what triggers it?"

"Not a clue. We tried to artificially stimulate several different spheres without success. We tried electricity, radiation, light, heat, cold – all the normal stuff – but nothing caused any activity. Then all of a sudden, when we were least expecting it, a sphere would start making a high pitched noise and emit a faint glow. Those are the same characteristics you observed from the twentieth sphere while it was still in the cave and there probably weren't any outside influences down there."

"That's true," said Frank. "In fact, if it hadn't been for the glow, I might have missed it altogether."

"Maybe it was calling to you," joked Tony.

Frank and Ben looked at each other and then at Tony. "What did you say?" they asked at the same time.

"I said, maybe it was... oh, come on! You don't really think it was trying to attract your attention do you?" laughed Tony.

Ignoring Tony's sarcasm, Frank turned back to Ben and said, "What do you think about that? Is it possible that the spheres have been trying to communicate with us, rather than with each other? Trying to get our attention or tell us something?"

Ben rubbed his chin in thought for a minute, and then said, "I suppose it's possible. They might contain some sort of sensor that detects the presence of a human, but for what purpose?"

"Maybe when one of these strange Indian characters came in to pick up a sphere, the appropriate sphere signaled to say "Pick me, pick me!" said Tony, still not taking the subject seriously.

"Well, it worked on me, that's for sure," said Frank. "I snatched up Number 20 and brought it right back here to the nest, apparently."

"And that means there's still an Indian down there somewhere waiting to deliver his sphere to Nevada," remarked Tony, suddenly more serious. "It's too bad we don't have some surveillance equipment in that cave. Maybe then we could learn who these guys are."

"But if your calculations are correct, the twentieth sphere isn't scheduled to be transported up here for another couple of years, at least," interjected Jim. "Isn't that the timing you guys worked out the other night?"

"Right, right. I guess that would be a pretty long stake out, wouldn't it?" laughed Tony.

"Still, you have a good point, Tony," agreed Frank. "There must be at least one of those guys still alive and kicking, somewhere. Let's select several of the most representative autopsy photos and pass them on to Edwards' buddies in Merida. Maybe they can turn up something."

"But what about the other activity?" objected Tony. "You said the sphere you grabbed was making noise in the car on the way back to Merida and again on the plane after you left Mexico. And I saw several of the spheres going off in the Yucca Mountain vault the night Carlson and I were down there. How do you explain that?"

"Well, I can't, right now, but give me some time to think on it," said Frank. "In the mean time, let's call Carlson and get some of those autopsy photos sent down…"

Frank was interrupted by the ringing of the FAX machine. "That should be the information about Carmen's boss," said Jim, as everybody gathered around and watched the pages arrive. The first sheet was a simple, hand-written note that said, in Spanish, "Carmen asked me to send this information to you." The note was signed simply, "Isabel."

As each sheet came out of the machine, Frank handed it to Jim, since he had arranged to have the material sent in the first place. Linda had squeezed in next to Jim, and the two of them scanned each page intensely. As they finished a page, Jim passed it to Tony and Ben, and they in turn handed it to Frank. When Frank had finished the third and last page, he looked disappointed.

"Well, this all seems to be pretty standard stuff, but at least now we know who we're dealing with," said Frank, as he handed the papers to Linda. "And this should make your research go a little easier."

"I'm on it," she said as she headed back to her computer with the personnel file.

Frank, Tony, Jim and Ben sat down at the near end of the conference table and continued to discuss Al Thompson's activities just prior to the time he was shot, but if Ben knew any more he wasn't admitting it and the conversation soon turned from fact gathering to speculation.

Given Thompson's age, it didn't seem likely that he would have made frequent long car trips, but if he had, his practical limit would have been about seven hundred and fifty miles in any direction from Beatty. Unfortunately, that included most of the western United States and a good part of northern Mexico. By airplane, Thompson could have easily reached any point in North America or the Caribbean.

Thompson had met with Tony and was later shot at the casino in Beatty on a Sunday night following one of his mysterious disappearances. Even though he only lived a couple of blocks from the casino, his car was found in the parking lot, indicating that he may have stopped at the casino on his way back into town. Since he gave Tony a sphere while he was in the casino, and since it was one of the previously recovered spheres on loan from the DOE, it seemed likely that he may have taken the sphere with him on his trip.

And then there was the discrepancy between the amount of money the DOE thought Thompson had and the amount that was actually found in his safe. Frank was reluctant to bring this information to light, but he wanted to take advantage of any information Ben might have before he was forced to return to his DOD duties.

As it turned out, Ben didn't know anything about the money. Carlson hadn't shared any information with Ben about Thompson's retirement cash-out and when Frank asked Ben if he knew where the old man might have come up with an extra $223,000, Ben just laughed.

"All he ever did was talk about how expensive things were compared to when he was younger. I had no idea he had hundreds of thousands stashed away. Maybe it had something to do with these trips he was taking."

"I've considered the possibility that he might be selling spheres to someone, but none of them seem to be missing," commented Frank. "And he didn't have anything else valuable enough to generate that kind of cash."

"How about information?" asked Tony. "He had access to the spheres, he had limited access to the Yucca Mountain facility, and who knows what else he may have learned by just being around that place. Maybe he was selling information to an enemy of the U.S."

Ben immediately came to the defense of the old man. "I didn't know Dr. Thompson all that well, but I'm certain he wasn't a spy or a terrorist or anything like that," he said. "He was passionate about his sphere theory, and I know he tried desperately to get people to believe him, but I don't believe for a minute that he would sell information about it for money."

"Just the same, let's ask Linda to do some checking when she has time. It's also clear that the key to a lot of things is finding out where Thompson went on his mysterious trips." Frank opened a large road atlas to a map of the United States, southern Canada and northern Mexico. "The answer has to be here somewhere," he said, as he folded his arms across his chest in thought.

Tony's eyes widened. "Not necessarily there," he said pointing to Frank's map, "but I remember seeing an atlas similar to this on the top shelf of the old man's closet! It might be a good idea if we had a look at *that* map, don't you think?"

"I agree," said Frank, "but how are we going to get inside?"

"Jill gave me her key just before the DOE spirited her out of town," replied Tony, pulling a brass key out of his pocket and showing it to Frank. "She guessed that we might want to get back in there at some point in our investigation."

"Okay, let's head up there right after lunch and see if the old man's mobile home provides any additional information. We should also try to talk to the Nye County Sheriff and see if they've turned up anything since Jill filed her burglary report. And maybe we can locate the old man's car and have a look at it, too. There might still be things in it from his last trip that would give us a clue as to where he had been."

"Well, let's get going," said Tony, ready to chase down the first lead that interested him. "I'm tired of being cooped up in this place."

"Hey, wait a minute!" cried Linda. "I'm going, too. Just let me print out this stuff for you."

Frank looked at Jim. "How about you, Jim? Are you up for a ride in the country?"

"Absolutely," he replied emphatically. "I agree with Tony – this place is wearing on me."

"Can I go along, too?" asked Ben sheepishly. "If you all leave, there won't be anything for me to do here."

Frank threw up his hands and said, "What the hell, let's make a field trip out of it. But if we're all going, we need to pick up our stuff. In fact, if there's anything you think we might need up there, bring it along."

"Okay, but you have to give me a second," protested Linda. "I've just found some info about your Sr. Garcia that I want to print out before I lose it. Oh, look! I just ran across a photograph of him on his high school's Web site."

Frank and Tony joined Linda at her computer and peered over her shoulder. The picture was dated June, 1971, and the caption read simply "Zuitok Garcia Garcia."

"What kind of name is Zuitok?" asked Tony. "This guy's parents must have really hated him."

"It's Maya," said Jim from the table. "And I believe it was also the name of the legendary founder of *Uxmal*."

"Well, that makes sense, because Sr. Garcia looks like he has a lot of Indian ancestry," said Frank, as he turned towards the door. "Gather that stuff up and bring it with you, Linda. We can study it on the way to Beatty."

As the others collected their things to leave, Tony motioned for Frank to follow him to the far end of the room.

"Did you see that photo?" whispered Tony, facing the wall so the others wouldn't overhear him.

"Yeah, he looks familiar, but I can't quite place him," replied Frank. "Maybe somebody I met in Mexico?"

"Of course he looks familiar, Frank! Our friend Garcia is a spitting image of the Indian we questioned in Al Thompson's mobile home and he also looks like all the ones I saw in Carlson's autopsy photos. Remember when I told you I thought they all looked like brothers? I'd be willing to bet that our Señor Garcia is part of that same clan!"

Chapter 30

As Frank pulled the Durango out of the Bechtel parking lot, he handed Tony his cell phone and asked him to call Carlson.

"Let him know that Ben is with us and give him my cell number in case he needs to reach us. If he asks where we're going, just tell him we're doing some research on Al Thompson's activities."

Tony made the call and then the conversation in the vehicle drifted to Jim's upcoming rendezvous with Carmen. Jim explained that they planned to meet in Miami, rent a car and drive back to Seattle so Carmen could see a large part of the United States since this would be her first trip north of the border.

"Doesn't the University object to you being gone so much?" asked Linda.

"I just started my sabbatical leave a couple of weeks ago, at the end of the last school term. For the next twelve months I am relieved of my teaching duties so I can concentrate on research. It's one of the few benefits of having a tenured faculty position at a major university – I basically get every seventh year off."

Frank made eye contact with Jim in the Durango's rear view mirror and said, "In that case, I'd like to talk to you about your plans for the next year before you make any other commitments, Jim. Maybe after we get this sphere thing resolved?"

"Okay, sure," replied Jim, "but I already plan to spend a couple of weeks with Carmen and I really do have to get cracking on some original research so I can get an article or two published before my year is up. At the University of Washington, the phrase "publish or perish" is taken very seriously."

Everybody in the vehicle had ideas about where Jim should take Carmen, and the next two hours passed quickly. Frank pulled off the highway at south end of Beatty and parked the Durango next to a building that housed the restaurant, casino and bar.

"Well, folks, this is where it all started," announced Tony, as he pointed to the front door of the establishment. "I ran into Al Thompson in this casino about two and a half weeks ago and I guess he was found shot a few hours later right over there. Frank, drive around to the side of that motel building, will you?"

Frank slowly drove across the large, paved parking lot on the north side of the restaurant/casino to the end of a two-story, Wild West looking building that contained about 30 motel rooms.

"According to Jill, this is where Al was found. Right here at the end of this building. He was probably on his way home, because he only lives a few lots down this road," said Tony, as he pointed down the street that ran along the north side of the motel property.

"Did you hear the shots fired?" asked Ben, from the far back seat of the Durango.

"No, I had only stopped for dinner. After the old man handed me the sphere and disappeared, I headed on up the road to Tonopah, where I spent the night at a truck stop. I was twenty miles north of town by the time the police say he was shot."

Frank headed slowly down the street and stopped in front of one of the several mobile homes that lined the northeast side of the road.

"This is Al Thompson's place. Let's check it out and then we'll pay the Sheriff a visit," said Frank as he turned into the short driveway that ended at the front of the mobile home.

Once inside, Tony went directly to the closet in the back bedroom to retrieve the old man's road atlas. It was right where he had remembered it being and he returned to the living room to find Frank bent over an old mechanical answering machine. Jim and Linda were going through drawers in the kitchen, and Ben was standing in the middle of the room looking lost.

"I've got it!" Tony announced proudly, waving the atlas for all to see.

"So do I, Tony. Listen to this," said Frank, motioning Tony to his side.

Frank turned a knob to the 'Play' position and made a shushing sign.

"Good morning, Mr. Thompson, this is Andy Willis calling and it's about 9:00 a.m. your time on June 21st. I'm going to be back in Nevada again next Thursday and I was hoping we could arrange another meeting. Everything from our last meeting has been transcribed and we'd like you to review the entire text one more time for accuracy. My publisher finds your theories very interesting, but he is eager to keep the process moving forward so he can realize some financial return to offset the rather large advances you have received. I think you have the number, but just in case, it's 212-555-3428. Please call me as soon as possible so we can work out the details."

"That was this morning," said Tony, checking the date on his watch. "It sounds like the old bastard was selling information after all, either in the form of an article or a book!"

Ben had overheard the answering machine message and he joined Frank and Tony. "I can't believe it," he said, shaking his head. "Dr. Thompson was getting a little unstable, but I certainly wouldn't have expected anything like this. All the information about the spheres is classified and he must have known that the government would prosecute if he went public. If I'm not mistaken, that's a New York City telephone number, so Dr. Thompson must have been working with a publisher back east."

"He might not have been doing it for the money, because we know he was very frustrated by the fact that the DOE wouldn't take his claims of an alien source seriously and he had apparently put in for his retirement. Maybe his mental condition, combined with his frustration with the DOE and the promise of a lot of money, altered his sense of right and wrong," said Frank. "Regardless of why Thompson did it, we need to get this process stopped immediately. Ben, get on the phone to Carlson and explain what we've learned so they can begin some damage control. I'll replay this message so you can write down the name and telephone number."

Ben jotted down the information and placed a call to Carlson on his own cell phone. While he was relaying the information, Tony said, "I suppose somebody should let Jill know that part of the money she has is going to have to go back to the publisher. I hope she hasn't spent it already."

"The DOE may not even be able to find her," said Frank. "From what you told me, they basically told her to get lost for a while. She could be anywhere by now."

"She could be, but I happen to know where that place is. She left me a voice-mail message a couple of days after she took off in which she indicated where she had gone in a way that only she and I would understand. I'll call her when we get back to town."

Frank smiled and said, "Okay, Romeo, I'll leave that to you. I guess our next stop should be the Sheriff's office, if there is one here in Beatty. Maybe we can get some leads on who shot the old man, and why."

Frank joined Jim and Linda in the kitchen and brought them up to date on the answering machine message. "Any luck out here?" he asked.

"Just this," replied Linda, holding up a small sheet of paper. "And it's certainly not as exciting as your discovery."

Frank looked at the paper and wrinkled his brow. "That looks like more hieroglyphics," he said. "What does it say, Jim?"

Jim studied it for a minute and then said, "I'm not familiar with some of the symbols, so I'll have to get my cheat sheets out of the car before I can tell you anything. Why don't I stay here while you go find the Sheriff?"

"Okay, if that's what you want to do. How about the rest of you? Going or staying?"

"I think I'll stay here and see what Jim turns up," said Ben. "Ancient languages fascinate me, but I've never had the time to study them."

"Well, I've <u>never</u> had an interest in ancient languages, so I'm definitely not staying here," said Tony.

"I think I'll go with you guys, too," added Linda. "Investigative work is more my style than languages."

"Okay, then, let's get going. We'll be back as soon as we can. Jim, don't forget your brief case before we go."

On the way out to the car, Jim pulled Frank aside and asked, "Does it seem to you that Ben is acting a little strange?"

"What do you mean?"

"He seems a little more nervous and on edge than normal. Ever since you decided to come up here to Beatty."

"No, I haven't noticed anything unusual," replied Frank, "but if you're uncomfortable alone with him, I'll make him go with us."

"No, no, I don't want to do that. You're probably right, I'm just getting spooked by being in the old man's place, that's all."

Jim collected his briefcase from the back seat of the Durango and walked back to the mobile home. As Jim opened the door, he glanced back over his shoulder and Frank could see a genuine look of concern on his face.

Frank got in behind the wheel and asked, "Have any of you noticed anything odd about Ben's behavior since we left Las Vegas? Jim sounds concerned."

No one spoke up, so Frank filed the idea away and headed back toward the highway. When he reached the stop sign, he rolled down his window and asked an elderly man who was waiting to cross the street how to get to the local Sheriff's office.

The man pointed south, back the way they had come in to town, and said, "It's that-a-way about two blocks. It'll be on your right. You can't miss it, sonny. Just follow the signs to the high school."

Frank thanked the old timer and turned right. It turned out to be three blocks, but the modern metal building was clearly visible once they got close. A sign on the door read *Nye County Sheriff – Beatty Substation.*

Frank, Tony and Linda entered the small office to find a uniformed man tilted back in an old wooden office chair with his feet resting on a desk that matched the chair. At the sight of the strangers, he snapped back into a stiff sitting position and said, "How can I help you folks?"

Frank explained that they were friends of Jill Harris, who had been called out of town unexpectedly, and that she had asked them to check on the progress of the investigation into her step-father's shooting.

"Shooting? You must be talking about that incident up at the Inn a couple of weeks ago. Thompson, I think his name was. That's the first murder we've had in these parts in almost twenty years," said the deputy, as he opened a drawer in the wooden desk.

"That's right, Al Thompson. He lived just down the street from the Inn," nodded Frank, trying to sound like he'd known the old man all his life.

The deputy removed a manila folder from the drawer and opened it in front of him on the desk. He pretended to scan the two visible pages as if studying the file. He would have fooled them, except that Tony noticed that his eyes weren't moving from side to side as they moved down each page.

"Well, there's not really any new information here," said the deputy. "The officer who investigated at the scene reported an apparent gun shot wound to the head from a small caliber gun, probably a rifle. A patron of the Inn found Mr. Thompson on the Third Street side of the property at about 10:15 p.m. Our paramedics arrived at 10:20 p.m. and the victim was transported to University Medical Center by Life Flight helicopter at 10:55 p.m."

"What makes you think it was a rifle," asked Tony.

"Well, since the bullet entered the head from above, we suspect that the shooter was on the hill across the highway and to reach a target from that distance you would need a high-powered rifle, probably one with a telescopic sight on it."

"Good detective work," lied Tony, trying to flatter the deputy. "Any idea what caliber it might have been?"

"No, I'm afraid the bullet was never recovered and we haven't received any additional information from the Medical Center. Las Vegas PD called us when the victim died but other than that we haven't heard from anybody. If I had to guess, though, I'd say it was probably one of those high-powered, small caliber varmint guns that everybody around here has – maybe a .17 Hornady or a .222 Hornet."

"And there aren't any suspects?" asked Frank, sensing that the deputy was about out of useful information.

"No, sir, not at this time, and no motive either. But the case is still under investigation by both Nye County and the State of Nevada," said the deputy confidently as he closed the folder in a way that said, "End of interview."

"Thank you very much for your help," said Frank. "I'm sure Miss Harris will appreciate knowing that both the county and the state are doing all they can to solve this terrible crime."

As the three walked back to the Durango, Frank said, "Well, that was certainly interesting."

"You're kidding, right?" laughed Linda. "I doubt if that man even knows what day of the week it is."

"Oh, he knows a lot more than that," said Tony. "And he gave us more information than he intended to. For example, Al Thompson wasn't the victim of a random act of violence. The fact that he was shot from a distance, probably with a telescope-equipped rifle implies he was specifically targeted. And since he had been out of town for nearly four days, the shooter had either been following the old man or knew his habits pretty well. I'd like to take a hike up onto that hill and see what I can find. I doubt if these cops even walked across the highway, much less conducted a search."

"What do you hope to find?" asked Linda.

"Footprints, a discarded personal item, maybe even a shell casing," replied Tony.

As Frank pulled away from the building, Tony noticed the deputy standing in the window watching the Durango.

Meanwhile, back at Al Thompson's mobile home, Jim had just completed his translation of the note Linda had found.

"Well, I'll be damned," said Jim softly. "This appears to be a death threat, of sorts."

"Written in hieroglyphics?" asked a surprised Ben. "That's a little bizarre, isn't it? What does it say?"

"A rough English translation would be 'Speak, and your blood will flow freely' but the choice of glyphs implies a stern warning rather than a statement of fact which is why I think it's a threat. And some of the symbols are odd, just like the symbols for *Loltún* we found on the spheres. They represent either a very early form of Maya writing or possibly even a different origin, such as Olmec."

"So you think this note may be related to the spheres?" asked an increasingly interested Ben.

"Indirectly, yes. And I would say that whoever wrote this note could probably read the messages on the spheres without needing the pile of reference material I have to use," replied Jim, indicating the papers he had scattered across the top of Al Thompson's table. I think I'm going to call Frank and let him know about this."

Jim used the telephone in the mobile home to call Frank's cell phone. "Where are you guys?" he asked when Frank answered.

"We're up on the hill across the highway from the Inn," replied a panting Frank. "And this is no easy climb, let me tell you! What's up?"

Jim described the message he had translated and his theory about the author. "And whoever it was written to would have had to be able to understand it," concluded Jim.

"So, if that note is a threat, there's a good chance that Thompson... hold on, I think Tony has found something."

There was momentary silence and then Frank came back on the line. "No, I guess it was nothing. You two sit tight and we'll be there in just a few minutes."

About fifteen minutes later, Frank, Tony and Linda returned to Al Thompson's mobile home. Jim handed Frank the original note along with a piece of paper on which he had written his translation. He pointed out several glyphs and said, "These are the ones I find unusual. I don't believe they're from the same period of time as the others. It's almost like the writer learned the newer form of the language late in life and slips back into his original dialect when he doesn't know a word."

"But by newer and original, you mean when? Aren't both of these forms of writing very old?" asked a confused Frank.

"Well, old is a relative term, but the more current form of hieroglyphics was probably developed near the end of what we call the Early Preclassic Period, which ended about 900 B.C. This other, related form of writing would date back before that. That's why I suspect it might be Olmec. Some researchers believe the Olmec taught their writing to the early Maya because the two are similar in many ways."

"So when an archaeologist tells me I look young, I shouldn't take that as a compliment, right?" laughed Linda. "Young to you guys could be anything after the birth of Christ!"

Jim smiled and replied, "I did say it was all relative, remember?"

"Jim, if we assume for a minute that the purpose of the spheres was to remind Maya priests of certain solar eclipses, and we know that the earliest sphere is dated 992 B.C., isn't it possible that the Olmec gave the spheres to the Maya?" asked Frank.

"Yes, I suppose so, but then the question becomes where did the Olmec get them?"

"Maybe they brought them with them," commented Ben from the kitchen.

Everybody turned at once and suddenly Ben was the center of attention. He reached behind himself and grabbed the counter as if the collective stares had knocked him backwards.

"What was that? Brought them from where?" asked Tony,

"Jim, please correct me if I'm wrong," began Ben, "but there's a lot of disagreement in the scientific community about the origin of the Olmec, right? There's a theory that they somehow migrated across the Atlantic from Africa, based on the giant stone heads they carved that seem to have Negroid features.

"Then there are those that claim the stone heads have Polynesian features. This group thinks the Olmec migrated across from the South Pacific and up through South and Central America. And there's still another group thinks the Olmec are actually the Jaredites, as described in the Book of Mormon."

"Yes, but the currently accepted academic theory is that the Olmec developed from much older civilizations of nomadic tribes who were part of the migration across the Bering Straits and down through what is now Canada and the United States," corrected Jim.

"But isn't it a fact that the Olmec are considered the first civilization of Mesoamerica? And they had highly developed systems of writing, mathematics and astronomy, all of which they passed on to the Maya," continued Ben. "None of the northern tribes had any such skills, Jim. Hell, most of them never even developed writing, much less mathematics and astronomy!"

"So what was your point again," asked Tony trying to break up the academic debate that was developing between Ben and Jim. "Oh, yeah, that the Olmec brought the spheres with them. And I think my question was 'Brought them from where?' wasn't it?"

"I have a picture on the wall of my lab back at Groom Lake by an artist named James Neff that shows a flying saucer crashed into a small hillside. In the background is a typical Maya pyramid and there are some Indians standing around looking at the wreckage. That painting may be closer to the truth than the artist ever imagined," replied Ben.

"Are you suggesting…" started Frank.

"I'm not suggesting anything. Officially, this conversation never happened, but you guys are getting pretty close to some extremely sensitive information, and you apparently have the DOE's blessing to pursue this line of investigation, so I'm going to save you some time.

"About three and a half years ago your tax dollars helped launch a very secret, very sophisticated satellite designed to survey the earth. The orbiter was equipped with devices designed to explore the optical, infrared, and several other spectrums and one of its first assignments was to look for underground facilities capable of manufacturing chemical, biological or nuclear weapons in the Mideast.

"To calibrate the instruments, the scientists decided to use the Yucatan Peninsula as a known "non-source" because the porous, non-metallic limestone composition of the land would provide a good zero point. Much to their surprise, they discovered what appeared to be a very dense object buried inside a remote hill near San Luis Potosi, Mexico. The hill turned out to be a large mound of rocks and dirt, and we now think it was originally an Olmec pyramid.

"Anyway, under the guise of building an astronomical observatory for the University of Texas, an American team of engineers and scientists was sent in to extract the object and secretly transport it back to the U.S. To be more precise, it was transported back to what is now my lab at Groom Lake."

Ben stopped for a minute to let what he had said sink in. Before anyone had time to start asking questions, he continued.

"The object I have been studying doesn't look much like the one in the Neff painting, but you get the idea. We don't know yet if it landed before the Olmec settled the area, after they arrived or if it came here with them on board, but carbon dating of pieces of wood found inside the mound around the spacecraft indicate that it was buried about 1,500 B.C., roughly the time Jim's academic buddies think the Olmec first appeared."

"I think I need to sit down," said Jim in a shaky voice. In a matter of minutes, the young scientist from the Department of Defense had turned his entire concept of Mesoamerican history upside down.

"That's probably wise," said Ben, in an unfamiliar, take-charge voice, "because I'm just getting to the good stuff!"

Chapter 31

Everybody except Ben sat down at the small kitchen table. They were all speechless, having just been told that the U.S. government had actually recovered a UFO and that they had it in a lab at the infamous 'Area 51' complex.

Frank was the first to break the silence. "You know, Ben, the UFO fanatics and Area 51 buffs would <u>die</u> if they heard the story you just told us! Everything they've been claiming for the past fifty-four years turns out to be true."

"Yes, I know, and the funny thing is, for fifty-one and a half of those years it was all myth and legend. Just about the time the whole UFO phenomenon was starting to choke itself to death, we had to go and find this damn thing," smiled Ben. It was the first time any of them had seen him smile all day.

"So, I guess the obvious question is do you have any spacemen or spacewomen to go with your spaceship?" asked Linda.

"No, that part of the Area 51 myth is still false, unfortunately. As an exobiologist, I'd much rather have little green men to study, but all I have is their little green wagon.

"I told you earlier that I was just getting to the good stuff but before we go any further, I must caution you that this information is highly classified. The DOE issued you temporary clearances a few days ago, but now those will have to be converted to permanent ones.

"That said, let me tell you the real reason I was sent over to the DOE to work with the late Dr. Thompson. I mentioned yesterday that the Atomic Energy Commission, now the Department of Energy, covered up the existence of the spheres for decades. By the time they finally shared their information with the DOD and a few other agencies, I had been working on the recovered spacecraft for more than a year. I had measured and cataloged every square inch of the interior in an effort to create a computer model of what the original occupants might have looked like and I had a pretty good idea of what everything in the cockpit was used for except for one item. Tucked away in the back was a rectangular box with a sealed lid that looked similar to an oversized egg carton and I just couldn't figure out what it was for."

"The spheres!" exclaimed Jim. "That's why you said maybe they brought them with them."

"Exactly. Once I received some physical data on the spheres, I was pretty sure they had arrived in the spacecraft. In fact, I had predicted there would be a total of twenty long before you guys came along, because my mysterious container had twenty positions. The DOD decided to keep this information to itself, of course, so the folks over at Energy have no idea how the spheres got here or how many to expect."

"So how much information regarding the spheres and your flying saucer <u>has</u> been shared between the DOD and the DOE?" asked Tony.

Ben smiled. "Practically none. I'm the only DOD researcher working on the spacecraft and, to the best of my knowledge, I'm the only individual working both sides of the fence. Energy knows I'm here to study the spheres, but they don't know the real reason why. It's been hard enough to keep information about the spheres from leaking. If word of an alien spacecraft got out, the social and political implications would be enormous."

"Okay, since you can see on both sides of the fence, what's your take on the spheres? You think you know how they got to the Yucatan, but who do you think was bringing them here to Nevada and why?" asked Frank.

"Based on what you and Jim learned in Mexico, and the information Linda came up with this morning, I'd have to say that the answers to both of those questions are in the Yucatan and it's beginning to sound like this Garcia guy may be involved on several levels. He's clearly protective of any information about the spheres, *Loltún* and Professor Torres' research. If he somehow learned that Dr. Thompson was planning to go public, who knows what he might do. I don't mean to step on your toes, but I think it's time we had our agents in Merida pick him up for questioning."

"I agree," nodded Frank. "Beside, Tony thinks Garcia is somehow related to the Indians who've been delivering the spheres to the Nevada Test Site, and that opens up a whole new set of possibilities."

"What?" asked Ben in surprise. "When and how did you come to that conclusion?"

"This morning, actually, when I saw the photo Linda found on the Web," answered Tony. "We've been keeping a few secrets of our own, Ben, because we haven't always been sure whose side you were on."

"I'm sorry, but I couldn't be more open with you earlier. Now, what about this theory of yours?"

Tony described the afternoon he had spent in Carlson's office with the autopsy files and his resulting observation that all of the deceased Indians looked uncannily similar.

"I made a table listing the heights and weights of each body and Jim was surprised at how similar the values were," explained Tony.

"Let me guess," interrupted Ben. "They were all about 5 feet, 10 inches tall and weighed approximately 155 pounds, right?"

Tony's jaw dropped. "How could you possibly know that?"

"Those measurements I took in the spacecraft, remember? Our computer modeling software developed a profile of a humanoid figure about 5 feet 10 inches tall and 155 pounds."

"Wait a minute," said Tony. "Are you saying that these delivery boys, possibly including Garcia, came to Earth in your spacecraft?"

"No, not at all," explained Ben. "In fact, it appears that the craft only carried two occupants. At least there were only two seats, and the craft certainly isn't big enough to hold twenty individuals of the size I just mentioned."

"But earlier you suggested that the Olmec brought the spheres with them. Weren't there lots of Olmec? I mean, like a whole civilization full of them?" asked a confused Linda.

"Yes, eventually, but what if the theories about the origin of the Olmec people are wrong?" challenged Ben. "What if a small group of individuals came here, not from Africa or Polynesia, but from outer space, to influence the population in this part of the world? The craft appears to have been intentionally buried around 1500 B.C. and there's no evidence that it crashed, so I believe it safely landed and was hidden to protect its secrets from future generations of what we now call the Olmec."

"And our delivery boys are simply the descendants of these aliens?" asked Tony, directing his question to Jim, the group's expert in anthropology.

"I guess it's possible," offered Jim, "but the similarity of their features doesn't suggest that they are the result of 3,500 years of evolution, even under very controlled, selective breeding conditions. It's more like they were ..." Jim's voice trailed off, as if the scientist in him were unable to complete the thought.

"Well, like what, Jim?" asked an impatient and still confused Linda.

"Like they were cloned, or something," Jim finally uttered.

Ben immediately stepped back from the group and dialed a number on his cell phone while Jim continued his explanation to the others.

"We only began to decipher Olmec writings in 1979, but what little we do know indicates that the Olmec religious leaders were members of ultra-secret societies called *gyo* or *jo*, in their inscriptions. The leaders of these societies apparently possessed immense mystical powers and were often depicted as shape-shifters, able to transform themselves between the form of a human and that of a jaguar."

"Are you kidding me?" laughed Tony. "This is beginning to sound more like a science fiction story every second. Come, on, Jim, shape-shifters?"

"Well, I, for one, have always believed that cats are really just aliens walking among us in disguise," added Linda with a grin, "and jaguars are cats, after all."

"No, seriously," continued Jim. "The more we learn about the Olmec religious and political systems, the less we understand them. It's a subject I've always wanted to explore, because so little is actually known about it."

"Maybe this could be your research project for the next year," suggested Linda. "Didn't you say you needed to do some original research so you could get published before your sabbatical is over?"

As Ben closed his cell phone and rejoined the group, he said, "But I'm afraid Jim wouldn't be able to publish most of what he's learned, Linda. Everything relating to a possible alien interference with the Olmec is highly classified."

"Well that's a bummer! Who was that?" she asked, indicating Ben's cell phone.

"I called Edwards and suggested that he have Garcia picked up immediately. We're going to try to bring him back to the U.S. for questioning if we can get the Mexican authorities to cooperate. I also asked him to initiate a DNA comparison on as many of the Indians as possible to see if there's anything to Tony's theory.

Edwards thinks they may have DNA samples from the last two or three autopsies, at least.

"Edwards also mentioned that the publisher's representative who called here has been contacted and there won't be a story. As it turns out, Dr. Thompson wasn't actually selling government secrets but he was working with this Willis guy on a book about his friend Dr. Torres' research and it hit a little too close to home."

"Wow, that didn't take long," commented Frank. "What kind of a tall tale did they make up to tell the rep?"

"Edwards was able to convince him that our poor Dr. Thompson was suffering from dementia and that publishing Torres' theories would make him a laughing stock. You mentioned something earlier about locating Thompson's car. Maybe we should try to do that now and then head back to the city. In light of what we've discovered this morning, I have some things I need to run down as soon as possible."

"Okay, but I think we'll have to go back to the Sheriff to find out about the car. If the old man left his car in the parking lot the night he was shot, they would have had it towed by now and when the local law learned who it belonged to, they should have impounded it as evidence in the murder case."

Satisfied that they had learned all they could from Al Thompson's place, Tony locked it up and pocketed the key. They made the short drive back to the Sheriff's office and Frank went in alone, so as not to intimidate the man. Frank was back behind the wheel within five minutes.

"That was quick," commented Tony. "So, where is it?"

"According to Barney Fife in there, they never found Al Thompson's car. I don't think it even occurred to them to look for it, but at least I got him to give me the license plate number." Frank handed Tony a piece of paper and put the Durango in gear. "I guess we might as well head back to Vegas, unless anybody has a better idea?"

Nobody did, and Ben was anxious to get back, so Frank turned onto U.S. 95 and headed south. Tony passed the Sheriff's note back to Ben and asked, "Can you get one of your people to run this plate and see if the car has turned up anywhere?"

"Sure," smiled Ben, as he took his phone out again. "Edwards' crew just loves running errands for the Department of Defense!"

After a brief conversation with someone on the phone, Ben disconnected with a puzzled look on his face. "Now that's a bit odd. It seems that Dr. Thompson's car was found abandoned in the parking lot of a place called the Gulf Marina in Port Isabel, Texas. The license plates, wheels and just about every other removable piece is gone, but the vehicle identification number checks out. It was impounded last week, but the Port Isabel authorities haven't gotten around to notifying Nevada yet, so I guess your Sheriff buddy back in Beatty is off the hook."

"Where the heck is Port Isabel?" asked Frank.

Tony pulled Al Thompson's road atlas out from under his seat and opened it to Texas. After studying the map for a minute, he said, "Port Isabel is on the southeastern coast of Texas, down in the very tip of the state next to the Mexican border."

"Interesting," said Ben, thoughtfully. "I wonder what our pal Garcia was doing the night Dr. Thompson was shot."

After a moment, Jim said, "You know, last Saturday when I returned to the library to finish my review of Professor Torres' notes, Carmen hid me away in her office so her boss, who we now know as Garcia, wouldn't know I was there. She told me he had just returned from a vacation and I think she told me later that he'd been deep-sea fishing."

"A fishing boat – of course!" shouted Frank, as he slapped his forehead. "Tony, how far is it by water from Port Isabel to Merida?"

Tony returned to the map and did some rough calculations. "It's about 620 miles, as the crow flies. At a modest 25 knots, that's a 24-hour trip but if you follow the coastline it's at least twice that far and with fuel stops it would probably take the better part of three days."

"So if Garcia <u>were</u> involved in the shooting, he would have had almost two weeks to get home. That would have given him plenty of time to drive the old man's car to Port Isabel, book a fishing charter and make a leisurely trip back to Merida," speculated Frank. "Linda, when we get back to the city, how about seeing if you can confirm any of this? If we can prove Garcia was in the U.S. at the time of the shooting, maybe Edwards' people can extradite him on murder charges."

As Frank slowed for traffic turning south onto Highway 160, Ben's cell phone rang. After finishing the call, he leaned forward between the front seats and said, "I've changed my mind about going back to the city. Would you mind dropping me at the Mercury main gate? The exit is just up the road a few miles."

"No problem," said Frank. "Something come up?"

"Yes, maybe. Those calls from the University of the Yucatan to Al Thompson's place were from Garcia's office, all right, and our people down there expect to pick him up within the hour."

After dropping Ben off at Mercury, Frank, Tony, Jim and Linda spent the next hour discussing the events of the day and catching their breath, so to speak. In less than twelve hours they had learned secrets shared by only a handful of other people on the planet. For Jim, especially, the revelations had come as an intellectual shock and he remained quiet most of the trip back to the city.

By the time they negotiated Las Vegas' afternoon traffic and reached the Residence Inn it was 6:30 p.m. All four of them were ready for some relaxation so Frank suggested an evening out and a ban on work-related discussions. After everyone had a chance to freshen up, they piled back into the Durango and headed to the Rio Hotel, a couple of blocks off the strip on Flamingo Road.

After a world-class meal in the fiftieth-floor VooDoo Restaurant, the four friends went upstairs to the lounge for a dessert of Bananas Foster. From their vantage point on the fifty-first floor outdoor terrace, they watched the lights of the city come on as the sun slid behind the mountains west of the city.

"I've always liked the desert," commented Tony, as the last sliver of the sun disappeared, "but I guess I like it best from the roof-top deck of a luxury hotel."

The stress of the day had drained away somewhere between the filet mignon and the lobster, and the four were in generally good spirits. Even Jim had managed to shake his depression and seemed to be having a good time.

"This has really been a kick," said Frank. "I'm not looking forward to going back to Seattle and an unknown retirement – I'd rather keep chasing mysteries like this one."

"Yeah, I know what you mean," nodded Tony. "I need to go back to Atlanta and take care of some business, but I think I'm pretty much finished with truck driving. Maybe I'll cash out my rig and go hang out with Jill for a while."

What about you, Jim," asked Linda. "This whole thing has been a real trauma to your academic background, hasn't it?"

"Yes, it certainly has," agreed Jim, sadly. "I don't know how I'll ever be able to go back to the University and teach anthropology without wondering whether or not the answer to every ancient question actually begins with the phrase 'Once upon a time, in a galaxy far, far, away.'

"I've never told this to anyone before, but one year when I was an undergrad in Spokane, two buddies and I went to the Washington coast for Spring Break. We couldn't afford the typical Florida party scene and that wasn't really our style, anyway, so we rented a beach house in Ocean Shores and just hung out for a week. The last evening of our stay we actually saw a real, live UFO fly in from the horizon, disappear behind the beach house for a few seconds, and then vanish back out over the Pacific Ocean."

Jim paused and took a sip of his drink.

"Did you ever find out what it was?" Tony asked.

Jim shook his head. "No, we never did. One of my buddies insisted we stop at the local Coast Guard station on our way out of town the next day and they told us that there had been several other reports of the sighting but that there had been no aircraft in the area the night before.

"We talked about our UFO sighting for days after we returned to Spokane, but pretty soon we had told the story to everyone we knew and we got tired of being laughed at, so the incident just faded into the past. By the time I got to graduate school, the idea of UFOs seemed ridiculous and I had convinced myself that there was a logical explanation, even if I didn't know what it was. After today, I'm not so sure."

"Well, on that note, I'd like to propose a toast," said Frank, lifting his gin and tonic. "To friends and aliens, and more of both!"

The four clicked their glasses together and Frank signaled the waiter for another round.

"I'd like to ask you all a big favor," continued Frank. "I'd like you all to promise me that we can meet in Seattle one month from today. I'm working on something pretty big and I'd like to discuss it with the three of you then."

Since Jim and Linda both lived in Seattle, they nodded without reservation, but Tony frowned and complained, "Ah, Frank,

I hope to be in the Caribbean soaking up the rays by then. Can't we discuss whatever it is now?"

"Sorry, but I'm not prepared to talk about it yet and I won't even pursue the idea unless I have your word, all of you, that we can meet next month. What do you say, Tony?"

After some friendly arm twisting by Linda, Tony finally agreed to the meeting, but not without a final protest.

"I don't see why you can't just e-mail me the information when you have it, Frank, but if you insist on seeing my smiling face, I guess I can arrange it." Part way through the next round of drinks Linda yawned and set off an epidemic around the table.

"Las Vegas may go twenty-four hours a day, but I sure can't do it anymore," said Frank, yawning for the third time. "You guys ready to call it a night and head back to the hotel?"

"Why don't the three of you go ahead?" replied Tony. "I think I'll stop downstairs in the casino for a while. I heard some Wheel of Fortune slot machines calling to me when we came in so I'll just grab a cab back when I'm done making my contribution to the local economy."

Frank, Jim and Linda said their good-nights to Tony in the casino and drove back to the Residence Inn in near silence, each one lost in their own thoughts about the day.

As Frank turned the Durango into the hotel parking lot, he stated the obvious. "Some day, huh?"

"Yeah, and I'm really beat," replied Jim. "What time do we meet in the morning?"

"Let's take it easy on ourselves, for a change. How about 8:30 a.m. at the Durango and everybody's on their own for breakfast?" said Frank.

"That sounds good to me. I'll see you two in the morning."

As Jim walked away, Linda turned to Frank and said, "Thanks for a really great evening, Frank. We're all so used to you picking up the tab that we don't even remember to say 'thank you' most of the time."

She kissed Frank on the cheek, patted him on the arm and started down the sidewalk to her room.

"Linda?" said Frank.

"Yes," she replied, glancing back over her shoulder.

"Can we talk for a while?"

At 12:30 a.m., Frank opened the door to the suite he and Tony shared and hung out the Do Not Disturb sign. Taped to it was a small note that read, "Tony: Linda's key is hanging on the door knob inside. Would you mind staying in her room tonight? See you at the Durango at 8:30 a.m."

Chapter 32

When Jim and Tony arrived at the Durango the next morning, Frank and Linda were already sitting side by side on the narrow back bumper sipping orange juice from plastic bottles.

"Good morning," greeted Jim brightly.

"Good morning, Jim," replied Frank. "You look rested and revived. I take it you slept well?"

"Yes, great, and I think I'm over that case of depression I was suffering from yesterday. I woke up this morning with a whole new attitude about the possibility of an alien influence on human history. Actually, I find it quite amazing, now that I've had some time to sleep on it."

"Well, would you mind keeping your enthusiasm down to a dull roar," grumbled Tony. "I have a huge hangover and I haven't had breakfast yet. I take it you two slept well?" he asked as he handed Linda her room key.

"Yes, thank you," answered Linda. Without any further explanation, she added, "Shall we go?"

The four climbed into the Durango and Frank drove away. Tony leaned his head against the window and closed his eyes with a groan. As they pulled up to the Bechtel guard shack, Tony opened his eyes and cried out, "Hey! What about breakfast? I can't work on an empty stomach."

After Frank pulled the Durango into a parking space just inside the gate, he tossed the keys to Tony. "Here, go get some grub. You look like you partied pretty hard last night. I thought you said you were just going to play some slots and catch a cab back."

"Well, that was the plan, but when I was down to my last few dollars I hit a $750 jackpot and ..."

"And you felt obligated to convert it all into alcohol?" laughed Frank.

"Well, I had some help, but, yes, that about sums it up. Oh, my head," moaned Tony as he put his hand on his forehead. "I'll be back in a little while. Don't discover anything exciting without me."

Frank, Jim and Linda entered the Bechtel building and showed their badges to the security guard, who handed Frank a folded piece of paper.

"Mr. Kingston would like you to call him at this number right away," the guard said mechanically.

"I wonder what this is all about," questioned Frank as he opened the door to the conference room. He put his computer bag on the table and picked up the phone to call Ben. Linda poured each of them coffee and Jim began spreading his translation notes out at one end of the table.

When Frank hung up the receiver, he said, "Well, that's certainly interesting! According to the folks at O'Callaghan, the DNA samples they collected during the last four Indian autopsies are absolutely identical. And get this – they all contain a nucleotide that they can't identify!"

Jim's eyes widened. "So they're alien after all! But Ben told us that the spacecraft he's been studying only carried two passengers, so how did these nineteen – or twenty, if you count Garcia – messengers get to Earth?"

"Maybe the spacecraft carried a pilot and the first messenger and the rest were brought in one at a time during each of the nineteen solar eclipse visits," offered Linda.

"Maybe," thought Frank out loud, "but I suspect the spheres are involved in this. I'm working on a theory."

"Is there any word on Garcia?" asked Linda.

Frank shook his head. "They can't find Garcia. Apparently he hasn't been seen since he left the library Monday afternoon."

"So we still don't know if he's Maya, Olmec, alien or just a regular guy, do we?" frowned Jim. "I sure hope they locate him because he could help answer some very important questions about the Olmec."

"Yes, and about Al Thompson and about the spheres and about the deaths of nineteen of his cousins," added Frank. "He's potentially the key to a lot of things."

Linda took up her position at one of the computers and began checking on boat charters in Port Isabel while Jim reviewed the photographs he and Ben had taken of the twenty spheres. Frank just sat at the end of the table and stared at the wall, lost in thought.

After about ten minutes of silence, Frank snapped his fingers and reached for the telephone. Thirty minutes later, when Tony arrived, Frank was still on the phone. He finally hung up and Jim slid down the table several chairs until he was directly across from Frank.

"It sounded like you were giving somebody pretty detailed instructions on how to get into the caves at *Loltún*," he said.

"I was," replied Frank. "It suddenly occurred to me that if Garcia were going to hide somewhere, *Loltún* might be a likely place."

"What's going on?" asked a still sluggish but improving Tony.

Frank explained the call from Ben and his idea about the cave while Tony filled a coffee cup.

"So Garcia and the pyramid disappeared the same night, huh? Does anybody else find that odd?" asked Tony. "What about the spheres themselves? Do we have a consensus on what their real purpose is, or was?"

"I thought we had agreed that they were designed to remind the Maya priests when and where certain solar eclipses were going to take place," replied Jim.

"But why only those nineteen eclipses" asked Tony. "Didn't you say there were a lot more eclipses than just the ones specified on the spheres?"

"Yes, a lot more," nodded Jim.

"So we're back to the theory that these nineteen spheres identify specific eclipses which coincided with the return of an alien craft, like the UFO sightings observed in Mexico City in 1991," said Frank.

"So much for the theory that the only purpose of the spheres was to serve as Post-It notes for the Maya?" laughed Tony. "Come on, what about the noise and the glowing? Those spheres must have another purpose!"

"You've got a point," agreed Jim. "They clearly have some sort of self-contained power source and they wouldn't need that if their only purpose were to display some hieroglyphics. A piece of rock could have accomplished that."

"Maybe they were some sort of data collection device," speculated Tony, "designed to record changing climactic conditions or something like that."

"Or maybe they were transmitters, or receivers, or both," added Jim. "Maybe they served as homing beacons for the ships that arrived during the eclipses."

"Maybe, but Carlson was really afraid of those things," remembered Tony. "When they started activating down inside the mountain I thought he was going to have a stroke. It startled me, too, don't get me wrong, but he was hyperventilating by the time we got to the surface. And the first time I met with Edwards and Carlson, right after you guys left for Mexico, they told me they believed the spheres posed a threat to national security. They acted like the spheres were bombs, or something."

"The only damage I ever saw them do was crack a couple of counter tops," added Frank, "and that's a long way from being a national security threat. Of course, we have the advantage of knowing that they've been here for nearly 3,500 years. Carlson and Edwards still think they started showing up in 1951, at the height of the cold war."

At her computer, Linda snapped the cover closed on her cell phone and called down to the three men. "I think I found Garcia's charter company. The third place I called confirmed that they had a passenger named Garcia on a boat that left Port Isabel the Saturday after Al Thompson was shot. The boat arrived in Celestún, a fishing town about 50 miles east of Merida, late the following Friday, which would have put him back in Merida the day of Jim's second visit to the Library."

"So we know he was in the U.S. at a time that would have allowed him to be in Beatty when Al Thompson was shot. That doesn't prove he pulled the trigger, but he certainly had the opportunity," said Frank. "I'm going to pass that info on to Ben. It may help convince the Mexican authorities to let them bring Garcia back here. Good work, Linda."

While Frank made his call to Ben, Tony, Jim and Linda continued to discuss the purpose of the spheres. Jim believed the spheres served a purely practical function but Tony was convinced they had a more sinister purpose. Either way, it was becoming clear that the spheres were the product of an alien race that had probably visited the Earth on more than one occasion.

Frank rejoined the debate and put forth a theory he'd been formulating for several days.

"Let's ignore Tony's *Alien Space Invaders* scenario for a minute and look at this from another perspective. What if these aliens, whoever they might be, decided to conduct an experiment in socio-cultural development. They looked around for a suitable site and ran across the planet Earth with a whole hemisphere that was inhabited but uncivilized. Oh, sure, there were some advanced cultures flourishing on the other side of the globe, but the year was 1500 B.C and these distant civilizations had no way to interfere with the experiment in Mesoamerica.

"What if a craft carrying the spheres was sent to Earth to influence the people we now call the Olmec and a supervisor was assigned to the project to check on the progress at specified times, as indicated by the dates on the spheres? What if each of the spheres was similar to a time-release capsule and contained a certain body of advanced knowledge about mathematics, astronomy and other subjects the aliens wanted to deliver to the developing Olmec. What if each of the spheres also contained the "essence" of an alien being – a teacher that materialized at just the right time to help the local population understand and use their new knowledge? You could think of the spheres as *seeds of civilization*.

"That might also explain why the aliens were so intent on returning their spheres to the buried pyramid. Maybe when they reached the Test Site the data collected by the spheres and the "souls" they had originally contained were somehow transferred to the pyramid for storage and transportation back to wherever they came from."

"But what about the relatively recent return of the spheres to Nevada?" asked Tony. "How does that fit into this fairy tale of yours?"

"I'm not sure yet, Tony. When did you say the spheres first started showing up?"

Tony checked the notes he had made from Carlson's autopsy files and said, "The first sphere arrived about April 10, 1951. The day I collected this data I remember seeing a picture on the wall outside Carlson's office that showed the first nuclear test, and that took place just a few months earlier, in January, I think."

Jim's eyes widened. "So let me get this straight. The government performs its first nuclear test in the atmosphere in January of 1951 and the first sphere shows up a few miles from the blast site less than four months later?"

"Right. Hardly seems like a coincidence, does it? I came to the same conclusion the day I was looking at the autopsy files," said Tony.

"And there's one more piece of information we didn't have until yesterday," smiled Frank as he continued to build his case. "One of the spheres is dated March 7, 1951 – that would put an alien visit right between the first nuclear test and the arrival of the first sphere!"

"So, we set off a nuclear blast in the atmosphere, your alien project supervisor returns to discover what we've done, and he starts the recall of his little black baseballs, right?" asked Tony.

"Something like that," nodded Frank. "It makes sense, don't you agree?

"And that would explain why the last sphere was on schedule to be carried back here about three years from now, long before its inscribed date of 2012 – because the project has been terminated early!" shouted Tony, slapping the table to make his point."

"And the asteroid that seems to coincide with the arrival of the spheres ..." started Jim.

Frank shook his head. "It probably isn't an asteroid at all. I'll bet it was discovered sometime after March 7, 1951 and I wouldn't be surprised if it has mysteriously disappeared by now."

"So now what?" asked Tony. "There isn't much more we can do here, and we may never know if your Seeds of Civilization theory is correct. The spheres are lying dormant at the bottom of Yucca Mountain and that's probably where they'll stay."

"You're right," agreed Frank. "Even if they find this Garcia guy we probably won't have access to him, so I'm afraid our work here may be done."

"And the buried pyramid?" asked Linda. "Is there any more we can learn about it?"

"Since it's apparently not buried any more, I don't know what we can do," smiled Frank. "If one of the functions of the spheres actually was data collection, perhaps the purpose of burying them in the sand was to allow them to download their information to the pyramid. Once the last sphere 'checked in', the pyramid may have been programmed to return home or rendezvous with the mother ship or something like that."

"And won't they be surprised when it shows up three years early, thanks to you and Jim!" laughed Tony. "I can't help wondering what kind of antennae scratching is going on back on the pyramid's home planet."

Frank smiled, acknowledging the humor of the situation, and then added, "But on a serious note, I feel like we've created more questions then we've answered – this has certainly been an interesting experience."

"So, shall we get out of here?" asked an impatient Tony. "This place gives me claustrophobia and we can wait to hear about Garcia above ground somewhere."

"Let me call Ben and Carlson and give them an update, and then we're out of here. Everybody please check around and make sure we aren't leaving anything because we probably won't be back."

While Tony, Jim and Linda gathered up papers, Frank placed a call to Ben. He explained his theory about the alien experiment, the purpose of the spheres and their sudden withdrawal after the 1951 nuclear test.

When Frank had finished, Ben said, "That certainly all makes sense, and there may be some checking we can do on this end to verify a few of the more speculative parts of your theory. Could I impose on you and your team to put all that into an informal report and get it to me before you leave town? And please tell Jim that I will do my best to salvage some unclassified, publishable material for him but remind him, and the rest of your team that all the information relating to this matter is still classified Top Secret."

Frank then called Carlson and relayed their feelings about Garcia and his involvement in Al Thompson's death, being careful not to mention anything about Ben's spacecraft or the Olmec theory. That would be up to the Departments of Defense and Energy to work out between themselves. Carlson thanked Frank and the team for their help and their patience, especially with young Ben Kingston.

"I'm sorry I had to force him on you," apologized Carlson, "but the DOD was pretty insistent. Every time they come snooping around these spheres, I get more apprehensive. I learned a long time ago that whenever the DOD gets interested in something, it usually means trouble."

"No apology necessary," replied Frank, smiling to himself. "Ben was very helpful and I have a feeling the two of you will be working together again in the near future."

After exchanging telephone numbers, the two said good bye and Frank hung up the phone.

"So how did that go?" asked Tony.

Before Frank could answer, his cell phone rang. The call lasted only a minute or so and he ended it with a frown.

"That was Carlson, again," said Frank. "He just got a call from Mexico. Garcia was found dead, face down and arms outstretched, in the small cave where we found the twentieth sphere."

"Just like the Indians that delivered the other nineteen spheres to Nevada!" shouted Jim.

"Well, there goes any chance of learning what this was *really* all about," sighed Tony. "How is Carlson taking this unfortunate turn of events?"

"I think the poor guy is more afraid of the Department of Defense than he is of aliens," smiled Frank. "Let's head back to the hotel to pack and make whatever travel arrangements you and Jim need for tomorrow. Then, how about if we spend the evening on the famous Las Vegas 'strip'? Linda hasn't had a chance to see the sights since she arrived, and I still have several thousand dollars of Jill's money left."

The idea of a night on the town appealed to everyone, even Tony who was still suffering from his previous night's partying.

"Oh, and Ben asked if we would summarize our thoughts and theories on paper before we leave, so how about if we take care of that before we do anything else? Linda and I can drop it off for him in Mercury on our way out of town tomorrow."

The prospect of writing a report was met with groans, but they all knew why it was necessary. If the Olmec theory proved to be true, a whole new era of scientific research was about to begin and it was due, in part, to their investigative work.

The evening out was a pleasant, and for some, profitable time. With the spheres and their mystery temporarily behind them, the four were able to relax and enjoy each other's company. Linda had never been to Las Vegas before and she was amazed by the scale of it all, especially the gimmicks used by the hotels to attract guests into their casinos. From the New York skyline appearance of the New York, New York hotel to the Eiffel Tower at the Paris hotel, to the gondola ride, complete with singing gondoliers, at the Venetian, everything was exciting to her. She even screamed and hid her face when a stunt man appeared to fall from the top of a mast during the mock pirate ship battle in front of Treasure Island.

Late in the evening, the group had worked their way down the strip to the Luxor, and decided that it was somehow fitting to end their night on the town by doing some gambling in the black, pyramid-shaped hotel. Tony soon hit a hot streak on a Wheel of Fortune nickel machine and Linda, who wasn't really into gambling, pulled up a chair to watch. As they chatted, Tony casually brought up the subject of the night before.

"Yes, poor Frank," sighed Linda. "I think he really has feelings for this woman he met in Mexico – Alex, I think her name is – but at the same time he is consumed with a sense of guilt that he is somehow cheating on Donna. The poor guy is driving himself crazy."

"Oh, I just assumed that you two…" smiled Tony.

"You thought Frank and I slept together? Oh, no, that could never happen, Tony. I don't see it, but Frank says I bear a strong resemblance to Donna and if sleeping with Alex troubles him, just imagine what a relationship with me would do to him! No, we just talked, mostly about Donna. She was my college roommate and best friend, and I think on some subconscious level Frank feels that I can speak for her. I care for Frank deeply, but as a friend, not as a lover."

Linda took three nickels out of Tony's hand, dropped them in the slot, and gave him a friendly kiss on the cheek. "For Luck," she said.

Tony pulled the handle and waited while the symbols came to a stop. As the last symbol clicked into place, a bell sounded and a light started flashing on top of the machine.

"I think we broke it," cried a startled Linda, over the sound of the ringing.

"No, actually, I think we broke the bank – we just hit the jackpot!" replied Tony.

The next morning the four friends met for a late breakfast before checking out of the Residence Inn. Linda was still on a high from her first night on the strip in Las Vegas and Tony was feeling pretty good about the $13,421 he had won at the slot machine. Frank and Jim had each lost about $100 and Frank assured Jim that, for Las Vegas, even they had done pretty good.

After breakfast, they loaded the Durango and drove down Paradise Road to the airport. After seeing Jim off at the Alaska Airlines gate, Frank, Tony and Linda walked slowly to the Delta gate where Tony's flight back to Atlanta was to depart. As they walked, Tony asked Linda about her plans, since she was the only one who hadn't commented the night the others were discussing their future on the terrace of the Rio's VooDoo Lounge.

"Well, I guess I'll go back to the newspaper and back to doing boring research on even more boring articles," she said with a pout. Jerking her thumb at Frank, she added, "And living next door to a globe-trotting multimillionaire is going to make my lowly job seem even worse. What about you?"

"I've thought about it a lot the past couple of nights, and I've definitely decided to sell my rig and ease into retirement. Maybe I'll call in a few favors and wrangle some kind of high-paying, low-stress consulting job out of the government. I've given them a lot of good years and a lot of hard miles – I think they owe it to me."

When they reached the gate, the plane was already boarding but Tony wasn't in a hurry to leave his friends so he decided to wait until the last minute. While the other passengers were getting on the plane, Frank's cell phone rang.

He closed the phone and scratched his head. "That was Carlson. Garcia's DNA is an exact match to the other four samples, so he was obviously supposed to be our twentieth sphere bearer. He's dead, and so is any chance of interrogating him, but when the Mexican authorities searched his office at the University they found a map of Nevada and a box of high-powered .22 Hornet rifle ammunition. That's exactly the kind the Sheriff in Beatty suggested might have been used in Al Thompson's shooting so it looks like we've found our murderer."

The last call for Tony's flight was announced, and he stood up to go. He hugged Linda warmly and shook hands with his old friend Frank. "Any specific plans for your retirement, old man?" Tony asked.

"Well, I've been interested in the unsolved mysteries of history ever since I was a kid," replied Frank. "Back in Seattle I have boxes full of research I did years ago and, in light of what we think we've learned about the Olmec, I'm anxious to get home and go through some of that stuff."

"Yeah, I'll bet there are dozens of ancient mysteries that could be explained if you're willing to accept your 'Seeds of

Civilization' theory," smiled Tony, as he collected his carry-on and headed for the door leading to his plane.

"Do me a favor, and hold that thought until our meeting next month in Seattle," called Frank, as Tony headed down the jet way and onto the plane.

THE END

Epilogue

(Seattle, one month later)

When Frank arrived at the old hangar at the south end of the King County Airport, also known as Boeing Field, Linda McBride, Tony Nicoletti and Jim Barnes were standing in front of the locked office door.

"Sorry I'm late, folks," called Frank, as he hopped out of his Durango. "I got stuck in a meeting with the bank. Thanks for meeting me here. Especially you, Tony. I hear you've been living it up in the Caribbean."

Tony, who had apparently been waiting the longest, grumbled, "What the hell is this all about, Frank? Why all the mystery, and why are we *here*! This place looks deserted."

"All in good time, my friend, all in good time," replied Frank, as he dug a key out of his briefcase and opened the door. He entered first and flipped on the office light switch. "Please come in!" he said, as if inviting guests into his new villa.

Warily, one after the other, Linda, Tony and Jim followed Frank into the dingy office in the corner of the small hangar. The place looked and smelled like it had been vacant for years. It was located at the far south end of the single runway, across from the Boeing facilities. From the side window there was a view of about a dozen new airliners awaiting their final test flights before being turned over to their owners. The logos on the planes were from all over the world and some were totally unknown. Directly across the long runway was the plant where Boeing puts the finishing touches on some of the large military aircraft it builds.

"I know it doesn't look like much, guys, but I'm going to have the place completely redone and it will be much nicer," announced Frank proudly, extending his arms to indicate the entire building.

"Why?" questioned Linda as she scowled and wrinkled her nose at the smell of old grease and oil. "Please tell me you didn't buy this dump – Oh, God, is that why you were at the bank?"

"Not so harsh, my dear," smiled Frank as he wagged his finger at her. "I asked the three of you here because I have a proposal for you that I hope you can't refuse. I bought this hangar a couple of days ago and I wanted you to be the first to see the new headquarters of the Northwest Institute of Discovery and Investigation – NWIDI!" beamed Frank.

"The what?" asked all three in unison.

"And why a hangar?" demanded Tony. "Couldn't you have rented some office space downtown? It'll cost a fortune to convert this old hangar into... well, into what ever the hell NWIDI is."

"Ah, but you see, my loud friend, they probably wouldn't let me park *this* in a downtown office building, now, would they?" replied Frank as he motioned the group through the back door of the office that led into the hangar proper.

There, parked in the middle of the dirty hangar, was a gleaming white Learjet 60 business jet with the letters NWIDI in black letters along the back portion of the fuselage.

"Wow, Frank, she's a beauty!" exclaimed Tony, as he crossed the hangar to the plane. "How fast does she go?"

"Top speed is 600 miles an hour, Tony. It seats six comfortably, has a maximum altitude of 41,000 feet, and a 2,500-mile range between refueling," beamed Frank, as if he had memorized the airplane's specifications guide.

The others followed Tony and when they reached the side of the aircraft Frank activated the cabin door and an electric stairway unfolded to allow them access.

"Please come in," waved Frank as he started up the stairs. "We can talk in here where there's a place to sit."

The interior of the plane screamed luxury. It was done in plush gray leather and burly maple wood trim. The six high-back passenger seats were arranged in three rows of two, one seat on each side of the aircraft with an aisle down the center, and the seats in the middle row faced backwards. Built-in pull out tables between the two sets of facing seats created a natural club car/conference room/dining area effect. Aft of the passenger area was a lavatory and luggage storage compartment. Forward of the passenger area, against the cockpit bulkhead, was a small galley and an entertainment center.

Once everyone was comfortably seated around the table, Frank began. "You all have to admit that we had quite an adventure as a result of Tony's mysterious black sphere, right?" asked Frank, making eye contact with each of them, one at a time.

The others all nodded and mumbled. Slowly, as they each remembered different incidents, a smile crossed each one's lips.

"Yeah, it was quite an adventure all right," laughed Tony, "But how does that, or this, for that matter, affect the three of us?" asked Tony, indicating the luxurious surroundings of the plane's interior.

"Good question, Tony," smiled Frank, leaning forward. "I have a proposition for you – all three of you. I have asked an attorney to formally set up a nonprofit corporation called the Northwest Institute of Discovery and Investigation and I would like the three of you to join me. I'll fund it in the beginning, but I expect it will become solvent fairly soon. You will all be paid well, I promise, and we'll work out of this hangar, once the renovations are complete. Tony, you'll need to move to Seattle, of course, and Jim, I assume you will have to carry on with some of your teaching duties at the University once your sabbatical is over, but otherwise we'll work together here! It'll be great fun!" Frank leaned back in his chair smiling from ear to ear.

There was absolute silence for several seconds before Jim finally spoke. "Frank, what on earth are you talking about? What would we do here, besides sit in your new airplane? Not only will I have classes, but I'm an archeologist and anthropologist. I dig things up. I do research," said Jim slowly, as if talking to a child.

"Yes, Frank, the adventure is over. We solved the mystery, sort of, and that's the end of it," added Linda. "We all have to work for a living – what would we do at this NWIDI thing?" she asked. The others nodded in agreement and started talking among themselves.

"Folks!" shouted Frank. "There are a lot more mysteries to investigate. This sphere thing is just the beginning. What I'm proposing is that the four of us, as the core group, select a 'project' and investigate it until we either discover the truth or decide it's not worth pursuing. Yes, you all have a specialty, and that's exactly the point. Linda, you're a researcher. The work you've been doing for the newspaper takes a special talent and we can set you up with all the computer equipment you'll need right here. Jim, like you said, you're an anthropologist and, as such, you have an incredible knowledge of languages and cultures – especially old ones. And Tony, you… well, mostly you save my ass when I stick my nose where it doesn't belong. There isn't a person on earth I'd rather have at my back. And you know your way around this country better then anybody I know. We'll need other expertise from time to time, of course, but we can hire that when we need it. What do you say?"

The others looked at each other and shook their heads like they were listening to a madman.

"Frank, we all had a hell of a good time banging around Nevada and the Yucatan, but the fact that I came to have the sphere at all was purely a stroke of luck. You can't just go out and make those kinds of things happen. Sure, I have to admit that I like the thought of doing this a lot better than the prospect of getting back behind the wheel of a big rig or sitting behind a desk, but come on, Frank! What *would* we do?"

Frank removed a manila file folder from his brief case and laid it on the table for the others to see. "This came to me indirectly, through our friend Edwards down at the Department of Energy, earlier this week. Open it and tell me what you think."

Linda opened the folder and the three of them started examining its contents. After they browsed the sheets and photos in the folder for a couple of minutes there were some murmurs, then pretty soon a gasp from Jim Barnes and finally a "Look at this one!" from Tony.

As the comments from the three grew to a loud buzz, Frank leaned back in his seat and said, mostly to himself, "So I take it we have a deal?"

R.J. Archer

Printed in the United States
56822LVS00008B/73